SAVAGE SCREENING

He hit a button on the computer keyboard. Music, slow, bassy, and sensual, filled the studio. Sixteen speakers' worth of sound that caressed and stroked. He stood and walked to the center of the room. "Do you remember I said you reminded me of someone?"

"Yes. Was she pretty?"

"Oh, she was beautiful."

"Do you still see her?"

"Why? Would that make you jealous?"

"Maybe. A little."

"I don't see her anymore. Come here."

Raven walked over to where he stood in the shadows.

Also by Stephen Smoke

Black Butterfly

Available from HarperPaperbacks

PACIFIC COAST
◆ HIGHWAY ◆

Stephen Smoke

HarperPaperbacks
A Division of HarperCollinsPublishers

This is a work of fiction. The characters, incidents, and dialogues are products of the author's imagination and are not to be construed as real. Any resemblance to actual events or persons, living or dead, is entirely coincidental.

HarperPaperbacks *A Division of* HarperCollins*Publishers*
10 East 53rd Street, New York, N.Y. 10022

Cover illustration by Kirk Reinert

First printing: April 1994

Printed in the United States of America

HarperPaperbacks and colophon are trademarks of HarperCollins*Publishers*

❖ 10 9 8 7 6 5 4 3 2 1

For Margaret
My best critic, my best friend.
Quite simply, the best.

one

It wasn't as though killing someone was a big deal.

He had done it lots of times . . . in the war. That was necessary. Acceptable. The right thing to do. People had bought him drinks in bars in exchange for details, details of the kill. *What was it like to fuckin' kill somebody, man? Were you scared? Did you feel guilty? Did you feel excited? Was there any blood? Did you get any on you? Did you bring back any "souvenirs"?*

It was cool. Correct. It was fuckin' patriotic.

And he had killed . . . after the war. When it was not acceptable. When it was not the topic of bar conversation. No one bought him drinks and asked him details. But they probably would have, if they had known. Known what he had done. To whom. And why. The details were much more . . . what? Provocative. Provocative in every way. The gooks he wasted in Nam were . . . what? Nothing. Nondescript.

All the same. Couldn't tell one from the other. Probably their own fuckin' mothers couldn't tell the difference. Big fuckin' deal.

But the people he killed after the war were . . . what? Women. White women. Guys in bars would have loved to hear the details. He wouldn't ever have had to buy a drink in a bar again. If he could tell. What he knew.

And why not? What he did was cool. Correct. Even fuckin' patriotic. If you looked at it the right way.

But not everyone looked at things the right way. The way Gino did. So he kept quiet.

That was okay. It didn't matter what other people thought. Gino lived in a world of his own. Yet he was not divorced from the rest of the world. He functioned well there. Did better there than most people. Had money. A glamour job. A little power.

Gino checked his watch. 2:15 A.M. He turned the key, and the Porsche engine started to growl. He liked the way the engine responded to his command. The sensation made him feel . . . what? Powerful. Which, of course, he was.

He pulled off the shoulder of the road onto the Pacific Coast Highway and headed south. The full moon tossed its light across the ocean like loaded dice, tumbling and rolling toward the shore, its number, its sum, predetermined. Always the same.

On the radio some left-wing bleeding heart was talking about meeting Jesus Christ. Said Jesus was a homeless man in Minneapolis. Lived on the street, playing guitar and singing songs like "These Are the Last Days."

Gino looked at the speedometer. Forty miles an

hour. Guy said Jesus dressed in jeans and a White Light Train T-shirt, worked doing day work at a Manpower job-placement center—usually unloading trucks.

The speedometer hit fifty. Gino felt the power. He had done . . . what? *This.* Before. No sweat. He laughed as a bead of sweat trickled down his forehead. He laughed again when he heard that Jesus was a big *Family Feud* fan and that the "Messiah" had been given backstage passes to every Prince concert.

The speedometer hit sixty. Over the speed limit. Especially for PCH. But it was late. He knew the highway. The California Highway Patrol didn't haunt the place. At this hour, almost any speed was safe. The guy on the radio was saying that Jesus wanted world peace, wanted people to learn to love one another, and wanted the Minnesota Twins to win the World Series. Again.

The speedometer hit seventy. This was definitely over the speed limit. Gino had promised himself he would not tempt fate. Not break the law. He laughed. Not break the law. On the radio, Jesus was being quoted as saying that frozen food and race riots were bad for the cumulative human soul, and it wasn't a good idea to mix Bailey's Irish Cream with Absolut Vodka, even though it tasted swell.

There she was.

In the headlights. She had done her job. Right on time. The digital clock on the dashboard said it was time. The two dots, the colon between the hours and the minutes, kept blinking on and off.

Like a heartbeat.

A hundred yards. Seventy miles per hour.
Seventy-five yards. Seventy miles per hour.
Fifty yards. Seventy miles per hour.
Twenty-five yards. Seventy miles per hour.
He saw her . . . eyes. . . .

Her body hit with a thud and bounced, almost as though in slow motion. Above and out of the path of light cut in the darkness by his headlights.

The impact sent the woman crashing against the windshield and, instantly, above and out of the head-lights' spectrum.

There was no telling where she would come down.

But it had been perfect all the same.

Gino slowed to a stop a couple of hundred yards on, pulled off onto the shoulder, parked the Porsche, and turned the engine and lights off.

It was over.

Finally.

It was a point of . . . what? Gamesmanship? Pride? Balance.

He had finally made things right.

Why should she be different from the rest?

The guy on the radio was saying Jesus had come back. For a reason. That there was no such thing as an accident. That everything had a purpose.

The woman thought it strange that she felt little if any pain when she hit the windshield. She felt her bones shattering, her flesh splitting, her blood being set free into a world in which it did not belong.

Yet she felt strangely peaceful. For the first time in a long time. Free.

She had not planned this, yet it was clear that this accident was no accident at all. It was as though it and everything else had a purpose that was just now becoming clear to her.

Suddenly she felt herself falling . . .

Falling . . .

two

Falling ...

She caught her by the head, trying not to hurt her.

"Don't do that!"

The girl turned to face the consequences.

"What do you think you're doing?"

"I'm sorry, Mommy." Erin held the doll in her hand contritely.

"That is a very expensive doll. You shouldn't play with it as though it were a ball."

"I'm sorry, Mommy."

"Don't be so hard on my granddaughter," said Cheney, walking onto the scene with a glass of '91 Burgess Chardonnay.

"Cheney, please," said Samantha, Cheney's daughter-in-law, who, like everyone else, called him by his last name rather than his first, which was Derek.

"I'm sorry," he said, his words putting him to some degree on an equal footing—at least in regard to Samantha—with his granddaughter, Erin.

"Don't be sorry. It's Erin who should be sorry. I know what you paid for that doll."

Cheney waved a hand, indicating that the price wasn't important.

"No, no. We all have to learn the value of a dollar."

"I was just having fun," said Erin.

Cheney raised his eyebrows in support. He knew that to raise a more stringent objection was pointless. Or at least it was pointless in the scheme of things. Family-wise.

"You can enjoy your toys without breaking them."

"Yes, Mommy," said Erin, after a while. After she recognized that resistance was futile.

Cheney just smiled at Erin and Samantha and walked away. He had learned long ago that taking sides in family disputes that did not involve the immediate family was always a losing proposition. In fact, it was often a losing proposition even when it involved the immediate family.

"You making trouble again?"

Cheney turned to see his wife, Elizabeth. She stood before him now, a glass of Evian mineral water in her hand. She did not drink it for any trendy reason, but merely because she wasn't much of a drinker, social or otherwise, and she eschewed the chemicals that made up most soft drinks.

"Not any more than usual," said Cheney.

Cheney and his wife looked out upon the back yard of their Pacific Palisades home. Their annual Fourth of July barbecue normally drew about fifty people: family, neighbors, and friends. This year there were about seventy.

"Having fun?"

"Sure," said Cheney. He was not a particularly social animal, although long ago, when he was chief of detectives for the LAPD, he had recognized that everyone, to a certain extent, was a social animal. Some decidedly more dangerous than others.

"What do you want me to do with these?"

Cheney turned and saw Petty, their feisty Mexican live-in housekeeper, approaching with a plate of thawed hamburgers. Over the years, five to be exact, she had been referred to as Hispanic, Spanish, and ethnic. She had informed Cheney that she had never been to Spain, didn't know "what the fuck" Hispanic meant, and wasn't in the least bit offended by the truth that she was Mexican, born in Tijuana, and came here legally in the mid-seventies, thank you very much.

"Just put them over by the grill," said Cheney.

"Funny," she said, with a cockeyed smile.

"What?"

"Your arms don't *look* broken."

Cheney took the plate from her. "You want me to do anything else?" he said with a sarcastic smile.

"I could use some help with the Caesar salad," she said, missing—or at least not acknowledging—Cheney's complaint.

"I'll see what I can do."

"The Stag's Leap is great."

Cheney looked like a child whose favorite toy had just been chopped up and spit out by a lawn mower. "What?"

"The Stag's Leap Reserve. It's fantastic."

"That's from my private stock," said Cheney, his eyes noticeably wider.

"Oh, yeah? Well, I didn't see no name on it."

"Petty—"

"It goes great with hot dogs," said the housekeeper with a smile and walked back inside.

"Cheney." Elizabeth knew best. She could also recognize a lost cause when she saw one. Better than Cheney.

"I've got to lay down the law," said Cheney.

"Give it up. You always say that, and you always end up going down in flames."

"She works for me," said Cheney.

"Life ain't fair, darlin'," said Elizabeth, kissing her husband on the cheek.

Cheney sipped his Chardonnay, still holding the burgers and, to a certain extent, the bag.

"Don't you think Diana is a little . . . well, underdressed?"

Cheney followed his wife's eye. Diana Fairchild, the wife of the Cheneys' next-door neighbor, Owen Fairchild, stood on the board preparing to dive into the pool. She was wearing a very small red bikini. It was not a thong bikini, but it was only a step removed. Plastic surgery—breasts and a nose job—regular aerobics, and running five days a week, plus two days a week at a "spa," had transformed Diana, especially from a distance, into a babe—that was what Cheney was thinking. She had become a woman who could wear that kind of bikini and get other women talking about it. Cheney could vouch for the fact that men were talking about it too.

"I hadn't noticed," he lied, his years of playing a political role serving him well.

"You noticed."

"Why would you say that?"

"Look at her."

Cheney focused on Diana as her tanned and toned figure bounced off his diving board, jackknifed in the air, and penetrated the surface of his pool. He could feel himself squinting.

"What's your point?"

"Does she really look that much better than I do?"

If ever a question deserved not answering, Cheney knew it was this one. And if it were to be answered, it was a question that would probably be cited as the exception to the rule that thou shalt not lie. Such a question not only deserved but required a lie.

"Of course not," he said, with as straight a face as he could muster.

"You really think so?"

"Of course I do."

"You know, I've been gaining a little weight lately."

"I hadn't noticed," said Cheney, the man who had made his living from his ability to perceive details.

"I'm sure you have, but I appreciate your tact. You know, I'm not the woman you married."

"Really? Who are you? Let's see some ID."

"You know what I mean. I've got to lose some weight. I've been putting in a lot of extra hours at work the past few months. I haven't been working out, and"—this was the hard part—"I am getting older."

"We're all getting older."

"Men don't get older," said Elizabeth disdainfully.

"Of course we do."

"Men get distinguished. Women get old."

"Times are changing."

"Not that much. Not fast enough, anyway. I know that I'm 'attractive for my age,' but that's not enough."

"For what?"

Elizabeth just looked at Cheney and sighed. She had that look in her eyes. Cheney recognized it. It was the look that said she thought he was an idiot. Or at least that he was acting like one.

"Elizabeth, I—"

"Look. There's Jim Sanford."

Cheney turned to see Sanford walking across the patio into the back yard. He looked a little lost. Disoriented.

"Maybe you should go talk to him," said Elizabeth.

Cheney didn't have to be asked twice. "Right. Could you take these over to the grill?" He handed his wife the plate of hamburgers.

Cheney hadn't seen Jamison Sanford since the funeral. They had never been close friends, but they had been neighbors for ten years, talked over drinks at a number of social occasions, and been paired in a couple of foursomes at the Riviera Country Club, where both were members.

The funeral service had been small and Cheney had offered his condolences perfunctorily. Perhaps that wasn't exactly the right word, he thought, as he moved toward his neighbor. He was not merely going through the motions. He had felt genuine sympathy for the man.

"Glad you could make it, Jamison." Cheney used

his full name, while his wife always referred to him as Jim.

Sanford nodded and smiled. It was a crooked smile, as if his muscles were unfamiliar with the command. Or at least out of practice.

"Thanks for inviting me."

"We always invite you," said Cheney. The implied *and Barbara* hung between them like a ghost.

An awkward moment of silence. Guests in bathing suits splashed water out of the pool. Children chased each other around, carrying objects their parents were sure would poke their eyes out. Life went on.

For other people.

"I've got to talk to you, Cheney."

"Sure."

"No, I mean I've really got to talk to you."

"What do you mean?"

"There's something strange about Barbara's . . . death."

"Look, Jamison, I—"

"No, I mean there's really something funny going on."

"Did you talk to the police?"

"Of course. They don't want to hear about it."

"I'm not sure there's anything I can do."

"Look, Cheney, people come to you all the time with crazy stories. I wouldn't impose if I wasn't sure."

Sanford looked around. Looked around at the happiness, the laughter. To him, it was as though they all lived in another world. Because his world was not a world of laughter. Not a world of happiness. Yet they shared the same air, the same ground.

But they could not have been farther apart.

"What do you want to talk to me about?"

"Barbara was murdered."

Cheney didn't know what to say.

"Let me buy you breakfast tomorrow at the club."

"Okay," said Cheney. Mainly because he didn't know how to say no.

"I thought the party went rather well," said Elizabeth when she got into bed next to her husband.

"Yeah."

"Something wrong?"

"Why do you ask?"

"I *am* a psychiatrist," she said.

"It's nothing."

"You mean nothing important. Which means nothing you want to talk about."

"Having a wife who's a psychiatrist can have its drawbacks."

"So can having a husband who has trouble communicating his feelings."

"C'mon, let's not argue."

"Why not? It's healthy."

Cheney had been around this track before. "Okay, what's wrong?"

"What's wrong with *you*?"

"You're trying to pick a fight." Cheney scanned his mental computer: Diana Fairchild. Bikini. Got to lose some weight. He leaned over and kissed his wife. "You looked great this afternoon."

"This afternoon?"

"Yeah."

"Why this afternoon? Not yesterday? What about

last night? You haven't said, `You looked great today' in a long time.''

"Are you having your period?''

"That's insulting, Cheney. You know how I feel about you saying that.''

"Are you?''

A little squinting of the eyes. "It doesn't make any difference.''

Cheney knew logic was not going to be his strong suit. He was destined to lose any argument his wife would start.

"I'm thinking of plastic surgery.''

"What?''

"Come into the twentieth century, Cheney. It isn't like I'm a teenager talking about a boob job.''

"Isn't this kind of sudden?''

"No. I've been thinking about it for a long time.''

"Really? You haven't mentioned it before.''

"I don't tell you every thought I have. And it's not like I'm overreacting. I've reached a time in my life when such a course of action is rational and the benefits very tangible.''

"That sounds so technical. You're talking about going under the knife.''

"Thank you, Cheney,'' Elizabeth said sarcastically. "I wasn't sure exactly what the procedure would entail.''

"You don't have to do this.''

"I know I don't *have* to do it. In case you're wondering, I'm doing it for myself. So you needn't feel guilty.''

"Guilty? Why should I feel guilty?''

"I'm not saying you should. I'm just saying you shouldn't.'' Beat. "If you do.''

Cheney knew his wife knew that he was scanning

all the possible past situations in which, from his wife's point of view, he could have been found culpable in causing her to feel insecure about her body.

He had never been unfaithful to Elizabeth. Not that he had not had opportunities. They both had opportunities. But nothing had happened, on his end at least. Still, he was not immune to the casual appreciation of an attractive woman.

But he had been discreet on those rare occasions. It had never been his intention to make his wife feel uncomfortable, less a woman. To make her feel that he might . . . stray.

No. That had never happened.

"I love you," he said as he leaned close to his wife and kissed her. Kissed her on the lips. Lingered there as if he meant it. Which he did.

"What did Jim want?"

"Nothing," said Cheney, leaning back and resting his head deep into the down pillow.

"I saw how you changed after you talked with him."

"What do you mean?"

"I know the look."

"What look?"

"You're interested, aren't you?"

"I really don't know what you're talking about," said Cheney as he reached over and turned off the light.

"Good night."

"Good night," said Cheney.

After a moment, in the dark: "You think we tell each other the truth when it really matters?"

"Of course," said Cheney.

Cheney thought about the look on Jamison Sanford's face. It was as though an invisible pain had him in its grasp, stretching his features and causing him to look gaunt and drawn.

As he got older, Cheney thought more and more about death. Not in an obsessive way, but rather in the way one recognized that night will eventually follow day and summer always ends.

And when he thought about such things, he hoped he would die before Elizabeth. He would not want to live in a world without her. Not want to have to cope with the pain of losing her. Not want to sit up nights, alone, with a bottle of good Chardonnay, trying to answer the unanswerable questions that accompanied such a loss.

Tonight as he lay there in the darkness, he thought about Jamison Sanford. Sanford was caught in that private hell right now. As Cheney lay in bed with his wife, Sanford lay in an empty bed a couple of houses away grieving and praying to his God for some peace.

Cheney turned over and spooned Elizabeth. She didn't move. She was already asleep.

But that didn't matter.

three

It was a glorious morning for golf. Cheney sat in the Riviera Country Club dining room looking out over the course. As a foursome of overweight business executives teed off, he recalled the old joke that God invented golf so white men would have a reason to dress like blacks. The joke wound up insulting both races, so it was probably acceptable these days.

He looked at his watch. Nine on the button. Sanford walked into the dining room and over to the corner. Cheney had chosen the table carefully, telling the waiter that, space permitting, he would prefer to have some privacy today. Everyone knew Cheney. Everyone liked him. He played three or four rounds a week and was a regular in the dining room and bar, where he could usually be seen sipping a Rombauer or a Burgess Chardonnay.

"Thanks, Cheney," said Sanford as he sat down.

Cheney and Sanford had never been close, but Sanford had always impressed Cheney as being a good-natured, friendly guy. A man who didn't look his age. This morning it seemed to Cheney that Sanford collapsed as much as sat down in the chair opposite him. He looked very tired. And suddenly he looked every month and day of his fifty-odd years.

The waiter arrived and poured Sanford a cup of coffee and a refill for Cheney.

Sanford played with his cup, unable to look Cheney directly in the eye. "This is really hard."

Cheney could only imagine what Sanford was going through. Losing a wife was obviously a devastating tragedy. Every ounce of that tragedy appeared to weigh on Sanford's face.

He finally looked up. "Look, I know you think I'm grasping at straws here, but this thing is driving me fuckin' crazy." Sanford took a deep breath.

"What makes you think Barbara was murdered, Jamison?" Cheney purposely used the man's name.

"A few things. First of all, they said Barbara was drunk and had staggered out into traffic when she was hit."

"The newspapers said her blood alcohol level was way over the legal limit."

"I know you and I have never been close over the years, but in all that time, whenever we socialized, didn't you notice that Barbara never drank alcohol?"

Cheney thought about it for a moment. He really hadn't noticed one way or the other. "Not really."

"Take my word for it. She never drank the stuff. Well, once, on our honeymoon, she had some champagne. Honestly, she used to smoke a little dope when she wanted to get high. Nothing serious, but she just was never into alcohol. It made her angry, hostile. And it also made her gain weight."

Cheney nodded. It was a minor point of interest that Sanford would admit his wife smoked marijuana. After all, Cheney was the former chief of detectives, and smoking dope was still illegal. Even in Los Angeles. Cheney took it as an indication that Sanford was willing to tell him everything.

"So what do you think happened to her?"

"I don't know. But there's more. Obviously, I had to identify the body. It was a horrible thing." Sanford shook his head and clenched his teeth before he went on. "What I saw made me retch. Literally."

"I'm sorry."

"It was more than what the car had done to her. Her body was covered with—"

This was tough. And Cheney could tell it wasn't going to get any easier.

"There were marks on her body."

"What kind of marks?"

"Burn marks. Little bruises and abrasions around . . . around her nipples and genitals."

Both men were silent for a moment. Cheney knew what to ask, but he decided just to let his friend speak. It was better that way, for both of them. At least for now.

"The police weren't interested in my questions about the marks. In fact, I think they thought I was responsible for them."

"And you weren't." It was not a question. Not quite.

"No. Barbara and I hadn't had sex in about a month when she was killed. In fact, I hadn't seen her naked in all that time. About a month before she died she seemed to change."

"In what way?"

"She became very distant. Remote. Preoccupied. That wasn't like Barbara. She had always been willing to communicate about what was bothering her. About a month before she was killed, she started staying up after I went to bed. Sleeping on the couch. Anything to avoid contact with me. She was going out at crazy hours, and when I confronted her about it, she just told me I was being silly and overly protective."

"What did you think was going on?"

"Naturally, I thought she had found someone else. Over the years I had tried to prepare myself for such a possibility. After all, I'm twenty years older than Barbara. At thirty-three she looked like she was in her mid-twenties. I . . . I adored her."

Cheney could vouch for Barbara's beauty. She had been a striking woman: slim, dark hair, green eyes, with an easy smile. Cheney remembered conversations he had had with other neighbors during which remarks were made to the effect that Jamison Sanford was indeed a lucky man.

But every refuge had its price.

For Sanford the price had risen by the minute.

"So you suspect that she had a . . . there was someone."

"Apparently. And whatever they did together was

certainly on the . . . what would you call it, the *rough* side?"

"And you told all this to the police."

"They weren't interested. Obviously the marks on her body had nothing to do with her death, not directly anyhow. She was hit by a car. And the marks were at least a couple of days old."

"I see. So what makes you so sure the marks on Barbara's body have anything to do with her death?"

"I'm not sure about anything, Cheney. I used to be sure of my marriage. Of my wife. None of my life makes much sense anymore. But my gut tells me something's not right. Our relationship had its ups and downs, no question about it. But we were always close. At least I thought we were. But for the month before her death, things changed. Drastically. Then suddenly she ends up drunk—a condition I can assure you she has not been in since we were married—then dead. I tell you, Cheney, something's just not right."

Cheney knew there was a lot about life, real life, that wasn't right. But that didn't make it illegal. Didn't make it murder.

"What do you want me to do, Jamison?"

"Look, I know I'm asking a lot. It's just that the police won't do anything. To them, it's just a hit-and-run, case closed. I know there's more."

"Maybe. But you might not like what I find out."

Cheney thought about saying what was on his mind. Which was, he knew damned well Sanford wasn't going to like what he found out. Knew damned well Sanford wasn't going to like knowing the name and face of the man who was marking his wife during some rough "sport sex."

But he also knew Sanford was going to get those answers one way or the other. So he just said, "I'll look into it."

"Thanks, Cheney. You don't know what this means to me."

"I don't know what I can do, but let me ask around."

"Great. Look, I expect to pay you for—"

"Forget it. I'm not a private detective, and I'm doing this because you're a friend. I don't need the money."

"So I've noticed. You live pretty well for a retired cop."

"City pension for a retired chief of detectives is pretty good these days. Besides, I made a killing in the real estate market in the late seventies, early eighties. That's how I was able to buy into the Palisades."

"Then how about a case of Stag's Leap?"

That was the closest thing to a smile Cheney had seen on Sanford's face. It wasn't a real smile, more a pale imitation of the old Sanford.

"Thanks," said Cheney. The gesture made Sanford feel better than it made Cheney feel, which was precisely why Cheney accepted it.

"So, how do we handle this?"

"I'll talk to a few people and we'll get together again. Then we'll figure out what to do next."

Sanford nodded, tasted his coffee for the first time, then stood. The two men shook hands. Sanford thanked Cheney again and left.

Cheney sat there for a while. Sipping his coffee.

And counting his blessings.

*   *   *

"Ten, fifteen"—Tony Boston looked up at Cheney in disgust and counted out the last ten dollars— "twenty, twenty-five."

Boston sat on the leather sectional just outside the plexiglass back wall of the racquetball court. Tony was about six foot three and had the kind of frame that baseball announcers refer to as lanky. His brown hair was short and his cheekbones high, the latter being the result of not eating regularly or well.

The two men drank natural fruit drinks they had purchased from the great-looking Chinese woman at the club's health food bar.

"You should give me points," said Boston.

"You always say that."

"Because you always beat me."

"But you're twelve years younger than I am."

"You've been playing longer than I have."

Cheney just smiled.

Tony Boston was Cheney's protégé. One of the conditions of his early retirement was that he could hand-pick his successor. Cheney had been Boston's rabbi. Beyond that, he had been his friend. Through it all. Including Boston's recent difficult divorce. Cheney often thought the term *difficult divorce* was redundant.

"So, what do you want to know?"

"What do you mean?" asked Cheney.

"You don't usually make the score that close unless you've got a reason."

"Am I that transparent?"

"Only because you want to be. It's friendly persuasion, Cheney, but you still want something."

Cheney drank his papaya juice and looked up at his sweaty friend. His very perceptive friend. "What do you know about Barbara Sanford?"

Boston squinted his eyes a little and finally said, "Hit-and-run. Nothing special. Why?"

"Her husband is a friend of mine."

"That's tough."

"What do you know about the case?"

Boston looked at his mentor and considered his answer. It was almost as though he were a student being presented a riddle. A zen puzzle. His mind raced through the data he knew about the case and, at the same time, he was trying to figure out why Cheney would choose this particular case to be interested in. Sure, it was his friend. But it was just a hit-and-run. Or was it?

"Actually, not much. I don't get involved in hit-and-runs. The only reason I even knew about it was that the husband was rich."

Cheney noted the words "the husband." So clinical. Removed. The chief of detectives saw all kinds of unspeakable things. It was best to develop a sterile vocabulary. It created distance.

"Would you look into it?"

"As a personal favor?"

"Yes."

"Done. Why?"

"My friend needs some answers."

"Don't we all," said Tony Boston.

"To answers." Cheney raised his plastic glass, touched it to his friend's glass, then drank.

"What should I be looking for?"

"Anything out of the ordinary. Something off-kilter. You know."

Boston smiled. He knew. Cheney had taught him to look for the wild thread, the odd piece that just didn't fit, a puzzle piece that looked like it should fit right in the middle of everywhere, but when you tried to place it, it fit nowhere.

Looking at it the right way was what made a good detective. Boston had learned that from the best. He had learned it from Cheney.

"So, how you doin'?"

"Okay, I guess."

"You like the condo?" asked Cheney, referring to the condo on Barrington in Brentwood that Boston had recently purchased. To people in the Midwest, it was a one-bedroom apartment with a den. To people in Los Angeles, it was a quarter-of-a-million-dollar home.

"It's cool. I run three, four days a week down San Vicente, and they got two or three bars where a large number of decent-looking women show up every night."

"Yeah, but they're all actresses," said Cheney. He knew the drill. He hadn't always been married.

"Right. When they find out I'm a cop they ask if I can get them on TV."

"So what do you tell them?"

"I tell them I was a consultant on *Hill Street Blues*."

"But—"

"Well, one episode, at least."

"Which never actually got shot."

"Still. . . ."

"Right." Cheney understood. In a town where people listed their own wedding videos as film credits, a person's résumé was merely virgin clay, ready to take shape as circumstances dictated. "You seeing any-body special?"

"Not really," said Boston with a sigh.

Tony Boston had been through the wringer, and Cheney had been there for every turn. Endless nights in bars detailing the injustices. A half dozen evenings putting Tony to bed, ignoring the tears, because men don't notice those things. One evening literally hold-ing Tony back from killing a man who was sleeping with his wife.

"I'm still looking," said Tony.

"For what?"

"I'd like to find someone like Elizabeth," said Tony. No one, even close friends like Tony, referred to Elizabeth by anything other than her full name. No Liz or Lizzie. No Betty or Beth. Elizabeth.

"I guess I'm a pretty lucky guy," said Cheney.

"You bet your ass."

Cheney toyed with his drink. "If I ask you a ques-tion, will you give me an honest answer?"

"Of course, why not?"

"You've known Elizabeth since we started dating, right on up through when we got married, right?"

"Right."

"Have you noticed any changes?"

"Changes?"

"In Elizabeth."

Tony pondered the question for a moment, then said, "Well, she does seem a little more philosophical these days."

"No, I mean, does she *look* different?"

"You mean like her figure?"

"Yes."

Tony thought about Elizabeth's figure for a moment, perhaps considering the possibility that he might be entering a quagmire in which there were only wrong answers. He had not risen to such high office without the ability to be a politician. "Elizabeth looks good."

"You mean for her age."

"I didn't say that."

"So, you're saying she looks as good as a twenty-year-old waitress?"

"Tell you the truth, she looks better than a lot of the twenty-year-old waitresses I know."

"You know what I mean."

"I'm not sure I do."

Cheney poured back another gulp of his papaya drink and set the large plastic cup down. "Elizabeth is thinking about having plastic surgery."

"Where?"

"In Los Angeles," said Cheney, keenly aware that he was not answering his friend's question.

"How do you feel about it?"

"I love her the way she is."

"Do you like the way she looks?"

"I said I love her."

"I know, but that doesn't answer the question."

"You think Elizabeth looks the same as when we got married?"

"I guess."

"Focus, Tony. You're an observant guy. Think about it. I'd really like to know."

After a moment, Tony said, "She looks a little different."

"Different?"

"Yeah, different."

"Different better or worse?"

"Define better or worse."

"This is bullshit, Tony. You know what I'm talking about. You know what I'm asking. Do you think Elizabeth looks more attractive now or seven years ago when I married her?"

"Look, Cheney, like they say, `Beauty is in the eye of the beholder.'"

"If I were a judge, I would order you to answer the question."

"People get older, Cheney. Not many of us look better than we did seven years ago, no matter how well we've taken care of ourselves."

"So what you're saying is that you don't think Elizabeth looks as attractive as she did a few years ago."

"Who does? Hell, you don't. Frankly, you don't look as good as you did last week."

"Thanks."

"So, is she getting a boob job?"

"I think that is the medical term for it, yes," said Cheney sarcastically.

"Cool. If you can afford it, you deserve it. That's what I always say. It'd be like making love to another woman."

It was the first time that thought crossed Cheney's mind. "Yeah?"

"Damned right. Think about it. Elizabeth has a certain body one day, the next day it's a different body. For you it would be like cheating, but doing it legally."

"Never thought about it like that."

"Eh, Tony?"

Cheney and Tony turned toward the voice. A slender woman with dirty-blond hair, wearing white terry-cloth shorts, a black midriff top and matching headband, bulky white socks and Nike tennis shoes, and carrying an attractive leather athletic bag, walked over and sat down next to Tony.

"Hi, Kim," said Tony, standing as she took a seat in a chair opposite the sectional.

Friends. Not hugging or kissing friends, noted Cheney. Perhaps a professional acquaintance. His mind never stopped. Even when it should.

"Kimberly Gary, I'd like you to meet my friend and mentor, Derek Cheney."

Kimberly offered her hand; then a look of recognition flashed across her face.

"Derek Cheney? Former chief of detectives?"

Cheney smiled.

"Kim works for the *LA Tribune*. She's a reporter."

"My son works for the *Trib*."

"Really?"

"Donald Cheney?"

Kimberly shook her head. "It's a big place."

"Person with your looks ought to be doing TV news." The words were out before Cheney had a chance to strangle them back where they belonged.

"Why, thank you. Actually, my agent says she's got something with one of the local independent channels in the works."

"Your agent? Guess the newspaper game has changed since my tour of duty."

"I'm really honored to meet you," said Kimberly. "Of course, I've read a lot about you. And that piece they did about you on *Sixty Minutes* was great."

"It was like a video gold watch. Hang around long enough, you get all kinds of things," said Cheney modestly.

"And that Yamaguchi thing. That was a tough one."

A tough one? Those weren't the words Cheney would have used. Tough was when you missed a putt on the last hole. In the Yamaguchi case, people had died. People who didn't deserve to die. Who deserves to die? thought Cheney. Such questions were not asked by sane men.

"Yeah, that was a . . . tough one."

Kimberly looked at her watch. "I've got a game in two minutes on court one. You can see how badly I play." She stood. "Nice meeting you, Mr. Cheney," she said, extending her hand.

"Just call me Cheney. Everybody does."

She smiled. "Call me," she said to Tony; then she left.

In less than a minute she appeared on the racquetball court directly in front of them.

"Friend of yours?"

"Not as friendly as I'd like."

"How do you know her?"

"She's a reporter, I'm a good contact. You know the drill."

"When I was chief, the drill was usually run by myself and a couple of guys who carried flasks of bad scotch and smoked cheap cigars."

"Times change."

"Nice to know some things change for the better."

"I dunno," said Tony absently.

"What do you mean?"

"It's hard to tell if I'm being used or not."

"Listen to your mentor. We all get used, kid. Sometimes it just feels better than others, that's all."

"Yeah, well, this doesn't feel like anything at all. We never went out, nothin'. Strictly business."

"So how're you getting used?"

"Skip it."

"You like her, don't you?"

"What's not to like?"

"Look, Tony, the divorce has only been final for six months. It's not like your cock is going to drop off at midnight. Lighten up. Let it happen. You don't have to marry the first good-looking woman you meet."

After a moment. "You're right. Maybe I am pressing a little."

"A little? Last week you were ready to buy some bullshit self-help book because that cocktail waitress at Nathan's wouldn't go out with you."

"I thought she liked me. The signs were there."

"She said she couldn't go out because she was married."

"She wasn't wearing a ring."

"Listen to yourself. Get a grip."

"Maybe you're right."

"Of course I'm right."

Through the glass, out of the corner of his eye, Cheney began to notice Kimberly playing against her male opponent. He tried to focus on his conversation with Tony Boston, but he found himself increasingly distracted. She looked to be about thirty. Her body was tanned and toned, typical LA specs. Although Cheney "appreciated a well-turned calf"—as they used to say in polite society before rock and rap music made it socially acceptable to say exactly what you meant, and loudly—he remained a spectator, not a player.

"What are you looking at?" asked Tony Boston.

Cheney turned his attention back to his friend. "Nothing."

"So, what are you doing home?" said Petty.

"I live here," said Cheney. "What are you making?"

She returned her attention to the mixing bowl. "Low-fat chocolate angel food cake."

"Really?"

"I'm using the fructose sugar, naturally."

"Naturally."

Petty knew Cheney was interested. What else did he do? Since his retirement he ran four miles almost every day, continued his quest for good under-fifteen-dollar Chardonnays, made pasta and other low-fat gourmet foods, and basically tried to stay busy. As long as he stayed out from underfoot, Petty didn't care what he did.

"The cake flour has no fat, the fructose sugar has no fat, and I'm using a nonfat hot chocolate mix."

"That's not in the recipe," said Cheney, referring to the hot chocolate.

"I'm going out on a limb."

"When will it be ready?"

"Gee, I dunno. When would you like?"

"I'm just curious, that's all."

"It'll be outa the oven in forty minutes. But it's gotta cool, and I don't think you should eat it right away."

"What do you mean?"

"You're so compulsive. I think you're substituting."

"What?"

"I know you think my world is limited to cooking shows and *Geraldo*, but I listen to talk radio sometimes too. I think you're substituting food for something that's missing in your life."

"That's ridiculous. I'm in great shape."

"That's what's so insidious about it."

"Insidious? I've never heard you use that word before."

"Talk radio's got this 'Vocabulary Word for the Day' thing. You know what *flatulent* means?"

"Yes. And I'm surprised they would use that word on radio."

"The airwaves are wide open these days, Cheney. Ever hear that Prince song 'Sexy M/F'?"

"Somehow it's escaped my notice."

"You know what M/F stands for?"

"I've got a vague idea. So what do you mean I'm substituting?" said Cheney, trying to steer Petty back on track.

"You're trying to pretend there's nothing missing in your life. So you spend your time running around buying, eating, and, even worse, *cooking* gourmet foods."

"It's a wonder they don't just come and take me away, isn't it," he said sarcastically.

"It could happen."

"Now that I've got my ten cents' worth of radio psychobabble, my day is nearly complete."

"Go ahead and laugh. Next thing you know you'll be making baskets in a rubber room."

Cheney just shook his head and started for the refrigerator.

Petty stopped him and handed him a glass of white wine. "Burgess, 1990."

"It's probably warm."

"I poured it when I heard your car."

Cheney looked at Petty and tried to think of something nasty to say. Instead he took the wine and left the room.

In the living room he sat down at the piano and started pounding out some tunes that made him think. Made him not think. Learning to play the piano had helped him retain some semblance of sanity over the years. Then he picked up the phone next to the white grand piano and dialed a number.

"Yes?"

"Elizabeth."

"Cheney."

"When are you coming home?"

"Soon."

"Like . . . ?"

"I should be there by *Nightline*. Is Petty making anything?"

"Some kind of nonfat chocolate angel food cake."

"Sounds great. I'll try to finish here as fast as I can. See you soon."

For some reason, the sentence "Is Petty making anything?" echoed in his mind. Why should it make any difference what Petty was making? Wasn't it enough that he was here, waiting?

Cheney drew a deep breath. He had been down this road dozens of times over the past few months.

Elizabeth was putting in long hours, working hard. She was committed. To people who needed her. She shared with him all the time she had left over. He was certain she loved him. No doubt about it.

He was making something out of nothing. That's what he kept telling himself.

Still. . . .

Cheney turned back to the keyboard and started playing the Eagles' "Desperado."

Outside it started to rain.

Cheney played.

Petty baked.

Elizabeth worked.

And the world danced in and out of light.

In and out of shadows.

The knife blade descended.

Quickly.

Piercing flesh.

Crazy eyes. Behind the knife. The knife slashed downward again.

And again.

Gino hit a key on the keyboard and turned toward the blonde. "So, what do you think?"

"Brilliant. As usual."

"I think the smash cuts work," he said, referring to the editing style, which employed quick, jolting cuts from one image to another, often accompanied by enhancing sound effects, such as a steel door being slammed shut.

The movie business being what it was, especially the low-budget movie business, Gino usually found himself in three stages of work simultaneously: shooting the current film, in postproduction on the last film, and in preproduction on the next one.

He turned his swivel chair away from the monitor and put his feet up on the console.

"How you doin'?" said the blonde.

"I'm tired. The movie's been—"

"You know what I mean."

Gino picked up his warm coffee mug and held it in both hands as though he were preparing to pray. "It's happening again."

The blonde sighed deeply. "I warned you not to go after Barbara."

"I know. But I thought that would be the end of it."

"I don't know how much I can help you this time, Gino."

"Does anyone suspect . . . about Barbara, I mean?"

"Not yet. But her husband still believes she was murdered."

"He's got no proof."

"But he's got money."

Gino stood and walked to the blonde. Put his arms around her. Put his head on her shoulder. Held her tightly. After a moment, he said, "I can't help myself. You know that, don't you?"

"I know, Gino. I know," she said, stroking his hair gently.

"You'll still love me?"

"Of course."

"You're the only one who really loves me. The only one who has never betrayed me."

"We understand each other," she said. She continued to stroke Gino's hair. "We understand what happened."

As he kept his head on the woman's shoulder, Gino wondered if anyone else would understand . . . if they knew what had happened.

four

Cheney was having the chocolate angel food cake for breakfast when Elizabeth walked in, poured herself a cup of coffee, and sat down at the kitchen table, which looked out on the back yard.

"What time did you come to bed last night?" asked Cheney.

"I think it was about twelve-thirty."

Cheney nodded. It had been one-fifteen. At least that's what the digital clock next to their bed had read.

"You're working too hard."

"It's coming to an end," she said, holding the hot cup with two hands, staring out at the pool.

"What takes till midnight? I mean, it isn't like you've got a patient who comes in that late."

"What are you saying?" Elizabeth turned toward her husband.

"I'm just curious what takes till after midnight to accomplish in your practice. It's never been this way since I've known you."

"I do have a nine-thirty."

"Every night?"

"Often. And you know things have gotten backed up since Nancy quit. By the time I'm done seeing patients, handling paperwork and insurance forms . . . it's just overwhelming. Plus I'm getting tax information together for Sal. Don't worry, things are changing."

"When?"

"Soon. Today I'm interviewing a receptionist/office manager Sal recommended. If she works out and I get the tax info all bundled up, things will get back to normal in a couple of weeks."

"Good," said Cheney. He drank some Ovaltine.

"Is something wrong?"

"What do you want me to say? Nothing's wrong, I don't mind going to bed by myself, night after night, week after week? It's been going on for nearly three months straight."

"I didn't react this way to your schedule when you were chief of detectives."

"You knew what my schedule was going to be like from day one. Now, all of a sudden, after seven years of marriage, your schedule has changed. Drastically."

"For three months. You know what I think is wrong?"

"What?"

"I think you're bored."

"That's another thing. A couple of years ago we made a *joint* decision that I take early retirement so we could spend more time together—"

"*And* so you didn't wind up getting shot. Don't forget that part."

Cheney decided not to mention, for the hundredth time, that that was more her concern than his. "Anyhow, I retire, and here I am with all kinds of time to spend with you; now you're too busy to show up."

Elizabeth turned away again. "I really think you're making way too much out of this. This is the first time in seven years my schedule's been like this. And I've promised you things are going to change soon." Elizabeth turned back toward her husband. "Trust me, okay?"

"Trust you? It isn't a question of trust, it's a question of time."

Elizabeth smiled. "I hate to say this, but I've got to run."

"Surprise, surprise."

"See you tonight," she said, and kissed him on the top of his head.

As his wife stood and walked away, Cheney noticed with a sense of pride that she was very well dressed today in her navy Donna Karan jacket with a matching skirt and Ferragamo pumps. Her cherry-colored leather attaché case completed a coordinated, if rather expensive, ensemble.

"Is that a promise?"

Her hand went up in a sort of wave as she disappeared through the door that led into the garage.

He heard a car door slam, her Mercedes engine turn over, the garage door open and close. Elizabeth was gone.

"So, what are you in such a good mood about?"

Petty walked in wearing a long blue robe over her nightgown. She was not a morning person.

"I'm not in a good mood."

"I was being ironic," said Petty. She poured herself a cup of coffee and sat down opposite Cheney.

"You were being a smart-ass."

"You know, Cheney, you're not a morning person."

Cheney just stared at her.

"What's on the agenda today, another search through some esoteric wine store up the coast looking for a fabulous Chardonnay? Or maybe it's trying to break twenty-eight minutes for four miles. Maybe you'll try to break seventy-five at Riviera. Or maybe this'll be the day you figure out how to make a great spinach egg-white-only pasta. The day is filled with possibility."

After a moment, Cheney said, "Are you through?"

"I'm sure I left something out. But you've got to admit you live a fascinating life."

"A lot of people would kill for a life like mine."

"And I'm sure they do," said Petty patronizingly.

"Do you have a point here, or is this just the daily public flogging?"

"You could always fire me."

"It'd be easier to get the Queen of England to step down."

Cheney drank some more Ovaltine. The phone rang. "I'll get it," he said as he stood.

"Slow down. It's not like I'm gonna race you for it."

"Hello?"

"I've got the information you wanted," said Tony Boston on the other end of the line.

"That was fast. When can we meet?"

"How 'bout lunch at the Brentwood Hamlet."

"Noon."

"See you there."

Cheney hung up and sat back down at the table.

Petty peered impishly over her coffee cup. "One of your buddies get a line on a secret pasta recipe?"

Fran Palmer was the manager of the Brentwood Hamlet, so she was often there when Cheney stopped by for lunch. She had organized several wine tastings at the Hamlet for Cheney over the years, and she was always willing to assist him on his well-known quest for good inexpensive Chardonnays. As he had explained to her one day, "Any idiot can find a decent twenty-five-dollar bottle. It takes time and persistence to find value." And Cheney had plenty of time on his hands these days.

Fran was a babe, even though she was pushing the age where women stopped giving their ages. Which, Cheney realized, was the day they turned twenty-nine. At least that was the way they played the game in Los Angeles. Women lied about their ages; men lied about everything else.

"You've got to try the Thai Chicken Caesar Salad," said Fran.

"It's good, Tony," said Cheney.

"Sounds good."

"And I've got a Clos Pegase that Jimmy says is exceptional. I'll give you a taste. Would you like a glass?" Fran asked Tony.

"No, thanks. I'm on duty."

Fran smiled and walked away.

"Is she married?"

"No," said Cheney. "But she's involved with a married man."

"Hmmm," said Tony, folding his menu and looking away.

Cheney knew how Tony felt about married people having affairs.

"So, what have you got?" said Cheney, trying to pull his friend back into present time.

"Nothing."

Cheney snorted. "Could've saved me a lunch tab by telling me that on the phone."

"A good cop can always use a free lunch. Especially if it's someplace other than a hot-dog stand. What's your interest in this case anyhow?"

"I'm just doing a favor for a friend."

"What are you looking for?"

"I don't know." Cheney toyed with his water. "Did you read the autopsy report?"

"Yes. By the way, it's rather strange to do an autopsy on a hit-and-run victim."

"Not if the husband suspects foul play."

"Not if the husband's rich, you mean."

"Did you read the report or not?" said Cheney, trying to get an answer to his question.

"You mean the marks on her body. The cigarette burns, the abrasions around her breasts and genitals."

"Yeah."

"So what? She didn't die of cigarette burns. Car hit her straight on, going around seventy miles an hour."

"Her husband hadn't slept with her in a month, and he tells me they weren't into rough sex."

"So she had a lover. It happens."

"Her husband also said she never drank."

"She drank that night. Her blood alcohol level was point-one-eight. Hell, that's legally drunk in Moscow."

"She could've been murdered."

"She could've been Ethel Merman, but she wasn't. Don't get me wrong, I'm not trying to be unsympathetic. I can relate to the pain of finding out your wife is . . . well, you know I can understand the guy's pain. But it's a real leap of faith to make this into a murder case."

"I told him I'd look into it."

"So you did, and you can tell him there's nothing to it. And as far as trying to find out who the other guy is?" Tony sighed deeply and shook his head. "Tell your friend the truth isn't all it's cracked up to be."

The awkward silence was broken when the waitress brought Cheney's wine, then left.

"Let me ask you a question. You saw the autopsy report. Would you say the 'rough sex' was consensual?"

"How the hell can I tell that?"

"Think. You've seen victims of the sadists who torture women. And you've seen a raid at an S and M parlor. There's a difference. For one thing, S and M play is usually more fantasy than reality. And even when it's reality, it's not usually something that leaves a lasting scar. People play at it, get close, a little closer, a little closer, then back off."

"The marks looked real."

"Scars?"

"Probably."

"Why would a married woman do that? She knows her husband is going to see the scars sooner or later. And when he does, the marriage is over."

"Maybe. Maybe not. Maybe her boyfriend just got carried away."

"I met Barbara Sanford several times. She was an incredibly bright person. I could understand her being passionate, but I find it difficult to believe she was stupid."

"Maybe she was planning to leave her husband. Look, Cheney, the thing is, she's dead. It's over. Nothing you can do will bring her back. And every piece of information you retrieve about her lover just becomes more glass her husband is going to have to crawl through," said Tony, with conviction.

"I can be discreet."

"There's no way to make shit smell sweet."

"Thai Chicken Caesar Salad," said the waitress as she set the plates in front of the two men and walked away.

"Oh, by the way, you remember Kimberly?"

"Sure, the girl from the racquetball court."

"She asked me for your number."

"Really?" Cheney picked up a fork and dug into his salad.

"Should I give it to her?"

"Sure, why not?"

"I dunno. Just wanted to check with you first."

"What does she want?"

"Who knows. She's kind of a cop groupie if you ask me."

"You ever go out with her?"

"Not yet. We've played racquetball a few times, but that's about it."

"You planning to ask her out?"

"When the time is right."

"I'll put in a good word for you if she calls me."

"Do that."

Cheney and Tony stopped talking and ate what they both agreed later was an excellent salad.

And Cheney was surprised to discover that the main thing he remembered about Kimberly Gary was the muscles in her thighs when she planted her right foot for a kill shot.

"Nice shot," said Jamison Sanford.

Cheney looked up from the third in a line of balls lined up on the Riviera putting green. "I've been having a little trouble with my putter lately. I'm trying this old blade putter I had when I was in college."

"Looks like you wrapped it around a tree."

"Actually, I did."

Sanford nodded and smiled politely.

"So," said Cheney. He picked up his brand new Titleist balls, walked over to his bag, which was leaning against an iron railing, and stuffed his putter and the golf balls into his bag, "you want some coffee?"

"Where does that leave us?" asked Sanford, when Cheney had finished telling him what he had learned from Tony Boston.

Cheney realized it left them in separate places, but he didn't say so. "I'm not sure."

Sanford put a couple of C & H sugars into his coffee. "What do you think I should do?"

"About what?" asked Cheney. He was thinking a lot of things and had arrived at several conclusions. But he would prefer not to say any of them to his friend.

"You think she was murdered?"

"I have no idea. There is no evidence to support that theory."

"What does your gut tell you?"

"Nothing," Cheney lied.

"I don't have a gut on this, Cheney. My insides have been ripped out and served up to me on a platter. I'm empty. I need answers."

"I don't have any answers for you, Jamison. I wish I did."

"You think I ought to let sleeping dogs lie. That I might get hurt by what you find out." Sanford didn't wait for a response. "How can I help you get me some answers?"

Cheney stared down at his coffee. He knew this was it—a turning point. He could still get away clean. Still skate on the surface of socially acceptable exit lines. *Nothing I can do. You know I'd like to help, but what can I do that the police can't?* Cheney knew them all by heart.

Instead he said, "Who was your wife's closest friend? Besides you, of course," he added quickly.

Sanford smiled. "I wasn't her best friend. I know it's fashionable for husbands and wives to be each other's best friend. Not fashionable, really. Maybe that's the way it's supposed to be. But that wasn't the way it was with us. You've got to remember, Barbara was twenty years younger than I."

Cheney noted the stilted grammar. Stilted? Correct grammar often sounded stilted in the nineties. It seemed to him as though grammar, art, and life in general were being leveled out at the lowest common denominator, and those who knew the way to the higher—or at least more traditional ground—had to apologize for that knowledge.

"So who was her best friend?"

"Kyoko Rabinowitz."

"How can I get in touch with her?"

"I've got her phone number."

"What can you tell me about her?"

"Kyoko and Barbara were in the same acting company in Vegas."

"I didn't know your wife was an actress."

"Yes, well, Barbara did a good many things before we met." Sanford toyed with his coffee, then looked up at his neighbor. "I'm not an idiot, Cheney. I know Barbara had a life before I met her. I know that; I know a lot of things. I can tell you honestly that nothing I know about her past seems to have any bearing on what happened to her on the Pacific Coast Highway."

"You say that . . . "—this was hard to say—"you say you didn't have sex with your wife in the month prior to her death."

"That's right."

"Was that unusual?"

"It was unusual for us. I'm not a sex machine, but even at my age I found Barbara very stimulating.

We always had sex two, three, four times a week. We would never let a week go by without having sex."

"I see. But you didn't have sex with your wife for an entire month prior to her death."

"That's right."

"Did you talk about that?"

"Of course. At least I brought it up."

"And?"

"Nothing."

"Nothing?"

"She wouldn't tell me why. And that was strange because we had always been able to communicate so well. Usually I'd come home at night and we'd talk about what we each did during the day, have dinner—which she would make—or we'd go out to dinner, which we did about four nights a week. She usually talked about her theater company."

"Theater company?"

Sanford smiled. For the first time, Cheney noted. It wasn't a big smile, but it was a start. "Well, it wasn't hers, actually. Although we—that is, I—contributed regular sums of money to keep the doors open. It was Barbara's way of staying involved. She knew she would never be an actress, but she loved the life."

"The life?"

"If you've been around live theater, you know what I'm talking about. If you haven't, I'm not sure I can really explain it. For Barbara, it was a connection to what she called her 'passion.'"

"Was Kyoko Rabinowitz a member of that theater company?"

"Yes."

"So, what do you want me to do, Jamison?" Cheney knew it was a loaded question. It meant more than *Do you want me to find out if your wife was murdered?* It meant more than *Do you want me to find out the identity of the murderer?* It meant filling in the blanks with answers that Sanford would have to live with forever.

"Give me the truth, Cheney." Sanford didn't flinch when he looked Cheney in the eye. He knew what it meant. Knew the implications.

He was over twenty-one. In all the important ways. "Give me Kyoko Rabinowitz's phone number," said Cheney.

"So, how was your day?" asked Elizabeth. She sat on the sofa in the living room. Home by ten-thirty. "A new record," Cheney had observed. Elizabeth had refuted his comment and asked him if there was something wrong.

He told her about his conversation with Sanford.

"I really want to watch *Seinfeld* before I go to sleep."

"Pardon?"

"It's a funny show. You like it too."

"I know, but I was talking," said Cheney.

"You taped it, didn't you?"

"Yes, but I was talking about one of our friends. The guy's in pain."

"Look, Cheney, it isn't that I don't care, it's just that watching something funny, after listening all day to people on the verge of putting guns to their heads, is a nice change of pace."

"Sorry." But he really wasn't. "Do you think we're connecting?"

"What do you mean by that?"

"I know we love each other. I know we're supposed to be best friends—"

"What do you mean 'supposed to be'?"

"We are," said Cheney.

"Which means?"

"That we tell each other everything."

"That's the litmus test for being best friends?"

"If someone is your best friend, what is there to hide?"

"Just because you don't say something doesn't mean you're hiding it."

"Sounds like gamesmanship to me," said Cheney.

"Well, luckily you aren't the only one who gets to make up the rules."

"You sound a little hostile tonight."

Elizabeth sighed and moved closer to her husband on the sofa. "I'm sorry, Cheney," she whispered into his ear.

"Really?" said Cheney, concentrating more on the heat of her breath than on her words.

"Really. I'm sorry. You like it when I say I'm sorry, don't you?"

Cheney thought about saying no, but he decided to come clean. "Yes, I do."

"Me too," she whispered in his ear. Huskily.

Cheney turned toward his wife. Looked her in the eye. "I miss you," he said sincerely.

"I'm here," she said.

Cheney held her close. Closer than he had in weeks. Then he felt her trying subtly to end the embrace.

"So, *Seinfeld*. . . ."

Cheney sighed, a beaten man, and reached for the remote control.

five

Kyoko Rabinowitz was a very good-looking woman. She had Japanese features, dark skin, and a dancer's legs. She was wearing white shorts and a bright yellow T-shirt with a Rolling Stones logo on it—the one with the tongue. She was barefoot. And she smoked a noticeably foreign cigarette.

"You Cheney?"

"Ms. Rabinowitz?"

"My first husband was Jewish. In this town, in the business I'm in—" She ushered him in without finishing the sentence.

Cheney sat in a large orange beanbag chair. Next to the chair, about eye level, was a terrarium. In the center stood a large tarantula. A large rubber tarantula.

"Can I get you something to drink?"

"No, I'm fine."

Kyoko sat on a couch opposite Cheney, curling her

legs up underneath her. "So, how's Jamison doing?" she said.

Cheney made a sympathetic face and shook his head. "It's tough."

"He really loved her."

Cheney noticed she did not say they really loved each other or that she loved him. "I appreciate your seeing me."

"Sure, no sweat. You're a cop, right?"

"I used to be."

"So, what's the deal? I thought Barbara was killed by a hit-and-run driver."

"That's probably what happened."

"Probably?"

"I'm a friend of her husband. I'm just tying up a few loose ends."

Kyoko looked Cheney in the eye for a moment, then turned and flicked an ash into a Caesar's Palace ashtray.

"Jamison said you were Barbara's best friend."

"That's true."

"How long had you known her?"

"More than ten years. We met in Vegas. We were in the same theater company there. That must've been '82, '83, something like that. The 'theater' was a dingy little hole in the wall that used to be an old strip joint on Paradise Road. Seems kind of romantic, thinking about it now. But I guess a lot of things seem that way when you put enough distance there."

Cheney knew that was true. "You two were actresses?"

"I still am. I was in a *Hunter* a few years ago and I did two *Magnums*. Couple feature roles. Not much work for Asian actresses unless you wanna be a hooker or run around a rice paddy wearing a big stupid-looking hat."

"It's a tough business."

"Life's tough. I got no complaints. Least none I'm planning to talk about with you." Kyoko took a drag off her cigarette, inhaled, and filled the air with smoke. "So, anyhow, Barbara and I came here to try and crack the big-time. We got an apartment together, not too far from here, really."

Cheney noted that Barbara had moved a world away, to Pacific Palisades, while Kyoko had traveled only a couple of blocks. But then, not all movement in life was defined by geography or the real estate contained thereon.

"Then you were around when Barbara met Jamison."

"Sure. He came to a theater where we were performing one night. Barbara and I and a couple of friends were doing a showcase."

"Showcase?"

"One-acts, blackouts, things like that. It's an opportunity to show off our talent for agents and people who can do us some good. But we always give out tickets, or sell them if we can, to other people so the house looks bigger. It's only maybe fifty or sixty seats, but even a little place like that looks empty when five people show up. I mean, it's embarrassing when the cast outnumbers the audience."

"So Jamison came to a showcase."

"Someone where he worked gave him a ticket. Apparently he and his ex-wife were big on the theater. Anyhow, he hung around outside after the show and asked Barbara if she wanted to have a drink. Naturally, I tagged along. It was a chance for a free meal, so what the hell, right?"

"Right. Did Barbara stay in touch with anyone besides you after she married Jamison?"

"That's a funny question."

Cheney knew it was a funny question, and he also knew that her response was not an answer. "I don't have a hidden agenda here, okay? I just never got to know Barbara and I'm trying to get a handle on the kind of person she was. Jamison said you knew her better than anyone."

"Barbara was not cut out to be an actress. You gotta be committed, you know what I mean? Even if you're committed and talented, chances are you're still gonna wind up waiting tables."

"So what you're saying is that Barbara used Jamison as her way out of a tough situation."

"I didn't say that. She was very good to him."

Again, Cheney noted, Kyoko had not used the *L* word, in a place where *love* would have been appropriate.

"How long after she met Jamison did she marry him?"

"About six months. He was crazy about her. I mean, you saw her, right?"

"She was very beautiful." Cheney felt uneasy about what he was going to say, what he must say. But if he was going to find out what happened to Barbara Sanford in the month preceding her death, he was going to have to say such things.

"I want you to know that our conversation is confidential."

"If you say so." Kyoko Rabinowitz was not a woman who trusted easily.

"Did Barbara confide in you?"

"As much as anyone."

"More than her husband?"

Kyoko flicked the ashes off her cigarette. "Probably."

"There is evidence to suggest—"

"You sound like Perry Mason."

"Sorry. Was Barbara seeing someone for the month prior to her death?"

"She was seeing me."

"Either you're trying to be humorous or evasive. Which is it?"

"I don't have to tell you anything."

"I know that. But I'm acting on your dead friend's behalf."

"No, you're not. You're acting on her husband's behalf. Don't get me wrong, I've got nothing against Jamison. He's a sweet guy. But we all have a right to our privacy."

"There are exceptions. Especially when what is done in that privacy impacts or hurts someone else."

"What if revealing that privacy will hurt someone else?"

"I thought you didn't care about Jamison."

"Look, I'm in a tough spot here. Barbara was my friend. I feel obliged. You got a question, ask me straight and let's go from there."

"I have reason to believe that Barbara was seeing someone, sexually, in the month prior to her death."

"Why do you say a month?"

"Because something happened, physically, that had never happened to her before."

Kyoko sighed, looked away, puffed on her dark cigarette. "She was acting strangely for a few weeks before her death."

"Strangely?"

"She was distant. She would cancel lunch dates, she wouldn't show up at the theater, she wouldn't return my calls." Kyoko shook her head.

"What did you make of it?"

"I don't know."

"Another man?"

Kyoko looked at Cheney and gave him a cockeyed smile. "If it was another man, I would have been the first to know."

That opened up an entirely different can of worms. To Cheney, that statement was as much as an open admission that Kyoko *had* been the first to know—about others.

"Did you ask her what was wrong?"

"Of course."

"What did she say?"

"What people always say when they don't want to, or can't, talk about it. Nothing."

"Did she ever regret giving up the theater?" asked Cheney, trying a different tack.

"Oh, she still kept her hand in. Last few years more as a patron, a behind-the-scenes person. But she still considered herself a part of our theater company."

"Which is?"

"The Sunset Players. We got a little theater on Sunset, just west of Gardner. She used to come by once, twice a week."

"When's your next performance?"

"Tonight, actually. We're doing a showcase. I play a whore in an original one-act called *The Off-Ramp Café*. It's about this bar under a downtown freeway off-ramp. Lots of traffic noise. It gets to be white noise after a while. Like it's irritating at first, really offensive, but then after a while you don't notice it anymore." Kyoko dropped some ash into the Caesar's Palace ashtray without looking. "Like a lot of things in life. You wanna come?"

"Maybe."

"I'll leave your name at the door."

"Here," said Petty, handing Cheney a piece of paper with a long list of items on it.

He looked at it. A grocery list.

"I need it by five."

"Anything else?" said Cheney sarcastically.

"Some oregano," she said. Missing, or choosing to miss, the sarcasm.

"Something smells good."

"Sit down."

Cheney sat. He often considered the irony that he was able, in the not too distant past, to walk into a building and cause several hundred street-tough men to snap to attention. And yet he was an underling in his own home. Long ago Cheney had come to the conclusion that, in spite of their combative banter, he simply liked and respected this woman. And he knew she felt the same way about him, though neither would admit that mutual admiration aloud if their lives depended on it.

Petty ladled some minestrone soup into a bowl she had set in front of Cheney. He tasted it, while Petty stood, waiting for her accolade.

"It's great."

"You said that about the lasagna yesterday." She turned and walked back to the sink. "You're an articulate man. Learn a new word."

"You're impossible. I tell you it's great, we got an argument. God forbid I tell you something's good."

"Everything I make is great, and you know it. This is more than a job. It's my passion. For nearly forty years, beginning with my sainted mother—" Petty stopped and genuflected.

Cheney had heard it all before. He ate his soup and tuned out Petty's voice.

The phone rang.

"It's for you." Petty covered the phone. "It's a woman."

"I'll take it in the other room," said Cheney. He stood and walked out of the kitchen.

"Naturally," said Petty, to his back.

"Hello?" said Cheney as he sat down in the leather chair behind his cluttered mahogany desk. The chair was big, the leather cracked, and it didn't really match the desk. But Cheney loved it, despite Elizabeth's protestations that he buy something more suitable.

"Cheney?" said a female voice.

"Yes."

"Kimberly Gary. I met you over at the racquetball club. Remember me?"

"Of course." He remembered her legs. Cheney shook his head and smiled at himself. He wasn't normally like that, and he did not find this mental process attractive in other men. "What can I do for you?"

"My regular racquetball partner just canceled, and—well, Tony said your wife's been working late these days. I was hoping you might be free, say around eight o'clock."

"Thanks for the invitation, but I'm going to have to pass. Elizabeth and I are going out to dinner tonight. Maybe some other time."

Pause. "Sure. Let me give you my number."

Cheney grabbed a pen.

"I live in Westwood. Same area code as yours. That's 555-9947."

Cheney wrote the number down and repeated it.

"Give me a call anytime. I could always use another racquetball partner, and Tony says you're pretty good."

"Tony knows it pays to say good things about me. That's why he's so successful."

"Anyhow, I hope you give me a call sometime."

"Will do," said Cheney and hung up.

He sat there for a moment. Was this attractive woman flirting with him? It sounded like it. Wishful thinking? No, she was clearly flirting with him. And the remark, "Tony said your wife's been working late these days." Did she ask Tony about his marital status, or did Tony just volunteer the information? It was not the kind of thing that would come up in normal conversation.

What did she want? Of course, she was a reporter. Still, she was very attractive. Big deal, a little racquetball game. What the hell, it would be fun.

* * *

Cheney's attention was focused on Sotheby's Preview catalogue. Moet & Chandon was offering vintage champagnes and Dom Perignon from Moet's Épernay cellars. For years he had been trying to get his hands on a 1914 Moet, the grapes for which were picked during enemy bombardment. He already had a 1911, which the late Andre Simon had simply labeled "The Best." He had given a friend, an LAPD lieutenant, a 1952 for his fortieth birthday in 1992; Cheney had kept two bottles of the same vintage for himself. Cheney's favorite champagne was the '69 Dom Perignon, which was renowned for its vanilla taste, among other attractive attributes.

In fact, Cheney did not particularly care for champagne and would, almost always, choose a decent Chardonnay over what most people called fabulous champagne. But there were exceptions, and Sotheby's catalogue contained some of those exceptions.

The phone rang and Cheney picked it up immediately. "Yes?"

"Hi, honey. What are you doing?"

"Figuring out how to spend some of our money."

"Hopefully it doesn't involve Sotheby's catalogue."

Living with someone, being open and honest, had its drawbacks. "So, we on for eight?"

"That's what I'm calling about. I'm afraid I'm going to be late again."

"I thought you said this kind of thing was coming to an end."

"It is. It's just that it isn't over yet. Work with me

on this, Cheney. I'll make it up to you."

Cheney thought about a lot of nasty things to say, but he bit his tongue. "What time will you be home?"

"Before midnight for sure."

"Okay."

Silence.

"Are you mad at me?"

"No. See you later," said Cheney, and he hung up.

Cheney closed the catalogue and tossed it across the desk. When he did, his note pad appeared. On the note pad was a number.

He picked up the phone and dialed. "Kimberly?"

"Cheney. I recognize that voice."

"How would you like to see a play tonight?"

The showcase was a series of one-acts and solo per-formances. A couple of guys did a scene from *Death of a Salesman*. There were several original one-acts deal-ing with life on the "mean streets of Los Angeles." Kyoko Rabinowitz played a whore in one and a lawyer in another; Cheney wondered if she thought she was being typecast. One singer/actor/waiter sang something that sounded like "Mack the Knife." One actress came onstage naked and did a performance-art piece entitled "Newed." She shaved her legs with an electric razor, read obituaries from the *LA Times*, turned on a large fan and ran toward it, her long black hair blowing wildly. She constantly referred to her breasts, which were, thought Cheney, quite attrac-tive. By the end of the piece, Cheney realized he was being lumped together in the mass of manipulative male figures who controlled women and saw them merely as breasts, cunts (her word), legs, and asses: body parts. Cheney found himself perusing the program in dim light during the final portion of the young woman's performance. But he did it surreptitiously lest he be considered even more despicably male than he had already revealed himself to be. Basically, by showing up and being a man.

"So, what did you think?'' asked Kyoko Rabinowitz as she came over to Cheney in the lobby after the show.

"Very interesting.''

"Not a very nice thing to say,'' she said, taking offense. "It was the nudity thing, right?''

"Well . . . ''

"It puts a lot of guys off. Makes them feel guilty.''

"I didn't feel guilty, really.''

"How did it make you feel?''

Cheney thought about saying that most of the show made him feel like sprinting to the rest room and grabbing a toilet bowl, but he said, "I understood it.''

"Understanding is not feeling.''

"Sometimes it's even better,'' said Kimberly, who was standing next to Cheney, sipping some jug wine in a plastic cup.

Cheney did the introductions.

"You know, you were very good,'' said Cheney.

"Really?'' said Kyoko, smiling now.

"Definitely. You had a certain . . . ''

"Flair?''

"Yeah, flair. I particularly like that little business you did with . . ."

"The thing with the phone and the ice cream?"

"Right," said Cheney, nodding.

"Everybody says that."

"And your closing argument in that case was so . . . what's the word I'm looking for?"

"Powerful."

"Exactly."

"*LA Cabaret Weekly* said 'powerful.' *Variety* said 'sexy'—about the whore character."

"Gotta agree. Can I buy you a drink?"

Kyoko looked at Cheney with a practiced eye. She might be gullible, but she wasn't stupid. "Business or pleasure?"

"Little of both. I promise to err on the side of pleasure."

"People usually do," she said, fixing him with her streetwise brown eyes.

He couldn't tell if she was smiling or not.

"Meet me down at Calais; it's a little French place two blocks south of here. It's kind of a theater hangout. You'll like it. Twenty minutes."

"Great."

Kyoko turned and started working the room, approaching anyone who looked like anyone in the crowd.

"I take it I'm invited too?" said Kimberly, her head cocked playfully to one side like a sad puppy.

"Try this," said Cheney, pouring Kimberly a glass of the Stag's Leap Chardonnay.

Kimberly held her glass to the light, even though she had no idea why she did so, swirled the liquid around, then sipped it. She smiled. She wasn't a wine expert. She couldn't tell which year or on which hill a particular grape was grown, but she could distinguish swill from the real thing.

"This is the real thing," she said.

"And then some," said Cheney.

"Cute place," said Kimberly, looking around the restaurant. It was low lit, everything in dark woods. A spiral staircase a few feet from the front door led to a second-floor bar, which was set apart from the large first-floor dining room. Upstairs there was a wood-burning fireplace, which now crackled with fading embers. All around the bar were black-and-white photographs of Calais, including a series of photographs of a ferry ride from Brighton to Calais. Cheney had taken that ride with his first wife nearly twenty years ago.

The French waiter had given Cheney a slightly condescending look when he ordered the California Chardonnay over several French wines the waiter had recommended. The young man's attitude had made Cheney feel as though he were actually back in Paris.

Kimberly raised her glass in a toast and clinked glasses with Cheney. "Thank you. This is very nice."

"I'm glad you could join me."

They made small talk about racquetball, the theater scene in Los Angeles as compared to New York, the recent heat wave, and the prices of the new Lexus 300SC and 400SC. Then Kimberly said, "Isn't this the same theater company Barbara Sanford belonged to?"

Cheney didn't respond immediately. Not because he didn't know the answer, maybe because he didn't know the *right* answer. "Why do I feel like you've got your hand down my pants?"

"Colorful way to put it, Cheney," said the young woman, unfazed.

"Tony told you."

"I ask questions. I'm a reporter."

"I'd almost forgotten that. Obviously you hadn't."

"Look, I'm not doing anything terrible here. If I didn't want you to know what I'm thinking, I wouldn't have said anything. I'm not an idiot."

Cheney was certain of that.

"What do you know about Barbara Sanford?" asked Cheney.

"Not much. She was killed in a hit-and-run accident on the Pacific Coast Highway a few weeks ago. She was married to a guy with money—a friend of yours, Tony said. There might be something more to it."

"And that sounds like a good story to you." It was not a question.

"Look, Cheney, I'm not here to bust your balls. I am a reporter. If there really is something more to the story, then I'm interested. Quite frankly, right here, right now, I'm more interested in you than I am in the story."

"Is that supposed to stroke my middle-age ego?"

"No, it's just the truth." Beat. "So, now that you mention it, what's with this Barbara Sanford case?"

"It's not a case," said Cheney. "I'm just doing a favor for a friend. I have no reason to believe that she was—"

"Murdered?"

"Absolutely nothing to lead me to that conclusion."

The reporter looked at Cheney suspiciously. "I know you must miss the job, but I doubt if you're desperate enough to start working hit-and-runs."

"Eh, Cheney!"

Cheney and Kimberly turned to see Kyoko Rabinowitz coming up the spiral stairs with a man on her arm. He looked to be in his late twenties. He had long black hair and Italian features. A good-looking guy. An actor. Cheney remembered him from the *Death of a Salesman* piece. LA was crawling with actors. The only things cheaper by the dozen were writers, or so Cheney had been told by a couple of Hollywood producers.

Cheney didn't usually order people by the dozen. He stood and shook hands as introductions were made all around. The Italian was named Bobby. Cheney asked the French waiter with the attitude for two more glasses and poured the new arrivals some wine.

They all talked about the show, and Cheney and Kimberly complimented Kyoko and Bobby on their various star turns, and everyone drank. Cheney ordered another bottle of wine, this time the more moderately priced but still excellent Au Bon Climat '91.

"I don't know whether or not Kyoko told you, Bobby, but I used to know Barbara."

Bobby looked up at Cheney. His expression changed noticeably. One moment he was having a good time; suddenly the smile was a distant memory. "How?"

"She was married to a friend of mine."

Bobby nodded. The answer seemed to make him feel better.

"You knew her?" asked Cheney.

"Sure, everyone knew her," said Bobby. "She was great."

"What was so great about her?"

"Pardon?" said the actor, genuinely taken aback by Cheney's pointed, almost rude question.

"I mean, I liked her too. But you said she was great. What do you mean by that?"

"Just a figure of speech. Maybe *great* isn't the appropriate word, according to Webster. But I liked her, we all did. Barbara had been with the company in one way or another for years. When someone you work with gets killed, it's personal. It affects you, you know?"

Cheney nodded. He knew. But as a cop, part of the uniform was a thick skin. "Who would you say was Barbara's closest friend?"

Bobby and Kyoko exchanged looks.

Which Cheney deciphered. Immediately.

"Probably Kyoko," said Bobby. "But Barbara and I were very close. She was . . ." He drank some wine and shook his head from side to side, searching for the right word.

"Great?"

"Yeah. She was great. She was someone who understood the creative process. She'd tried to be an actress. She knew what we were all going through. Most angels—people who put money into a production or a company—don't have a fuckin' clue what we go through. They just buy a ticket to the show, if you know what I mean. But Barbara knew. That's what set her apart.''

"Because her husband gave the company money and she didn't make you jump through hoops for it.''

"Kind of. Look, I gotta go.'' Bobby finished his wine, shook hands, exchanged meaningless good-byes, and walked down the spiral staircase into one of the genuinely meaner streets of Los Angeles. The meanest streets, reflected Cheney over his fourth glass of Chardonnay, were often the ones where people knew you by your first name and greeted you with a smile.

"So, was he sleeping with Barbara?'' asked Cheney.

Kyoko Rabinowitz winced as if he had tossed a drink in her face. "Why would you say that?''

Cheney knew it was not an answer. "I'm curious. I want to find out everything I can about her. Look, I'm not trying to hurt anyone. I don't sell stories to the tabloids. I'm doing a favor for a friend. That's all there is to it.''

Kyoko assessed Cheney. "They were good friends.''

Cheney didn't ask what that meant. He knew. Just like he knew that was all he was going to get from Kyoko.

Tonight, anyhow.

"So what do you think about all that?'' said Kimberly as she walked with Cheney to her car.

"What do you want me to say?''

"The truth.''

Cheney stopped. Kimberly stopped and turned toward him. "Don't bullshit me and I won't bullshit you," he said. "Trust is earned, you understand?"

"I understand."

"Maybe. Maybe not. Don't tell me you want the truth when what you really want is a story."

"Sorry."

"Doesn't cut it," said Cheney.

"So where do we go from here?"

"Where's here?"

"You, me, present time. I'm looking for a story that would be a feather in my cap, but I don't want to step on your toes to get it."

"You step on my toes, you don't get it. Guaranteed."

"Is that a warning?"

"It's the truth. That's what you want, right?"

Silence. "So what's the deal?"

"The deal is, I tell you what I want to tell you, you don't push me for the rest. And if I ever read a word of something that came from me, through you, that I didn't okay, from that moment on I'm deaf and blind, and you end up looking dumb."

"Interesting ground rules."

"You don't have to play."

"Don't I?"

"This isn't a page-one story."

"It is if it's murder."

"You think Barbara's husband loved her?" asked Cheney.

"I do."

"You think she loved him?"

After a moment, she said, "I don't know. Love is a funny thing."

"What do you mean?"

"I mean, you talk to twenty people, you get twenty different definitions. Let me give you an example. What does love mean to you?"

"I don't know. A lot of things."

"I do believe thou waxeth poetic," said Kimberly sarcastically.

"I don't know. . . . Trust. Trust is a big part of it. Caring, companionship—that's a big thing."

"You're pathetic, Cheney," said Kimberly with a wicked smile.

"What do you mean?"

"I mean, let's say I asked you about love twenty years ago."

"Yeah?"

"How far down the list would sex have been?"

Cheney didn't answer.

"Fifteenth? Twentieth? Would it have been in the top one hundred?"

"What's your point?" asked Cheney, although he thought he knew.

"My point is, if sex and passion would not have been the top two, they both would have finished in the top five. Now you talk about your lover as though she's a companion on a long ocean cruise."

"That's not fair."

"Why? Because I'm not married?"

"First of all, you don't know a damned thing about me or my wife."

"So why did you invite me out tonight instead of your wife?"

"She had to work."

"Is that the only reason?"

"Of course."

"Tony's a better friend to you than I am. You didn't ask him to go. You hardly know me."

Cheney sighed. He knew when he was trapped. "I thought you were nice—of course, that was before I got to know you," he said with a charming smile.

"I'm not nice. I'm not bad either. In fact, I'm probably a lot like you."

Cheney gave in. A little. "After you've been married for a while, even with a very good marriage—which, by the way, I consider mine to be—things change."

"You mean you lose the passion."

"No."

"Then you lose the lust."

"Society often confuses lust for passion. Lust is not the end-all emotion that movies make it out to be. Married people live together seven days a week, not just Saturday nights. Things change. Doesn't mean they change for the worse."

"You're probably right, Cheney," said Kimberly. She took the keys out of her purse, opened her car door, got inside, and rolled down the window.

"Thanks," she said and then drove off.

Cheney watched her drive away. And while he did, he was thinking about what she had said. About passion. About lust.

About love.

He had never said the word *love*. To anyone.
Except the blonde.
And the other one.

People took advantage of you when they knew you loved them. Better to keep a person guessing. After you said *love*, the other person always took you for granted. Started to let herself go. Expected things. Became another person, not the person you fell in love with.

Love was a fool's game. And he was not a fool.

Love.

The word appeared on the screen. Isolated. Black on white.

Became crimson on white. On black.

Two screens. Four. Eight.

Sixteen screens. Surrounded: 360 degrees.

Music. The sound, the *feel* of a single bass note. Deep bass. Pulsating rhythmically. From two speakers.

He pressed a button. Sixteen speakers.

He stood in the center. Maestro to all sensation. Sensation at the stroke of a key.

Gino pressed a function key. Love faded.

Image. Woman. A woman he knew from the old days, from Las Vegas. A woman he could never forget. He had touched her. Touched her as he had touched the others. But not quite. Now she was his. Finally.

Image. Woman. He moved the mouse on the pad, selected the woman's face, clicked on it. Clicked twice. The woman's face became bigger. On sixteen screens.

Keystrokes. His hands played the computer keys like a concert pianist caresses the keys of a Steinway. Grand. Oh, God, was it grand! Caressed them knowingly. Confidently. Lovingly.

The woman's face began to change, to be transformed. Subtly at first. But noticeably. Slowly she began to look like she *should* look. In his mind.

On sixteen screens.

He pressed more keys and handled the mouse like a surgeon handling a scalpel. A new background. Video. Movement. There she was. Not in the place he had seen her last, but where she was *supposed* to be.

He fiddled with size, scale, perspective, and color. While the music blasted.

He was a performer. The ultimate performer, a kind of god, creating a universe in his own image. The way it was supposed to be. The way *she* was supposed to be.

And those images moved and danced to the cadence, *dec*-cadence, he commanded.

"Bravo! Bravo!"

The man turned toward the woman, the woman in the shadows. The blonde. She stepped out into the light, the flickering light of the images on the screens. She moved closer to him until she stood directly in front of him.

"What do you really think?"

She took his head in her hands, her manicured red nails knitting together at the back of his neck in his long, wavy black hair. She opened her bright red mouth wide and kissed him. Deeply.

He ran his fingers through her blond hair.

"May I?" she said.

He touched her lips with his finger. Slowly ran it along her wet mouth. Nodded.

She moved in front of the computer terminal and put her hand over the mouse. She clicked on the woman's face. Enlarged it.

"What was her name again?"

"Barbara."

The man moved around behind the blonde. Reached his hands around her, unbuckled her belt.

The woman enlarged the face on the screen a little more.

Gino unzipped her jeans.

Raised the cheekbones just a little.

Gino pulled her jeans down.

Made Barbara's lips a little fuller.

Gino pulled her G-string panties down.

Made the image's eyes green. Emerald.

Gino unzipped his pants.

Changed the nose just a little.

Gino put himself into the warm dew between the blonde's legs. Neither of them could take their eyes from the screens. The images.

And as he moved in and out of her, his hand reached for the keyboard and hit a key. The word LOVE faded onto the screens and overlaid the woman's new face.

Love.

They were looking at the word on sixteen screens when they climaxed.

"Still awake, eh?" said Cheney when he walked into the bedroom.

Elizabeth looked up from the book she was reading. The TV was going in the background. Muted. The latter-twentieth-century electronic fireplace. "Yeah," she said, taking off her reading glasses. "I got home about thirty minutes ago. What kind of trouble have you been getting yourself into?"

"Funny thing to say."

"Just a figure of speech, darling. I'm not accusing you of anything. So, where have you been?"

Cheney undressed and laid his clothes over a chair. "I went to see a play."

"Really. I didn't know anything about it."

"Kind of a business and pleasure thing. Barbara Sanford belonged to a theater company, and one of the people I interviewed this afternoon left my name at the door. I think maybe Barbara might have had a relationship with one of the actors in the company."

"You really think she was having an affair?"

"It happens," said Cheney as he got into bed. "Even in the Palisades."

"I know that, Cheney. I'm a psychiatrist."

"You knew Barbara better than I did. How would you describe her?"

"I didn't know her all that well. We served on a couple of committees together, but that's about it."

"I thought you had coffee with her a couple of times last year."

"I did. She wanted to come over and talk. Everybody wants to talk when they find out you're a psychiatrist. But she never really opened up. She didn't tell me anything particularly revealing."

"You think she was capable of having an affair?"

"Anyone is capable of having an affair."

"Even you?"

"We're talking hypothetically here. Given the right—or wrong, depending on your perspective—circumstances, anyone is capable of having an affair. Marriage in modern-day America is a perilous business."

Cheney's attention drifted back to Barbara and Jamison Sanford. "There was the age difference. I mean, he was twenty years older than Barbara."

"Age can play a part, but it isn't the primary factor."

"What is?"

"I've been a psychiatrist now for nearly fifteen years, and a lot of people I see are dealing with this issue one way or another. I'd say the biggest factor in people having affairs is . . . " She paused for emphasis.

"Yes?"

"Opportunity."

"Opportunity?"

"Interesting, don't you think?"

"What about integrity, love, commitment?"

"They all play a part. But I have several patients, very religious, who demonstrate integrity in virtually every other aspect of their lives, who cheat on their husbands—or wives. Women who don't work, who have a lot of time on their hands: kids at school, a few bucks in the bank, work out at the health club regularly. They have lots of opportunity. More opportunity than a woman who has kids at home and works to support her family. A salesman is more likely to have an affair than a factory worker. A salesman makes his own schedule. Plenty of time for fudging here and there."

"Is that why actors and actresses are always having affairs?"

"Exactly, my darling," said Elizabeth, in a mock pedantic tone. "They're usually out of work. And what better way to pass the time, right?"

"Can't argue with that."

Elizabeth closed her book and set her glasses down on top of it. "I've made a decision, Cheney."

"You're going to have an affair."

"Better than that," she said with a smile. "I'm going to have the plastic surgery."

"You're kidding."

"I'm serious. That's one of the reasons I was late tonight. I stopped by to see Steven—"

"Steven?"

"Blomberg. He's the plastic surgeon on the second floor of the building. He and his wife came to our Christmas party last year. He was the guy who invested in baseball cards."

"Ah, now I remember. I feel a lot better now."

"He did a preliminary exam, and I'm scheduled for next Wednesday."

"That's . . . " Cheney couldn't think of the word.

"Great?"

"Yeah, I guess. What exactly are you going to have done?"

"Breast augmentation."

"Augmentation?"

"We're not talking Goodyear blimps here, Cheney. We settled on 34-C's."

"Sounds like something that drops bombs out of the sky."

"Steven said I have enough 'jacket' to accommodate 34-C's perfectly. Don't worry, you'll like them."

"I like them already."

"Now there will be more of them to like. I'm actually excited about this, Cheney. You should be too."

"Why?"

"Because I'm your wife. And in a few days I'm going to look more voluptuous than I ever have."

Cheney nodded. "I hope you're not doing this because of anything I've said or implied."

"I'm doing it for myself." She leaned over and kissed Cheney. "And for you too."

They turned out the lights and fell asleep.

On opposite sides of the bed.

six

"I always like having breakfast with you, Cheney," said Tony Boston, as he finished off one of two croissants in front of him. They sat opposite each other at a tiny table in Emil's, a small but renowned bakery on the West Side.

"Why's that?"

"Because you always pay."

"Thank you, I enjoy your company too," said Cheney, as he pulled on some vanilla-flavored coffee. "So, how's it going? Personally, I mean."

"I dunno. Still haven't heard from Dorie. Been over six months."

Cheney just nodded, but he thought about grabbing his friend by the lapels and saying, *So fucking what? You're divorced! She left you for another man! Get a grip!* Instead he said, "You seeing anyone special?"

"A secretary. She works for the DA's office. Pretty

cute, but it's nothing, you know, hot or anything like that.''

"You go out regularly?"

"Semi-regularly. We went out last Friday. To see a movie. We haven't—"

"You haven't gone to bed with her," said Cheney.

"Right. We're just friends, I guess. Maybe I'm not ready. It'll take some time to get over Dorie."

It'd take me ten seconds, thought Cheney, but he bit his tongue. Even very bright people seemed to take a vow of idiocy when it came to sex. Clearly, that's what the hook had been with Dorie. Clear to Cheney. It had not been nearly that clear to Tony.

"So, how you comin' on the Sanford hit-and-run?"

"Nothing, so far."

"Which brings you to your next question," said Tony, smiling and knowing he was earning his croissant.

"I'd like to find out who Barbara Sanford was."

"What do you mean?"

"I know she was my neighbor's wife. I saw her around here and there for the last seven years. Before that, even during that time, who knows? Not me."

"So you want me to put the department's resources to work to find out who she was."

"Right. I know she came here from Las Vegas, according to her husband."

"You say 'according to her husband' as though that might not be accurate."

"I don't know. That's the point."

"You think she was fooling around with someone before she was murdered?" Tony didn't like women who fooled around on their husbands.

"I don't know, Tony. Maybe she was as loyal as the day is long. I just want you to run her through the computers, okay?"

"Okay."

"Today?"

"Today."

"Guess who I was with last night," said Cheney.

"Who?"

"Kimberly Gary."

"You went out with Kimberly Gary?"

"I don't mean 'went out with.' She called and asked me to play some racquetball. I had an invitation to a play and Elizabeth was busy."

"She's great, isn't she?"

"Kimberly? Yeah, she's very bright."

"Now there's someone I could go for," said Tony Boston. He shook his head in awe at the possibilities.

"I want to ask you something," said Cheney, fidgeting with his coffee cup. "When I talked to Kimberly yesterday, she said she knew Elizabeth was busy a lot of nights."

"So?"

"How did that come up? I mean, did you volunteer the information or what?"

"I'm not sure, really. We were just talking about you. She seemed very interested, very impressed. She knew your famous cases; it was like she was a fan. She wanted to know all about you: what part of town you lived in, what kind of car you drove, all about your wife. I wish she felt the same way about me."

"Hang in there. Sooner or later you're bound to become a broken-down old has-been too."

"That's one of the things I like about you, Cheney. You don't have an ego."

Cheney smiled and noted, not for the first time, that Tony often took him too literally. "So, call me tonight with whatever you've got."

"Sure, no problem."

Cheney paid the check and the two men walked out of the pastry shop. Cheney caught his reflection in the mirror. Checked his look. Pretty tricky footwork for a man without an ego.

"Eh, Kyoko."

Kyoko Rabinowitz turned around. She was watering flowers in her tiny garden in back of her tiny house. "Cheney."

"I knocked on the front door."

"No problem," she said.

"I wondered if I might have a word with you."

"Do I need a lawyer?"

"Only if you've done something wrong."

"Don't bullshit me, Cheney. More people go to jail for being stupid than for breaking the law."

"I'm not here as a cop. I'm here as Barbara's husband's friend. I'm trying to find out what happened to her the night she was killed. Any other subplots don't interest me. Officially or unofficially."

Kyoko set down her watering can and breathed a deep sigh. It was not a sigh of relief.

"Bobby didn't kill Barbara. He loved her," said Kyoko later, sitting across the kitchen table from

Cheney, a cup of tea in front of each of them. "I know that. I'm sure of it."

"Being sure of it and knowing it are two different things."

"They don't sound like two different things."

"The way you mean them, they are. What you're really telling me is you believe he didn't kill her. You're not offering an alibi. It's just a gut feeling."

"My gut is almost always right."

"And not admissible as evidence in a court of law. How long had Barbara and Bobby been seeing each other?"

"By 'seeing each other' you mean fucking, right?"

"More or less," said Cheney, never ceasing to be amazed at the great strides accomplished in the battle for equality of the sexes.

"Three years, maybe."

"Everybody knew?"

"Not everybody, I guess."

"Everybody in the company knew."

"Yes."

"How did this work? I mean, she was married."

"Obviously. But there were lots of late nights."

Cheney recalled his wife's comment regarding opportunity being a key element in infidelity. *Infidelity.* Even the word sounded like something from a different era, thought Cheney. Like talking about a Model T. Today when someone mentioned the Lindbergh baby, half the room thought you were talking about some kind of miniature cheese. Infidelity was a joke to the MTV generation. Probably had been a joke for a long time, unless a person was on the receiving end. It never seemed funny then.

Cheney knew that. Learned it up close and personal many years ago. It was the kind of thing that stayed with you.

"Men have affairs for very different reasons than women, in case you didn't know."

"How's that?" asked Cheney.

"Men, well. . . . A woman, any woman, stands still long enough, some guy'll fuck her; that's basically the male prerequisite. Women are usually more picky. And they make an emotional investment."

"At least you're not bitter," said Cheney sarcastically.

"I *am* bitter. Men are animals."

"Some women like animals."

Kyoko drank her tea before she spoke. "I know you're trying to be clever, and I know what you're saying. Quite frankly, I like a man to be a man—you can read that any way you want, it's not open for discussion, at least not with you. But I don't like rolling around with pigs. Some men are pigs."

"Is Bobby a pig?"

"No way. He . . . "

"Yes?"

"He isn't a wimp. He's a tough guy, but he isn't a pig."

"What do you mean, a 'tough guy'?"

"I don't want to talk about it."

"You're going to have to talk about it with someone, now that you've said it. I'm the easiest guy to talk to. Were you and Bobby—"

"Lovers?"

"Okay," said Cheney, figuring the word worked as well as any other.

"We used to be. He treats a woman like a woman."

"Which is how?"

"He listens to her, respects her, puts her in her place when she *wants* to be put in her place. You noticed I didn't say *needs* to be put in her place."

"I noticed."

"Some women want their men to draw a line. You know what I'm saying?"

"I think so."

"They want to know he's in control. I'm not saying every woman feels this way, just some. A lot. I do."

"Barbara did?"

"Yeah, I guess so."

"And she didn't feel that with her husband." It was not a question.

"Her husband filled in a lot of the missing pieces for Barbara. But what man can be everything to a woman, right?"

Cheney didn't answer. But he thought about the question. All kinds of theoretical answers came to mind. Nothing that held any weight.

"Bobby didn't kill her."

"How do you know?"

"I know people."

"You ought to get a job as a professional juror."

"He's a good man," said Kyoko, ignoring Cheney's sarcastic remark.

"You've got his home address and phone number." Again, it was not a question.

"Sure. I told him you'd probably be by."

"You're a pretty smart lady."

Kyoko Rabinowitz stood and walked out the back door of her house. Cheney followed.

In the middle of her back yard was a small pond.

In the pond were about a dozen large goldfish. Cheney saw two turtles.

Kyoko knelt down beside the pond and Cheney stood behind her.

"Snakes come around here all the time."

"I don't like snakes."

"Really? They don't bother me. Maybe it's because I've lived in LA too long."

"What do you think happened to Barbara?"

"She's dead. Nothing can bring her back."

"That's not an answer. You say you're sure Bobby didn't kill her. Then you must have some other theory."

"Police say it was hit-and-run."

"That's the police theory. What's yours?"

"I don't know."

"I'm not asking for a sworn statement. I *know* you don't know. I'm asking you what you think happened."

No one spoke for a moment. Fish swam, turtles moved slowly, and snakes slithered in the grass.

"I think somebody killed her," said Kyoko finally, as she tossed a pebble into the pond. "And I hope you catch the guy and cut off his balls."

"I was expecting you," said Bobby, when he opened the door.

Bobby Charles lived in a one-bedroom apartment in West Hollywood. Nothing fancy, nothing to be ashamed of. His name was on about a dozen posters on the wall. Not always—rarely, actually—in the starring role. The posters on which he had star billing were for small productions at the Circle Theater in

Cleveland, Ohio: Ibsen, Shakespeare, Chekhov. All the roles that prepared actors to play the challenging parts made famous in such TV classics as *Three's Company* and *My Mother the Car*.

Bobby Charles drank from a glass of red wine. He sat on his ragged couch opposite Cheney, who sat in a ladder-back chair. "In TV, people's lives and careers are decided on what one family in Des Moines happens to watch. The Nielsen Family. If you knew the names of those people and had a few bucks, you could own the fuckin' world."

Cheney had spoken with two actors today. Two bitter souls. Besides cops, he thought, actors must be the most cynical people on earth.

"So, you were expecting me?"

"Yeah."

Neither man said anything. Neither man was stupid.

"You were having an affair with Barbara Sanford." It was not a question.

Bobby smiled as though Cheney had used some quaint term. "I guess you could call it that."

"What would *you* call it?"

"We cared about each other."

"You loved each other?"

"I didn't say that."

"I know. *I* did."

Silence.

"What do you want me to say? I didn't kill her, if that's what you're after."

"When's the last time you saw Barbara?"

Bobby walked over to his exercise bike, got on, and started pedaling. "You mind?"

"No."

After he got up to speed he said, "I saw her a coupla days before she was killed."

"You say 'killed.'"

"You get hit by a car going seventy miles an hour, that's killed, right?"

"So, you think it was a hit-and-run."

Bobby pedaled some more. "I dunno."

"You said you saw her a couple of days before she was killed. Did you have sex with her?"

"That's kind of a private thing."

Cheney shot Bobby a hard look. "Listen, pal, I can dump your life with Barbara Sanford and any other man, woman, or child you've been to bed with in your whole fuckin' life all over the front pages in this town tomorrow morning." He played the beat, let it sink in. "Or . . . it's just you and me talking. It's up to you."

"That'd be the best press I've had in ten years."

Cheney didn't say anything. For two reasons. First, he knew enough to let the other guy talk. Second, he knew Bobby Charles was right.

"No, we didn't have sex."

"Was that unusual?"

"As a matter of fact, it was. We usually had sex when we got together."

"Which was how often?"

"You really need the details?"

"I don't know what I need. Tell me the truth and I'll cover your ass. Lie to me and I'll nail it to the wall."

"Usually three times a week. Monday, Wednesday, and Friday. Weekends she spent with her husband."

Cheney thought of several sarcastic replies but decided such remarks were not in his—or his client's—best interests. "When was the last time you had . . . made love to Barbara?"

"Is this really necessary?"

Cheney just looked at him.

"You know, now that you mention it, it *is* kind of strange. . . ."

"What's that?"

"Well, like I said, we used to make love three times a week, like clockwork, you know. Then, for about a month or so before she was killed, it kinda petered out."

Kind of a peculiar choice of words, but Cheney didn't mention it. "What did you make of it?"

"I don't know."

"You must have had some reaction. You make love to the woman three times a week for a few years and all of a sudden nothing for a month. Then she winds up dead. You never thought about it?"

"Yeah, I thought about it."

"So what did you think?"

"I don't know."

"I know you don't know. I'm asking you what you *thought*."

Bobby pedaled faster, glancing at the gauges on the cycle, then out the window. Not ignoring Cheney, but rather trying to come up with an answer.

"Did you think she was seeing someone else?"

Bobby pedaled faster. "No."

"Why not?"

"Because."

Cheney went for the jugular. "Because she didn't

need to fuck anybody else but you? Because she told you you were the best?"

"She did," said Bobby, turning to Cheney with a defiant scowl. "And she meant it."

Cheney smiled. "Maybe you weren't the only actor in the family."

Bobby stopped pedaling, got off his bike, and moved toward Cheney. He was breathing heavily. When he looked Cheney in the eye the bravado drained out of him. The old detective hadn't slashed the jugular, but he had sure as hell touched a nerve.

Bobby walked over to the couch and sat down. "I loved her," he said simply.

"What do you mean?"

"I mean, I loved her. I wanted her to leave her husband and marry me."

"Did she say she would do that?"

"Not in so many words. But we were getting there. Slowly but surely. I could tell."

"What could you tell by the fact that she wouldn't make love with you during that last month?"

"I don't know. I thought maybe she—"

"Wanted to remain with her husband?"

"That never occurred to me," said Bobby.

It had never occurred to Cheney either, but he said it just the same. "Did she say anything or do anything to give you an idea who this other person might've been?"

Bobby leaned back against the couch, relaxed into it. "Not really."

"Think about it. Something insignificant to you might mean something to me."

"All I know is that she changed that last month."

"Changed? How?"

"She seemed distant, you know? But the really strange thing is, she wouldn't let me have sex with her. I mean, that had never happened before."

Cheney recalled Sanford saying he had not had sex with his wife for a month before her death.

"Did you ask her what was going on?"

"Of course."

"And what did she say?"

"She just said she was going through something. You know women."

Cheney knew women. As well as any man thought he knew them. Which, Cheney had concluded some time ago, wasn't very well at all. "Did you notice anything else about her during that last month?"

"Like what?"

"Did you ever see her naked during that time?"

"That's a weird question," said Bobby, looking at Cheney as though he were a dirty old man.

"If you've been having sex three times a week for two years and you don't see the woman naked for an entire month—because she wants it that way—yeah, that is weird."

"What does seeing her naked have to do with anything?"

Cheney ignored the question. "Was Barbara seeing someone else?"

"I don't know."

"For the sake of argument, let's just say it crossed your mind. And because you loved Barbara so much, let's just say you started thinking about where and with whom she might be spending her time. It did cross your mind, right?"

"So?"

"So when people ask themselves questions like that, they usually fill in the blanks. Who did you *think* she was seeing?"

Bobby breathed deeply and looked out the window. Then he looked back at Cheney. "I don't know, but . . ."

"But?"

"But whoever he was, I think she was afraid of him."

"What makes you say that?"

"She was really more than just distant. She seemed scared. Barbara didn't scare easy, you know? I mean, we snuck around a lot—sorry, I know her husband is a friend of yours. But Barbara was . . . tough. I'd never seen her scared of anything until that last month."

"What did she say when you asked her about it?"

"Nothing. Like I said, she just said it was something she was going through and it would be over soon."

"You didn't press her on it?"

"Barbara was the kind of person who only said what she wanted to say, when she wanted to say it."

Cheney thought about pointing out that Barbara wasn't saying anything anymore, but he figured he'd done enough damage to Bobby Charles for one afternoon. He also figured that was all Bobby had to give.

seven

The building in which Elizabeth Cheney practiced was located in Westwood on Westwood Boulevard, just south of Wilshire. It housed medical specialists whose expertise ranged from psychiatry to pediatrics and from gynecology to ophthalmology. It wasn't a tight-knit community, but everyone knew one another by name and exchanged polite smiles and small talk in the elevator.

"Is Dr. Blomberg in?"

A woman in her mid-forties looked up from her computer, through an open window in the wall. "May I help you?"

"My name is Cheney, *Detective* Cheney." He wasn't above pushing buttons he knew always worked. "My wife is a patient here."

The woman disappeared into the back offices. Cheney walked around in the empty waiting room.

On the walls were numbered Stobart lithographs. On the table were pamphlets regarding cosmetic surgery: breast augmentation, breast reduction, liposuction, rhinoplasty, tummy tucks, eyelid surgery. There was even a pamphlet on breast reduction for men.

"Mr. Cheney?"

Cheney turned. Dr. Steven Blomberg was an attractive man. Younger than Cheney had anticipated. He looked to be in his mid-thirties. His long hair was tied in a ponytail. He looked tanned and healthy. He looked more like a tennis pro than a doctor.

"Yes," said Cheney, moving forward and extending his hand. "My wife is a patient of yours. Elizabeth Cheney?"

"Yes. I know Elizabeth quite well."

"You do?" It was a knee-jerk reply.

"Of course. She has the office above mine, and our parking places are right next to each other. In fact, I met you at your Christmas party last year."

Cheney smiled, remembering the doctor's interest in baseball cards. "Right."

"Have I done something wrong?"

"Pardon?"

"My receptionist said that there was a detective here to see me."

Cheney smiled again. "I just said that to get her attention."

"I see." Blomberg was not smiling back.

Cheney noticed that Blomberg had not asked him to come into his office.

"I'd really like to talk with you privately."

"About Elizabeth's surgery."

"Yes."

"That's a little unusual. Maybe we can call Elizabeth, and—"

"I'd rather talk with you privately, if you don't mind. Don't worry, I'll just take a minute of your time."

Blomberg appeared to consider the request. Unlike many people Cheney interviewed, Blomberg continued to look him in the eye. Cheney knew a lot of doctors, some through Elizabeth, some he'd met on the job. Most of them felt superior to the rest of the world. And when they looked you in the eye, it wasn't because they didn't think they had anything to hide, it was usually because they didn't give a flying fuck what you thought.

"All right. I've got a patient in fifteen minutes."

Blomberg's office was dark. The shades were drawn. Track lighting highlighted lithographs of country cottages in a smoky mist. The carpet was thick, the piped-in music classical. The chair in which Cheney sat was real leather, and he sank down into it for a second before he came to rest.

Blomberg sat behind his desk and waited for Cheney to speak.

"I wanted to talk with you about Elizabeth's surgery."

"Obviously."

The remark stung Cheney. "Do we have some kind of problem, you and me?"

"I don't think so. It's just that I'm a doctor. You're seeking confidential information about your wife. Naturally, I'm conflicted."

Cheney didn't give a fuck how conflicted the guy was. Yet, begrudgingly, he took the point. "I was just rather surprised by her decision, that's all. I want to know a little bit about the surgery. Risks and so forth.''

"The surgery is strictly routine. As you know, Elizabeth is in excellent physical health.''

"If she's in such excellent physical health, why is she having surgery?''

"A person can be in excellent physical health and still have room for cosmetic improvement.''

"Improvement in whose opinion?''

"Elizabeth's, obviously. Look, Mr. Cheney, I understand your apprehension—''

"You do? Tell me. I'd like to know.''

"Well, first of all, Elizabeth is younger than you are.''

"So?''

"Please don't be offended. You're the one who wanted to talk. I'm just giving you my free opinions and insights, having worked in this field for many years.''

"Sorry,'' said Cheney, though he really was not.

"I can understand how you might feel threatened. Elizabeth will look even younger than she does now, more attractive.''

"I hadn't thought of that,'' said Cheney. "Quite frankly, I feel very secure in my marriage. What I want to talk to you about are the risks to Elizabeth.''

"Every time a patient has surgery, there is a risk. Anyone who tells you otherwise is not being honest. However, the procedure Elizabeth has chosen involves minimal risk.''

"There was something else I wanted to ask you.'' This was a tough one.

"Yes?"

"Did Elizabeth say why she wanted the surgery?"

"Yes."

Silence.

"You're not going to tell me?"

"I believe that is privileged information."

"It wasn't because of anything I said, was it?"

"I'm not sure what you mean."

"I mean, it wasn't because she was feeling insecure about our relationship."

After a moment, Blomberg said, "No."

The intercom came alive on the doctor's desk. He pressed a button. "Yes?"

"Mrs. McPherson is here."

Blomberg looked at Cheney.

Cheney thought of saying thanks, but he just nodded, stood, and walked out.

"I wish you hadn't done that."

"I'm sorry. I was just concerned about you, that's all."

"What did Steven say?" Elizabeth sat behind her desk in her office, the window behind her looking out over Westwood Boulevard.

"Not much. He was very loyal to you."

"What's that supposed to mean?"

"He seems to take the doctor-patient relationship very seriously."

"What exactly were you trying to prove?"

"Nothing. Except maybe that I love you. Look, Elizabeth, I worry about you going under the knife, okay?"

"There's nothing to worry about. Steven's the best. And Cheney . . . "

"Yes?"

"Try to focus on the positive aspects. You're the one—besides myself, of course—with the most to gain."

"It's hard for me to look at it that way."

Elizabeth smiled a crooked smile. "I'm paying a lot of money to make myself look more attractive. You're my husband. We go to bed together every night. Do I have to draw you a picture?"

"I just don't want to lose you, that's all."

"You're not going to lose me, Cheney. I'm getting new boobs, not a new brain, for chrissake."

"Maybe I'm overreacting."

"I think so."

"So, you got time for dinner?"

"No, I'm afraid not. I've got a patient at six."

"Maybe we can catch a late dinner at the club. I've got—"

"It's gonna be another late night. I'm sorry, Cheney, but I've got to do this. With the surgery next week, things are even more jammed up. Don't worry, it'll all be coming to an end soon."

Cheney didn't ask what exactly was coming to an end. Soon.

Elizabeth got up from behind her desk, walked around to her husband, and sat on his lap, putting an arm around his shoulder. "Tell the truth. Don't you really want a babe?"

"I've got a babe."

"Don't make me jealous," said Elizabeth playfully.

"I've got you." Beat. "Babe."

The intercom buzzed. Elizabeth kissed Cheney, got up, and answered the phone.

Within minutes Cheney was in his car, on his way home, listening to talk radio. Some guy was talking about spray-on hair for prematurely bald men. Premature? If you wanted hair, going bald at a hundred would be premature.

So then, thought Cheney, what was *mature* baldness?

Cheney picked up his mail and, in a matter of ten seconds, dunked it like Shaquille O'Neal into the wastebasket he had several years ago strategically placed next to where Petty always set the mail.

"You have some messages."

"Anything urgent?"

"Tony called. And somebody with a very sexy voice."

"Man or woman?" said Cheney uninterestedly as he perused an inordinately large phone bill.

"Some woman named Kimberly Gary. She said you had her number."

"If you're just going to sit at home and watch TV, you oughta get out and do some exercise."

"I dunno. Maybe."

"You do play hard to get, Cheney."

"I'm not playing."

"Does that mean you're *serious* about playing hard to get?"

"You know what I mean."

"C'mon, I need some exercise and I've got the court reserved."

"You seem to have a lot of courts reserved."

"I've got a friend at the registration desk."

"Friends in high places. Look, Tony called. Let me call him and see if I can meet him; then I'll meet you afterward. I'll call you back."

"She used to be a hooker," said Tony Boston, sipping on his Absolut vodka. He and Cheney had a table next to the window at the Rolls Royce Club, which was located across the street from Samples Racquetball.

"A hooker? Are you sure?" Cheney was genuinely surprised.

"No doubt about it. I talked with a guy who worked Vegas vice. He looked through the files for me."

"I appreciate that."

"I'm sure you do. That's why you're gonna pick up the tab tonight."

"For a change," said Cheney sarcastically. "What else?"

"She wasn't big-time. She was only arrested once. She paid a fine and officially fell out of the system."

"That's it? You better nurse that drink."

"There's more. She was attacked and nearly killed eight years ago."

"By a john?"

"Who knows? I know the Vegas cops didn't make a big deal about it. Hookers get attacked all the time. It's the cost of doing business, as you and I know. It might not be pretty, but it's the truth."

"The truth can be a very elusive quantity," said Cheney.

"No wonder she left town and came to LA."

"Right. Somewhere she could feel safe."

"Do you think your friend knew his wife was a hooker?"

"I don't know. If he did, I doubt if he would have brought it up at our Fourth of July barbecues."

"Maybe you should ask him."

"Right."

"No, I'm serious. This guy comes to you and wants the truth. It works both ways. Or at least it should."

Cheney nodded.

"You gonna work out?"

"Oh, I don't know," said Cheney. He knew. What he didn't know was why he didn't tell Tony Boston. Partly it was because he didn't want his meeting Kimberly for a game of racquetball to be misunderstood. Partly it was because he knew he wouldn't have to explain it, since Tony was already drinking vodka and therefore not planning to stop by the club.

Cheney huffed and puffed his way through three sets of racquetball, winning each set but by declining scores, 21–7, 21–11, 21–15. During the match he couldn't keep his eyes off Kimberly's tanned and toned legs, which were displayed to their best advantage in a pair of brief white terry-cloth shorts. Her body was not perfect, Cheney noted. Yet it was young, and youth forgives the errors of indulgence graciously.

"I'll beat you one of these days," said Kimberly, after they each had showered and were ensconced in a corner booth of the now nearly deserted Rolls Royce Club.

"Don't count on it," said Cheney.

"I like this wine."

"Rovelle '91. Underrated and moderately priced. It's an excellent Chardonnay for the price."

"You know a lot about a lot of things."

"You live as long as I have, you will too."

"Most people just grow older, not wiser. Besides, you're not so old, Cheney; don't give me that bull. You just beat me three straight sets."

"You're a girl."

"I'm a woman," said Kimberly, looking Cheney in the eye. "In case you hadn't noticed."

"I noticed."

"Naughty, naughty, you're a married man."

"Look, don't treat me like an idiot and I won't treat you like a little girl."

"Fair enough. To treating each other . . . well," said Kimberly, when she had decided upon the right word. She raised her glass.

Cheney wasn't sure he knew what he was drinking to, but for some reason the term "slippery slope" kept running through his mind.

"So, how long do you have tonight?" asked Kimberly.

"What do you mean?"

"I mean how long can you stay out?"

"What kind of question is that?"

"You're married. I just thought . . . I don't know."

"My wife and I are not each other's keeper. We come and go as we please."

"But you always end up going home."

"Not always," said Cheney.

Silence.

Followed by a hasty explanation. "What I mean by that is sometimes I go out of town. Sometimes I'm working a case and I'm out all night. We trust each other."

"Sorry, I didn't mean to pry."

"Really?"

"Maybe I should change the subject."

"Let me guess. Barbara Sanford."

"I talked to Tony. He said your friend's wife used to be a hooker."

Cheney let it slide. He wasn't sure if he did so for his or her benefit. "Yes."

"Does that surprise you?"

"I suppose so."

"That's a strange response."

When Cheney thought about it, he decided it probably was. But finding out that a good-looking woman who had been an aspiring actress had also turned a couple of tricks in Vegas, while trying to make her way, didn't really come as a total shock. Maybe he was jaded. Maybe he was just realistic.

"People do all kinds of things when they're young. Can't hold it against them forever. People have a right to keep their pasts private."

"That's very magnanimous of you, Cheney. You think you'd feel the same way if you found out your wife had been a prostitute?"

"Elizabeth was never a hooker."

"That's not an answer."

"It's the closest thing you're gonna get."

"So, what do you think? About the case."

"There is no case."

"If Barbara Sanford was murdered, there is."

"There isn't the remotest bit of evidence to indicate that."

"Not yet. But I've got a feeling."

"You've just got hunger pangs. You need a story. You want it to turn out sordid and lurid so it'll fit into some neat tabloid package that'll get you noticed."

"So?"

"At least you're honest about it."

"Why shouldn't I be? The woman's dead. Nothing's going to bring her back. But if she was murdered . . . well, I get a chance to show what I can do."

"What about her husband? He's the one with the rope around his balls, being dragged through the mud."

Kimberly leaned back and sighed. "You don't like me much, do you, Cheney?"

"I like you fine. It's just that I don't like hurting innocent people."

"Nobody's completely innocent. If you learned anything being a cop, you must've learned that. You talk to the sweet cookie-baking housewife long enough, and out falls somebody who thinks blacks are genetically inferior and ought to be sent back to where they come from, wherever the hell that might be. You talk to a liberal off the record and he'll tell you every anti-Semitic joke in the catalogue. We're all covered with shit. Every cop knows it, every reporter knows it. Anybody who walks the street for a living knows it. Barbara Sanford knew it too. I don't look down on her. She did what she felt she had to do."

"Just like you."

"Just like me."

"How did you get so cynical?"

"I'm an umpire, Cheney. Life is full of close calls, and somebody's got to make them. Sometimes you're right, sometimes you're wrong. Any way you cut it, it's better to make a call—even if it's wrong—than stand around with your hands in your pockets waiting for life to begin."

Cheney drank his wine and watched Kimberly speak animatedly, passionately. Maybe it was the wine, maybe it wasn't, but she looked very attractive.

"Why did you meet me tonight?" she said.

"You said you wanted to play racquetball, and I needed the exercise."

Kimberly nodded. "You saw Tony first."

"That's right."

"Did you tell him we were getting together?"

"No."

"Why?"

"No particular reason."

"Really?"

"No. Feel free to mention it to him tomorrow. It isn't like I'm hiding anything."

"No, I suppose not. Look, I gotta call it a night."

Kimberly got up and grabbed her sweater and her duffel bag. "Thanks for the wine. And the game."

"You're welcome," said Cheney, rising politely.

Kimberly just stood there looking at Cheney for a moment. Then she turned and walked away.

Cheney sat down and finished the rest of the Rovelle by himself.

*　*　*

Elizabeth was asleep when Cheney got home. He crawled into bed quietly without touching her. Convincing himself that he did so because he didn't want to wake her.

"I really like your stuff."

"Stuff?" asked Gino.

Raven, the brunette, looked intimidated. Gino liked that. Was used to it. Made him feel . . . what? In control? Yes, but it was more than that. Much more than that.

"I mean, it's like a multimedia work of art. It's more than a painting, it's computer art, it's magic . . . it's great. I love it."

"Thank you."

"What do you call it?"

"It's a . . . correction."

"What do you mean?"

"Look around you. God's mistakes are everywhere. I correct God's mistakes. I make what is ugly look beautiful."

"I never thought of it quite like that before."

"I'm sure you haven't. You see that building over there?"

The brunette looked over at the First Interstate Building, a steel and glass giant in the downtown skyline.

Gino and the woman were sitting on the roof of his building, which was located in Chinatown in downtown Los Angeles. A bottle of wine he'd told her to buy on the way over sat between them, half empty.

"I did an industrial film for a contractor in that

building," said Gino, pointing toward First Interstate.

"No kidding."

"They didn't buy it, though. Paid the money, refused to use it."

"Why?"

"Why?" asked Gino with a mixture of bitterness and condescension. "Because they don't know what the fuck they're doing, that's why." He drank liberally from his glass and held it out for the brunette to refill. She did. He didn't acknowledge her doing so. Calculation. Every move was a calculation.

"I've got a surprise for you."

The brunette smiled.

Gino picked up his guitar, which lay next to the checkered tablecloth that was sprawled out over the tar on the roof. He strummed it and began to play. Beneath the full moon. Beneath the stars. Beneath the looming monoliths that made up the LA skyline.

After the song, Gino put the guitar down and drained his glass. Held it out for another refill, which was eagerly offered.

Calculation. Indoctrination. Execution.

"I wrote that for you."

"Really?"

"Of course."

"But this is only our second date."

"Artists don't punch a clock. Inspiration happens when it happens." Gino drank from his glass, not taking his eyes from Raven. "You inspire me."

"That's the most romantic thing anyone has ever done for me."

Gino raised his glass, and Raven clinked it with hers in a toast.

"Do you write the music to your films?"

"Sometimes. What films have you seen?"

"I only saw the one, over at UCLA, the night we met."

His films had screened at several film festivals around the country and in Canada and Japan, even in Australia. But no major distribution deals had come out of those showings. Some rave critical reviews. A couple of runner-up awards and some honorable mentions. But he had never hit the home run.

But there were other rewards.

"You must be talking about *Black Heart*."

"Yes, that's it. The one about the LA riots. I remember the score because it was so . . . "

"It served as a counterpoint."

"Exactly. I mean, a film about the riots, you naturally expect a score full of rap or some other very urban-sounding music. But I remember thinking it was as though Dylan—the acoustic, pre-electric Dylan—had done an honest cut-through-the-shit poetic soundtrack. It was brilliant. Very different."

"Yes," said Gino with a bitter smile. "The *LA Tribune* thought the score was 'too white.'"

"I know, but that's exactly the point. The urban score, the politically correct score, was obvious. Too obvious. It's like putting the *Rocky* theme in every fight film. It's a no-brainer."

"Critics are just frustrated artists. God forbid an artist has a name the critic can use as a play on words. I know these bastards. I know how their minds work. I can picture a critic saying, 'I really liked this work, but you know, this guy's name would work so well in this funny word-play headline. Then more people will read my column. More people will think I'm clever. So fuck this guy who's spent a fucking lifetime working on this project.'"

Gino finished his wine and held out his glass. Again.

Calculation. Indoctrination. Execution.

"You a sports fan?"

"Some sports," replied Raven.

"I mean, think how many sportswriters are waiting for Houston Oiler quarterback Warren Moon to have a great day against the Miami Dolphins, just so they can top a story with the line MOON OVER MIAMI."

"You're probably right."

"You bet your ass I'm right," said Gino with passion.

"Are you working on a movie now?"

"I've got one movie in post and I'm shooting another one. And I'm working on one of my own projects too. Something very special. It's an idea I've been working on, one way or another, for about eight years now."

"Really?"

"I don't mean to sound immodest, but I believe it's my masterwork. An artist knows. You work and you work, and the work gets better. Then there comes a time, a single project, when all the hours, the talent, the hard work, the inspiration come together. And this is it."

"When will it be done?" asked Raven excitedly.

"Soon. Very soon."

"What's it about?"

"It's not a linear plot. It's not something I could tell you in a ten-second pitch. But it's important. Something you could relate to. It's about a woman."

"Who?"

"Someone I used to know. Someone very much like you. In fact, you remind me of her."

"Really?"

"Definitely. That's what attracted me to you originally. I'm obsessed with this project—I get that way when I really get into something. And when I saw you . . . well, I can't tell you what went through my mind."

eight

"I kind of enjoy watching big-screen TV," said Petty as she put the batter in the Belgian waffle maker.

"You watch it every night, what's the big deal?"

"With you and Elizabeth out till all hours, I own the remote control. Makes a big difference."

"You've got a TV in your room, for chrissake."

"Once you've had big-screen, it's hard to go back."

"What time did Elizabeth get in last night?"

"I don't know. I went to sleep after Jay Leno's monologue. What time did you get in?"

Cheney sipped his coffee. "About twelve forty-five."

"Then she arrived home sometime after eleven forty-five and before twelve forty-five."

"Thank you for the clarification."

"Don't get sarcastic. The waffles aren't ready yet. Anything can happen."

"Good morning," said Elizabeth as she breezed into the kitchen, grabbed a Firestone Winery mug, and poured herself a cup of coffee. She walked over to Cheney, leaned down, and kissed him on the cheek. "Gotta run. I'm late."

"Maybe you should get more sleep," said Cheney, to his wife's back.

"From your lips to God's ears."

"You'll be home for dinner tonight?"

"I hope so. I'll really try." She disappeared into the hall leading to the garage.

"Maybe you should take up a hobby," said Petty. She handed Cheney a plate with two waffles on it.

"I have enough hobbies."

"I mean something you can do at night."

"Maybe I should."

"Maybe you already have."

"What is that supposed to mean?" said Cheney as he poured the nonfat strawberry syrup on his waffles.

"Nothing. It's just that Elizabeth isn't the only one who's coming in late these days."

"What do you expect me to do? Stay home and watch TV with you?"

"I really appreciate your coming by the office, Cheney," said Jamison Sanford. His twenty-second-floor Century City office looked out west toward the ocean, with Santa Monica in between. On a clear day he could see whitecaps on the waves. This morning was not such a day.

"No problem. I was in the neighborhood. Look, Jamison," began Cheney nervously, "when a person does an investigation, that is, when you start turning over stones, all kinds of things are bound to show up. Things that may or may not be—usually aren't, as a matter of fact—relevant to the investigation."

"What are you trying to say?"

"I'm basically asking you, how completely honest do you want me to be with you?"

"I trust you. I know you have my best interests at heart and that the information is confidential."

"Hold on. You're making an incorrect assumption there, Jamison. The public has ways of finding out all kinds of things I don't tell them. What I'm about to tell you now, a reporter already knows. And she didn't get it from me."

Sanford lowered his head a little and massaged his temple with his right hand. He appeared to be thinking. Cheney knew he was trying to brace himself.

"Tell me," he said when he looked up. It was a deceivingly simple statement.

"How much do you know about your wife's past?"

"Not a great deal. I know she came here from Las Vegas. Wanted to be an actress. Not a terribly original story. Beautiful women always have a past, Cheney. I'm not naive."

"Did she ever talk about her life back then?"

Sanford took a deep breath and let it out. Looked Cheney in the eye. "Just tell me, okay?"

"Did you know she'd been arrested for prostitution?"

Sanford ran his left hand across his mouth a couple of times. Said nothing. Pursed his lips. Stood. Walked to the window and stared out at an ocean that was not in sight. Stood there for a while. Put his hand to his face again and wiped something away. Cleared his throat. Turned back around to face his friend.

"No, I didn't know that."

"Look, Jamison, I'm sorry—"

Sanford held up a hand and shook his head from side to side. "No apologies. If I want answers, I've got to be prepared for something like this."

Cheney had been around, seen more than Sanford, and he knew there was no way to prepare for "something like this."

"Is there a connection between her being—well, you know—and her murder?"

"I have no idea. I doubt it. It's just another lead, that's all. You gotta follow every lead because you never know where it'll take you."

"I understand." Sanford walked back to his desk and sat down. "You said something about a reporter already having this information."

"She's a beat reporter for the *Trib*."

"Do you trust her?"

"I trust her to do what everybody does—whatever is in her own best interest."

"Which means?"

"She won't run the story if it turns out your wife really was a hit-and-run victim."

"If it turns out she was murdered?"

"That depends. If it has anything to do with motive, or if it ties your wife to the murderer, she'll print every word."

Both men sat silently for a moment.

"I can stop here," said Cheney. "Quite frankly, I'm the only one looking into the case."

"What about the reporter?"

"She's a reporter, not a detective. If I pack it in, chances are it all ends here."

"Then I'll never know."

"I know this sounds a little corny, Jamison, but you're playing in my ballpark now and I know what I'm talking about. Sometimes it's best not to know. Nothing's going to bring Barbara back. And whatever you find out could rip your heart out."

Sanford looked levelly at Cheney. "I'm a bottom-line guy, Cheney. That's what helped me get all this." He raised his hands to take in the office, his empire, which, Cheney had heard, was worth something close to a billion dollars. "I always need to know where I stand. Got to have the facts, the real untampered-with facts. Not just what I want to hear. I demand it of other people, and I've always demanded it of myself. I know what you're thinking."

Cheney *was* thinking something, something he didn't dare say out loud. Out of respect.

"You're thinking I broke that rule with Barbara. How else could things have gotten so far out of control?"

Cheney said nothing. That was exactly what he was thinking.

"I suppose people make exceptions to rules for people they love. It usually turns out badly, but sometimes your heart offers you no other choice. I've made two exceptions in my life. Jenny, my first wife, helped me build the business. She supported me when we had nothing. She was the most devoted and good-hearted woman I have ever known. In the last years of her life, she wanted for nothing, but all the money in the world couldn't beat the cancer. Losing Jenny taught me a lot about love and about the finite quality of life and time.

"Several years later, when I found Barbara, I was determined to love her, help her in any way I could, and protect—" Sanford paused and looked at his friend. "There are days, Cheney, when life seems like it's far, far too long."

He leaned back in his chair and took a deep breath. "Bring me the truth."

Cheney stood, nodded, and let himself out as Sanford swiveled his chair around toward the window and dove into his own private hell.

While Cheney stood waiting for the elevator, he was thinking about Sanford's last words. Cheney would bring his friend the truth. But he knew that the truth, contrary to popular belief, rarely sets people free.

Cheney rang the doorbell for the fifth time and was just about to turn and walk away when he heard a voice calling, "Who's there?"

Following the voice around to a redwood fence that surrounded the back yard, Cheney looked over and saw Kyoko Rabinowitz holding a towel in front of her.

"What do you want?"

"I need to talk to you."

"I'm sunbathing. In the nude. It doesn't bother me, if it doesn't bother you."

"No problem," said Cheney. *I guess*, he said to himself.

When he sat down in the rickety white-vinyl lawn

chair next to where Kyoko had sprawled out again, face down on the towel, Cheney noticed that it *did* bother him. Certainly more than it bothered her.

"I time myself, okay? I need another fifteen minutes on my stomach, then a shower, and I'm outa here. I don't want an uneven tan. I mean, you walk *toward* somebody, you got tanned legs; you walk away, you look white. It looks weird, you know what I mean?"

"Yeah," said Cheney, even though he hadn't the foggiest idea.

"Don't get any ideas."

"Pardon?"

"Don't take offense, but you're from like an older generation. I mean, you equate nudity with sex. I'm nude, right?"

Cheney offered no argument.

"But I'm not coming on to you and I don't want any misunderstandings. Okay?"

"Gotcha."

Cheney forgot what he was going to say.

"So? You wanted—no, you said you *needed*—to talk to me."

"I've been talking to some people, and it's obvious that Barbara was seeing someone besides Bobby for maybe a month before she died."

Kyoko said nothing. Took in the rays.

"It makes sense that she might, well, spare her boyfriend the details. But you? You were her best friend."

"You mean like guys' locker-room talk?"

"Something like that."

"And you're an expert on what women say to each other?"

Cheney thought about saying that he used to think he was an expert, but he really felt out of the loop on such things these days. However, he was playing the only card in his deck. "I'm a cop," he said, as though that were an answer. "I figure she told you what was going on."

"Like what?" asked Kyoko, turning her head and looking up at Cheney.

"Like maybe she was fucking some other guy," said Cheney, regaining his bearings in very choppy water. "She's fucking some guy, she's going to tell you. That's what I think."

Kyoko turned over on her side, exposing medium-sized breasts that were slightly upturned and a patch of neatly manicured pubic hair—which Cheney tried not to notice. Tried very hard not to notice. "Well, she didn't tell me, okay?"

"She didn't tell you about the guy, or she didn't tell you his name?"

Kyoko looked at Cheney for a moment, made some kind of decision, and ran her suntan-lotioned fingers through her hair. She didn't change her body position. "She didn't tell me the guy's name, okay? And I don't think he was a lover."

"What do you mean?"

"Barbara already had a lover, okay?"

"You mean Bobby? I hate to burst your bubble," said Cheney, "but there are some women who have more than one."

"Not Barbara. She was strictly a one-man woman."

"According to my count, she was already one over the limit."

"You mean including her husband?"

"Color me old-fashioned."

"No need to get sarcastic."

"I'm trying to find out what happened to your best friend. Nobody wants to talk to me, and everybody figures they're doing the right thing. I have no ax to grind. I'm not running for office. I'm not writing a book. I'm just trying to get at the truth. I'd think if your friend was murdered, you'd like to know who did it."

Kyoko turned a little more toward Cheney. "You really think she was murdered? Is that what this is all about?"

"I don't know. If that's not it, and it's just an indiscretion on Barbara's part, or if it's something that has nothing to do with her death, it'll probably just die with her husband."

"And if she was murdered?"

"Then I'll do my best to strap the guy into the electric chair."

Kyoko stood, wrapped the towel around herself, and sat down in a matching lawn chair opposite Cheney. "Barbara trusted me."

"For good reason. You're a tough nut to crack. You show them a badge, a lot of people spill their guts."

"I've seen badges before. And I've known the guys who flash them. They're just guys."

"And you always had what they wanted?"

"Something like that. Sex is like money, especially when you don't have any—money, that is. Everyone uses what they've got to get along."

Not everyone, thought Cheney, but he didn't argue the point. "So, who was Barbara seeing?"

"I don't know. Honestly. But she was seeing someone for a few weeks before she was murdered. It really shook her up, too."

"What did she say about him?"

"Nothing specific. Not really. She told me the less I knew, the better off I'd be. I know she was scared. It wasn't like a romantic thing. Over the years Barbara was—well, she was kind of a romantic person. And she would always tell me who she was involved with. But this was different."

"Then why was she seeing this person?"

"I don't know. All I know is she seemed scared."

"Of what?"

"I don't know."

"Did you know if this person was hurting her? Physically?"

Kyoko looked out over her redwood fence toward the Los Angeles skyline. Through the smog. Through the grayness that obscured the city, made it vague and unclear. "One afternoon she came over here and she was crying. She said she had to use my bathroom. After about an hour, I opened the door and briefly, just before she quickly covered herself up, I saw there were marks on her chest. Like burns."

"Did you ask her about them?"

"Yes. But she told me she couldn't tell me anything."

"What happened?"

"I just held her for a while, and she cried."

"What did you think was happening?"

"I didn't know."

"You said that. But what did you *think* was happening?" Kyoko not only knew Barbara better than he did, but the more he got to know her, the more he respected her opinion.

Kyoko rubbed her greasy hands on the towel before she spoke. Then she looked up at Cheney. "I thought she was in trouble. In over her head, you know? She told me it would be over soon and not to worry about it."

"What did she mean by that?"

"I don't know. I wish to God I knew."

Both were silent for a moment.

"Look, I gotta get going."

Cheney stood. He took out a piece of paper, scribbled his home number on it, and handed it to Kyoko. "I'm not the enemy here, Kyoko. I know you cared about Barbara. So does her husband. So do I. If you think of anything, call me, any time. You can speak to me on or off the record."

"What does that mean?"

"It means you might want to tell me something that will help the investigation, but you might not want Barbara's husband to know about it. You call me, you want to talk. You can make the rules. I'm just looking for the truth."

"Good luck, Cheney," she said with a smile. "That's the most dangerous job in the world."

nine

"Sounds like she was being blackmailed."

"Yeah, but by whom, and why?" said Tony Boston between mouthfuls of pasta. Marino's was a restaurant a few blocks from Parker Center. Lots of cops went there, lots of lawyers and local politicians. Vito Marino was in his seventies now, and would smell like garlic, sweat it, breathe it, fart it till he died, even if he never ate another clove. He still wore an apron under his brown jacket—synthetic in the spring and summer, tweed in the fall and winter. Vito glad-handed movers and shakers, smiled at their friends. Took time to ask how a patron liked the meal. In LA, such traditions were either gone, or alive only on the West Side for a hundred bucks a pop. At Marino's, the customer got pasta, rolls, and a dinner salad for $8.95. Dinner. Lunch was two dollars less. Cheney and Tony were having lunch.

"I don't know who was blackmailing her."

"Maybe it was somebody who knew she was a hooker back in Vegas."

"Maybe. But it doesn't add up. For one thing, blackmailers don't usually end up killing a goose that lays golden eggs. If she can't lay golden eggs, he usually settles for silver."

"Maybe her lover . . . no, that doesn't make sense either," said Tony, thinking out loud.

"Now, if she were blackmailing someone and ends up dead, that makes sense. It doesn't make any sense if she's the one being blackmailed."

"But you're right," said Tony, rolling angel-hair pasta around his fork, "it does sound like blackmail. Or at least the guy had something major hanging over her head."

"But what?"

"Like I said, the hooker thing sounds possible."

"Maybe. It explains why she met with someone she didn't want to meet with—even though I have some problems with that too—but it makes no sense whatsoever, tying it together with her getting run over by a car on the Pacific Coast Highway."

"Maybe there's no connection. Maybe the official report is correct. Maybe she was being blackmailed. Maybe she was being tortured by someone. Maybe she couldn't take it anymore, got drunk one night, and staggered out in front of a car. No particular connection, but all true. Maybe the husband wants one answer when it's really all of the above."

"But it seems like quite a coincidence that within a few weeks of being blackmailed she winds up dead," said Cheney.

"It happens. You know it and so do I. You walk out of here and get killed by a drive-by shooter. The papers are going to write about you being an ex-chief of detectives. Quite a coincidence, Cheney having lunch with the current chief of detectives, walking out of that lunch, and getting shot. Life is full of coincidences. They don't mean shit unless you tie them together with facts. Hell, according to some lunatics, the only people not involved in the JFK assassination are the ones born after November 22, 1963."

"I know what you're saying, but I've just got a feeling."

"You've got a friend. A friend who's in a lot of pain. A friend who wants some answers to questions most people never get answers to. Life has more questions than answers. That's just the way it works."

"Is good?"

Cheney looked up. Vito stood hovering over their booth.

"Everything's great, Vito. As usual."

"I miss you, Cheney. You a good man."

"Thanks, Vito."

"Eh, Tony, you lika da angel hair. I make it al dente, justa for you."

"Perfect, Vito. Fuckin' perfect."

Vito laughed so that the belly beneath his tomato-sauce-spattered apron jiggled noticeably. He shook hands and walked to the next booth.

Tony tasted his Chianti, set it down. "Kimberly says you two played racquetball last night."

Cheney didn't respond immediately. "Yeah, well, Elizabeth said she was going to be late and Kim said she needed somebody to play. I didn't really make up my mind until the last minute."

"What do you think of her?"

"What do you mean?"

"I mean, I think she's great. She seems good at her job and she can keep her mouth shut when it's appropriate, when it might compromise a case." Tony looked up at Cheney. "And she's got great legs."

"Really? I hadn't noticed," lied Cheney.

"Check 'em out. She's a babe."

"So what are you trying to say?"

"Nothing, just making conversation."

"You gonna ask her out? On a date, I mean."

"Never know."

"Look, Tony," said Cheney, changing the subject, "if I wanted to go to Vegas, you think you could hook me up officially with somebody?"

"Sure, no problem. Are you going to go?"

"I'm thinking about it. First I've got to talk with Sanford again."

"I'm thinking about going to Vegas for a couple of days."

Elizabeth looked up at Cheney. She had made it home before nine, and they were sitting at the kitchen table eating. Petty had cooked a pesto sauce and boiled some garlic pasta Cheney had made a couple of days earlier.

"I thought you didn't like Vegas," she said as she sipped an '89 Rombauer Chardonnay that Cheney had uncorked for the occasion.

"I'm not going for fun. In fact, I might not go at all.

Barbara Sanford used to live there, and"—Cheney grated some fresh Parmesan he had picked up at Nick's Italian Deli in Brentwood that afternoon—"she was arrested for prostitution there."

Elizabeth stopped eating. "Are you sure?"

"Positive."

"How long ago?"

"A year or two before she came out here."

"Does Jamison know?"

"He does now."

"That's a tough thing to hear. Especially about your dead wife. Who has no way to defend herself."

"He wants the truth."

"Do you think her having been a prostitute has anything to do with her death?"

"I have no idea. I'm just gathering facts at this point. Besides, there's another reason I want to go soon—your operation."

"That's very thoughtful of you."

"Even though you downplay the risks, it's surgery. I'll be there."

"You sound so traditional, Cheney."

"And you love it."

"That's true. And I love you. Very much." She raised her glass of Chardonnay to him.

"I'm sorry about going behind your back to your doctor yesterday, but I just wanted—"

"You wanted to be reassured. That's natural. And you did it the way you always do things—you just plunged ahead, directly from point A to point B."

"Sometimes I hate being married to a psychiatrist."

"I'm a lotta fun, Cheney. At least that's what you say." Elizabeth smiled. "Or was that just bedroom talk?"

"No, it's true."

Elizabeth looked at her husband thoughtfully. "Is it as true today as it was when we were first married?"

"Of course."

"Answer me honestly, Cheney. Look, there are no right or wrong answers. When we first got married you couldn't get enough of me. Morning, noon, and night. You were a fucking animal."

"Nice choice of words. Is that a medical term?"

"You know what I mean."

"Honey, you're the psychiatrist in the family. Tell me, isn't it natural for things—"

"You mean sex."

"Sex things, yes. Isn't it natural for things to kinda calm down?"

"Yes, it is. I just want to know if you're as sexually attracted to me as you used to be."

"Of course."

"Then why haven't you been as sexual with me lately as you used to be?"

"It's natural, Elizabeth. Things change."

"Don't you wish they didn't?"

"Wishing is something I used to do when I was a child. When I became a man, I stopped acting like a child."

"But don't you miss it? I mean, don't you miss being the object of someone's sexual obsession?"

"You mean like in *Fatal Attraction*?"

"You know what I mean. I mean like it used to be with us. It was healthy, lustful, and fulfilling."

"So what are you saying here?"

"Nothing, really," said Elizabeth. She drank her wine and pushed her plate away.

"Is that what this plastic surgery is all about?"

"What do you mean?"

"Now who's being evasive? Are you getting plastic surgery to recapture some moment in our past?"

Elizabeth looked at Cheney. "I'm not sure. But don't go whipping yourself to death. I'm doing this for me. I want to look as young as I can for as long as I can. Is there any sin in that?"

Cheney did not respond.

"I'm not hurting anyone. I know it's a vain thing to do. But it's my money, it's my body—"

"I love your body. Really."

"Look, I know you're a great guy and you wouldn't leave me just because I've put on a few pounds. But let's face it, I'm not in the shape I was when we got married."

"Neither am I."

"Quite frankly, you're not that far from it. Anyhow, I devoted a great deal of time and energy to practice-building over the past few years, and I stopped working out the way I used to."

"It doesn't matter."

"It does matter. At least it matters to me. Like I said, Cheney, you're off the hook."

"What if I told you I like your body better now than when we got married?"

"I'd say you were lying."

"Some guys love husky women."

Elizabeth just looked at Cheney in disbelief, as Cheney's life flashed before his eyes.

"I don't mean to imply for one minute, one second, that you're the *slightest* bit overweight," said Cheney, backpedaling as fast as he could. "All I'm saying is that there is no one specific perfect body type. Look, we're getting older. Both of us. No matter how much we work out, how well we eat, we're never going to look twenty years old again."

"All I'm saying is, I feel I have a legitimate, ethical option and I'm going to exercise it."

Cheney had no argument with his wife's logic. And in a vague and interesting way that he found difficult to admit to himself, he was curious about how his wife would be sculpted by the cosmetic surgery.

"There's something I want to discuss with you, Elizabeth."

"All right."

"When we came to a joint decision that I would retire from the force, I had no idea I was going to be sitting home every night while you were putting in late hours."

"That's not fair, Cheney. You retired for a lot of reasons."

"And one of those reasons was so we could spend time together."

"How many times do I have to tell you, this is just an aberration? It'll end soon. I promise."

"I hope so. I have to admit that when I see Tony doing the job I used to do—quite well, I might add— while I'm sitting around making pasta, playing golf, and tracking down Chardonnays, it just . . . this isn't what I signed up for."

Elizabeth stood, walked over to her husband, and extended her hand. Cheney stood. Elizabeth took his hands and placed them between her legs. "This is what you signed up for, isn't it?"

"Yes, ma'am, it is," said Cheney, bringing his right hand to his forehead and saluting.

Elizabeth looked up into her husband's eyes and licked her lips. Slowly. "Well, a person should get what he's been promised."

Cheney took his wife in his arms.

And was glad he had given Petty money for the movies.

He slapped her hard across the face.

Raven grabbed her cheek and looked at Gino in shock. "What did you do that for?"

"Because I love you," said Gino.

Calculation. Indoctrination. Execution.

Raven felt the heat of the impact of flesh on flesh. She had never felt that before. As she stroked her cheek and looked into the eyes of the man she admired, she tried to reconcile the sensations.

"What's the matter?"

"You hit me," she said.

Gino laughed. It was not the laugh of a monster. It was the laugh of a father whose child has asked why the sun comes up every morning. Toleration.

Indoctrination.

"You hurt me."

"Did I? Let me tell you what hurt is," he said, a fire in his eyes Raven had never seen before. "Hurt is drawing blood. Hurt is having to call an ambulance. Hurt is whaling on you when I'm out of control." He paused to let the words sink in. "Did I hit you as hard as I could?"

"No, but—"

"Is it going to leave a bruise?"

"I don't—"

"Do you think I really meant to hurt you?"

"Then why did you hit me?"

"Because I love you."

Indoctrination.

"I don't understand."

Gino sighed and looked at Raven patiently. "Let me ask you a question. The first time you saw my work, did you understand it? I mean, completely. Every nuance. Every subtlety."

"No."

"Yet you knew, you *sensed* there was an overall truth there."

"Yes."

"Something greater than you. Something you could not understand. Yet something you gradually came to understand."

"Yes."

Gino smiled. "Which one of us do you think is smarter?"

It occurred to Raven to say they were equally intelligent, or that no one could measure such things, but such answers sounded unrealistic. Vapid.

"You are," she said finally.

Indoctrination.

"But that doesn't mean I'm stupid," she added.

"Do you think I would waste my time on some stupid bitch?" Gino leaned over and kissed Raven on the forehead, anointing her.

Making her feel smart. Intelligent. That she wasn't a stupid bitch.

Indoctrination.

"So why did you hit me?"

"I touched you in a different way, that's all. It was sensation. It all depends on how you interpret that sensation."

"What do you mean?"

"I mean, some people pay for the kind of sensation I just gave you. Some people find it pleasurable."

"I don't."

"You will," said Gino with the confidence of a man playing with a marked deck of cards. "You've been programmed to interpret those sensations in only one way. That's all. Trust me. I used to feel the way you do right now. We're all young and naive once in our lives. No harm in that. I don't hold it against you."

Gino put his hand on Raven's hand.

Indoctrination.

Suddenly Gino removed his hand from Raven's and slapped her again.

She started to answer.

He slapped her again.

She started to answer.

He slapped her again.

She sat there. Silent. Motionless.

"That's better," he said, smiling knowingly. "I love you," said Gino, not taking his eyes from Raven.

After a few seconds, she said, "I love you too."

"Tell me again."

Indoctrination.

"I love you."

Gino leaned across the table and kissed Raven hard on the lips.

"Tell me again like you mean it."

"I love you, Gino," said Raven. She felt a whirlpool of sensation inside her beginning to swallow her up.

"Nothing is dirty when it's done in the context of a loving relationship."

"I don't know about that," said Raven. She sat next to the stage, finishing the second drink Gino had ordered for her, Long Island something or other. All she knew was she was feeling a little tipsy.

"So?"

"So what?" she asked, even though she knew.

"Are you going to do it or not?"

"I don't—"

"You don't what?" said Gino belligerently. "Do you love me?"

"Yes, but—"

Indoctrination.

"Then show me," he said, looking her in the eye.

She tried to focus. "I've never done anything like this before. I'm not sure—"

"Are you sure you love me?"

"Yes, but—"

"But nothing. Either you love me or you don't. Simple as that."

It didn't seem that simple, but in her state of mind Raven really wasn't sure. Of anything.

"So, you gonna do it for me?"

"Gino, I—"

"For me," he said and smiled. "Just for me." Gino handed Raven a fresh glass.

She drank. To please him. "Maybe some other night—"

"Tonight. Now."

She drank some more.

Gino stood and extended his hand as though asking m'lady for a dance. She stood and walked up the steps to the tiny stage.

The music kicked in and the place went dark.

Gino sat down.

In the spotlight, Raven looked uncomfortable. As though she had never done this before. Which, of course, she hadn't.

Above the music, she heard the cheers of what she knew to be about a dozen men scattered throughout the tiny club.

The light shone in her face. She could not see Gino. But she knew he was there. And she knew what he wanted her to do.

What she *had* to do.

What she had been *indoctrinated* to do.

She was wearing a short black dress, a dress bought for her by Gino, and matching high-heel shoes. She began to move her body to the pulsating rhythm of the music. Maybe she had drunk too much. She felt herself riding the waves of sensation that flowed into and out of her: music, applause, cheering, alcohol. . . .

She was dancing. And when her fingers touched the hem of her dress, the cheers and applause intensified. And she thought, although she could not be certain—because of the blinding spotlight, because of the alcohol—that she heard Gino's voice the loudest.

She felt her eyelids getting heavy, but she continued to dance. Again she reached down and touched the hem of her dress.

Applause.

Slowly she began to pull the black dress up her thigh, to her hips.

Applause.

Approval.

Over her hips. Over her shoulders. Her head. Dropped it on the floor.

Applause. Approval.

The bra went next.

Applause. Approval.

She was moving as though in a dream. On automatic. As though she were trying to feel in the darkness for what was right. And she could tell what was right, because when she did the right thing she heard the applause. Received the approval.

When her fingers looped inside her G-string panties, the cheers intensified.

Approval rose like a fountain in front of her.

As her panties fell onto the stage and she bathed herself in the admiration that flowed toward her, she was certain she had done the right thing.

When it was over, Raven said, "You don't think I'm a slut, do you?" She was back at the table, fully dressed again, sitting close to Gino.

"Of course not. You were *great*."

Gino ran his fingers through Raven's hair, which was wet with sweat. Petted her.

"So, would you like to see my new movie?"

Raven perked up like a dutiful child. "Really?"

"Why not?"

"I thought you said you never showed anyone a work in progress."

Gino did not speak immediately. Then he smiled.

"You're not just anyone. Not anymore. Besides, maybe you'll inspire me." Suddenly he reached down between her legs and grabbed her.

Raven reacted. More slowly than she thought she would have. More slowly than she would have before. Before tonight.

"That's what all those dogs were howling for," he said, not letting go his grasp.

Raven tensed up. But she was not afraid.

"Are you turned on?"

After a moment, Raven said, "Yes." She put her head on his shoulder. Put her arms around him.

She did not see him smile. Take a drink.

And watch the next dancer.

With disgust.

ten

"What do you think you're going to find in Vegas?" asked Jamison Sanford. He was sitting in a white wrought-iron chair looking out over the vast expanse of his back yard.

"I don't know. Maybe nothing. All I'm saying is that, as an investigator, I should check it out. Personally. And I want to do it soon. Elizabeth is having surgery in a few days, and—"

"I wasn't aware of that. I hope it's nothing serious," said Sanford, genuinely concerned.

"No, it's . . . nothing serious," said Cheney, not wanting to get into it.

"It's tough to hold on to the things you love, Cheney. But then, I'm sure you know that."

Cheney knew that.

"Give me a minute." Sanford stood and walked from the large patio into his house.

As Cheney looked out upon the gardens and the two ponds in Sanford's back yard, he thought about Sanford's comment. It *was* tough to hold on to the things you love, particularly the people you love. In the late twentieth century, divorce was the rule, not the exception. The American Dream was broken, and no one knew how to fix it. The world was changing, way too fast for a man in his fifties who remembered a world without CD players. Cheney had walked into a music store recently and asked the clerk where the record album section was. The guy had looked at him as though he had asked for a ticket to the Gettysburg Address. Life didn't work the way it worked when Cheney was growing up. It didn't work the way he figured it was going to when he got to be this age.

And it never would again.

Sanford walked back outside to the patio, sat down, and handed Cheney twenty thousand-dollar bills.

Cheney took them and started to say something.

Sanford held up his hand. "The amount of money is not important to me, Cheney. What you do with it is. If there's a surplus, I'm sure you'll give me the change—minus your fee, of course."

Cheney pocketed the money. He knew this was small change to Sanford. He was going to need some expense money in Vegas, as well as here in town. And he was going to charge the man. But Cheney knew the price didn't make any difference to Sanford as long as he got his answer.

"What can you tell me about Barbara and Vegas?"

"Apparently you already know more about what she did there than I do."

"What do *you* know?"

"She told me she grew up there. She told me she went to college there but didn't graduate."

"You say she grew up there. Do her parents live there?"

"No. They're both dead."

"Any other relatives?"

"She was an only child."

Cheney didn't say so, but he had heard this kind of case history before. There was a reason for it, and he thought he might know what it was.

"Is there anything you can tell me about her life in Vegas that might give me someplace to start?"

"Not really. She never talked about her past."

"Didn't you think that was odd?"

"Not really."

"You seem to have cut your wife a lot of slack."

"Look, Cheney, I may not be able to play the game as spryly as I used to, but I still know the score. I was fifty when I married Barbara. She was in her twenties. If she wanted to keep certain things private, that was okay with me. I knew I wasn't marrying Mother Teresa."

Cheney leaned forward. "Are you being glib, or are you just not leveling with me?"

"What are you talking about?"

"What I'm talking about is you're the richest guy I know, and I've met presidents. You didn't make that kind of money being stupid. A man in your position doesn't marry someone he doesn't know a fucking thing about."

"Even smart people get stupid when it comes to sex. Or maybe you're immune to such things."

Cheney had never met anyone who was immune to such things. Only people who were between addictive episodes.

"To be honest with you, Kyoko probably knows more about the things Barbara didn't want me to know about than I do."

"But you could have found them out."

"That's true. Perhaps there are certain things a person doesn't want to know."

"So why hire me now?"

"The circumstances are different. When Barbara was alive, I allowed her freedom and privacy. She gave me a considerable amount of happiness. There was no reason to pry. But now . . . now she's dead, I need to know what happened."

"You need to know who her lover was."

"No. I need to know who killed her. That's what I'm paying you to find out." Sanford stood. "And I'm quite certain you will be able to do so. Now, if you'll excuse me . . ."

Cheney stood. Sanford walked him to the door and closed it behind him before Cheney was in his car, which was parked in the circular driveway that emptied onto Sunset, about five miles from the Pacific Ocean.

From the Pacific Coast Highway. Where Barbara Sanford had been run down.

By someone Cheney had just been officially hired to find.

It was nearly two. Everyone he knew had a job. He had a job too. He could tell by the bulge in his pocket.

Big money. For some. For most people Cheney knew. For him too. He steered the black 1991 300E Mercedes onto Sunset and drove west until it dead-ended at the Pacific Coast Highway.

As he drove north toward Leslie's, he passed the spot on the road where Barbara Sanford had been run down and killed. There was still a dark patch where her blood had stained the pavement.

Leslie's was a little shack of a place, at least compared to the moonlight-over-the-water mega-restaurant on stilts about two hundred yards south of it. Cheney occasionally frequented Leslie's for three reasons: they served good wine by the glass, the view was fabulous, and he liked Michael, the bartender, who at this time of day still served food from the lunch menu.

"Haven't seen you in here for a while," said Michael. He slid a bowl of Manhattan clam chowder on the bar in front of Cheney. Michael was tall, a little out of shape. Today he was wearing a Hawaiian shirt that hung down over a pair of old jeans, which was exactly how Cheney remembered him from the last time he was in. And the time before that.

"Ah, well, you know . . ."

"Sure."

The place was empty at two-thirty in the afternoon, so Michael felt comfortable leaning over the bar and chatting with the ex-LAPD chief of detectives.

"How's Elizabeth?"

"She's fine. She's . . ."—this was not the time or place—"fine."

"So, whatcha workin' on?"

"Littla this, littla that."

"Can't talk about it, eh?"

"It's not that. Life can get pretty boring when you retire."

"Especially after a job like yours."

"Ain't that the truth." Cheney tasted the chowder. He made a sound that described his pleasure. "You know, I really would like this recipe."

"I know, Cheney. We go through this every time."

"And you always promise you'll ask Leslie."

"I forgot, okay?" Michael poured Cheney a Burgess and set it on the bar. "Forgive me?"

"Forgive what?" Cheney picked up glass number one, turned around, and held it up toward the window, the ocean, and the sunlight. He sipped and savored, then turned back around toward Michael. "So, I hear you had a little excitement out here a few weeks ago."

"What do you mean?"

"The hit-and-run?"

"Oh, yeah. Hell of a thing. I was working that night. In fact, I closed up, so I saw all the flashing lights on my way home."

"Cops come by the next day?"

"Yeah. They called me at home; I was off the next day. Showed me a picture of the woman. Never saw her before. Lotta blood. Car that hit her must've been going pretty good."

Cheney nodded.

"You know, it's a crazy thing. . . . "

"What's that?" asked Cheney, feigning a lack of interest, or at least moderate-to-polite interest, while he sipped his chowder respectfully.

"I've worked out here on PCH nearly ten years

now. Never heard of a hit-and-run like that. Oh, every now and then in the summer when the beach is packed. But late at night? C'mon. It's four to six lanes, and it ain't exactly rush-hour traffic. Crazy."

"So what do you hear about it?"

"What do you mean?"

"I mean, you talked to people about what happened, right?"

"Sure."

"Anybody think there was something more to it than hit-and-run?"

"You mean, like was it intentional? Nah. Didn't hear anything like that. Why?"

"No reason. You busy that night?"

"Nah, pretty dead, really. There was one guy. . . . "

"Yes?"

"Closed the place."

"Notice anything unusual about him?"

"Not really. Well, one thing. He wasn't drinking alcohol."

"Really. You'd think a guy hangs out here till you close, he's drinking."

"It's unusual but not unheard of. I mean, Malibu is a decent drive back to LA. We don't encourage people to drink and drive back ten miles of winding road."

"You say it's not unheard of. What kind of people come in here and don't drink?"

"People who come for the view. Designated drivers."

"Was he alone?"

"Yes."

"So he wasn't a designated driver. Did he seem interested in the view?"

"Not really. He sat at the bar. Can't see the ocean from here, unless you turn around."

"So what other kind of person comes in here and doesn't drink?"

"Some people come for the chowder," said Michael, smiling and looking at Cheney.

"Did he have any chowder?"

Michael thought about that a moment. "Can't say for sure. I don't have a photographic memory, but I don't think so."

"So if he didn't come for the view and he didn't come for the chowder, what kind of person does that leave?"

"I dunno. Maybe he was just on his way home and stopped by for a . . ." Michael's voice trailed off. "Hell, I dunno."

"What did the guy look like?"

"Average."

"Thanks. I'll put out an all-points bulletin. Was he white?"

"Yeah. Tell you the truth, Cheney, if the person had been a woman, I'd have been a helluva lot more attentive, you know what I'm sayin'? All I remember is the guy had like medium-length hair, no beard, and he wore a black leather jacket."

That narrowed it down to about two million guys in LA between the ages of eighteen and fifty.

"You think this guy's got something to do with the hit-and-run accident?"

"I have no idea," said Cheney. He slid his empty bowl across the bar in Michael's general direction. "You think if I brought in a photograph of the guy you could ID him?"

"I doubt it. Like I said, if it'd been a woman . . ."

"Thanks. Great chowder."

Cheney tossed a twenty-dollar bill on the bar and held up his hand. The chowder and the wine came to about nine dollars. The information was on the house. But Cheney appreciated good wine. And good information.

Before he pulled back onto the Pacific Coast Highway, he used his car phone to call his answering machine. Two messages. Tony Boston had the name of a Vegas detective, and Kimberly Gary wanted Cheney to call her. She said it was urgent.

Cheney called the number she had left on his machine and told her he would be right over.

"Thanks for coming. Sit anywhere," said Kimberly.

The apartment was smaller than Cheney had anticipated. Modern, neat, efficient, all wrapped up in pastels and chrome. Sterile was the word that came to Cheney's mind.

"So what's so urgent?"

"Tony said you might be going to Vegas."

Cheney said nothing, knowing she was waiting for him to speak.

"Are you?"

"Yes."

"I think I should go with you."

"I can't think of why."

"I'm the perfect person."

"Why?"

"First of all, I'm from Vegas. I grew up there, went to UNLV, the whole nine yards."

"Pretty bold request."

"If you don't ask, no one can say yes."

"I don't think so."

"Why not?"

"Why should I let you come?"

"I'll pay my own way. I know the turf. In fact, one of the guys I went to school with is managing editor of the *Vegas Chronicle.* I'm sure you're talking to someone there in the department, but if Barbara Sanford was an area resident, it wouldn't hurt to have a friend in the morgue." She was referring to the voluminous amount of newspaper material on microfiche in a newspaper office's basement.

Cheney knew he didn't have time to search through those archives. And he knew Kimberly was motivated—for several reasons.

"You've got nothing to lose. If we come up empty, no harm, no foul."

"I might come up with something and you still might come up empty. I'm under no obligation to share my information with you."

"Understood," she said, willing to take her chances. In fact, besides a few dollars, she had nothing to lose and a lot to gain.

"I don't know."

"C'mon, Cheney. You're going anyhow. I can only be a help. Besides, you're not going to be working twenty-four hours a day."

"What does that mean?"

"It means I know the city."

"I have to think about it."

"When are you going?"

"Tomorrow, probably."

"Let me know either way, okay?"

"Sure."

"How long will you be gone?"

"Couple, three days."

Cheney and Elizabeth lay in bed, Cheney on his side, looking at his wife.

"So where is this going, Cheney? Do you really believe Barbara was murdered?"

"I don't know."

"What do you think you'll find in Vegas?"

"Maybe nothing, but it's a string I have to play out."

"What does Jamison think about you digging around in Barbara's past?"

"He wants to know who killed her, and digging up her past is a legitimate line of inquiry."

Elizabeth and Cheney were silent for a moment. Then she leaned over and kissed her husband gently on the lips. "I'm glad you're coming back for the operation."

"Nothing could keep me away."

Cheney made love to his wife in a way he hadn't made love to her in . . . he couldn't remember the last time it had been quite like this. Where had this new passion come from? Cheney could only speak for himself. There was going to be separation. But he had taken trips without Elizabeth before.

It was something else. Perhaps, considered Cheney as he lay spent and sated next to Elizabeth, the renewed passion had not come solely from himself.

Cheney turned onto his side and slid his right leg over Elizabeth's lower abdomen. "That was good."

She kissed Cheney on the mouth. She was heavy-lidded. Fatigued and satisfied.

"You sure about . . . you know?"

"I'm sure, Cheney. Look at it this way: whatever you just had fun with is going to be more fun to play with soon."

"Is that any way for a psychiatrist to talk?"

"It's the truth. Men are very visual—sexually, that is. Why do you think they want an eighteen-year-old bimbo over a bright, mature, intellectual woman?"

"They're idiots?" said Cheney.

"Right answer, my darling," she said with a smile. "Most men are idiots when it comes to choosing a woman. So I'm just hedging my bets against you becoming an idiot. In the very, very distant future, of course," she added quickly. And somewhat sarcastically.

"If that's really the reason, I want you to cancel the surgery."

Elizabeth looked her husband squarely in the eye. "No. I'm doing this for myself, Cheney. There's nothing wrong with what I'm doing."

"Then don't make me out to be the villain. The idiot villain."

"I try and try to manipulate you and what do I get?"

"Fucked?"

"Is that any way for a man to talk?"

"To his wife, maybe. To a wife like you, definitely."

Elizabeth put her arms around her husband and pulled him close to her. "You're such a sweet-talker, Cheney."

And they gave each other another sweet goodbye.

*　　*　　*

Cheney stood dressed in his navy blue Pierre Cardin robe, a snifter of Armagnac in one hand, looking out over his back yard through the open patio door. It was three in the morning and he couldn't sleep. He didn't know why. His mind was filled with crazy images. He had noticed that when he was supposed to be asleep, according to his body clock, and he was not, he could often just close his eyes and images would appear as though he were actually dreaming. He first noticed this phenomenon twenty years ago on his first stakeout. At four in the morning, as he stared, as he had for hours before, at an apartment building, he noticed that he was so fatigued his mind was already dreaming, even though his body was fully awake. And for reasons he had never figured out, whenever this phenomenon occurred, the dreams were always in color.

Cheney closed his eyes.

Barbara Sanford was flying through the air on the Pacific Coast Highway. In slow motion . . . her body covered with burns. On her face was a black mask.

Some "average" guy was closing a Malibu bar, his back to the Pacific, drinking soda.

Elizabeth was walking into a roomful of people wearing a low-cut red dress. She too was wearing a mask, a red mask.

Color. Images.

Cheney opened his eyes. Tasted his drink and took a deep breath of chilly night air. Five miles from the ocean, the air was clean. Cleaner than in the city.

And for some reason the image of Kimberly Gary's legs kept flashing in his mind.

Like a red light. Flashing in the darkness.

Even with his eyes open.

*   *   *

"I don't usually allow people in my studio. It's my secret place."

"I feel honored," said Raven. She leaned down and kissed Gino. In less than twenty-four hours she had recognized a major change in herself. Something was different. The way she related to men? No. Today at work, she still felt repulsed by the way her boss had looked at her. She was not turned on by the way the security guard in the parking lot had held on to the parking ticket for that extra second.

The way she related to men had not changed.

The way she related to Gino had changed.

Dramatically.

She felt about him the way she had never felt about anyone. Never before had she entertained the thought of dancing naked in front of other people. At a nightclub? Unbelievable. That was not her. Not the way she behaved. Not the way any of her friends behaved.

Yet it *was* the way she had behaved. No gun had been held to her head. Why had she done it?

She had lain awake all night trying to figure out why. No "right" answer had come to mind. And the more she thought about it, the less she required an explanation.

Sensation. That was what it was all about. But the sensation of being slapped? Of dancing naked in front of drunks? She had never sought such sensations. In fact, they were sensations she not only would have avoided but would have found repugnant.

Before last night.

What had changed?

It was Gino. He had changed her. He had shown her that what she had considered dirty was just sensation. What she had considered painful was merely an interpretation of that sensation.

Sensation capable of being interpreted in any way a person wished.

"I hope you can appreciate my work."

"I do." She squeezed his hand. Feeling safe and secure. "This is incredible," she said, turning in a circle, looking at the sixteen screens that formed the circular theater.

"Do you know why I asked you here tonight?"

"No," said Raven. She moved close to him and kissed him hard on the mouth. "Why?"

"Because you inspire me."

Raven smiled, basking in the compliment. "You inspire me, too," she said, looking Gino in the eye, her heart starting to race.

Gino hit a button on the computer keyboard. Music, slow, bassy, and sensual, filled the studio, sixteen speakers' worth of sound that caressed and stroked. He stood and walked to the center of the room. "Do you remember I said you reminded me of someone?"

"Yes. Was she pretty?"

"Oh, she was beautiful."

"Do you still see her?"

"Why? Would that make you jealous?"

"Maybe. A little."

"I don't see her anymore. Come here."

Raven walked over to where Gino stood. That was

when she noticed the leather restraints directly above his head.

In the darkness, she had not seen them. In the shadows.

eleven

"I appreciate your letting me come along."

"Just so we understand each other. You help me with your connections, and I tell you whatever I want to tell you."

"Sounds fair," Kimberly said. She wore a beige skirt that didn't touch her knees when she was seated—as she was now, next to Cheney on Southwest flight 415 to Vegas—and a white blouse, open at the collar.

And perfume. Usually Cheney found women's perfume overly sweet. Not Elizabeth's, of course, but they had been down that road together to make a selection that produced what Elizabeth referred to as the desired result. The result being that it aroused her husband.

But Kimberly's perfume did not smell overly sweet, thought Cheney. It was, well, provocative. Pleasant, at least. Not oppressive.

"Would you like a cocktail?" said the flight attendant, a black man in his late twenties.

"What kind of wine do you have?" asked Cheney.

"Chablis and Burgundy."

"I'll have a diet cola."

"And for you, ma'am?"

"I'll have a Bloody Mary."

"Very good."

"It's only ten in the morning," said Cheney, as the man turned his attention to the passengers across the aisle.

"It's six in the evening in London."

"You're not in London."

"I'm not in LA either. What's the big deal, Cheney? You sound like my—"

"Father?"

"I was going to say something else. But the idea's the same. Lighten up. I promise not to take off my clothes and run down the aisle naked."

Cheney thought about saying something humorous but decided against it. He pressed a button on his armrest and pushed his seat back from the upright position to a more comfortable one. "You seem to know a lot more about me than I know about you. We've got an hour plane ride. I'm all ears. You said you went to UNLV?"

"Yeah, it was great. Especially if you like basketball."

The flight attendant returned with the drinks and set them on their trays.

"People always put Vegas down. They think it's such a sleazy place."

"It isn't?"

"Yes, but it has its bad points, too." Beat. "Seriously, I grew up there. People usually just come for a weekend to see the Strip. It's like someone going to LA, hanging out down at Venice Beach, and thinking everybody in LA gets around on skates."

"Some of my friends do."

"I'd get some different friends if I were you."

"I'm thinking about it."

"Anyhow, I liked the place. Your personal experience of a place is the important thing. Most of my friends couldn't wait to get out of Vegas. I've seen a lot of those same people in LA. They can't wait to get out of LA."

Cheney nodded.

"When I was in college I always dreamed of writing for a big-time newspaper."

"So what do you do now that you've accomplished your goal at such a young age?"

"I'm thirty-two. That isn't as young as it used to be, especially in LA. What do I do now? Simple. Set new goals."

"And when are you going to do that?"

"I already have." She drank her Bloody Mary and smiled at Cheney.

"What are you smiling about?"

"I was thinking about someone. A guy I dated when I went to school there. His name was Brett. He was my journalism teacher."

"You're kidding."

"It happens, Cheney. Or don't you watch the soaps?"

"I don't, actually."

"Trust me. It happens. I was crazy about him. He

knew everything about everything I wanted to know about. That's not a great sentence, but poetic in its own way, don't you think?"

Cheney nodded again.

"He was thirty-one and I was twenty. He knew all the rules I needed to learn, he had clippings of his work—he had been published in dozens of newspapers—including an article in *The New York Times*. And he knew about sex. It was all there, Cheney. And it was mine for the plucking. He thought I was the sexiest thing that ever came down the road.

"The first six months were blissful. Stolen moments, weekends holed up in his apartment fucking hour after hour after hour, not able to get enough of each other. The apartment was lined with books. He had a fireplace. It was fucking idyllic."

"At least you're not bitter."

Kimberly smiled again. "We split up after a year. I found out he was teaching because he couldn't get a job—on *The New York Times* or any other paper, including the local ones. The books he owned, except for a dozen or so, were books he scammed from various publications saying that he, as a college journalism professor, would review them, but he never did. Even the fireplace was fake."

"How about the sex?"

"It lost its charm."

"It often does."

"You mean sex eventually fades?" asked Kimberly, looking up at Cheney over her Bloody Mary.

"It fades with someone you really don't love."

"I agree. People confuse love and sex." Kimberly finished her drink and looked at Cheney. "But there's no harm keeping in training while you're waiting for the Olympics."

"I never looked at it that way."

"Men always look at it that way, Cheney. Never met a man who didn't." She smiled. "But that's okay. You can't help being a man. Besides, sometimes that way works out best."

"I'm not sure I know what you mean."

"I'm not sure you do, either." Kimberly pressed the button on her armrest, leaned back in her seat, and closed her eyes.

Cheney drank his soda, looked out over the clouds, and tried to figure it out.

Cheney picked up the keys to a Caprice at the Avis counter, and drove Kimberly to the Maxim Hotel. The hotel was located just off the Strip, within walking distance of all the more high-profile places.

Las Vegas was like an adult Disneyland, thought Cheney. Like Disneyland, the rides in Vegas cost money, but if you were over twenty-one and had cash in your pocket the rides were often a lot more fun.

Cheney didn't used to like Las Vegas, but his last few visits had been enjoyable. On one visit he had stayed at Caesar's with Elizabeth. They had spent a great deal of time and money shopping at the Forum, an indoor shopping mall that appeared as though it was really outside. Clouds crawled across the ceiling, and day changed to night and back again. The last time, two years ago, Cheney had come with a couple of cops who knew the town, so they went mostly to places off the Strip, places where the locals hung out.

Cheney and Kimberly went their separate ways in the lobby. Cheney unpacked in his room and called Detective John Hanna to let him know he was on his way over.

Hanna took him to Tony Wojnowski's, a Hungarian chili joint near the Showboat. It was the kind of place that sponsored a bowling team, maybe even two. It drew an ethnic crowd, in the old sense of the word, meaning Polish and German: lots of people with names that ended in *ski* who talked about football and baseball and weren't afraid to get into a public conversation about professional wrestling.

Hanna had chosen Wojnowski's for two reasons. First, for the chili. Second, he knew LAPD was picking up the tab.

"Don't you just love this shit?" asked Hanna rhetorically, referring to the chili.

"Great." Cheney coughed, his mouth on fire. "You eat here often?"

"Every Friday, come hell or high water."

Cheney figured he could use a little high water about now.

"So, you're stayin' at Maxim."

"Yes."

"There's a bar a couple blocks from there. Cop bar. Kelly's. Try it. Tell Tim I sent you; he's the bartender. He'll take care of you."

"Thanks."

Cheney let Hanna eat in peace. A side of sauerkraut and knockwurst and a beer, added to the chili, seemed to induce some type of culinary nirvana in him. He sighed deeply and shook his head appreciatively with nearly every bite.

When the dishes had been cleared away and the second Bud from the tap set in front of Hanna, Cheney said, "So, you worked the Barbara Holgate case?"

"Yeah. That was during my first year as a detective. I remember almost every detail of every case my first year. After that—well, it starts to blur, you know?"

"Yeah." Cheney knew. But it wasn't so much the blur as the numbness. A cop had to put on armor to keep himself from being ripped apart by real life. Chandler's mean streets were parade routes compared to what it was like out there in the nineties. Even in Vegas.

"So, what was Barbara like?" asked Cheney.

"Pretty. Lost. Naive."

"Naive? I thought you said she was arrested for prostitution."

"She was. That doesn't mean she wasn't naive. Just because a person shoots heroin don't make 'em an expert on drugs. Besides, she was in way over her head."

"What do you mean?"

"I mean she was smack dab in the middle of a serial murder case."

"A serial murder case?"

"Maybe not big-time, but yeah. That's how I met her. I wasn't involved with the prostitution bust. That's Mickey Mouse, especially here, except maybe during certain election years."

"This serial murder case. . . . Obviously she wasn't the murderer, and since she left here alive I have to deduce she wasn't a victim either."

"Well, your deductions would be a little off, Cheney. May I call you Cheney?"

"Everybody does."

"Then I will too. She was one of the *intended* victims. In fact, she was the only victim who lived."

"How many people did the guy kill?"

"Guy? How do you know the killer was a man?"

"You ever know a serial killer who was a woman?" asked Cheney.

"Not personally. But I read about a couple." Hanna drank his beer. "Still, I take your point. Don't make much sense looking for a woman serial killer."

"How many victims?"

"Three. Barbara would have been the fourth."

Cheney thought about saying something like *not exactly a reign of terror*, but he stopped himself. Any murder is a reign of terror to the victim and to surviving family members. Instead, he said, "What makes you think a serial killer was responsible?"

"He was trying to do to her what he did to the other girls. The victims were tortured, then murdered. Tossed like garbage in downtown dumpsters."

"When did the murders occur?"

"Summer of eighty-four. Barbara Holgate was a good-looking woman, as I recall. Brunette. Great legs. Not too top-heavy, if you take my meaning, but that never mattered much to me anyhow. But I digress," said Hanna, putting his beer mug to work again. "On the report she listed her occupation as *Model*. I'd actually seen her in a couple of local ads: bra ads in the newspaper for a department store, as a dancer on a billboard for a local club, that kind of thing. Not much action for a model in this town. Enough to blow a little air up your skirt, but if you wanna really take off you go to LA or New York."

"Was she from around here?"

"Born to working-class parents in a working-class neighborhood. Kinda home with framed pictures of the saints on the wall. Her mother was always praying to them for help; her father was always knocking them down when he slammed his wife's head against the wall in a drunken rage."

"You talked to her parents?"

"After she left town. I went over there to get a number where I could reach Barbara if I had any questions. They had no idea where she went."

"I was told her parents were dead," said Cheney, remembering what Sanford had said.

"They weren't eight years ago. Might as well've been, though, as far as the girl was concerned. I got the address from the report. They didn't look like they were going anywhere."

"You said there were three victims."

"Local girls. Early to mid-twenties."

"Any similarities among the four women?"

"All of them were models. Well, kinda. Barbara was the most legit. The others went the massage parlor/outcall massage/take-a-picture-of-me-in-your-hotel-room route. They all also had photos shot by the same local photographer. Guy who ran a skin tabloid. He didn't take anything particularly hardcore. Not of those girls. Least nothing we could turn up."

"He still in town?"

"Yeah. So is his rag. I'll get you his number."

"What can you tell me about the killer's MO?"

"Like I said, he tortured the women before he killed them."

"What do you mean, exactly?"

"Cigarette burns on the nipples and genitals."

Cheney knew there were similar burns on Barbara's body. But she had not been killed and dropped in a dumpster. And as horrible as burns to the nipples and genitals were, it was not exactly a unique MO.

Especially not these days. Still . . .

"You said Barbara managed to escape."

"The guy attacked her in a downtown alley, grabbed her off the street late one night. Started to burn her but got scared away when someone turned down the alley and shined a pair of headlights on the scene."

"Barbara get a look at the guy?"

"He was wearing a mask. The only thing we know about the attacker is he was white."

"So what happened with the investigation?"

"Not much. Guy stopped after that. Least he stopped here in Vegas. And, quite frankly, you don't get the public clamor about solving a dead hooker case, even if it's a serial murder, that you do with . . ." Hanna searched for the right word.

"Real citizens?"

"You know the drill."

Cheney knew it. Didn't like it, but he knew it. Hooker gets killed, live with it; she's not one of us. Inner-city kid gets gunned down, maybe even twelve in a weekend, live with it; they're not like us. One white guy gets gunned down on a street corner in Beverly Hills, they call out the National Guard.

Cheney knew it.

From both sides.

"Barbara left town a month or so after she was attacked. Frankly, besides being scared shitless, I don't think she was too happy about a spotlight being shined on her private life."

"Did you ever come up with any suspects?"

"Just the usual. Nothing, really. You think this old case has something to do with the one you're working on in LA?"

"I don't know. That's what I'm trying to find out."

Cheney got Hanna to give him directions to Barbara Holgate's parents' house and drove his rental car to 499 North Charter Street. As Hanna had said, it was a working-class neighborhood, heavy on the working, not so heavy on the class. A black wrought-iron gate that needed painting separated the one-story brick house from the potholed street.

Cheney hadn't called ahead. He wanted to catch the Holgates a little off guard. No big deal if they weren't home. He'd just come back. Vegas wasn't that big a city. Even now.

A man who looked to be in his middle fifties opened the door. He said nothing, just stared at Cheney.

"Lawrence Holgate?"

"Whaddaya want?"

"My name's Cheney. I'm from Los Angeles. I'd like to ask you a few questions about your daughter."

Holgate looked like he wanted to say something, but he swallowed it. "My daughter's dead."

"I didn't think you knew." The words were out before Cheney realized what he had said.

Something changed in the man's face. Suddenly he didn't look so tough. "What did you say?"

"Your daughter was killed last month in Los Angeles."

Holgate opened his mouth. Not so much to say something; it was more an attempt to hide what the words had done to him. Quick, jerky twitches on his face betrayed the emotions vying for position.

"Come in," he said in a voice that cracked.

Inside, Lawrence Holgate sat shakily on a ragged green couch. Alone, he looked small, even though Cheney figured he stood at least six feet and weighed over two hundred pounds. He was not nearly as tough as he had been just minutes earlier.

"You say she was married to a friend of yours?"

"A neighbor."

"Was she respectable? I mean—"

"I know what you mean. Yes, she was respectable."

Holgate didn't say anything. He just ran his fingers through his hair and sighed deeply.

"Is Mrs. Holgate here?"

"No. She hasn't been here for about five years. She ran off with some guy she met at church bingo. Hell, I don't blame her." He shook his head and sighed again. "I used to—blame her, that is. I was drinking night and day. Knocked her around a little. Sometimes more than a little. I wasn't a good man back then. Hell, I'm probably not a good man now. Maybe now it just don't seem so bad 'cause there's nobody around for me to hurt." Holgate looked out the window and breathed quick and deep, trying to get his bearings. "You wanna beer?"

"I'm fine."

Holgate stood and walked out of the room. When he came back he was carrying a can of Diet Pepsi. And his eyes were red.

"You're trying to catch the guy who killed Barbie?" he said as he sank down into the couch again.

"That's right."

"So what are you doing back here?"

"At this point I don't know what's relevant and what's not. I'm just collecting all the information I can."

"Nothing round here's gonna make her look too good." Holgate shook his head again. "She was better than all that."

"At the door you told me your daughter was dead."

"I'm sorry." Holgate couldn't stop shaking his head. "To me, she was. We had a falling out a long time ago. And—" He couldn't get the words out.

"When she left town you considered her dead?"

"No, it was before that. It was when she got into— you know, what she was doing. I couldn't abide it. Just couldn't."

"What was she doing?"

Holgate looked at Cheney strangely. Cheney couldn't tell if it was surprise that the cop didn't already know or if it was fear that Cheney was going to make him say it aloud. "You don't know?"

"I know she was arrested for prostitution."

"Then you know." Holgate started shaking his head again. "Why? I'm not made of money, but I get by. She didn't have to do that. She didn't have to." Holgate reacted as though he had tasted something bitter and was trying to spit it out.

"Did your daughter have any boyfriends?"

"She had lots of boyfriends," said Holgate, some of the edge coming back into his voice.

"I mean anyone special."

"I dunno."

"I'd appreciate it if you thought about it for a minute. It might help."

"Who?"

"It might help Barbara's husband find out who killed her."

After a moment, Holgate said, "She used to have a boyfriend. Before she got into all that shit. Kid from down the street. Tommy Clegg was his name. Family moved away. Last I heard he was selling cars over on Central."

"How was he involved with your daughter?"

"They were high school sweethearts. They knew each other since they were kids. It was a healthy relationship. Probably the last one she ever had."

"I think the one she had with her husband for the last seven years was a healthy relationship." Cheney said it more to make Holgate feel better than from conviction.

Holgate took a swig of cola and nodded his head. "God, I hope so. I really do."

"What happened between Barbara and Clegg?"

"The real world happened to Barbie. She was a pretty girl, as I'm sure you know. People notice pretty girls. She just wasn't ready, you know?"

"Tell me." It wasn't that Cheney didn't understand, he just wanted to hear Holgate's version. The long version.

"Thing that started it all was she was chosen

Homecoming Queen. No big deal, right? Didn't used to be. Anyhow, the local businesses came around and wanted her to pose for pictures to put in newspaper ads. Then the photographers filled her head with all kinds of promises. Pretty soon her head got too big. Too big for people like her mother and me. According to her, we didn't know what we were talking about. It was like we lived in two separate worlds.

"Then came the drugs. First time, second time— hell, the fucking hundredth time—I yelled at her, I screamed at her, I warned her, I threatened her. But she wasn't scared of me. There was nothing I had she wanted anymore. Her new friends were willing to give her everything she thought she needed.

"One night—sorry, one *morning*—she came home at seven, just before I was supposed to go to work. I hadn't slept all night. Through the window I saw a guy in some expensive foreign job drop her off. She looked like she'd just gotten dressed before she walked in the door. I started reading her the usual riot act, but this time she just laughed at me. The madder I got, the harder she laughed. Meanwhile, her mother is in the bedroom crying.

"I opened her purse and inside were two vials of crack and a roll of cash like I'd never seen. Maybe you get used to that kinda thing in LA, but it hit me like a ton of bricks."

"Nobody gets used to that kind of thing," said Cheney.

"So I told her to get out. She stumbled into her room, packed a bag, and I never heard from her again."

"Never?"

"Oh, I know she talked to my wife now and then, but that's about it."

"Where does your wife live now?"

"I don't know. She don't keep in touch."

"Nice family," said Kimberly Gary.

Kelly's wasn't a fancy bar; most cop bars weren't. But it was close to the hotel and Tim Kelly, the owner's nephew, was generous with the scotch. Just like Hanna had said.

"Not the kind of family I grew up in," said Cheney.

"It's a different *world* from the one you grew up in. Most kids today don't grow up with two parents, let alone their biological parents. And the problems in school aren't smoking, talking, and chewing gum. They're drugs, rape, and murder."

"I remember times when music was something more than a drum machine beat and a bunch of guys and girls grabbing their crotches and leaping at the camera saying 'Comin' to get ya, muthafucka!'"

"Chill out, okay?"

"I'm tired of chilling out. I'm tired of being retired. I'm not eighty years old. I'm only fifty-three. I'm bored outa my fuckin' mind."

"You're working now. And I'm helping you," she said with a smile.

"Yeah, right." Cheney drank some of his Glenlivet. It tasted good and felt good going down. Better than he would have liked it to feel. "How are you helping me?"

"I found out Barbara Holgate was a victim of a

serial killer—obviously she wasn't murdered, but she was attacked by a guy the cops think was the serial killer."

Cheney said nothing.

"So you already know that. Big deal. I know it wasn't part of our deal that you were going to tell me anything, but you ought to at least give me an A for effort."

"A-plus."

"Thank you very much."

"What else did you find out?"

"You know about the reporter who did an article on 'The Only Woman to See the Killer and Live'?"

Cheney's face betrayed him.

"I didn't think so," said Kimberly.

"You got a name?"

"By tomorrow I'll have the reporter himself."

"Let me know."

"You bet your ass I'll let you know. I'm trying to impress you here, Cheney. In case you haven't noticed."

"You hide it well," said Cheney.

"Sounds kind of promising, don't you think? I mean, she was attacked by a serial killer in Vegas, then she ends up murdered in Los Angeles."

"After eight years? Quite a stretch. And serial killers don't usually run their victims down with a car. It's usually something more . . . personal."

"Tell me about serial killers, Cheney."

"I'm not an expert."

"You're not a novice, either."

"To be a serial killer you've got to kill four or more people. In this case Barbara would have been the fourth."

"Why four?"

"I don't know, really. Some experts say three or more. Anyhow, another criterion is you've got to put some time between the killings. You kill eight people in drunken rage one afternoon, that doesn't make you a serial killer. There's a cooling-off period. Then it starts up again."

"And?"

"There must be premeditation. And there's usually a sexual component. Often the killer was abused physically, sometimes sexually, as a child."

"Lots of people are abused as children—if you listen to the talk shows, figure about ninety-nine percent. Damned few of them turn out to be serial killers. What makes the difference?"

"I don't know. Profiles, generalities, can only take you so far. But it can be a piece of the puzzle."

"You don't think there's any connection between what happened to Barbara eight years ago and what happened to her in LA?" Kimberly looked disappointed.

"I don't know. I really don't. I admit it's a coincidence, but people being touched by violence in this country more than once in a lifetime is not the coincidence it used to be."

The jukebox came alive with Eric Clapton's acoustic version of "Layla."

"When did you leave Vegas?"

"In 'eighty-five."

"You're about the same age as Barbara. You ever meet her?"

"No, why?"

"You wouldn't lie to me, would you?"

"No, I wouldn't, Cheney. Not about anything important."

"Sane people only lie about important things."

"Sane people?"

"I didn't say good people."

"You ever lie, Cheney?"

"Sure. But not lately."

"Maybe nothing's been that important—lately," said Kimberly with a smile.

It was not a humorous smile, and Cheney felt himself getting a little uncomfortable. He took advantage of a yawn he felt coming on. Played it for all it was worth. "I'm tired."

"Really?" Kimberly checked her watch. "It's only ten o'clock."

"I think I'll call it a night."

"I wish you would come out with me."

"Where are you going?" said Cheney, in spite of himself.

"This is America's only true twenty-four-hour town. There's this little coffeehouse I used to hang out at."

"Thanks, but I think I'll turn in."

Kimberly stood, the slit in her dress breaking open as she did. "Let me give you the number in case you change your mind. It's open all night. I'll probably be there till three or so." She scribbled a number on a cocktail napkin and slid it across the table to Cheney. "Just in case you can't sleep."

"Thanks."

Kimberly leaned down and kissed Cheney lightly on the cheek. "I hope to see you later," she said with a smile.

Then she walked away.

Cheney tossed down the rest of his scotch and tried to remember when he had seen another woman as good looking as Kimberly Gary. One who had paid this much attention to him.

He was still trying to answer that question when he walked back to his hotel.

twelve

The digital clock next to Cheney's bed read 1:00 A.M. In blue. The bed was hard, the pillows soft. He couldn't sleep. He usually went to bed between twelve and one.

He tossed and turned. A little. Mainly he just lay in the shadows of the moon and the city lights. And the blue digital clock.

His mind was churning. He thought about Lawrence Holgate and how he probably wasn't sleeping either. He thought about Elizabeth and how she probably wasn't even home yet. She hadn't been home forty-five minutes ago when he'd called.

But mainly he was thinking about Kimberly Gary.

The directions Cheney got over the phone led him down an alley to a sliding-glass patio door next to a five-story industrial chimney. A young woman with long black hair looked up at him with big eyes, made bigger, Cheney suspected, by something a little more potent than peace, love, and understanding. "May I help you?"

Cheney thought that an odd greeting. This was a coffeehouse, not a department store. But then he suddenly realized he was over fifty years old and not a typical patron.

"I'm looking for Kimberly Gary."

"She's inside with Kelsey."

"Kelsey?"

"He runs the place. They're upstairs in the musicians' room."

Cheney plunked down the five-dollar cover and got the grand tour. The Trick of the Light coffeehouse consisted of five rooms. The main entertainment room was immediately to the left of the entrance. People wanting to go in that room had to remove their shoes and, according to the sign, not talk during a performance. A second room consisted of chairs, a long table with pastries, donated by local bakeries acknowledged by name on small placards, and coffee—three different kinds. Tonight it was regular, decaf, and nutmeg. The third room was a game room, which was like a small study with books and board games available to anyone who wanted to read or play games. The fourth room was the foyer, where he had met the girl with the big eyes. It was filled with about a dozen people, all of whom seemed to enjoy good conversation as long as the Republicans were made out to be neo-Nazis.

The fifth room, where Kimberly was, was on the

second floor. A teenager with a skin condition stood guard at the base of the stairs. Somehow Cheney talked his way past the acned sentinel.

"Cheney!" Kimberly stood when she saw Cheney and walked toward him.

The upstairs room was dark, lit only by a few candles and two strategically placed desk lamps. A long-haired mid-twenties guy remained seated on a couch in the middle of the room, his guitar resting on his knee.

"I hoped you'd come." She kissed him on the cheek again. This time a little closer to the mouth.

Cheney wondered if she really knew the difference. The way he knew the difference.

"Let me introduce you to Kelsey."

The young man stood and shook hands with Cheney. Then they all sat down: Kelsey on the couch and Cheney and Kimberly on a love seat opposite him.

"Interesting place," said Cheney, making conversation.

"Yeah, I like it. The big bands come through town, play the big arenas for the big bucks, then they come down here and play for free."

"That's great. Why do they do that?" said Cheney. Not because he was trying to be a wise guy; he really didn't know.

"For art. They play in front of twenty thousand people, they make money. But nobody really hears the music and nobody wants to hear the new songs. They come down here, and all we got is listeners. You'd be surprised how bad these people, even the superstars, wanna be heard."

"I see." Cheney nodded his head as though he had compassion for the deprived rock gods who had to endure such tribulation.

"This really brings back memories," said Kimberly. "I used to come down here all the time." She reached behind the couch, withdrew a bottle of wine with a ribbon stuck on its neck, and handed it to Cheney.

"What's this?" he asked, taking the bottle. He knew what it was, but he didn't know why she had given it to him.

"Just a token of my appreciation. You didn't have to let me come."

Cheney inspected the label: 1990 Burgess Chardonnay. "I'll bet this wasn't easy to find. In Vegas, I mean, on such short notice."

"It wasn't that hard. You gotta know where to look."

"Thanks." Cheney turned his attention to Kelsey. For a couple of reasons. "You ever meet a woman named Barbara Holgate?"

"No," he said, shaking his head. "Doesn't ring a bell."

"That'd be a few years back. Say 1984 or before."

"That was before my time. I just took over here in eighty-nine."

"But you knew Kimberly."

"She's been here since then."

"I came back for Christmas to visit some friends a couple of years ago."

There was a knock at the door, and everyone turned toward the sound.

"Come in," said Kelsey.

Cheney immediately started thinking about why the guy had to knock, and what might go on in the musicians' room that made knocking essential. Cheney hadn't knocked.

A young man opened the door and stuck his head inside.

"There's a hundred people downstairs in the main room."

"Thanks, Danny."

Danny nodded and left, closing the door behind him.

"I tell whoever's downstairs to let me know when the room is at its peak; then I go down and play."

"What goes on before that?" asked Cheney.

"We have an open-mike policy. If someone happens to be billed to play, they can go on just before or just after I do."

"Sounds like a good deal."

"Look, it's not as manipulative as it sounds. I don't earn a bundle from this gig. I'm trying to make it, you know? People actually come in here and request my songs. *My* songs. I used to play at the Holiday Inn down the road. I made more money, but I had to sing Michael Bolton songs all night long. Give and take, you know?"

"Yeah, I know."

Kelsey stood, guitar in hand, and started toward the door.

Cheney started to get up but felt Kimberly's hand on his knee, holding him down.

"See you downstairs," said Kelsey as he exited and closed the door behind him.

"You don't want to hear Kelsey?"

"Sure. Later."

Kimberly took a corkscrew out of her purse, opened the wine, poured some into two plastic cups, and handed one to Cheney.

"To you," she said.

Cheney didn't argue. They touched plastic glasses and drank. "Thanks."

"You're welcome."

As the wine began to heighten certain senses and dull others, he became aware of how dimly the room was lit. In fact, they were virtually in shadow.

And she was looking at him. Unflinchingly. At two in the morning. In a strange city. Drinking wine she had purchased. And they were alone. Because she wanted it that way.

"How do you feel?" asked Kimberly.

"What do you mean?"

"What do you *think* I mean?"

"I'm not sure."

"Cheney, one thing you're not is stupid. You're a street-smart tough guy who cuts through the shit. So don't pretend to be dumb, okay?"

"I'm not pretending to be dumb. Maybe I'm just being discreet."

"You mean tactful?"

"I don't know exactly what I mean."

"Maybe this will help."

Kimberly leaned forward and kissed Cheney on the mouth. He felt a kind of spark when her lips touched his. Fully touched his lips. The sensation was warm. Electric.

Erotic.

The surprising thing, to Cheney, was that he had done nothing to stop her.

"What's that all about?" he asked.

"What do you *want* it to be about?"

"What a person wants and what a person gets are often two different things."

"Often, but not always."

Cheney smiled and tried to cool things down. "Are you really trying to come on to me?"

"I'm not trying."

Cheney couldn't argue with that. She had graduated, with honors, beyond trying.

"Why me? I mean, you're already involved in the case."

Kimberly moved a little closer to Cheney. "Aren't you ever just sexually attracted to someone?"

"Sure, but—"

"But what? I don't have AIDS. I don't imagine you do either. I might be wrong, but knowing what I know about you, I'm willing to roll the dice."

"So now we're talking about sex," said Cheney, mainly because he couldn't think of anything else to say.

"*You're* talking about it. I'm—"

"I've never done this before."

"Really? I have some books back in my room," said Kimberly with a smile. A confident smile.

"No, I mean I've never cheated on Elizabeth."

"Cheated? I don't like that word. Too negative. I want to make love with you. And you—well, maybe I'm reading you wrong, but I get the distinct impression that to choose between the Chinese water torture and having sex with me you wouldn't have to hire a counselor."

Cheney coughed before he spoke. "Look, I'm not

exactly a pilgrim here, but I just don't feel right about this."

"How do you feel?"

"About what?"

"About me?"

"Well, I certainly think you're attractive—"

"Are you attracted to me?"

"Yes, but—"

"But what?"

"I'm married."

"I'm not asking you to leave your wife. I'm just talking about sex. I'm not going to hound you for the rest of your life."

When she used the word *sex,* Cheney's head filled with images of the two of them in bed together. He felt a tingling in his groin. Started to feel flushed.

"Why me?" asked Cheney again.

"Why is anyone attracted to anyone else? Chemistry, who the hell knows."

Kimberly set down her plastic cup and moved closer to Cheney. She kissed him full on the mouth. Again.

Cheney could not deny the feelings that were building inside him. Nor could he deny the guilt.

"I can't do this," he said. He stood, his body pulling him one way, his conscience another.

"You can, Cheney. And you probably will," said Kimberly. She remained seated, looking up at him. Her legs were crossed provocatively. The look in her eyes was pure confidence. Uncut and shot up raw.

"I'll see you tomorrow morning," said Cheney, and he left.

He drove around for a while before he went back

to the hotel. He rolled the windows down, let the air in. Tried to think thoughts that made him feel as though he had done the right thing.

After a while he managed to convince himself that he had.

He drove into the parking lot, parked his car, and took the elevator up to his room.

He turned on the TV. An old black-and-white movie from the forties was on *The Late Show*. Cheney started to watch it, but his heart wasn't in it.

He hit the remote control and the room went dark.

And he lay awake.

For two hours.

Thinking about Kimberly Gary and what it would feel like to be between her legs.

"What was her name?"

"Raven," said Gino.

"Are you okay?"

Gino held the phone close to his mouth. "Not yet," he whispered.

Silence.

"What should I do?"

"Look, Gino, you know I'll do everything I can. I always have, but . . ."

"But what?"

"Do you think this is the last one?"

Gino thought about the question for a moment. "I don't know."

"You're getting to a place where I can't help you anymore."

"Maybe I'm already there," he said softly. After a

moment he whispered, "Do you still love me?" It was more a plea than a question.

"Of course. Look, I can't get to you right away. Go out and get some bags of ice. Put the body in the bathtub and keep it packed in ice. I'll take her out into the desert and bury her. They'll never find her out there."

"Thank you, baby. I love you."

"But Gino."

"Yes?"

"From now on, you will have to dispose of the bodies."

"How do you know there will be more bodies?"

"I know you, Gino. I'm the only one who does, remember?"

Gino swallowed hard and took a deep breath. She knew. "Yes," he said finally.

"Will you be all right?"

Gino thought about saying that he was now almost certain he would never be all right again, but he just said, "Yes."

"I love you."

"I love you too," said Gino.

He hung up the phone and walked across the room. Got down on his knees. Reached out and stroked Raven's hair as her dead eyes stared into another world.

And said, "I love you."

To an empty room.

thirteen

The phone rang and Cheney answered it groggily. "Hello?"

"I got the name of the porn photographer guy you want to talk to," said Detective John Hanna. "Don't be fooled. He can come across as a normal human being."

"I take it you're not a subscriber," said Cheney as he wiped some sleep from his eyes.

"I'm no prude. I like a good piece of ass as much as the next guy and I'm not going to puke in a sack at the sight of a naked woman, but a person has to draw the line. This guy crosses it. Seven days a week."

"So, you have his name."

"Name's Larry Taylor. Phone number 555-8795. He's in the Bradford Building at the corner of Kansas and Ninth."

Cheney scribbled the information on the pad next to the phone.

"He's a creep, Cheney."

"So why don't you lock him up?"

"You mean like the way you lock up all the creeps in LA?"

It was a rhetorical question, so Cheney didn't respond. "Ever hear of a guy named Clegg? Tommy Clegg?"

"No, why?"

"He used to be Barbara Holgate's boyfriend before she—" Cheney tried to find the right word, but it eluded him. "Barbara and Clegg were childhood sweethearts. Last her father heard of the guy, he was selling cars here in town."

"Of course you already checked the phone book."

Cheney started to say something.

Before he did, Hanna said, "Just kidding. I'll look into it."

Larry Taylor worked in a two-story building about as far off the Strip as a business could be and still get a Las Vegas zip code. A pawnshop took up the entire first floor. Guns and guitars dominated the window space. Strange combination, thought Cheney as he passed the window and headed for the entrance to the upper floor. Unfortunately, not as strange as it used to be.

The directory listed Larry Taylor and his *Flesh Pot* tabloid next to the number 214. The second floor was lined with frosted glass doors upon which had been stenciled the names of the businesses that clicked and clattered away in the shadows behind them. There were three bail bondsmen, two lawyers, and Flesh Pot Publications.

"May I help you?" said the blonde. The black blonde. The black blonde *man*. With the red lips and the baritone voice.

"I'd like to speak with Mr. Taylor."

"Who shall I say is calling?"

"Mr. Cheney. I'm from Los Angeles."

"Ooohhh," said the receptionist with a smile and wink. He stood and metronomed a rather rotund butt, which was packed into a short black skirt, toward an inner office door, opened it, and walked inside.

After a moment, he returned and, with a wink and a nod, said, "I told him you were cute."

"Thanks."

"You can go right in," he said and sat down behind the desk.

Cheney walked into Taylor's office and closed the door.

Larry Taylor sat behind a large desk piled high with paper and photographs. In back of him was a wall of windows that looked out onto a vacant lot where a group of black youths were spraying graffiti on a wall.

"Who are you?" Taylor looked to Cheney to be in his early fifties. He might have been younger, but he carried about fifty extra pounds and his face was puffy from cheap whiskey, a bottle of which sat on the windowsill.

"Derek Cheney."

"So?"

"I'm from Los Angeles and I—"

"Hold on, hold on," said Taylor, holding up his hand, shaking his head. "You a cop?"

"I used to be chief of detectives for the LAPD."

"Yeah, and Jimmy Carter used to be the fuckin' president. I don't have to talk to you."

"If you prefer, I can come back later with Detective Hanna."

Taylor recognized the name. "Let's see some ID."

Cheney flashed his credentials, then put them back in his pocket.

"So what does the LAPD want with little old me? We don't sell outside the state of Nevada."

"I just want to ask you a few questions."

"About what?"

"You remember a woman named Barbara Holgate?"

"Sure, she was a babe. Why?"

"She died recently in Los Angeles."

"Died? You mean she was murdered?"

"What makes you say that?"

"If she died of a heart attack I don't think you'd be here tryin' to bust my balls."

"Answer a few questions and I'm outa here."

"I got nothin' to hide."

It was amazing, thought Cheney, not for the first time, how often people said exactly that. "You said you remember her."

"Sure. I took some pictures of her. I take pictures of a coupla hundred girls a year. You're talkin' seven, eight years ago. That's a lotta pussy."

"But you remember Barbara out of more than a thousand women."

"So?"

"What made her so special?"

"I didn't say special, okay? I said I remembered her. The reason I remember her is probably the same reason you're here now. She was attacked a few months after the pictures were taken."

"The other victims who were attacked also had their pictures taken—by you."

"Yeah, well, don't break your leg jumpin' to conclusions. In case Hanna didn't tell you already, I had iron-clad alibis for the nights of the attacks. And let me tell you something else. A lotta girls posed for me at one time or another. You're a pretty girl in Vegas, chances are you're gonna wind up posing for me. And it don't have to be showin' pink or havin' sex with a dog, either. Most of the pictures I take are for the cover, just basically your tasteful topless shit. This ain't Hollywood. I can't get away with the crap they get away with out there. In Vegas, it's tease more than anything else. Otherwise they'd run me outa town on a fuckin' rail, okay?"

Cheney refrained from saying that it was, in fact, okay with him. "How well did you know Barbara?"

"Not too well. She posed for me a coupla times. The cover I did with her was the most popular cover I did that year. I keep track of those things. I mean, I didn't plan to be a pornographer when I was a kid. It's just that nothing else I did paid nearly as well. Point is, I'm a businessman. I track how well every cover does. I note the color, the model, the pose, the type style, the subject matter of the headline and subheads. Blondes are almost always better sellers than brunettes."

"Almost?"

"Barbara was a brunette. Like I said, best cover of the year."

"Did you see her socially?"

"I never dated her, if that's what you mean. But she came up here every once in a while and I kept in touch with her—especially after I found out how well the cover did."

"What about the other women who were attacked?"

"I only remember them because the police asked me about them."

"Were the others cover girls?"

"Yes."

"But their covers didn't do so well."

"That's right," said Taylor, missing Cheney's sarcastic tone.

"Do you have any of those covers handy?"

Taylor sighed, stood, and walked over to a wall of file cabinets. He started muttering to himself. "'Eighty-five, 'eighty-five, 'eighty-five. . . . Here we are."

He pulled open a long drawer and started flipping through what looked to Cheney to be copies of his tabloid.

In less than two minutes Taylor tossed four copies of *Flesh Pot* on the desk, then sat back down in his chair.

Cheney picked them up and looked at the covers. Each was dominated by the figure of a woman in a small bikini bottom. In one, the woman had her hands on her hips and looked boldly into the camera, breasts exposed. In another, the woman was holding a champagne bottle in one hand, an empty champagne glass in the other, and was looking directly into the camera. In the third, the woman was holding the nozzle of a fire hose, looking boldly into the camera. In the last one, Barbara Holgate was holding a beach ball over her head and looking directly into the camera. Each woman wore high heels. Each was a brunette. Each was looking into the camera, as though daring the reader to challenge her.

"The covers look so similar."

"I know my business," said Taylor.

"No, I mean, why did Barbara's cover sell so much better than the others?"

"What made Marilyn Monroe immortal? She wasn't the best actress, she didn't have the best body, and she wasn't the smartest person ever to come down the pike."

"Marilyn's dead."

"Nothing like dying when you're on top to make you live forever."

"In someone's imagination."

"Better than being forgotten altogether."

Cheney almost said, Better for whom? but instead said, "Did the girls get fan mail?"

"Fan mail?" said Taylor, as though Cheney had just asked him if there was a real Santa Claus. "They got jerk-off letters, shit like that."

"So you kept no record of the correspondence?"

"The correspondence became instant wastepaper. Fact is, the secretary I had at the time, the one who handled the, uh, 'fan mail,' used to wear rubber gloves when she opened the envelopes, if you get my drift."

"Was there any way someone could have contacted these women through you?"

"Anything's possible, Mr. Cheney. It's possible the

sun might not come up tomorrow morning. But it sure as hell ain't likely. To answer your question, short of bugging the place or being a fly on the wall, I have no idea how anyone could have used this office or me to get to those girls."

"What about someone who worked for you? Freelance writers, layout artists, people like that."

"They don't work out of this office. I farm all that stuff out to independent contractors and stringers. It's just me and the receptionist. I'm a lean, mean capitalist machine."

"What about the pictures you didn't use on the cover?"

"What do you mean?"

"I mean, you took a few rolls of film, right?"

"So?"

"What happened to the pictures?"

"Who knows?"

"You don't?"

"They're lying around somewhere, someplace. Maybe. What difference does it make?"

"Who develops the pictures you take?"

"A local processing house."

"So they see everything you shoot."

"So?"

"I'm just asking."

"Yes, they see everything I shoot. You think the killer was some crazed person working at the photo developing house?"

"I don't know what to think. My job is to ask questions."

"Well, my job isn't to answer them. I've got a deadline and a business to run."

Cheney picked up the cover of Barbara Holgate holding a beach ball in a tiny string bikini, her breasts sticking straight out, nipples hard. Suddenly he felt strange, like a Peeping Tom, ogling his friend's wife. In a way, he was.

Cheney set the cover down and repeated an earlier question. "Why do you think this particular cover was so popular?"

"I don't know."

"What's your professional opinion?"

Taylor picked up the cover and took a long look at the photograph, assuming the expert's pose. "She's gorgeous. What can I tell you?"

"Anything else?"

After a moment, he said, "She looks hard. Tough. Some guys like that."

And some guys don't, thought Cheney.

The used-car lot at Sahara and Lucky Drive was deserted at two in the afternoon, a ghost town littered with castoff tin and rubber. The cars showed their age despite considerable effort by the dealer to hide that fact. Pennants snapped in the breeze as Cheney walked onto the lot and into a trailer that served as an office.

Because of a preliminary background check, Cheney knew Tommy Clegg was only thirty-two years old. But he looked small behind his desk, and when he glanced up at the detective, he did so through ancient and watery eyes.

"Tommy Clegg?"

"Yes?"

"I'd like to talk to you about Barbara Holgate."

Cheney noticed Clegg's facial muscles start to twitch. "Is she dead?"

"Why would you say that?"

"You're a cop, right?"

"Yes," said Cheney, not bothering to offer the complete and unabridged definition of who he was and why he was there.

"Have a seat."

Cheney sat down opposite Clegg, with a pile of *Sports Illustrated* magazines, a digital clock, and a tablet of contract forms between them on the desk.

"Why would you assume Barbara was dead?"

"The last time I saw her, she'd narrowly escaped being murdered, and now, almost ten years later, you show up here, out of the blue. You're not from here, are you?"

"I'm from Los Angeles."

"I always had a bad feeling about Barbara. I knew her looks would ultimately betray her."

"What do you mean?"

"Well, I imagine you're here because you know that Barbara and I were once engaged."

"I heard you were childhood sweethearts."

"We didn't feel like children when we were seventeen years old, I assure you. Anyhow, Barbara was starting to bloom, as they say, and she liked the attention. She found it all quite flattering, which I suppose is natural. But she didn't know how to handle it. No one does, at least at first. At that age. Add to that the fact that she started doing drugs and running with the wrong people. She was drowning, drifting away from the people who cared about her. Like her parents."

"And you." It wasn't a question.

"I got married a couple of years ago," said Clegg, turning his head and looking out the window. "It took me awhile to get used to the idea Barbara wasn't coming back. You ever love somebody, Mr.—?"

"People call me Cheney."

"You ever love somebody, Cheney?"

"Yes."

"I've been in love only once in my life. I know, you're thinking I just said I was married. My wife loves *me*. Don't get me wrong, I think she's fantastic, and we've got a whole helluva lot in common, including a beautiful daughter. My wife would do anything for me, and I'd do just about anything for her too." Clegg's smile was humorless. "Love is a very strange thing."

"Why's that?" asked Cheney, simply because it was his line.

"It's a rare thing when two people love each other the same amount at the same time. One person usually holds the upper hand. And human nature being what it is, you give somebody a club, they're gonna use it. You know what I'm saying?"

"Did Barbara Holgate use that club on you?" asked Cheney, trying to steer clear of philosophical discussions and put the focus back on Barbara.

"She beat the shit out of me with it, quite frankly. Now I know you think that sounds very bitter. Well, it is, I guess. But that's what happened. I would have done anything for her. Any fucking thing in this whole fucking world."

Cheney recognized what was happening to Clegg. All the grief, all the anger, the pain, was coming back to him now and exploding through the cracks in his otherwise even-tempered exterior like a long dormant but volatile molten volcano. Cheney had to get as much information as he could before Clegg blew sky high.

"You say she started doing drugs and running with the wrong people. Could you be more specific?"

"Crack, smoke, whatever. I don't think she was shooting up, if that's what you mean. But even getting stoned makes you do things you might not do otherwise, especially where appetite is concerned."

"Appetite?"

"You know exactly what I mean."

"Who was she running with?"

"She was modeling. So she was hanging out with photographers, actors, musicians. You know the crowd."

"Where does that crowd hang out?"

"Trick of the Light, for one. It's a local coffeehouse." Clegg shook his head and gave a bitter laugh. "You wanna hear a crazy story?"

"Sure," said Cheney. Rule number one: keep the guy talking.

"I remember one night, toward the end of our relationship, I go out with Barbara to a local dance club. Everybody knows her there. For the first hour or so we have a great time. Then we get into an argument. For the life of me I can't remember what the hell we argued about. Anyhow, I say some nasty things and take off.

"So I go over to a friend's house to cool off. I realize that maybe I said some things I shouldn't, although I was not completely in the wrong. Who is, right? Anyhow, I go back to the club and she's gone. I ask a few people where she went and I find out she left with some guy—I remember him because he was giving her the eye from the bar.

"So the bar closes and I'm frantic. I call her father and she's not home. Naturally, he's pissed, me calling at two-thirty in the morning. But I'm crazed, you know? Until this time I'm completely certain Barbara's never had sex with anyone but me. That kind of thing makes a difference. Especially when you're young. First times. . . . " Clegg shook his head and looked out the window again.

He turned his attention back to Cheney. "I call all her friends, but I still can't find her. Finally, and I know this sounds stupid, I end up going to all the hotels within a mile of the dance club. I describe Barbara and tell each of the desk clerks that I'm her brother and that our father has just had a heart attack.

"No one believes me, of course. I get home just as the sun's coming up. For another three hours I sit by the phone, shaking. Finally, she calls. I ask her where she's been and she says she's been in a hotel. I ask her if she spent the night with the guy she met in the bar, and she says yes. I ask her if she had sex with the guy. I'll never forget her answer. Never as long as I fuckin' live. You know what she said? She says, 'Of course. What do you think?' So I hang up and go into the bathroom and throw up. Dry heaves. For almost an hour."

"Was that the end for you two?"

Clegg gave another bitter laugh and looked Cheney in the eye. "Two days later I begged her to marry me. Love's a crazy thing, Cheney. It's not something you can add up in a column and have it come out the same every time."

"But she slept with another man." Cheney found himself caught up in Clegg's story.

"Men idolize women who flaunt their sexuality, Cheney. Last I heard, Madonna was the highest paid female entertainer in the world. You tell *me* what she does better than anybody else."

"But it's different if it's your girlfriend or your wife."

"I could argue with you all day long. All I can say is how I handled the situation in real life."

"But you two didn't get married."

"No. Actually it got pretty pathetic after that. I lost all control in the relationship. She knew she could humiliate me, do anything and get away with it, and I would still take her back. I wish I could say I came to my senses. Quite frankly, it was just a matter of her growing increasingly bored with me."

"She took another lover?"

"Several."

"Anyone in particular?"

"As a matter of fact, yes."

"Who?"

"I really don't know. All I know is he was an older man."

"A sugar daddy?"

"No. At least not from what I could figure out. She was very secretive about the relationship, which led me to believe the guy was married. But I didn't notice that her lifestyle, in terms of clothes, jewelry, residence, whatever, really changed. I don't think she was getting money from him."

"And you two drifted apart."

"We stayed apart for a couple of years. Then suddenly she came knocking at my door one night at three in the morning. That was the night of the first attack."

"First?"

"She was attacked twice. The second time she was attacked, she called me from the airport and told me she was leaving town. That was the last time I ever heard from her."

"That first night, what did she say about her attacker?"

"Nothing she didn't tell the police. I drove her to the police station a few hours later."

"Did she give you any indication as to who the attacker might be?"

"No. He wore a mask."

"Did she consider herself a random target?"

"I think so. After all, she was attacked early in the morning. A woman walking the city streets at that time of night, well . . ."

"Well, what?"

"Nothing."

"She deserves it?"

"Maybe she doesn't deserve it. But at the very least she's being careless, you know what I mean?"

"Tell me."

"Well, a woman walks by a bunch of construction workers in a miniskirt up to her ass, the guys go crazy and she cries sexual harassment. Okay, I understand it. Maybe nobody should be human. But most people are. Any woman knows the effect she's going to have when she dresses like that and walks by a bunch of guys. For her to say they shouldn't act that way is one thing. But unless she's mentally deficient, she shouldn't be surprised.

"So if Barbara's walking around in the middle of the night, by herself, dressed the way she usually dressed, she's got to have known there was a risk involved. That's all I'm saying."

"That it was her fault."

"It wasn't her *fault*. No one has the right to do to another human being what that guy tried to do to Barbara. All I'm saying is people should be more realistic, more careful."

"You say you never talked with Barbara after she left town in 'eighty-four?"

"That's right."

"That sounds strange, you being so forgiving and crazy about her."

"I didn't say I haven't tried to contact her. I didn't know where she went."

"Did you contact her family?"

"You mean her father? Sure, I called him. But he never heard from her either."

Cheney stood, thanked Clegg for his help, and started for the door.

"Cheney?"

He turned around. "Yeah?"

"This guy Barbara married."

"What about him?"

"Was he . . . ?" Clegg's voice trailed off.

Cheney realized there wasn't a thesaurus in the world with the words Clegg was looking for. But Cheney knew them just the same. "He was good to her. He really loved her."

He didn't bother to mention that he was beginning to think maybe Barbara didn't love her husband all that much.

But then, he figured Tommy Clegg already knew that part of the story.

There was a message waiting for Cheney when he got back to the hotel. He was to meet Kimberly at an address she had left for him, if he got in before four. It was three-thirty. Cheney asked the guy behind the desk for directions and hopped back into the Caprice.

"Glad you could make it," said Kimberly. She met him at the top the stairs and ushered him into a huge living room bathed in natural light by windows that opened on three sides to a large front yard.

Cheney sat down on a burgundy chesterfield next to Kimberly.

"Geoffrey Marks is upstairs working. He operates a video business out of his attic. It's really something. Runs the length of this place. It's more like a big studio."

"Why am I here?" asked Cheney.

"Shortly after Barbara Holgate was first attacked, Geoffrey interviewed her. For reasons you and I both know, the papers weren't real interested in the story. I mean, it wasn't like the guy broke into her house while she was nursing her baby. She was just another hooker walking the streets at two-thirty in the morning."

"And Geoffrey?"

"He's a reporter for some local fringe tabloid. At least he was then."

"What tabloid?"

"A now-defunct rag called the *East Side Gazette*. He tracked her down."

A sound came from another room, and a few seconds later a man walked into the living room. He came over to Cheney, extended his hand, and said, "You must be the LA cop."

"Cheney." They shook hands.

Geoffrey Marks sat down in a chair opposite Cheney and Kimberly. He looked to be in his early forties, lean, fit, and tall. He had a clean feel about him that told Cheney, the trained observer, that he was drug and alcohol free.

"Kimberly told me about poor Barbara. Terrible thing. I thought she was going to outrun it all."

"Outrun what?"

"Someone tried to kill her a few years ago, but I'm sure you already know that. That's how I met her. And just after the article I did on her was published, she was attacked again."

"Tell me about that."

"Shortly after Barbara was attacked I contacted her. I have, or at least I had when I was working for the *Gazette*, a number of contacts in the police department. She grew up on the east side, so it seemed like a good story for the paper."

"How did she react?"

"She didn't want to talk about it at first, but I met with her a few times and finally convinced her it was better to go public about what happened to her."

"Do you have a copy of that article?"

"Yes. I gave a copy to Kimberly."

"It's a very good piece," said Kimberly, flattering

Geoffrey purposely, yet effectively. "Since she couldn't identify her attacker, the article focused on warning women in town that there was a madman on the loose and to be careful."

"That's right," said Geoffrey.

"Do you think your article led to her getting attacked a second time?" asked Cheney.

"I'm not sure. How can anyone be sure about something like that? Besides, a person can assume just so much responsibility. I mean, it isn't like I attacked her myself. I really thought I was helping."

"Of course," said Cheney, trying not to make it sound patronizing. "You must have gotten to know her."

"I'd say there weren't many people who got to know Barbara Holgate very well. Certainly I didn't. But I did get a story that was well received, one that I actually thought would do some good."

"When was the last time you heard from her?"

"The night of the second attack. She told me she was going to leave town right away."

"Without going to the police?"

"She thought it was useless."

"Did she say why?"

"Did she have to? I mean, she went to the police the first time and nothing happened."

fourteen

"The surf and turf is good," said Kimberly.

"Maybe I'll have that."

"And I'll have another glass of wine, kind sir," she said, holding her glass for Cheney to refill.

Theodore's was the kind of place locals, locals with money, gravitated to in Vegas. It was off the Strip and all but off the map to tourists. Hanna had recommended the place "as long as you got an expense account." Cheney didn't have an expense account, but he had the next best thing: cash. They took it here.

Cheney and Kimberly sat at a corner table. The place was all wood and track lights. Very intimate. Waiters, no waitresses. Menu prices that made you feel comfortable about lingering awhile after your meal.

"That's it," Cheney said, after he'd filled Kimberly's glass, turning the bottle over and putting it, neck down, into the ice bucket.

"To us," she said, lifting her glass toward him.

He didn't respond immediately. He looked into her eyes. She didn't look away. "To us?"

"We're good together, don't you think?" she asked with a smile that was playful and humorous.

"I suppose."

They clinked glasses and drank.

"You know, it's funny you and Barbara never ran into each other. I mean, you were in Vegas at the same time and you both frequented the same coffee-house."

"Maybe we did, but I don't remember. Look around you, Cheney. There are a lot of people in this restaurant. Someone years from now could say you were in the same restaurant at the same time as, say, that couple over there." She nodded in the direction of a man and woman sitting at a table near them. "It's true, but you won't remember what those people looked like. You won't remember anything about them."

Kimberly scooted over in the booth so her hips touched his. The initial sensation seemed electric to Cheney. He was surprised at his reaction. He had been approached by other women over the years, but truthfully, since he had retired, such options presented themselves less and less. Even so, for some reason he was tempted by Kimberly as he had not been tempted in the past.

"You okay?" said Kimberly. She placed her hand gently on Cheney's hand.

"Yeah, I'm fine." What he really wanted to say was, Yeah, but I'm fucked.

"Look, Cheney, I'm attracted to you, okay?"

"Okay," said Cheney, even though he knew it sounded stupid. He was a little out of practice.

"I can tell when a guy's attracted to me too. There's no shame in it, Cheney. Sex is a healthy thing."

"For single people." Cheney caught himself. "And, of course, for married people, between themselves."

"You're really uncomfortable, aren't you?" she said with a self-satisfied smile.

"A little, I guess."

"It's interesting. I mean, I see you act so confidently all the time, and now—well, you don't seem so confident."

"I'm not. I haven't done this in a long time. I've been completely faithful to Elizabeth."

"Don't worry, they haven't changed any important rules."

She was right about that, thought Cheney later.

What had changed, of course, was not the game but the uniforms. In one key moment, Cheney had switched teams. He was no longer a team player but a free agent.

"Completely faithful" was an arbitrary term that was usually invoked by someone seeking to soothe an uneasy conscience.

Cheney knew he was wrong.

But he knew he was going to do it anyway.

The bathroom door opened and Kimberly walked out into the bedroom. The room was lit only by the streetlight spill, but his eyes had already adjusted.

She lay down on the bed, on her side, cocking her

leg as though she were posing for a magazine. One of *those* magazines. She was nude. "So, what do you think?"

"Very nice," said Cheney, as though commenting on a piece of art. He could tell she enjoyed his admiration and was not unaware of the attraction her body held for him. He leaned close to her. To her body. Her nude body. Felt that body against his nude body. He reached out and touched her knee. Slowly slid his hand up her thigh until it stopped in the moistness between her legs.

Kimberly made a sound. Her eyes closed and her head rocked back.

Cheney positioned himself on top of Kimberly, between her legs, and put himself inside her.

"Ahhhhh. . . ." Again Kimberly's head rolled back.

Cheney could not get enough of this new body. Even while he moved in and out of her tight femininity, his hands scoured her body for sensation. The taughtness in her upper thighs. The smoothness of her buttocks, which he grabbed hold of with each hand, lifting her up as he drove himself deeper and deeper into her. The sweet smell of her neck. The taste of her lips. Above and below. The power he felt when he flicked her clitoris with his tongue and she jerked once, twice, on cue, as though her nerves were electrified by some erotic prod.

Cheney had her with her legs up over his shoulders. He had her from behind. He had her from the side. He had her in his mouth, and he looked down on her as she got on her knees and had him in hers.

She said things to him that no one had ever said to him before. He wasn't sure if what she was saying was true. But, in that moment, he could not have cared less. It was as though these sensations were being experienced for the first time.

When it was over, she licked him clean. Licked him in places he had never been licked before. Made him feel sensations he had not felt in a long time. Made him wonder if he had ever felt them before.

Even as he experienced it, he knew this was an aberration, a blip on the radar screen. And it was probably never going to happen again.

Cheney looked down at the manicured patch of hair between Kimberly's legs. Looked at her heaving chest. Touched her body, which was still twitching with involuntary contractions. And reminded himself that this was a night that would have to end. The thought inspired him.

He smiled confidently, amazed at his resiliency. Felt himself beginning to swell again.

Cheney could not get enough of this new body.

fifteen

When he awoke the digital clock read 6:30. Cheney usually got up or at least woke at about this time, regardless of when he went to bed.

Through the part in the curtains, the morning sun pierced the darkness like a righteous sword, cutting across the bed.

Cheney blinked the sleep from his eyes and oriented himself. At first, he didn't know where he was.

Then it all came back to him. He turned his head and saw Kimberly lying on her stomach, nude and minimally covered by the white bedsheet.

Cheney took a deep breath, stared at the ceiling, and sighed.

Guilt. Must've been drunk outa my fuckin' mind. No, if I was that drunk I probably wouldn't have been able to perform.

What time was it in LA? Same time. Elizabeth

would be just getting up. Completely unaware of what he'd done. Completely innocent.

He felt so guilty!

Cheney looked over at Kimberly. At her body. He felt himself becoming aroused. He touched her thigh. Heard her moan.

She started to wake up. She turned her head toward Cheney and through heavy-lidded eyes looked up at him and smiled. "Hi."

I feel so guilty, said Cheney.

To himself.

"I know you feel guilty," said Kimberly.

"No, it's not that," said Cheney. Trying his best to convince himself.

They were sitting next to each other on the plane back to Los Angeles.

"Then what is it?"

"What do you mean?"

"I mean, a few hours ago you had your cock between my legs and you were making sounds as though you had a direct line to God."

After a moment Cheney said, "I'm sorry."

"You have nothing to be sorry about. At least not with me."

"You mean I have something to be sorry about with my wife?"

"No, I don't mean anything of the kind. As far as I'm concerned, Cheney, we're even. I'm happy. I had a great time last night. I'm satisfied, and I feel very comfortable sitting next to you on the plane. But for some reason you don't feel the same way."

Cheney thought about arguing, but he didn't. Kimberly was right. He was happy, but he felt bad. And the reason he felt bad was the same reason he was happy. What business did a happily married man have being happy about having sex with a woman who was not his wife? The answer was obvious. Simple.

And damning.

"It's not your fault," said Cheney.

"Fault? What are you talking about?"

Cheney was obviously out of his depth. Uncharted waters.

"I'm not used to this, okay?" said Cheney.

"Don't feel bad. Most guys are much more of a challenge."

"You do this a lot, do you?" said Cheney, not managing to hide his sarcasm.

"I don't go to bed with most guys, if that's what you mean," she said evenly. "I'm just saying that you're different, that's all. We had a great time; we gave each other a lot of pleasure and no diseases. That's more than a fair exchange these days. Let's just leave it at that."

"So you don't plan on . . . continuing?"

"You're a married man. If we went on seeing each other in Los Angeles, you'd have to start lying. I can't see you doing that."

"I'm already lying."

"Not really. You're just not telling the whole truth. When you see a friend whose tie you don't like, you don't feel compelled to go over and tell him you don't like it, do you? Some things are just better left unsaid."

There were a number of holes in Kimberly's analogy, but Cheney knew what she was trying to say. It was a type of logic many men and not a few women used so they could look at themselves in the mirror in the morning.

They both ordered drinks. It was only ten in the morning, but Cheney was trying to put alcohol on his wound. Trying to find something to stop the bleeding.

As he sat in his window seat staring down on the clouds, he felt lower than he had felt in years. Had it been the alcohol last night? Was that it? he asked himself as he sipped scotch, aware of the irony of that thought and his immediate action.

No, he decided. He had been fixated on Kimberly Gary for some time. Fixated, yes, but motivated enough to actually cross the line?

Cheney had done the right thing most of his life and almost all of his married life—from his wife's point of view. But he had not done the right thing last night. There was no getting around that fact. He had broken a vow. There were no particularly good reasons why he had done so. It was not as though he had a reason he could present to his wife as proof that his actions were warranted.

No, it was clear to Cheney that he had transgressed.

The question now was how he would handle that transgression.

As he finished his first Chivas Regal and poured himself another, he turned to look out the window into the clouds.

And realized he didn't have a clue.

*   *   *

"So, you think Barbara Sanford was murdered?"

"I still don't know," said Cheney, huffing and puffing. He wasn't used to running after having a couple of scotches.

Cheney and Tony Boston were running down San Vicente toward the ocean. It was a beautiful run. Two two-lane one-way roads were separated by a wide median strip of grass and trees. Part of the 1984 Olympic marathon had been run down San Vicente. Off to the side were big houses and manicured lawns and lots of gates with security company signs prominently displayed. During daylight hours runners, joggers, and walkers were always in evidence.

Cheney remembered, when he had started walking on San Vicente, he always envied the men and women who actually ran. Now he was one of those people.

"I envy you."

"Why's that?" asked Cheney, even though he knew.

"Spending a coupla nights with Kimberly."

"What does that mean?"

Tony ducked under the branch of a tree and looked at Cheney strangely. But he still kept pace. "I'm not accusing you of anything. I was just thinking I would like to have been in your shoes. Coupla nights outa town with Kimberly, that'd be all right with me."

"Oh," said Cheney. He was wondering if he were increasing his chances of having a heart attack by drinking alcohol and then running. He stopped thinking about it.

"So you think it was worth going to Vegas?"

"Yes."

"Why?"

"What do you mean? You're very inquisitive these days," said Cheney.

"And you're pretty touchy."

"Sorry," said Cheney, shaking it off.

"Probably because of Elizabeth's surgery."

"Yes. That's probably it."

"So when is it?"

"Tomorrow morning. She's taking off early today so we can spend some time together."

"You make it sound like it's pretty serious."

"All surgery is serious. You know that. I mean, people can die from an improperly administered anesthetic. You never know."

"That's right, you never know."

Cheney felt himself getting winded, while Tony was running smoothly, breathing evenly—much the way Cheney ran when he didn't get drunk first. This was grueling.

"So, what do you think of Kimberly?"

"She's okay, why?" asked Cheney.

"You must have spent some time alone with her. I'd like your opinion."

"About what?"

"I'm not asking about her sexual prowess, Cheney. I'm just asking what you think of her, that's all. After all, you're a trained observer."

"She's attractive," said Cheney, trying to keep up with Tony and speak at the same time. "She's bright. What else do you want to know?"

"I don't know. I just like her, you know. I've decided I'm going to ask her out."

Cheney tried his best to breathe normally.

When they arrived at the place where San Vicente dead-ended at Ocean Avenue and a park that ran south to the Santa Monica Pier, Cheney and Tony walked for a while, then sat down on a bench that looked out over the Pacific Ocean.

A homeless man sat beside them reading a Ross Macdonald novel. He was wearing a fedora, an old brown suit, and tennis shoes. His bicycle was lying on the ground next to him. Occasionally he would look up at the two men on the bench.

"I'm not sure it's such a good idea to start seeing Kimberly," said Cheney.

"Why not? Dorie and I are divorced. I'm lonely, Cheney. And I'm sick and fucking tired of losing myself in my work. The only women I meet, I meet on the job. I met Kimberly because she's a reporter, but what the hell. She's not married; she's got a body to die for. What else is there?"

Cheney considered saying that his friend was a little short on objective criteria, but he decided to keep the moralizing to a minimum. For a number of reasons. "Maybe you should get together with someone who doesn't want something from you."

"What's wrong with that? I mean, who doesn't want something from someone? You see a woman from across a crowded nightclub floor. You don't know her IQ, you don't know what she's 'into' spiritually." You like the way she looks and you want something she's got. It's biological. There's no shame in that.

"So Kimberly butters me up because I'm the chief of detectives. Big deal. You think a big-time basketball player turns down some woman who comes up to him and says she wants to have sex with him just because he's famous? Hell, no. People are attracted to other people for all kinds of reasons. I'm not Tom Cruise, but I'm not the Elephant Man, either."

Cheney could find no fault in his friend's reasoning. He still wasn't crazy about Tony asking Kimberly out, but he could not possibly explain why to his friend. What the hell, thought Cheney, Kimberly would probably turn him down.

"So, when are you going to ask her out?"

"I don't know. Soon. Real soon."

"What do you think of sin?" said a voice.

Cheney and Tony turned around to look at the homeless man.

"What did you say?" asked Cheney.

"Sin. What do you think of it?" said the man.

"I think it's highly overrated," said Cheney glibly.

"Sins of the fathers. In Ross Macdonald's books people can never outrun their past."

"It's just a book."

"Yeah, but he seems to know what he's talking about. The characters seem so real."

"Look," said Cheney, trying to ease into it, "what makes you such an expert on Ross Macdonald?"

"I'm an English professor at UCLA. At least I used to be."

"What happened?" asked Cheney.

"Who knows? California government, declining social and family values." The man pocketed his book, picked up his bike, and got on. "Sins of the fathers. Who the fuck knows, right?"

The man pedaled away.

"Strange guy," said Tony. He stood up and started walking back toward San Vicente.

"Yeah," said Cheney, following Tony.

"What do you make of him?"

"I don't know. Glad my father wasn't a sinner," said Cheney, starting to jog alongside Tony.

"Everybody sins, Cheney. You know that. You can't spend twenty years as a cop and not know that."

"I know that. It's just that every sin doesn't have to come back to haunt you like it does in the movies."

"I agree with you."

"Good."

"But you never know."

Cheney picked up the pace and started running beside Tony. Neither one said a word all the way back.

Cheney had never been to the Bel Air Athletic Club. It was rumored that Ronald Reagan was a member. But then, it was rumored that every powerful white male in the western world had been a member at one time or another. And there was no way to check.

A valet took Cheney's Mercedes after he had pulled into the semicircular driveway up in the hills above Sunset. It was a strange feeling for Cheney to feel somewhat out of place with a two-year-old Mercedes. Yet as he made his way to the front door past 560s, Ferraris, and Rolls-Royces, the thought occurred to him.

But it did not linger. Cheney was too old to be intimidated by such superficialities. At least for very long.

The man behind the desk gave Cheney a pass and directions to the steam room. As he changed into a towel and left his street clothes in a locker with a computer lock—the combination to which was written on his pass—Cheney took the place in. Not exactly the YMCA. Designer soap. Designer brushes and combs, towels and cologne. A shoeshine guy sat in the corner reading *The Wall Street Journal*.

When he opened the door to the steam room, Cheney expected to find a dozen rich fat guys sitting around in towels talking about mutual funds. The room was hot; waves of steam rolled up rhythmically from various places in the floor. But it was deserted, except for Jamison Sanford, who sat against the far wall.

Music was piped in. The music was Bruce Hornsby's "The Way It Is." Sanford was holding a snifter in one hand. With his other hand he waved Cheney over to him.

"Quite a piace," said Cheney as he sat down on the second level of marble seats that ringed the room.

"You like Bruce Hornsby?"

"Yes."

"Good. I requested his first CD, beginning to end."

Cheney thought about putting in his own request but decided against it. He had come here for a reason.

"Well, what did you find out about Barbara?"

"Not much."

"Not much of an answer."

"For the money?"

"Even for free. Look, Cheney, I'm paying the tab and I don't expect you to shortchange me, even if you think you're doing me a favor. Understood?"

"Understood."

So Cheney told his employer everything he had learned in Vegas—except, of course, what he had learned about Kimberly Gary.

"Do you think the attacks in Las Vegas have anything to do with her death?"

"I don't know, but I'm looking into it."

"What was her father like?"

"Like a man waiting to die."

"Sometimes, Cheney, I think most of us are just waiting to die. We sure as hell don't know how to live. We put off our happiness. We believe we have all the time in the world."

"I don't know about that," said Cheney. "We seem to live in a world that, if anything, is drowning in pleasure."

"I didn't say pleasure. I said happiness. There's a difference. If you don't believe me, look it up in the dictionary."

Bruce Hornsby was playing a piano solo on "The Way It Is" when Sanford smiled. It was not a happy smile. "I have a great deal of time to reflect on life and death these days. To me, pleasure was having sex with Barbara. Happiness was strolling with her on the beach, watching her laugh, holding her hand, and knowing that she loved me. That was pure joy."

Sanford brought the snifter to his lips and drank. "Don't get me wrong, Cheney, there's nothing wrong with pleasure."

Cheney nodded. And thought about Kimberly. But he thought more about Elizabeth.

Sanford leaned back on the marble slab behind him. "I can buy all the pleasure I want. Tonight, if I wanted to, I could have two of the most beautiful women in the world. Three. Four. And pay them to do whatever I wanted them to do to me. Pleasure, Cheney. It can be bought with cash or plastic. But"— Sanford shook his head—"happiness is an entirely different matter. I have not experienced a moment of happiness since Barbara was killed."

Even in the sweltering heat Cheney felt a chill run up his spine. He looked at the clock on the opposite wall. Elizabeth would be home soon.

"I've got to get going, Jamison."

"I understand. Cheney . . ."

"Yes?"

"You will stay with this?"

"Yes."

"Thanks. This is more important to me than you know."

Cheney thought about telling Sanford that he had a pretty good idea exactly how important it was to him, but he just shook hands and walked out of the steam room.

sixteen

"So how was your trip?"

"Fine," said Cheney.

"I gave Petty the night off."

Cheney and Elizabeth sat alone in their living room, which included a white baby grand piano, a Kitmun original, and two numbered Byersly lithographs.

"How do you feel?"

"You mean, do I feel scared?" asked Elizabeth.

"Well, yeah, I guess."

"I feel good. This is not high-risk surgery, and I'm focusing on what I'm going to look like afterward. It's going to be a new me," she said with a smile. It was a youthful smile, the kind of smile children have when they talk about what they're going to get for Christmas.

"I'm sure it'll be great."

"Aren't you excited? I mean, you're the one who's going to get to test the merchandise."

"I have to admit, I *am* a little curious," said Cheney. He had thought about it, though not as much as Elizabeth figured he had thought about it. New breasts. Lifted, firmer, larger. What was there to argue with?

And, quite frankly, Cheney was looking forward to making love to Elizabeth with her breasts looking much the same as they had been when he had met her.

"How long do we have to wait until—you know, we can . . ."

"Fuck?" said Elizabeth, smiling because of the effect her saying the F-word had on her husband. "What's the matter?"

"You don't usually talk like that."

"You hear the word every day."

"Not from you."

"How does it feel?" Elizabeth was still smiling.

Cheney smiled back. "I'll get over it."

"Take your time," she said, putting her hand on Cheney's thigh.

When her hand reached inside his pants and grabbed his rising penis, a strange and unique thought hit Cheney like some kind of errant lightning. He felt unclean. As though responsible for every type of bacteria or virus that had made headlines in the past hundred years. As though some type of plague clung to his penis at this very moment. And, if there really was any bacteria or virus alive and kicking down there, and he spread it to Elizabeth, he knew he would, in fact, be responsible. The thought sent shivers through him.

His penis recoiled at the thought of that potential responsibility.

"What's wrong?"

"Nothing," said Cheney.

"Look, Buster, I got the proof right here," she said, still holding Cheney's wilting penis.

"Maybe I'm just not in the mood," he said.

"Get in the mood," replied Elizabeth.

And she gave him at least four good reasons to do so.

Gino did not believe he was mad. On the other hand, he thought, if you were really insane you were often the last to know. Yet what other proof did he need? He had killed. Not once but several times. With his bare hands.

Gino had not grown up with the intention of being a murderer. And he did not consider himself a victim, as he had heard many criminals describe themselves. Even though he knew that injustice had always stalked him, until . . . until he had decided there was no rhyme or reason to life. No God. No official score-keeper tallying up the points of the angels and debiting the sinners' ledger. Sinners did pretty damned well in this world, and no one, with all the scientific tools and philosophic arguments at their disposal, had ever proved there was another.

Gino kept score his own way. And the angels, for all their good work, always seemed to end up with the short end of the stick. Perhaps it was because they were content to wait for their reward in heaven. Perhaps heaven was a wonderful place, where good people who did good works lived happily ever after with other good people who did good works.

Perhaps heaven did not exist.

The world Gino woke up to every morning existed. Injustice existed. Manipulative people existed. Existed and touched his life and the lives of innocent people.

Perhaps there was no heaven, but there was a hell and Gino was a citizen. And good citizens took responsibility. It had taken him time to understand such things, but he had learned. The hard way.

He had learned that in this world grace was precious and usually absent, but evil was everywhere. In every TV newscast, in most big box office movies, evil was often the star. In real life, evil motivated people more often than good. How often did a person determine his or her actions on the basis of how those actions would positively impact another person? Gino had often considered these things, added them up, and the final score was always the same.

And his own actions? The cleansings? Would it have been right or wrong to have killed Hitler at the beginning of World War II? Gino had often argued. Some things were obvious; the rules of the angels were too limiting. They allowed others to take merciless advantage.

Gino would not allow such people, evil people, to take advantage of him. Not anymore.

Where he saw evil he would eradicate it, before it touched him. It was not insane to preempt disaster. It was not madness to cleanse the moral landscape.

Someone had to. The world was drowning in compromise. Someone had to take a stand. It was not a radical position. Everyone could see evil, but it was quite another thing to *do* something about it.

Gino was strong.

Finally.

He could not turn water into wine, but he could carve out a piece of heaven from a little bit of hell.

And if not heaven, he could at least carve out the cancer.

The Orange Seahorse was a Chinatown nightclub just off Broadway, down an alley. It was peopled by "club youth," although the mix was somewhat different from the mix on the East Coast, where the phenomenon of dressing in outrageous costumes, body paint, and makeup really got started.

Gino walked inside and smiled. It was a vision that could have been conjured up by Dante on LSD. The club was filled with about two hundred decked-out participants, many smiling, when you could distinguish their mouths beneath the makeup, with a teeth-clenched, Ecstasy-induced grin.

Two men wore bird cages on their heads, like helmets. They were dressed in gladiator leather, criss-crossing belts, and knee-high sandals. Their bodies were painted white, their lips bright ruby red, and their shaved heads were adorned with a number of canaries. Hence the bird cages.

A woman was covered in gray body paint, her entire body shaved except for her eyebrows and the close-cropped carrot-colored hair on her head. She wore platform shoes the color of her hair. Her teeth were a brilliant white, especially in contrast to her gray body paint.

The place was like a Dali cartoon, at once disorienting and exhilarating, stimulating in its decadence. A subtle madness flowed like a river that led, ultimately, to broken hearts of darkness. This madness flowed freely because the masks, the costumes, hid identity and therefore, to a certain extent, responsibility. Here, in the Orange Seahorse, the social personality was checked at the door.

A young brunette who was not dressed like an art object, but rather like a sex object, smiled at Gino from the bar. Instead of alcohol, the bar offered "smart" drinks. The man behind the bar, who was made up to look like a clown, served beverages containing herbs, enzymes, and fruit juices. The idea was still to alter one's consciousness, but in a "healthy" way. And whereas alcohol helped a person forget, many smart drinks were supposed to improve one's memory.

"Hi," said Gino as he sidled up next to the girl at the bar. She wore brown suede knee-high boots and a loincloth that was made up of two squares of leather held together by a leather string that encircled her waist. It appeared to be a matter of considerable interest to many of the men, and some of the women, around her to determine if the brunette was wearing anything underneath. Whenever she walked, it became apparent that she was not. She had topped off the ensemble with a bra made up of two more pieces of leather. And, of course, another string.

"Hi," she said with a smile that stretched across her face like a taut rubber band.

Gino knew the signs. She was on Ecstasy. Although he had never done the drug, he had done MDA, a version of it, years ago. The smile was a result of the amphetamine-derivative rush that came with Ecstasy, which was also known as the love drug because it made the user very horny. Even the act of breathing felt somewhat orgasmic. At least that's the way Gino remembered it. Such a quality made Ecstasy a popular drug in clubs. Kind of like a psychedelic Spanish Fly.

"You come here often?" asked Gino. It was not an original line, but he wasn't trying to break into a safe. The equipment needed would be minimal.

"Do I *come* often?" she asked, her grin remaining in place while her tongue moved.

"That's close enough."

They both smiled and laughed at nothing for a moment. "So, what do you do?" asked Gino.

"I'm a model."

"Really. You're very pretty."

"I know," she said. And she did.

"What's your name?"

"Jane. Jane Dumont. What's yours?"

"Gino."

More smiling and laughing. About nothing.

"So, what do *you* do?"

"A little of this, a little of that."

"C'mon, tell me."

On the right beat Gino said, "I'm a director."

"No kidding."

And that was usually all it took.

* * *

Tony Boston sat staring at the TV, drinking luke-warm beer from the can. So many options, sixty—count 'em, sixty—channels, and all of them available at the press of a button. Power.

On one channel some guy was selling something in a tube that was supposed to grow hair. On another channel, a guy on a yacht, surrounded by beautiful women, was selling tapes and seminars that were supposed to make you rich. Then there was a doctor who was talking about a simple outpatient operation that was supposed to make your penis two inches bigger. And there were two beautiful girls in bikinis looking right into *your* living room, at you personally, telling you with a straight face that they wanted to meet you and were ready—no, *anxious*—to give you their "personal" phone number. "Call 1-900-4-A-LOSER," said Tony aloud to no one. He had noticed he had begun speaking aloud when he was by himself. Not all the time, but every once in a while. Was he going crazy? Maybe he just needed some nonelec-tronic companionship.

He took another swig of beer and watched some guy on TV pour lighter fluid on his car, set it on fire—while the audience oohed and aahed—then put out the fire and smear some miracle wax on the burn spot.

If this ain't the end of the world, thought Tony, it's gotta be the commercial before the last act. He picked up the remote control but couldn't pull the trigger. It was easier to kill somebody than it was to turn off the fucking TV. When you had nothing else to do. When its noise, talk, and music camouflaged the fact there was no real noise, real talk, or real music in your life.

The phone rang. Tony gratefully hit the mute button, not the off button, on the remote.

"Hello?"

"Tony?"

"Yes?"

"This is Kimberly. Kimberly Gary. I hope I'm not disturbing you."

Tony decided not to tell her how thankful he was that she had freed him from sixty channels of hell-in-a-jar. "No, I'm just watching some TV."

"I'm over at the club. Just finished a racquetball game."

"Did you win?"

"Actually, I did. Anyhow, I was wondering if you'd like to join me for a drink next door?"

"Sure, I guess I could tear myself away. Thirty minutes?"

"Great."

"See you soon."

Tony hung up, picked up the remote, aimed it at the TV, and pulled the trigger. Black screen. Silence. Silence was hard to take when you knew it was all you had. It enveloped and drowned you until you cried out for a sound to break that silence. Even an artificial sound. When loneliness was all you had.

Tonight Tony had plans.

"It isn't like I planned to be a waitress, you know," said Jane Dumont. "Person's gotta pay her dues."

Gino sat in his director's chair, a real director's chair, while the brunette in the suede boots sat on the couch opposite him.

"Nice loft."

"Thanks."

"I've actually seen some of your movies," said Dumont, as she took in the walls with posters on them. Posters that included Gino's name as either editor, writer, or director or some combination of the three.

Gino nodded. "You want some more wine?"

"Nah, I'm fine. I'm actually pretty high," she said.

Like he didn't know. Her sitting there in her loincloth, casually exposing her femininity as though it meant nothing. Gino knew exactly what it meant.

"I like your look."

"Really?" she said. She had heard that all her life.

"Yes. In fact, I'm working on a project now that requires someone with that look."

"Really?" she said enthusiastically. That was what she needed to hear.

What Gino *knew* she needed to hear.

"They say Vegas is a pretty nice place when you get away from the neon and the casinos."

"It's okay. Going back reminded me of why I left."

"That bad, eh?" said Tony, taking a hit off his Samuel Adams beer.

"Not really. There's just nothing there for me anymore, that's all. If I'm going to be a writer, I have to live in New York or Los Angeles."

"So how come I hear about all these writers who live in the country, in little rustic out-of-the-way places?"

"They move there after they make it."

"Why LA instead of New York?"

"I tried New York first."

"I didn't know you used to live in New York."

"This is the first time we've really talked. There are all kinds of things you don't know about me," said Kimberly with a smile.

Tony couldn't read the smile. Which struck him as odd because that was a big part of his job—reading people. Of course, he knew why he was having trouble. Keen insight was almost always the first thing to go in a personal relationship, especially when that relationship involved sex or the desire for sex.

"How long were you in New York?"

"Three, three and a half years. I lived two blocks from the Dakota. You know, the place where John Lennon used to live?"

"Yeah," said Tony, nodding, although he hadn't been to New York for fifteen years and the information was wasted on him.

"Three blocks from the park. I ran around Central Park five days a week. Past pretzel vendors, hot-dog vendors, even booksellers with portable stalls. I remember I bought a 1916 *Leaves of Grass* with hand-pasted pastel illustrations. You ever read Whitman?"

"I'm not much for poetry."

"Least you know it's poetry. I was talking about Walt Whitman with a guy once and he told me he was a big Whitman fan. Turned out the guy was into *Slim* Whitman and had just purchased the singer's CD from an eight hundred number on some home shopping channel."

"That's funny," said Tony.

"Not really. He was pretty cute."

"So what made you leave New York? I thought it was the publishing capital of the world."

"It is. But I got tired of doing freelance work and editing a martial arts magazine—"

"A martial arts magazine?" said Tony incredulously.

"I got the job because I had my own camera. I could take pictures and do the interviews at the same time. That plus I could tell the difference between a noun and a verb. The clincher was the fact that English was my first language. Oh, yeah, it was a highbrow operation."

"It's funny thinking of you writing about the martial arts."

"It was kind of funny, really," said Kimberly with a disarming smile.

She had a beautiful smile, thought Tony.

"All those martial arts guys had the same story— got beat up as kids, learned the martial arts so they could defend themselves, then when they knew they could kick ass, they didn't have to do it anymore, and now they're at peace with themselves. I just changed the names and juggled a few facts and kept writing the same article month after month. Nobody noticed.

"And naturally, I always got saddled with writing the annual obligatory women's self-defense article. Which was always a short piece about the importance of being able to defend yourself from sex-crazed men, accompanied by a number of photographs of men getting kicked in the groin."

"How could you leave all that behind?"

"Just stupid, I guess. A guy I met at a publishing company in New York got a job as an editor for the *Los Angeles Tribune*. He called me one day and asked if I'd be interested in hanging out in police stations. The rest, as they say, is history."

"Is that where you want to end up? In the newspaper business?"

"Hell, no. I'm like everybody else. I want to be rich and famous and end up talking to Oprah and Phil. What the hell, maybe even Geraldo—although I might have to undergo a sex change for that."

"That'd be quite a waste."

"Why, is that a compliment, Mr. Boston?" said Kimberly coquettishly.

"If it walks like a duck and quacks like a duck . . ." The two were silent for a moment. Then Tony said, "How are you planning to win the lottery?"

"True crime is always the flavor of the month for TV, books, and movies. Can't go wrong sniffing around real-life murder cases."

"Is that why you're pushing so hard on Cheney?"

"I'm not pushing that hard. Besides, he's a big boy, he can say no. People say no to me all the time."

"I find that hard to believe."

"Trust me. This case Cheney's working on is an opportunity. The department has all but erased it from the books. Let's face it, a really high-profile case the whole city knows about, some New York publisher is going to assign a writer to it and I'm squeezed out. Nobody knows about this story yet. Short of committing a crime myself, finding a case like this is the only way I'm going to get a piece of the pie."

"Sounds a little mercenary."

"What does?"

"Capitalizing on other people's pain."

"Don't make me sound like some vampire. I'm not

the one killing people. And if I don't write about it, someone else will."

"If it's actually a murder case."

"It is."

"How do you know?"

"Trust me. I've got a feeling."

"You mean you want it to be."

"No. I know it."

"Women's intuition?"

"Something like that."

"I don't know if I can do something like that."

"It's just a role. In your acting classes you might have to be a seagull. Or a rock. Doesn't mean you have to be that thing forever. It's just acting."

"Yeah, I guess." Jane Dumont stood in the room Gino called his studio. "But I've never done anything like this before."

"Acting?" said Gino.

"No, I mean . . . you know."

"Let me set up the camera."

"Really? You're going to film this?"

"Of course."

Jane Dumont got a funny look on her face, shrugged, and said, "Okay."

She held her hand above her head, as Gino buckled her wrists into the leather restraints.

"Relax. This is going to be fun."

"That was fun," said Tony, after he had walked Kimberly to her car.

She put her duffel bag into the back seat and turned back toward Tony. "I'm glad you could make it," she said.

"Me too." Silence. "Kimberly . . ."

"Yes, Tony?"

He liked the way his name sounded when she said it. "I'd like to see you again. On a date."

"Fine. When?"

"When's your next free night?"

"Could be awhile. You know the newspaper game. Let me check."

Tony could feel his heart falling through his feet into his shoes.

Kimberly plucked her appointment book from her dashboard and starting leafing through the pages. "Well, let's see. No. No," she said mumbling to herself, not looking at Tony. Then she looked up at him. "How about tomorrow night?" she said with a playful smile.

Tony's heart rocketed back up to where it used to be and started beating strongly again. "Great," he said. And he meant it.

Kimberly scribbled something on a piece of paper and handed it to him. "That's my address and home phone. Give me time to work out. Come by around nine, okay?"

"Okay."

Kimberly leaned over and kissed Tony very briefly on the lips, smiled, got into her black four-wheel-drive Prelude SI, and drove away.

It was not a passionate kiss, thought Tony, as he wandered through the parking lot in the general direction of his new Lincoln Town Car—being chief of detectives had its rewards. But it was not a Hollywood phantom air kiss either. Somewhere in between. And she had initiated the kiss, however insignificant it was. Why was it insignificant? He was always thinking the worst about himself when it came to women. But living with Dorie, going through the divorce, listening to her lawyer, reading her complaint, walking in on her with another man—all that got a guy to thinking maybe there was something wrong with him. His lawyer had told him not to think that way. Had told him not to believe anything that was written in Dorie's complaint. Which seemed strange to Tony. But his attorney assured him that was the way the game was played.

Cheney had tried to convince Tony that there was nothing wrong with him; he had simply made a bad choice with Dorie. Most women were not cut out to be cops' wives. Certainly Dorie hadn't been.

Tony had dated a few other women since the divorce, two of them women Cheney and Elizabeth had set him up with. The blind dates had not turned out to be disasters, but neither were they successful. He never saw either of the women a second time.

Kimberly was the first woman he had been interested in who showed some interest in him. After all, she had called him for a . . . was this a date? It felt like a date. At least it felt like a date to him. He wondered how it felt to Kimberly.

Was she using him? Perhaps.

Under the stars in the parking lot, a chill night wind coming in off the Pacific, which was only a couple of miles down the road, Tony listened to the ping-ponging chatter in his head. He was out of practice.

Not very comfortable with women. He had never been really comfortable with them. And for the past year or so he had buried himself in the job. Content to leave questions unanswered. Content to put that part of his life on hold.

Tonight Kimberly Gary had punched the right buttons. He was no longer on hold.

She did not know how much longer she could hold on. Even through the drug haze, Jane Dumont heard screams. Her own screams. Saw blood. Her own blood.

Even through the drug haze, Jane Dumont knew she was dying. Dying! *Oh, God, no! Please let this be a dream. A role. Anything but real life. My life. No, no, no!*

Her breasts had been . . .

Oh, God, no! Please let this be a dream!

seventeen

"So today you get your new boobs," said Petty to Elizabeth as she put a waffle on Cheney's plate.

"Another sensitive quarter heard from," said Cheney.

Because she was not supposed to eat anything before surgery, Elizabeth just sipped some weak hot tea and stayed above the fray.

"More hot water?" Petty hovered over Elizabeth, who held her hand over her cup.

Petty sat down to a plate of low-fat Jimmy Dean sausage and a low-fat pancake. She poured some low-fat fake maple syrup over everything. Then she put some nondairy creamer into her coffee substitute and stirred.

"You ever consider plastic surgery?" said Cheney.

"Nah, I'm into natural things," said Petty.

"Really," said Cheney, his ironic tone lost on her.

"Besides, sagging tits is God's way of preparing you for the change."

"The change?"

"You know. Less sex. You got sagging tits, you're gonna have less sex, let me tell you."

"I see," said Elizabeth, trying to hide a slight smile behind her teacup.

"Look, Petty, we respect your opinion—" said Cheney.

"Why shouldn't you? Just because I'm your live-in slave doesn't mean I haven't lived."

"You're not a slave."

"Oh, yeah, I've lived on the edge," she said, setting down her fork to concentrate. "Raised two daughters who are both married, thank the Lord." She raised her eyes to the ceiling or somewhere beyond. "They weren't conceived by angels. Men found me attractive. Lots of men. Too many men, let me tell you. Three husbands, God rest their souls." Again the raised eyes; this time she crossed herself for good measure. "All that without store-bought tits."

Cheney and Elizabeth sat looking at her incredulously. Then Petty looked at Cheney accusingly.

"It wasn't my decision, okay?" he said defensively.

Petty snorted, picked up her fork again, and resumed eating, continuing to look at him admonishingly out of the corner of her eye.

Cheney's appetite vanished. "You about ready to go, honey?"

The drive over was uneventful, except for some guy who came over to Elizabeth's Mercedes, squeegee in hand, asking if he wanted the windows washed. Cheney shook his head, and the guy went to another car.

Carjacking was, in effect, domestic terrorism. Cheney had not wanted to buy this car, partly because he didn't want to put Elizabeth at risk. She often worked late and the car stuck out like a wallet hanging out of somebody's pocket. He didn't give a fuck about the car, but when somebody waved a gun in your face, Cheney knew anything could happen. And it often did.

But Elizabeth usually got what she wanted. She got him. She got her car.

And today she was getting new breasts.

"This is a very simple procedure," said Steven Blomberg. Cheney thought he looked even younger than the last time they met. Not old enough to shave, but old enough to do surgery. On Elizabeth.

"I don't want either one of you to worry."

"I'm not worried," said Elizabeth.

Cheney said nothing.

"Usually it's the boyfriend or husband who worries," said Blomberg, as he smiled and looked at Cheney. "Really, it's a standard procedure. I've done over a thousand."

Cheney wondered if he counted each breast augmentation as two, but he decided not to ask.

"Don't worry, Cheney," said Elizabeth, taking her husband's hand. "I'm gonna be fine. In fact, I'll be better than fine."

"You're better than fine now," Cheney said and kissed his wife.

"She'll be pretty groggy when she comes out of surgery. I'll give you some medication for her to take every four hours for a couple of days. Don't be surprised if she experiences some initial pain. It's natural. As I'm sure you know, we're using saline implants so you won't have to worry about silicone problems down the road. Any questions?"

"How long before—"

"Before you can play with them?" asked Blomberg with a smile.

"No," said Cheney irritably. He felt like reaching over and slapping the guy.

"Sorry."

"How long before she can get up and around?"

"Day or two. She should stay in bed for twenty-four hours, then get back into the groove slowly. I'll want to see her next week for a checkup. Don't worry, everything's going to be fine."

Cheney nodded. No one said anything for a moment.

Blomberg looked at his watch. "I'll go in and get things set up. My nurse will come in to prepare you when we're ready, Elizabeth." He smiled and walked out of the room.

"You sure you want to go through with this?"

"How many times have you asked me that?"

"Doesn't make any difference. I just want you to know you can change your mind."

"Cheney, read my lips. I'm doing this for me. Me. Do you understand?"

"I know, but—"

"No buts about it. It's my decision. I want your support. Buck up, kiddo. This is going to be your favorite Christmas present ever. And tomorrow you can unwrap it." She smiled. "It's the gift that keeps on giving. Year after year. Cheer up." Elizabeth leaned over and kissed her husband.

Cheney took her in his arms and held her close. Ran his fingers through her hair. Felt her heart beating against his chest. He loved her very, very much.

The nurse walked in, smiled, and asked Cheney to leave. Elizabeth nodded.

Cheney left. Slowly.

The knife went into the nude woman's breast up to the hilt. Blood pumped from her chest like a geyser.

The woman screamed and blood spurted out of her mouth.

The man stood over the writhing woman triumphantly. And laughed.

"Cut!"

"Shit!" said the man. "I've got blood all over my pants. Fuck!" he said, bending over and shaking the fake blood from his trousers.

The nude woman got to her feet, walked over to a chair, and put on a cheap terry-cloth robe. No one seemed to notice the nude woman or the blood.

"We can't shoot that again, Gino. Wardrobe doesn't have another pair of pants."

"Don't worry about it. I'll shoot around your pants."

"Looked good to me," said Harry Corbin, the movie's producer. "It'll do."

The actor walked away. He knew Corbin didn't want to talk to him anyhow. He knew the producer was not concerned with performance. Like people who determine the quality of a smorgasbord by the weight of food per dollar, Corbin gauged the success or failure of each day by the amount of film exposed.

"Gino, Gino, you're killin' me here. You know what time it is?"

"Yeah, I know, but—"

"There you go using the 'but' word again. 'Buts are for Buttheads.'"

"Yeah, yeah, yeah," said Gino. He had heard it all before. Before lunch.

"You think some guy who picks up this video gives a flyin' fuck about whether the lighting's just right? You think he notices if some actor's got blood on his pant cuff? Hell, our continuity person doesn't even notice those Mickey Mouse details. Lighten up here, pal. This ain't brain surgery."

It was barely moviemaking, thought Gino, but he held his tongue. He never confused what he did with high art, nor would he be on the edge of his seat when the Academy Award nominations were announced. But he wanted to do the best work possible. For under three hundred thousand dollars, creating a movie that was also good work was quite a challenge.

Gino had gained a reputation for directing decent down-and-dirty slasher movies. For under three hundred grand, he couldn't be beat. He took ten to fifteen thousand for himself, wrote the damned things, and directed them. He did four or five a year.

But it was always a struggle. Never enough money. Never enough time. Never enough of anything to make the kind of movie Gino really wanted to make. A couple of years ago he had hoped that doing these movies would lead to bigger and better things, but he was starting to believe he might be stuck here in no-man's-land. Listening to guys like Corbin talking about Buttheads.

The money he made from doing these movies, which were shot in less than two weeks, plus the money he occasionally made as a film editor, allowed him to finance his own projects, buy computer equipment, and maintain his loft. Gino didn't really care about anything else.

"I thought we were going to spend a little more on this movie," said Gino.

"We?" said Corbin. "I don't remember seeing your name among the investors, Gino."

"I'm investing my time and talent—"

"Whoa, now. Just a minute here. Every fuckin' waiter in town—hell, even my fuckin' gardener's fuckin' son's got talent. Big fuckin' deal. You know what I'm sayin' here? I don't make art. I stuff splashy video boxes with eighty-five minutes of exposed tape that has some relation, however remote, to the art on the video box. You know what I'm sayin'? Talent's a dime a dozen. You can't spend it. Money, you can spend. We go out to lunch, the tab comes, I look up at the guy and say Gino's gonna exchange some talent for lunch. Fifty fuckin' bucks' worth of his talent. The guy laughs in my face, you know what I'm sayin'? But they take my plastic. They take my money. On a fifty-dollar tab, the difference between your talent and my fifty-dollar bill comes to exactly fifty bucks. You know what I'm sayin'?"

Gino just took a deep breath and nodded. He had no lines in this script.

"Hey, don't get me wrong here," said Corbin, putting his arm around Gino and giving him a little hug. "I respect you. I really fuckin' do. I wouldn't have hired you unless I respect you."

"As an artist?"

"Whatever. You get the job done, bring the fuckin' film in on time, on budget. That's what counts. The rest—well, leave that to Paramount and Disney, you know what I'm sayin'?"

Gino nodded.

"Sorry I had to get heavy with you, Gino. Look at it as a lesson, you know? I'm tellin' you the truth here. Money'll put a roof over your fuckin' head, get you a car, get you fucked. Talent? Well, a lot of real talented people starve in this town. Give me a pocketful of money any day. Somethin' to think about, Gino. You know what I'm sayin'?"

Corbin didn't wait around for an answer. A production assistant was running toward him with a portable phone. He patted Gino on the shoulder and was off to put out another fire.

"Gino?"

Gino turned and saw a young dark-haired woman standing in front of him. She looked nervous.

"Yes?"

"You probably don't know me. I'm Vampire Number One."

Gino smiled. "What's your real name?"

"Jenny. Jenny Clarke."

Gino sat down on an apple box and crossed his arms. "So, what can I do for you, Jenny Clarke?"

"Well, I know this might sound a little bold, but, you know, a girl's gotta look out for herself, you know?"

"Tell me."

"I've noticed you looking at me."

"Is that so?" Gino was not going to make it easy. Why should he? he thought.

"Yeah. I could tell."

"I like your look. You remind me of someone I used to know."

"Really? Who?"

"An old girlfriend."

"Really? That's nice," said Jenny with a smile.

They were both silent for a moment. Gino knew he held the upper hand, so he just waited. Being a film director, no matter how unimportant, was one of the few remaining jobs left in western civilization wherein one could be an absolute dictator and still get away with it.

"So, you wanna get together?" she asked.

"What for?" said Gino.

"I don't know, maybe we could go see a movie."

"I'm actually very busy, Jenny, and if I go out with someone on a first date, I prefer to do something that provides us an opportunity to talk, to get to know each other."

"That sounds good too."

Gino looked at Jenny Clarke. And made a decision. "Give me your address and I'll pick you up around ten."

"Great."

"I hope you're not the inhibited type."

"I'm very open," she said. She scribbled down her address and phone number and handed the piece of paper to Gino.

"See you tonight."

"Look forward to it," she said, looking back over her shoulder and smiling as she hurried away before he could change his mind.

But Gino knew he wouldn't change his mind.

"We gotta talk," said Corbin, walking back over to Gino, a production assistant in tow.

"What's the problem?"

"We got the cop and all three vampire girls coming back tomorrow. We gotta lose somebody."

Gino took a look at the shooting schedule. "We can lose Vampire Number One. I'll do a rewrite. We won't need her tomorrow."

Corbin nodded his head cheerfully. "That's why I like having a director who's also a writer. You know what I'm sayin'?"

Cheney sat in the waiting room for the next two hours. The operation itself would only take sixty minutes or so, but the nurse had told him he would not be able to take Elizabeth home for at least another hour after that. So he had brought a book. Blomberg's nurse had suggested he go out and do something for a while, then come back.

But Cheney couldn't do that. He wanted—no, he needed—to be there. Just in case he was needed. In case Elizabeth needed him.

Cheney opened an Ed McBain 87th Precinct novel and started to read. It was the kind of easy reading that got the reader involved immediately. But Cheney couldn't concentrate. His mind started to do a negative sort of times when he had sat and waited while people he cared about went under the knife. Standard operations. Simple procedures. Something could always go wrong. His first partner's wife went into the hospital to have her tonsils removed. Standard operation. Simple procedure. His partner had kissed her as they wheeled her down the sterile hallway. He and Cheney had joked about which ice cream parlor he was going to buy her "dinner" at. Cheney had sat in the waiting room with his partner, talking about the job, sports, his partner's two-month-old baby. Cheney would never forget the look on the doctor's face when he came through the door and started walking slowly toward the two cops. After having performed the standard operation. The simple procedure.

Two months later Cheney's partner had taken his wife home, but she was no longer his wife. Brain damage incurred during the anesthetic had left her unable to recognize her husband or her child. Unable to walk or to control her bodily functions.

Cheney still could not shake the look on the doctor's face. He had walked as though in slow motion, to the cadence of a dirge, a black messenger delivering a requiem. Cheney and his partner had known what the man was going to say. Not the exact details, but they had known the man held death in his hands. Cheney remembered something strange that he had forgotten until now. He remembered wanting the scene to slow down and stop, as though if the doctor had not reached them, had not spoken the unspeakable, the horror would not have existed. It was as though it would not have become real until the man's words sculpted the nightmare into flesh and blood.

"Mr. Cheney?"

Cheney looked up at Dr. Blomberg, who stood in the doorway.

"Yes?"

"Your wife is out of surgery and everything went perfectly."

"Thanks," said Cheney.

Blomberg smiled a little and disappeared into his office.

Cheney looked down at his book. It was shaking visibly in his hands.

"How do you feel?"

"Kinda groggy," said Elizabeth. She looked up at Cheney from her pillow.

Cheney sat on the edge of the bed. "If you want anything . . ."

"I just wanna sleep," she said with a lazy tongue.

"Sure. If you need anything, just holler. I'll be right outside."

Cheney tucked his wife in bed, kissed her on the cheek and forehead, then walked out into the living room.

"So?" said Petty, hitting a button on the remote. Phil Donahue went mute. He was talking to a bald man dressed like a Vegas showgirl.

"So what?"

"How'd it go?" Petty turned her attention away from the TV and swiveled her body around in the chair to face Cheney.

"One hundred percent success."

"I had an uncle once. Doctor said the same thing—"

"Petty, stop it. I don't want to hear this story."

"You're right." She paused. "So, you like the new boobs?"

"Petty, please."

"They big enough for ya?"

"C'mon, Petty."

"I mean, did you get your money's worth?"

"You know this operation was strictly Elizabeth's idea."

"Yeah, and if I leave my dentures under my pillow, I'm gonna wake up a millionaire."

"What are you talking about?" said Cheney, leaning back in his chair. Out of the corner of his eye, he couldn't help but catch the bald guy dancing like a Vegas showgirl, complete with high heels and a big headdress.

"What I'm talking about is what you put that poor woman through."

"Look, you heard what Elizabeth said. You know it was her idea."

"What is she gonna say?" said Petty, looking at Cheney as though she were explaining two plus two equals four.

"Elizabeth is an independent woman. You know that."

"So tell me, Mr. Know-It-All, why is she getting new tits?"

"You heard what she said."

"I wanna hear it from you."

"She said she was doing it for herself."

"Translation?"

"I don't think it needs any translation."

"For herself? You mean she wanted to spend money, go through the risk and pain of major surgery—"

"*Minor* surgery," said Cheney.

"All surgery is major, Mr. Smarty-Pants," said Petty, referring to Cheney by one of his apparently infinite number of names. "She wanted to go through all that because she could not live with her tits the way they were? Do you really think Elizabeth is that insecure and unhappy with her self-image?"

"Maybe she just wanted to look the best she could."

"So the way she looked wasn't good enough for you?"

"I never said that."

"Not in so many words, but maybe your words and actions implied what you couldn't bring yourself to say. Wake up, Cheney. Smell the Chardonnay. A woman doesn't go out and get big tits for herself."

"Lots of women do."

"No, Cheney. They get them for men. It may enhance their self-image, but if it weren't for men," said Petty with disdain, "do you really think women care about the size of their tits? I don't think so. They do it for men, pure and simple, case closed."

"But I'm her man."

"Exactly," said Petty accusingly.

"I'm telling you she doesn't have to do that for me."

"Apparently she thought she did. There are many ways to communicate besides verbally. You know that. But then, you wouldn't have to say much. After all, you're a man."

"What does that mean?" asked Cheney, although even as he asked the question, he was pretty sure he didn't want to know the answer.

"It means you're a pig. You look at a woman, tally her up. Breasts: 'eight on a scale of ten'; legs: 'I'd give 'em a nine'; face: 'it'll do.' Maybe Elizabeth thought her value was falling in your eyes, and she figured she could bring it up a couple points with a boob job."

Cheney was silent for a moment. "This is all speculation, right?"

"Speculation?" said Petty, as though her intuition was beyond challenge.

"I mean, Elizabeth didn't tell you these things."

"Some things don't need to be said."

Out of the corner of her eye she saw a bunch of bald men dressed like Vegas chorus girls doing the can-can.

"I gotta watch this," said Petty, turning her attention back to the TV.

Cheney sat there for a moment thinking about what Petty had said. Had he given Elizabeth subliminal signals that led her to choose cosmetic surgery? Certainly her body had changed since they were married. But he was not unhappy with Elizabeth's body.

Cheney stood and walked to the doorway of their bedroom. He stood watching his wife sleep. She looked peaceful and happy.

It was how he wished she would always be.

"How's Elizabeth?"

"She's fine. She's resting."

Cheney remembered when this office had been his. For seven years. They were, if not the best, at least the most challenging years of his life. Now pictures of

Tony Boston's parents sat on the desk where photos of Elizabeth and of Cheney's son and daughter by a previous marriage used to sit. Even the smell was different. The clutter was there, but there was less of it than when the office had been his. A computer terminal that provided instant access to literally millions of pieces of information sat on a leaf that, when attached to the large oak desk, formed an *L* butting up against a window that looked out over an ocean of black-and-whites with numbers on their roofs.

"I thought you might be interested in this," said Tony, handing Cheney a file.

Cheney opened it. It was the paperwork on a murder victim named Jane Dumont. The photographs attached to the autopsy report indicated that the nineteen-year-old woman had been found nude in a vacant lot in Silverlake, near downtown. The knife wounds were clear and vicious. They mutilated the woman's breasts almost beyond recognition. He scanned the autopsy report. While it detailed a tragic and brutal murder, he wasn't sure why Tony was showing him the file.

"Look at what they found under her toenails."

Cheney scanned the page. Finding DNA under the fingernails was often helpful in cases like this, but that information was not listed. What was listed was "chocolate, Karo syrup, red food coloring, and detergent."

"So?" said Cheney.

"You know what that is?"

"Doesn't mean anything to me."

"It's fake blood," said Tony with a smile.

"Fake blood?"

"Yeah, like in the movies."

Cheney shook his head, puzzled. "That doesn't make any sense. I mean, from the look of things, there must have been plenty of real blood to go around."

"Yeah. The reason I showed it to you is because we found the same thing under Barbara Sanford's toenails. By itself, it didn't seem to mean anything. But when you link everything else up with this victim . . ."

"What do you mean, everything else?"

"Look at the photographs again."

Cheney looked at one of the photographs and began to see what Tony was getting at. Both Barbara and this woman were brunettes, with similar facial bone structure. And while Barbara had not had her breasts ripped up, they had been abused.

"I see what you mean, but there are also some huge differences. First of all, the physical abuse is different. Second, Barbara died of injuries directly related to being struck by a car."

"I know. I'm not saying this is a definite match. I just wanted you to take a look."

"The thing that bothers me most is the method of killing. You get some lunatic who likes to see a woman bleed to death, hitting her with a car just isn't the same—"

"Thrill?"

"Yeah, I guess," said Cheney, not wanting to use that exact word.

"I know. And maybe I'm way off the mark here. God knows mutilation of the genitals is not exactly an original crime."

Cheney nodded. He knew that was true. The practice was, unfortunately, almost commonplace. It served no purpose to announce to the public exactly what had happened to a murder victim's body, particularly a woman's body—although men's bodies were sometimes mutilated also, especially in gay-related murders. The genitals were frequently the target of rage. Cheney had attended a seminar once that examined this phenomenon. The psychiatrist, a short bald man with a Boston accent, had said that sexuality was often used or perceived as a source of power. Whereas it was common for men to use power in the form of money, women often used access to their sexuality as a source of power. A man who suffered a real or perceived wrong at the hands of a lover—particularly a lover who either denied access to her sexuality or gave it to another—often became obsessive about the lover's sexual hold over him. Great significance was then assigned to the sexual organs themselves. This, of course, the doctor had said, grew out of a basic dynamic of supply and demand. That is, that which is scarce has increased value. When sexuality is denied, that sexuality becomes more valuable.

And when in pain, the doctor had explained, logic was almost always secondary to impulse. That being the case, many irrational conclusions could be drawn. It was very common for cuckolded lovers to become obsessive about their former lovers' sex organs. And taken to its extreme, as in the case of a murderer, it was rather logical, really, the doctor had said with a wave of his hand, that the rage, the pain felt by the betrayed lover, would be directed toward the objects of sexual power, the genitals.

Cheney had attended that seminar during the first year he was a detective. Subsequent years in the field had taught him that the theory had considerable basis in fact. It was very common in violent crimes to see genital mutilation. He remembered a case where a jilted homosexual castrated his former lover. There had been a lot of jokes around the station house about that one. But the thing he remembered most was his feeling about how misguided the action had been. As though it solved something. As though it had really been about something physical. Cheney knew that when a relationship, heterosexual or homosexual, went sour, it usually had something to do with people growing apart and not communicating about it fast enough to keep up with the changes. The sex—more or less, good or bad—was often just a symptom of what was going on.

But then, Cheney also knew that sex made everybody crazy, and no doctor, no book, and no amount of insight was ever going to change that.

"You got anything else to tie Barbara Sanford and Jane Dumont together?" asked Cheney.

"Not a thing. You know how Barbara Sanford lived. Dumont lived life at the other end of the spectrum. About twelve years younger, no rich husband, aspiring model and actress by day—well, at least on days when she went out for auditions—and clubber by night."

"Clubber?"

"Get with it, Cheney. I'll bet you're old enough to remember all five Beatles' first names."

"Four."

"See?"

"Hell, I remember Elvis Presley when he was thin."

"Shit, Cheney, you're so old it's a wonder Elizabeth lets you out without one of those homing devices."

"Look, I'm less than ten years older than you, so fuck you."

"At least you're not sensitive about it."

"So what's a fucking clubber?"

"Actually it's called 'club youth.' People dress up and go to these youth-oriented clubs. 'Youth-oriented' is a euphemism for the fact that the clubs don't serve alcohol."

"Cheap way to open a club."

"Right. Also, there are a lot of party drugs at these places. Ecstasy's a popular menu item."

"Yeah, I read about it. People refer to it as the love drug."

"Exactly. Few years ago I was at a party unofficially, and some people were taking it. They ended up fucking right there in the living room in front of everybody. Un-fucking-believable."

"Two people, doing it right there in front of you?"

"Eight people."

"And you didn't make any arrests?"

"You should've seen the five women."

Cheney just shook his head.

"I'm going down to the Orange Seahorse. You wanna come?"

"Pardon?"

"There was a stamp on the dead girl's hand—almost invisible unless you held it under infrared light. Orange Seahorse. It's a nightclub in Chinatown."

* * *

An ordinary person would need a map, a guide, and a lot of luck to find the Orange Seahorse. With directions and a decent knowledge of Chinatown, it took Cheney and Tony Boston nearly an hour. It was down an alley, past a bakery, turn left at the neon sign—which didn't work—turn right at the live seafood store, then down another alley, past the fireworks company, and so forth.

Cheney knew that teenagers could find the place in two minutes with their eyes closed.

But it was daylight, and neither Cheney nor Tony were within wishing distance of nineteen. They were happy when they finally found a door with an orange seahorse stenciled on it. Tony knocked. Several times.

Finally a man opened the door. He squinted into the light and said, "We're closed." He started to shut the door, but Tony stuck his foot between the door and the frame and withdrew his shield.

It was usually a universal free pass.

Ten minutes later the three of them, Tony, Cheney, and John B. Anthony, the club's owner and manager, were sitting around a table in the deserted club talking like they were old friends. Anthony was tall and about as thin as a person could get and not be dead. Cheney and Tony knew the guy was on something, probably heroin. It was making a comeback.

"I love it when cops come down. Tell your friends. No problem. Fact is, most of the security people I got are moonlighting cops or ex-cops."

Cheney and Tony had heard it all before, but they just nodded and listened. There was no point in arguing. They were there to get the guy talking.

Anthony smoked while he talked. Constantly

tipped the ash off his long black gold-filtered cigarette.

"Never got busted," said Anthony after a long-winded monologue.

Which didn't mean nothing illegal was going on, thought both cops. But they weren't there to make an arrest. They were there to talk. Or at least to listen to Anthony talk. And whether he was just intimidated by cops—it was easy to feel that way when he and his club were full of drugs—or whether it was a manifestation of some speedball he had just done, Anthony was talking a mile a minute.

Tony Boston took two five-by-seven head shots out of his pocket and handed them to Anthony. He took the photographs in one hand, still holding his visibly foreign cigarette in the other.

"Ever see them before?"

For the first time since Tony stuck his foot in the door, Anthony was quiet. He looked the photographs over carefully. Both cops saw a spark of recognition and waited to see how truthful the guy was going to be. Which, in effect, would be a gauge of how difficult they were going to have to be with him.

"Yeah, I seen one of them," he said, flicking an ash into the ashtray directly in front of him. "This one," he said, indicating Jane Dumont and handing both photographs back to Tony Boston.

"When?"

"Not sure, really."

"Think about it. It's important."

"Why? She some kinda druggie or somethin'?"

"She's dead," said Tony. Knowing the anvil-dropping effect such words had on most people.

"No shit!" said Anthony. He drew on his cigarette. Hard. "Fuck!" he said as he ran his free hand through his long, unwashed hair.

"So?" said Tony.

"Look, man, I don't know nothin' about no fuckin' murder, okay?" said Anthony, holding up his hand, genuinely freaked out.

Cheney recognized the reaction. Anthony had not exactly "left the building," but due to the effects of whatever drug he was on, he was not completely there either. The drug jacked up the impact of the bad news, and the adrenaline caused Anthony a few problems in effective public speaking.

"Relax," said Cheney. "We're not here for you. We just want to ask you some questions. You understand?" He spoke firmly, trying to get Anthony to focus on him.

"Okay," said Anthony, dropping ash on the floor now. "Okay," he repeated, in case anyone hadn't heard him.

"So, when was she here?" said Tony.

"I dunno. Last night, night before. I really can't remember."

"Did she come here often?"

"Yeah. Couple times a week. That's how come I recognize her."

"Do you remember anyone she was with the last time she was here?"

Anthony tilted his head back and stared at the ceiling.

"I'm not sure," he said when he came back from the trance.

"Think about it," said Tony. "The LAPD would be

very grateful for any cooperation you might be able to provide." He did not have to say that the LAPD would not be very grateful for his lack of cooperation.

Anthony didn't need a translator to get the message. He went back into a trance.

Cheney had been through this a million times. If not a million, then several hundred for sure. It wasn't that Anthony didn't remember anything important, he was merely sifting through the details to make sure he could cover himself. As a businessman, Anthony knew—and Cheney knew he knew—that people were more often harmed by what they said than by what they did not say.

"I remember he was older."

"He?"

"The guy with . . . what's her name?"

"Jane. Jane Dumont."

"Right. Most of the people who come in here are pretty young. Unlike a lotta clubs," said Anthony, flicking ash in the glass ashtray again, "we don't keep older people out. Besides, the way some of these people dress up, you couldn't tell Princess Di from Ronald Reagan."

"But you could tell the guy with Jane Dumont was older."

"Yeah. He wasn't wearing any makeup, and he wasn't decorated like a fuckin' Christmas tree."

"So, what did he look like?"

"Who the hell knows? Older, that's all I can tell you. I'm trying to be helpful."

"And you are. Was he white?"

"Yeah."

"Short, tall?"

"Medium height, medium weight."

"That's very interesting," said Cheney sarcastically.

Tony Boston shot Cheney a look, then turned his attention back to the club owner. "He have a mustache?"

"No. Clean-shaven."

"But you say he was old. What gave you that impression?"

Anthony shrugged his shoulders as though such things were obvious. "He had some gray in his hair—"

"Long hair, short hair?"

"Long."

"Over his ears? Down the middle of his back?"

"Over his ears. Not over the shoulders."

"He as old as me?" asked Tony.

"No, man, he wasn't that old."

Although he knew he should not have, Tony felt a little stung by the remark. "He seem fit or overweight?"

"Like I say, medium weight. Not particularly muscular." Anthony pulled on his cigarette.

"He a regular?"

"Never saw him before. Reason he stuck out is because, like I said, he was older, you know."

Tony knew. Old, but not as fucking ancient as me, right? Fucking asshole, thought Tony. But he said, "Anyone associated with the movie business come in here regularly?"

Anthony's eyes got wide and he looked at Tony as though the detective had just asked him to recite the names of all fifty states. Backward. "You serious?"

"What do you mean?"

"Everybody's in the movie business, man. Least

they like to think they are. Every pretty piece of—I mean every girl likes to think of herself as an actress in waiting. Especially people who come in here. They're exhibitionists. And the guys, hell, they're the next Jean-Claude van whatever-the-fuck-his-name-is. Or they're a screenwriter who's got some big deal in development at one of the studios. Or they're some artsy-fartsy director who's looking for the next Madonna. The old guys are usually producers. Which means they probably optioned some poor schmuck's screenplay for ten bucks in the bathroom. Now they're big-time."

"So, you figure this old guy with Jane Dumont was a producer?"

"Who the fuck knows."

"He been in here much?"

"I dunno. Only reason I noticed him is because he was old and because he was with the babe. I don't focus much on guys, if you know what I mean."

"Yeah, I know what you mean." Tony took a card out of his wallet and handed it to Anthony. "Call me if he comes in again."

"Sure, no sweat. Always like to help the cops," said Anthony.

Outside in the alley, Tony caught his image in a window. "You think I look old?"

"You look younger than me."

"Fuck. I really *am* getting old," said Tony, shaking his head and walking quickly toward the car.

It was nearly dark by the time Cheney got home. He poured himself a glass of wine and walked out into the back yard, where Elizabeth was sitting in her robe, a cup of coffee in front of her.

"How do you feel?" asked Cheney, as he sat down at the white wrought-iron table with its four matching chairs.

"Great," she said with a smile.

"You in pain?"

"Just a little twinge now and then when I raise my arms. I've got some pills for that. But all in all, I feel fantastic."

"You look pretty chipper, considering."

"I didn't have open-heart surgery, Cheney, I just got a boob job."

It was like Elizabeth to minimize the seriousness of things, particularly when it had to do with her own health. That attitude had its advantages and disadvantages. She never complained, which was nice, but then she never went to a doctor until she had no choice. So far she had managed to dodge any fatal bullets.

"You want to see?"

"What do you mean? Here?" said Cheney, checking the back yard with a swivel of his head.

"We have ten-foot hedges. And I don't see any helicopters or *National Enquirer* photographers snooping around."

"I don't know."

"You want to see, don't you?" said Elizabeth playfully.

Cheney thought about arguing, but the truth was he really did want to see. "Okay."

Elizabeth parted her robe. "Close your eyes while I undo my industrial-strength bra."

Cheney did as instructed. He felt like a kid on Christmas morning waiting to unwrap his presents. He heard her working with her bra for what seemed like an eternity.

"Okay, open your eyes."

"Holy shit!" said Cheney. This was his best Christmas ever.

"You like?"

"Holy shit!"

"Your needle's stuck, Cheney."

"They're fabulous."

"And they're yours as long as you continue to be a good boy," she said, amused by Cheney's reaction. She could not recall seeing him so genuinely happy.

Cheney moved closer. "They're much bigger than I thought they'd be."

"Steven said they're a little swollen now, so they'll go down a bit."

"They . . . they stand right up there, don't they?"

"They're real breasts, Cheney, just like in the movies," said Elizabeth, gently refastening her bra and pulling her robe closed.

Cheney sat back in his chair and tried not to look disappointed.

"What's the matter with you?"

"Nothing."

"You have the look of a child whose toys have just been taken away from him."

"Sorry. This is going to take some getting used to."

"I hope so. Those things weren't cheap. Think of them as an extended vacation from which we'll both receive a considerable amount of pleasure."

Cheney was already thinking something like that.

And more. At the moment, however, he was thinking about how he could convince Elizabeth to quit her job and stay home with him. Forever. He shook his head and drank some wine. Perhaps he was being unrealistic.

"I can't wait to show them off at the Muldaurs' party tomorrow night," said Elizabeth with an arrogant smile.

"Are you sure you're up to it? I mean, you just had surgery."

"Cheney, I'm not planning to run a marathon, and I promise not to get into a fight. We're just going to go to a party and do a little slow dancing."

"And show off your tits."

"You bet your ass. You think my tits are better than Gloria's?"

Elizabeth was referring to Gloria Muldaur, wife of Benjamin Muldaur, the computer tycoon. Something Gloria had said to Elizabeth several years ago had rubbed her the wrong way, and ever since then the two had not gotten along. A couple of years ago, Gloria had gotten a boob job and had been flaunting her breasts at social functions ever since.

"Much better than Gloria's," said Cheney. He would have said so even if it weren't true. But it was, in fact, true.

"Good. I think so too."

The childishness of the discussion occurred to Cheney, and he asked his wife, "Do you think you're acting like a psychiatrist?"

"I act like a psychiatrist with my patients. That's enough. Would you rather I act like a psychiatrist in our personal life or a big-breasted tart?"

"Come to papa, you big-boobed babe," said Cheney, leaning over and kissing his wife passionately on the lips, careful not to jostle the precious merchandise.

eighteen

"I like your loft," said Jenny Clarke, as she walked in and looked around at the coliseum circle of screens that comprised most of the visible space.

"Thanks. It's very functional."

Gino took Jenny by the hand, led her through the circle of screens to the other side of the loft, and hit a light switch.

"Wow," said Jenny, genuinely impressed. The wall opposite her was hung with movie posters. Some she recognized, some she didn't. "You work on all those?"

"In one capacity or another."

"This movie, the one we're working on now, is the first movie I've been in."

"Really?" said Gino, waving a hand toward the white couch that ran along the poster wall.

Jenny sat down.

"Hey, I saw that one with my boyfriend when I turned sixteen," said Jenny, pointing to a poster of a werewolf fighting with a karate guy who was flying through the air, kicking and punching as he flew. "At the drive-in."

"I don't think I've ever been to a drive-in."

"Oh, it's great. Lotta privacy, if you know what I mean."

"Yeah, I think I do. Like some wine?"

"Sure."

Gino didn't ask whether she wanted red or white, chablis or cabernet. He would bring back a glass filled with wine, and she would take it and smile as though he had returned with the Holy Grail filled with Dom Perignon.

Gino hit another switch and a light came on in the kitchen. He poured two glasses of wine from an already open bottle, put the bottle back in the refrigerator, hit the light switch again, returned to the living room, handed one glass to Jenny, and sat down next to her.

"To the movies," he said.

Jenny smiled and drank as Gino drank. "This is really wonderful, you know?"

"How do you mean?"

"Well, I mean, here I am hanging out with a Hollywood director, drinking wine in his loft. I was in my very first scene this afternoon. . . . I mean, it doesn't get any better than this, does it?"

"I don't imagine it does," said Gino, smiling, trying not to let his condescension show. "Where are you from?"

"Michigan."

"Whereabouts?"

"Canton. Near Detroit."

Gino shook his head and smiled. He didn't know what the fuck to say about that. He had never been to Michigan. Probably had known people from there, but no one ever brought up the fact. Until tonight.

"You know, you've got great eyes," said Jenny, drinking liberally from her glass.

"Really?"

"Oh, yeah. I know eyes. My father is—well, he was; he's dead now—an optometrist. Your eyes kinda suck a person in, you know?"

He knew an ophthalmologist was a medical doctor and an optometrist wasn't. Or at least he didn't have to be. "Is that good—that my eyes 'suck you in'?"

"Sure, I guess. I mean, you're a director. You gotta have good eyes."

Gino nodded, not completely certain what to make of Jenny's comment. She was nervous and she wasn't making total sense. By nodding, not responding verbally, not trying to extricate her from her conversational awkwardness—which would have been the easy and polite thing to do—he made her even more nervous. Which was okay with him.

"I knew this guy, an amateur hypnotist," said Jenny, trying to keep the conversation going. "Name was Michael—well, that's not important. Anyhow, he made it so some guy lost all his four's."

"Pardon?"

"He hypnotized the guy and told him the number four didn't exist."

"You're kidding," said Gino. He had to smile. He had never heard of such a thing.

"Yes. I mean, no, I'm not kidding."

"So what happened?"

"When the guy came out from under hypnosis, he counted from one to ten and left out the four. Some guy held up two fingers and asked him how many fingers he saw. The guy said he saw two. Then someone held up four fingers and asked him how many fingers he saw, and the guy didn't answer."

"Hope the guy wasn't an accountant."

"Or had an appointment on the fourth floor," said Jenny, smiling, partly from the wine, partly from the humor of the hypothetical situation, partly from the giddiness of being here in a Hollywood director's loft. Okay, so the guy wasn't Scorsese or Spielberg, but hell, she wasn't Michelle Pfeiffer either. Not yet, anyhow.

"That's really wild. Wonder whatever happened to the guy."

"I dunno. Never saw him again."

The two were silent for a moment.

"You said this morning that I reminded you of an old girlfriend," said Jenny, after she had taken a healthy swig of wine.

"Yes. But she was more than a girlfriend."

Jenny thought about asking how much more, but she realized it would have been just as easy for Gino to have told her how much more as it was to give the vague answer he obviously wanted her to have.

"What about me reminds you most of her?"

"Your face."

"When's the last time you saw her?"

"She's . . . well, she passed on."

"I'm sorry," said Jenny, fearing she had put her foot in it. "I didn't mean to—"

"Don't worry about it. It's a logical question."

"Sometimes I just don't know when to keep my big mouth shut."

"I told you, don't worry about it. Let's talk about you. You said this was your first scene today?"

"In the movies. I did a lot of theater back in Michigan."

"Theater?"

"High school stuff mainly."

"What made you decide to come to Los Angeles?"

"There wasn't any other choice, right? I mean, if you wanna be in the movies, there's no place else to go. Also"—Jenny smiled and lifted her eyebrows in a philosophical gesture—"there was this guy. . . ."

"There usually is. Especially with someone as attractive as you."

Jenny smiled widely. "Thanks. I know I get jobs because of the way I look, but I can really act. Honest," she said, as though convincing Gino of that fact, at that moment, was the most important thing in the world. Perhaps it was. To her.

"I'm sure you can."

"Did you see—well, anything today when you were directing me?" There was a longing in her eyes that Gino had seen in the eyes of a thousand hungry actors. They were scaling a mountain on hands and knees, across broken glass. All they had to keep them going was their own confidence—which most of their acquaintances wrote off as wishful thinking—and the occasional compliment. Such compliments took the place of money; a compliment from a "real director" could sustain the pursuit of the elusive summit for . . . well, at least for another month or so.

"The camera loves you," he said. What he meant was, *The camera loves your chest*, but he didn't say that.

Jenny nodded good-naturedly and smiled. She had heard it all before, and she was determined that her body would be an asset, a door-opener, and that her talent would eventually outshine her 36 double-D's. "I'm having a showcase next Tuesday over at the Calabash Theater. It's a little hole in the wall on Cahuenga just off Hollywood Boulevard. I'm doing *Streetcar*. . . . I'd love for you to see me in it. I can leave your name at the door."

"I'll see what I can do. Jenny?"

"Yes?"

"Did you do what I asked you, about not telling anyone that you were coming here?"

"Of course."

"Good. You know how jealous people can get when they think a person might be getting the benefits of . . . favoritism."

"Boy, do I. Don't worry, I didn't even tell my roommate. She's a struggling actress." Jenny didn't say "too." No point in projecting a negative image. "I told her I was going to a movie and not to wait up."

"Good. You know, Jenny, all artists, or most *true* artists anyhow, want to do something meaningful. Something they can leave behind that outlasts a fad or a box office gross."

"A masterpiece?"

"Exactly. And I'm working on something, have been for some time now. I was thinking you might be perfect for one of the characters."

"You're kidding!" Jenny was overcome with a wave of possibilities. "What makes me . . . perfect for the part?" she said, unashamedly mining for compliments.

"The look."

"You mean I look like her." It was not a question.

"Yes."

"So the movie is about her?"

"Not exactly. It's about what life is ultimately about. Love. Trust. Betrayal. Pain. It's an endless cycle we go through."

"We?"

"Artists. We're very sensitive."

"Do you think a person can be too sensitive?"

"An artist must not shut down his senses. And that openness makes him vulnerable to heartbreak and pain. It's just the way of life. When a person loves you, she knows she can abuse you and you will forgive her," said Gino, not looking directly at Jenny.

"Do you really believe that?"

"Don't you?" Gino didn't wait for an answer. "There's no doubt about it. Giving your love to someone is like handing them a dagger and exposing your heart."

"That sounds very depressing."

"You're young. Idealistic. Let me ask you a question. When was the last time someone was in love with you?"

Jenny thought for a moment. "Fred. A guy I knew about a year ago."

"Was he really in love with you?"

"Yeah, big-time."

"You're not with him now, are you?"

"No."

"Who loved whom the most?"

"He loved me more than I loved him."

"And you left him, right?"

"Yeah, but there was a reason—"

"There's always a reason. But it's always the same result. The person who loves the most is always the person who gets his heart served up to him on a platter."

"I never really thought of it that way before. Is that what your movie's about?"

"In a way. You want me to show you?"

"What do you mean?"

"I've got a set for the movie in the next room."

"No kidding! Sure. Can I have some more wine?"

"You can have anything you want," said Gino.

"You know, this is like the greatest night of my life."

Gino just smiled and went to get the wine.

"More wine?"

"Not yet. I've got another sip or two left. This is quite a place," said Kimberly, looking out over the airport runway and a Cessna that was just now taxiing by their window.

"I like it."

"Kinda pricey," she said, referring to the menu.

"I can afford it," said Tony Boston.

The Hangar was located at Santa Monica Airport. Windows on three sides provided a view of small aircraft taking off and landing. Tony had called ahead and reserved a window table.

"It's risky taking a woman to an expensive restaurant on the first date."

"Why's that?"

"Because it's tough to top."

"Then I'll just have to be very imaginative."

"You come here often?"

"Once."

"How did it work out?"

"I went home alone," said Tony.

"Too bad."

"Not really. I came with Cheney."

They both laughed. Tony loved her laugh. But there wasn't much about Kimberly Gary he *didn't* like. Not now. Not in the beginning.

"I want to thank you for including me in the investigation as much as you have, Tony. I really didn't—"

Tony held up a hand. "No business tonight, okay?"

"Deal," she said with a smile. "No business. So, what else is there?"

"Pleasure," said Tony. Because she had given him his cue.

Kimberly finished the wine in her glass. Tony removed the bottle of Brander Chardonnay she had chosen and filled her glass. He was doing a lot of things on cue tonight.

"I love this wine. I did a story on Santa Barbara wineries about a year ago. Brander was my favorite winery. Very small. Friendly people. It's rare to find one of their bottles in a restaurant."

"I didn't know wine cost so much. I'm basically a beer and cocktail guy."

"Really? I would never have noticed," said Kimberly with as straight a face as she could muster. "Actually, I find it's better to judge a man less by *what* he drinks and more by how *much* he drinks."

"Why's that?"

"I don't like a man who falls asleep before his shift is over."

Right then Tony had the first thought that he might be getting himself into trouble.

Kimberly sipped silently, never taking her eyes from him. "You attracted to me?"

"Promise me something," he said.

"Tell me what it is first."

"Don't underestimate me, and I won't underestimate you."

"Fair enough."

"Yes, I'm attracted to you," said Tony. "You already knew that, didn't you?"

"I had my suspicions."

"But you like hearing me say so out loud."

Kimberly smiled.

"Look, Kimberly, I'm a little out of practice doing this kind of thing."

"What kind of thing?"

"Dating. Don't get me wrong, it isn't like I haven't dated before, it's just I haven't been very interested in anyone since my divorce."

"You want to talk about it?"

"Not particularly. It's not that I *don't* want to talk about it. You want to know anything?"

"How long were you married?"

"Four years."

"Any kids?"

"Nope. Kind of a blessing, I guess, the way things worked out. What about you?"

"No kids. Never married, really."

"Interesting way to put it."

"I met a guy in New York and we were married for a few minutes—a month, actually. Big mistake."

"What happened?"

"I stopped drinking vodka, for one thing," she said, smiling. "Amazing how different things look when you don't drink for a few days in a row. He was an unemployed actor—kind of redundant, don't you think? Anyhow, we were crazy about each other. I was working on creating a new novel form—something about a mosaic, each chapter seemingly having nothing to do with the others until a final chapter made them all fall together in a complete whole."

"Sounds fascinating."

"Sounded like downright genius, three A.M. in some actors' bar, bottle of vodka three-quarters dead, a bunch of drunks who hadn't read anything more weighty than *Variety* in the past ten years cheering me on, patting me on the back, pouring my vodkas neat.

"Meanwhile, through the drunken haze, I think I'm shacked up with the next James Dean. Now that's an original fantasy," said Kimberly.

In a way, as bad as he knew the story would end up, Tony found himself envying Kimberly. Envying the fact that she had lived, and lived through, that lifestyle. For all its dead-end streets and long odds, such a life sounded romantic. It was the kind of adventure most people, including Tony, would only read about or see in the movies. He supposed lots of people looked at *his* job the same way.

"When you're young, you believe in dreams," said Kimberly. "Every failure's just part of the process at twenty-one, twenty-two. Every tiny success, every little victory, is an obvious stepping stone on the road to glory."

"You sound a little bitter."

"Just because it all turned to shit? Maybe it was because I came home early—from the job I had supporting myself and James Dean—and found him in bed with my best friend."

"I've heard that tune."

"Really? My best friend was a man."

"Well, that *is* a variation on a theme," said Tony, trying to keep a straight face. He was not entirely successful. "You seem to have come through it okay."

"Yeah, well, I'm a survivor."

"Takes courage."

"Not really. Not when you consider the alternative. I'm just like everybody else my age, except maybe I've got a feeling that some of my dreams can still come true. Not all of them, but enough so it makes it worth getting up in the morning. What about you, Tony? You got any dreams still standing?"

"I used to dream about being married, having a beautiful wife and a couple kids, and being the chief of detectives. Got one out of three."

"If you were a baseball player, those kinda numbers would get you five million a year."

"But I'm not a baseball player. I'm just a cop. A good cop, but something's missing."

"Maybe you need a dream."

"Nah," said Tony, shaking his head. "I think what I need feels a little more like flesh and blood."

They looked at each other as a prop job landed and

made its way to the hangar. Tony had liked this woman before they sat down to dinner, and he liked her more now.

And he had the distinct feeling that she liked him too.

Tony picked up the last french fry from his plate and put it in his mouth. Despite his desire to look cool in doing so, a drop of ketchup dripped from his mouth onto the plate.

The blood dripped from her breasts. She writhed in agony, her hands secured in leather restraints above her head. She screamed as the blood poured from her mutilated breasts, down her stomach, her legs, and onto the floor.

"Ahhhhhh!" she screamed again, as loud as she could. Then, much more calmly, she said, "Is that more like it?"

"That's good," said Gino, as he looked up from where he was adjusting a light, just off to Jenny's right. He stood and walked over in front of her. "Are you sure you understand what to do?"

"I'm writhing and screaming; then you come in through the window. You're coming through the window out of frame, right?"

"Don't worry, I've already shot that part of the scene. It'll cut together perfectly. Let me worry about that. I'm just going to come through the window to give you a more realistic cue to play off."

"Okay, so you unfasten my hands from the leather restraints, you say a few things to me, you kiss my breasts, and then you wipe away the blood."

"Right."

"You sure this isn't just another slasher flick?"

"You're looking at just one level. There's a metaphor at work here. I heal you with my kiss. With my love. I take away the pain."

"But it sounds like the opposite of what you told me before. That all love eventually turns to pain."

"Maybe I just can't stop trying to find a happy ending."

Gino walked back to the camera and looked through the lens. "Fabulous. You ready?"

"Ready."

Gino picked up a plastic squeeze bottle full of fake blood and walked over to Jenny. "I'm only going to shoot this once, so make it great!"

"Don't worry."

"I know you can do it. Otherwise I wouldn't have asked you," Gino said, as he squeezed blood all over Jenny's chest. Then he removed a knife from his pocket.

"What's that?" asked Jenny nervously, even though she could clearly make out what it was.

"A knife." He grabbed it by the handle.

Jenny gasped.

Gino smiled and demonstrated the knife with the retractable blade by shoving it into the palm of his hand several times. He hit a tiny button on the side of the knife and the blade stayed inside the handle. Then he removed some adhesive substance from his pocket and put a dab on her chest, right around her nipple, and smeared another dab on the knife. Then he put the knife on her breast, where it stuck out straight. "Voilà!"

"Looks like the real thing," said Jenny, looking down at the fake knife on her chest.

"Movie magic. You ready?"

"Let's do it."

"Okay, I'll start the camera and give it a verbal slate. Start screaming immediately afterward. I won't yell action. Got it?"

"Got it."

Gino walked back to the camera, looked through the lens one more time, made sure the microphone and boom were out of the picture, then started the camera.

He raced over to where he had a window set up, the glass inside it already shattered. "Scene seven, Take one!"

Jenny had had her eyes closed from the time Gino started back toward the camera. She was getting into character. She began to scream and writhe again. She started to howl, to moan, all the time struggling in vain against the restraints.

She jerked suddenly when she felt Gino's lips on her breasts. She looked up into his loving eyes as he removed the fake knife from her chest, tossed it on the floor, and kissed away the blood until she was healed.

And as he unfastened her hands from the leather restraints Jenny fell into his arms, clinging desperately to him, clinging to life, to the safety of his love, as her chest heaved with giant sobs of genuine gratitude.

"I really appreciate you taking me to such a nice restaurant."

"My pleasure," said Tony as he stood in the living room of Kimberly Gary's Westwood apartment. He thought it was a well-appointed place, decorated in grays and pinks and chrome, with framed prints on the wall that were probably chosen more to fit into the color scheme than because of any preference for the work itself. Chosen by the building's interior designer, probably. The apartment looked neat, certainly much neater than his own place, but it didn't look lived in. There was nothing here that looked or felt like Kimberly Gary. It felt like a nicely decorated storage facility where she stashed her things.

"You want something to drink?" she said, her head stuck into the refrigerator in the kitchen area, which was separated from the one-step-down white-carpeted living room in which Tony stood looking at the reading material on her coffee table.

"You wouldn't happen to have any of that Chardonnay we had for dinner, would you?"

"I'm a working girl, not a rich cop like you," she said, closing the door, wedging a bottle under her arm, picking up a corkscrew and two glasses from the countertop, and heading into the living room.

"*Esquire*," said Tony, referring to a magazine on the coffee table. "I thought that was a men's magazine."

"I like the writing. Here, would you open this?"

Tony took the chilled bottle of wine and opened it.

Kimberly held out the two glasses, one at a time, for Tony to fill. "It's not Brander, but it has a similar oaky flavor."

Tony set down the bottle on one of the *Esquire* magazines and held out his glass. "To the prettiest reporter I ever met."

Kimberly held out her glass. "To the nicest cop I ever met."

"Not very ego-stroking."

"To the sexiest cop I ever laid my eyes on—or anything else, for that matter. How's that?"

"I'll drink to that."

"Tastes like butterscotch to me," said Tony, making sure to exhale some of the aroma through his nose the way Kimberly had instructed him at dinner.

"Have a seat."

Kimberly sat down on the couch. Tony sat down next to her. Close enough so that their knees almost touched.

"You really mean that? I mean, about me being the sexiest cop you ever met?"

"I meant the sexiest cop I met *today*. Besides, I had to say something, otherwise we'd still be standing." Kimberly looked at him playfully, just to make sure his feelings weren't hurt. "You are a sexy man. Trust me." She leaned over and kissed him very lightly on the mouth, withdrew, and drank some wine.

"That was nice."

"Yes, it was. I've got to warn you, I may come across like a highway to hell, but I'm really more like a yellow caution light when it comes to sex. I don't hit the sheets on the first date."

"In that case . . ." He faked a move to leave.

"Very male."

"Count on it," said Tony confidently. It was a confidence he hadn't felt with a woman for some time. Maybe it was the wine, he thought. Maybe it was something else.

"I like you, Tony. Let's just—"

"Whatever you do, don't tell me you want to be friends. Last woman who told me that took all my money and almost killed me."

"She must've been pretty mean."

"She was. And whatever instinct for the jugular she lacked, her attorney more than made up for."

"Sounds like you don't like women much."

"I like them fine. Maybe too much." Tony exhaled deeply. "It's not easy being a cop's wife."

"That's bullshit."

"Pardon?" said Tony, genuinely taken aback.

"I said that's bullshit. Your wife doesn't need you to make excuses for her. She knew you were a cop when she married you, right?"

"Right. But sometimes you just don't know what you're getting into until you're into it."

"She was over eighteen when you married her, I presume."

Tony nodded.

"She was an adult, for chrissake. Capable of making decisions. Lawyers could make Hitler sound like a victim. Maybe she believes it, but you don't have to. Give yourself a fucking break."

Tony nodded. What she said made sense. He had heard it before, but no one had made the case so forcefully.

"So, Tony, I don't want to be your friend. At least not *just* your friend. I promise that if things don't work out for us romantically, you can never count on me to help you move, to be a shoulder to cry on, to remember your birthday, or any other nice thing friends do for each other. Fair enough?"

"Sounds fair," said Tony.

"So let's just let it happen, okay?"

"I'd like it to happen," said Tony.

Silence.

"Maybe I'd better get going."

"I had a nice time, Tony."

"Me, too." Tony put his arm around Kimberly and held her body close to his. He was aware of her breasts, her perfume, her moist lips, the smell and texture of her hair. His senses drank in the experience of her.

Tony got yet another good-night kiss at the door and left, walking slowly, rather aimlessly, toward the elevator, looking back over his shoulder and smiling at Kimberly, who stood in front of her door smiling back at him.

As he rode down in the elevator, alone, he tried to quell some of his enthusiasm. He didn't want to set himself up just to get knocked down. He had done that before. More than once.

So when he walked out of the apartment building, he waited until he got into his car and closed the door, before he let out a verbal high-five at the top of his lungs.

"All right! That was great!"

"Really?" Jenny looked up into Gino's eyes. They really were hypnotic. And, she noticed now, very kind. She had lost herself in the part, and it was taking some time to slip back into reality. "I felt like I really *was* that woman."

"I know. And I love you for it. You were brilliant."

The smile came back to her face again. "Thanks." She was beaming.

"How did it feel?"

"It was horrible."

"No, I mean, how did it feel when I released you?"

"It was . . ." Jenny took a deep breath, tilted her head back, then forward again. She shook her head. "I can't find the words."

"Try. Think about it. It's important to me."

Jenny took a deep breath and focused on the nightmare again. "It was . . . obviously it was a relief, but it was more than that. Much more than that. It was like . . ."

"Redemption?" Gino said the word as a holy man might whisper the secret text of a sacred prayer.

Jenny started to shake her head, then stopped. She considered the word, its meaning, the context, and her smile returned. Slowly. Spreading across her face as the recognition dawned inside her. "Yeah. It was like a new life. Like falling off a cliff into endless darkness and then suddenly being pulled back into the light."

"Redemption."

"Yeah, redemption."

Jenny leaned forward and put her arms around Gino's neck. Looked him straight in the eye. Feeling as though she were an equal for the first time. And if not an equal, certainly closer to it than she had been when she had walked through the door an hour earlier.

"Did you really mean what you said?"

"What?" said Gino.

"About me being brilliant," she said. Although she also meant about him saying he loved her. Or, more precisely, that he loved her *for it*. Same thing, on a night full of wine and promise. A night when she felt like a star, like it could really, really fucking happen, for the first time in her life.

"I meant it."

Jenny kissed Gino again. This time a little more fully on the mouth. Lingering a couple of seconds longer. She did not feel used. Not after he told her she was brilliant. Because she knew, fucking knew, that it was not some bullshit lie to get between her legs. It was the truth. And she could not remember feeling better about herself or her chances to redeem her life. Redeem? Fallen from grace, fallen from parental and personal expectation. She knew she was talented. Knew she would eventually rise to the top. Redemption. She was redeeming a life of failure for a life of success. Redemption. Salvation from a life of, if not sin, then at least slumming expectations. Deliverance from a type of hell that people who did not risk never really knew. She had risked. Everything.

"So what now?" asked Jenny, her eyes on fire.

"I just need to shoot one more scene."

"What scene is that?" she asked, leaning back from her embrace. She was not put off, not disappointed, she merely wanted to concentrate, focus.

"It's the scene that immediately leads up to the scene we just shot."

Because all movies are shot out of sequence, the idea of shooting the scene that preceded the one they just shot seemed perfectly natural. "Do I have lines?"

Gino smiled. "Very important lines. Let me get the script and explain the scene to you."

Jenny was daydreaming about acceptance speeches when Gino came back with a piece of paper and handed it to her. She read it over. Focused on it. After a few moments she looked up and said, "Kind of graphic, isn't it?"

"Graphic?"

"I dunno, it seems . . ."

"Think about it. It's important. You must be this person."

Jenny read the lines over again. And again. She looked up into Gino's hypnotic eyes. "She seems so . . ."

"Yes?"

"Cruel."

"You really think so?"

"Yes."

"Why?"

"I think that's obvious," said Jenny.

"Why? Because she was lost to her passion? Is that bad?"

"No, it's just that—well, the things she says must make her boyfriend . . ."

"Yes?"

"It's gotta be tough to hear that kind of thing from someone you love."

"Tough?" said Gino. "Tough?" he repeated, raising his voice.

"Well, maybe that's not exactly the right word."

"What *is* the right fucking word, then? You're supposed to be her, right?"

"Yes, but—"

"But what? Are you an actress or what? Tough? Is that really the word?"

"No."

"Then what is?"

"Horrible."

"Horrible? From whose point of view? You aren't her lover. You are the woman. She's not thinking that what she says is horrible. Concentrate. Concentrate!" said Gino, standing and starting to walk, to stalk around the young malleable actress.

"Okay, okay." Jenny tried to focus. On the character. On the process. Gino was trying to help her. To help her find her best performance. Focus. Concentrate. On the character. On her art. On Gino.

"I'm waiting!" shouted the director as he circled Jenny.

"She's a slut!"

"Is she?"

"No."

"Focus."

"She's lost."

"To what? Tell me who she is! Tell me who you are! Tell me!"

"I'm someone who is a slave to my body."

"Good! Tell me! Tell me!"

"I'm a good girl. I want to do the right thing, but something . . ."

"Yes?"

"Something's stopping me. I don't want to hurt anyone. But—"

"But what?"

"It's unavoidable."

"Because?"

Jenny didn't know.

"Because!" pressed the director.

"I don't know."

"Tell me!"

"I don't know. I really don't know!"

Gino reached out and slapped Jenny across the face.

Her immediate reaction was submerged by the whole experience, and oddly she did not take it personally. She started to cry. In character. "I don't know. I don't know why I did it."

"Did what?" shouted Gino.

Jenny did not answer. Through her tears.

"Did what!"

"Have sex with another man," she whimpered.

Gino slapped her again.

"Did what!"

"Hurt you."

Gino did not slap her again. He got down on his knees in front of Jenny, gently took her face in his hands, and lifted it so her eyes were now even with his own. "You're incredible," he said.

Jenny grabbed Gino and pulled him as close to her as she could. Sobbing, dripping tears on his shoulder, she felt at once destroyed and re-created.

Never more alive.

"I want to get this on film," said Gino, wanting to capture the genuine moment before it disappeared.

Jenny sat up straight, wiped her eyes, and nodded. She was clay, Gino the artist.

"Let me put you in the restraints again and I'll use a verbal slate. When I come to you this time, I'll be wearing a mask. Don't let that throw you."

Jenny nodded and moved back into the middle of the set.

"Just one more take and it'll all be over," said Gino, as he secured her wrists in the leather restraints. He kissed her lightly on the lips and said, "You're fabulous."

Jenny closed her eyes, put herself in trance. Focused on all the emotions she had just experienced. Tried not to let them escape. Tried to bottle them up for one final explosive performance. A performance that must be more than a performance. It must appear real. Be real. She knew she could do it. Knew she could do anything. After all, Gino had told her she was fabulous.

Jenny could not recall being this attracted to a man for a very long time. How else could she explain what she was feeling?

She looked at the masked man, her eyes fluttering under the sheer weight of the sensuality called for in the script. When she spoke her last line, the man moved forward, knife in hand.

"I can't help myself," she whispered.

As the man raised the knife in the air.

It lingered there a long moment, she thought. She looked into the masked man's eyes, and in that instant she knew.

She screamed as the knife penetrated her breasts.

Over and over again.

The blood dripped from her breasts. She writhed in agony, her hands secured in the leather restraints above her head. She screamed as the blood poured from her mutilated breasts, down her stomach, her legs, and onto the floor.

"Ahhhhhh!" she screamed again as loud as she could.

Finally the screaming stopped.

And the camera continued to roll.

nineteen

Cheney spent most of the rest of the next day running errands for Elizabeth and jogging six miles instead of the usual four so he could comfortably fit into the suit he was planning to wear to the party that night. At various times during his run Cheney found himself fantasizing about what it was going to be like to have sex with the "new" Elizabeth.

Tony called when Cheney got back from his run. He had nothing new to report about the case, but he could not stop talking about his date with Kimberly Gary and the fact that they were getting together again that evening.

When Tony asked Cheney if there was something wrong, Cheney said he hadn't slept well. Then he hung up and took a long hot shower.

Two hours later, Cheney was pacing the living room floor looking at his watch. It was nearly eight-fifteen, and they were supposed to be there by eight-thirty. Even though they were only five minutes from their destination, he was getting anxious. He had not heard a sound from their bedroom for nearly thirty minutes.

Finally the door opened. Cheney looked up.

And Cinderella emerged.

"Wow!" said Cheney. Elizabeth was wearing a knee-length black velvet Christian Dior dress, black stockings, and shoes. Her hair was teased into a younger look. She was wearing the diamond earrings he had bought her for their fifth wedding anniversary. But all those things were just side dishes to the main course. The black dress was low cut—not down to her pubic bone, but lower than any other dress Cheney could remember Elizabeth wearing. Women usually knew their strengths and weaknesses. Smart women accented their strengths and downplayed their weaknesses. Elizabeth had always had good legs, but her breasts, although Cheney had never had any complaints, were clearly not her best feature.

Until now.

In anticipation of this party, Elizabeth had obviously purchased the dress before her operation. It now fit her as though it had been made for her.

Elizabeth walked over to Cheney, very sexily, he thought, moving her hips from side to side a little exaggeratedly. Her confident eyes never left his as she kissed him, her mouth open. Like the old days, thought Cheney.

For some strange reason the image of Frankenstein's monster flashed in his mind, then was gone.

"You like?" she said, nearly an octave lower than her normal voice.

"We don't have to go to the party, you know," said Cheney hopefully.

"I wouldn't miss it for the world." She kissed her husband again. "I'll be right back. Save my place." Then she walked back into the bedroom to get something. Cheney couldn't figure out what it could be. She looked like she already had everything. And then some.

Petty came into the room just as Elizabeth left. "So, she gonna let you take 'em for a walk?" she said as she passed Cheney. She just kept going, not waiting for a response.

He hoped she liked it. He had slaved over the special sauce for nearly three hours. Everyone and his brother said they made pasta sauce, whatever the hell that meant these days, but Tony used his mother's recipe. He used real anise seeds. Not anise flavoring, not anise drops, not essence of anise. Real fucking anise. Sugar. Olive oil. Not olive oil from some supermarket, but from an Italian deli. Wine. Sautéed carrots. Sautéed onions, mushrooms, and peppers. His own personal contribution was sun-dried tomatoes marinated in olive oil, a mild rice vinegar, and garlic. And when he sautéed his ingredients in the correct order, in the right combination of wine and olive oil, it was not so much cooking as it was a form of art.

And he made his own pasta. Didn't just *boil* it, *made* it. Cheney had turned him on to making pasta. After the divorce, Tony had time on his hands. And the extra time he had at home, he tried to fill with something besides TV. Making pasta relaxed him. Killed some time. That was how he had looked at it at first. But then he had gotten into it.

In fact, he had two pasta machines, a hand crank and an electric model. Truth was, he used the electric model more than the hand crank. But he had made an exception tonight. This was an occasion.

The good news was that Kimberly Gary had agreed to have dinner at his condo.

The bad news was that she had passed up his invitation to pick her up.

Tony, who was not at his most secure with women yet, had immediately seen the negative. Kimberly was willing to come to dinner but wanted to have the option of beating a fast retreat if he started coming on to her.

Tony checked his watch. She should be here any minute. The sauce was ready and the pasta was hanging limply over the slats in the wooden pasta rack.

The doorbell rang. Tony took off his apron and went to the door.

"Hi," said Kimberly.

"Hi," said Tony. He was glad he didn't have to say much more than that. Kimberly was dressed in a black vest with a white long-sleeved shirt underneath, a flower-print skirt that was sheer and positively seethrough when she stood between him and the floodlight that lit the stairs, and black stockings and cowboy boots.

"Come in."

Kimberly walked inside and set down her purse on

a table as Tony closed the door. "Something smells wonderful."

"Just a little something I whipped up. Hope you like pasta."

"I love pasta."

The party was going strong at the Muldaur home when Cheney pulled the 300E into the semicircular driveway, got out, and let a young red-suited valet park the car. Maybe it was just his imagination, but Cheney could swear the valet gave him a wink as he handed him a claim check after letting Elizabeth out the passenger side. Cheney wondered if Elizabeth was wearing underwear. He shook his head and tried to get a grip. His mind was definitely adrift in unfamiliar waters.

Cheney wasn't sure if the room went silent when Elizabeth walked in, but it seemed that way. Cheney was a firm believer in the idea that we all see what we believe, that we select bits of information from the tidal wave available to us, and the information we select is information that tends to verify what we already consider to be true.

And so tonight, whenever Cheney would catch someone staring, they would always be staring at Elizabeth. At Elizabeth's chest.

Cheney was not the jealous type. Never had been. He was completely secure in his relationship with Elizabeth. He knew other men were attracted to her, and he liked that. Partly, he assumed, because he knew she was completely devoted to him, partly because he was a man and he liked the way she made him look.

When Benjamin and Gloria Muldaur approached from across the room, Cheney got the distinct impression that Benjamin was pulling his wife much the same as a person would pull a stubborn animal by the leash, the animal's feet planted in the earth, ripping up turf as it was being pulled along.

"Cheney, Elizabeth," said Benjamin, extending his hand to Cheney and bussing Elizabeth on the cheek.

Gloria stood there looking like a rabbit caught in the headlights.

When Benjamin said, "There's something different about you, Elizabeth," it looked to Cheney as though Gloria might faint.

"I've been working out a little more," said Elizabeth, trying her best to conceal a smile. If the moment could be compared to a sporting event, thought Cheney, it would have been like hitting a grand-slam home run in the bottom of the ninth to win the World Series.

"Cheney, I've got a Chardonnay I'd like you to give me your opinion of. A client sent me a case of it. It's from a boutique winery in Napa. I think it's quite wonderful, actually," said Muldaur.

"I'd love to try it," said Cheney, who was known to his friends as the resident wine expert, or wine snob, depending on whether or not the person approved of Cheney's penchant for the grape.

The two men walked away, trading words like *vanilla* and *French oak*. Which left Gloria alone, still caught in the headlights. She smiled in a very strange way. Her lips curled upward, but all her other features remained down-turned and, Elizabeth thought, etched in genuine terror.

"Glad you could come, Elizabeth."

"I wouldn't have missed it for the world. Your party, that is. You've put on quite a spread."

Gloria's attention turned quickly to her body. Was Elizabeth referring to her hips? Of course, she had put on a couple of pounds, but she hadn't thought it was noticeable.

"I think I'll grab something to eat," said Elizabeth. "I'm famished. That's the great thing about working out." She leaned conspiratorially close to Gloria. "You can eat anything you want." Pause. "By the way, I haven't seen you at the club lately."

"I've been busy," said Gloria defensively.

"Of course," said Elizabeth with an understanding wink. Then she walked slowly away toward the buffet table. She felt like running, she was so hungry, but she played it cool. Take it all in, she told herself. Moments like this don't come around very often.

Tony tried not to trip over his expectations, but he looked at Kimberly Gary as a once-in-a-lifetime experience. It was difficult to determine whether he was attracted to her because she was so intelligent or because she was so beautiful. With the women he had dated in the past, there was always a clear-cut choice.

Kimberly Gary had both. In spades. Tony had never known anyone like her. He was hypnotized by her: by the way she walked, by the way she held her own in conversation without being contentious, by the way she laughed.

"Great wine," said Kimberly. She sat on the love

seat in Tony's living room, next to Tony. Not close enough so that their knees touched, but close.

"Something Cheney turned me on to."

"I like him."

"Cheney? He's the best. He's been my mentor. Besides that," said Tony, pausing for emphasis, "he's been my friend. Helped me through some pretty tough times."

"Does he think the Barbara Sanford case is related to the other murders?"

"So, we're talking business now?"

"We're just talking. If you don't want to discuss it, we won't."

"It's hard to tell what Cheney thinks. He usually doesn't share his opinions until he's on solid ground. By the way, if I ever read in the newspaper anything I tell you in off-the-record situations like this, we have no relationship—friend, business, or otherwise."

Kimberly smiled. "I like it when you talk tough."

"I'll keep that in mind."

"Do that," said Kimberly. She leaned over and kissed Tony lightly on the mouth.

"She wasn't doing any kind of movie I was aware of," said Jamison Sanford. He had caught Cheney's eye and rescued him from what was becoming Benjamin Muldaur's seemingly endless pedantic monologue on the state of California Chardonnays compared with French whites.

"Do you think you would know if she was?"

Sanford didn't answer immediately. "Obviously, there is a great deal I did not know about my wife. I purposely tried not to pry. As you can well imagine, a man with my means could have hired a detective and had her followed twenty-four hours a day. That's just not my style. All I knew, all that was important, was that she was a person with a good heart, that she loved me, and that we were together. I could count on one hand the number of evenings she wasn't waiting for me when I got home. What she did during the day was her business. I trusted her."

Cheney thought about asking him what he trusted her to do or not to do, but he didn't. Cheney knew guys like Sanford. They were realists. Young wife, secure in himself, he did not want total disclosure. He expected certain things, and as long as those require-ments were met cheerfully, lovingly, no questions would be asked. If there was another life, if there was someone else, it was the wife's responsibility to be discreet, to make sure nothing unpleasant washed up on the shore of an otherwise happy relationship.

"Who do you think would know what Barbara did during the day?"

"Kyoko. But you've already spoken with her."

"Maybe I need to ask her more specific questions."

"By the way," said Sanford, "Elizabeth looks stun-ning this evening."

"Yes, she does, doesn't she?" said Cheney as he spotted his wife standing by the punch bowl talking animatedly with another woman, whom Cheney did not recognize.

"Here's to appreciating life as it happens, not leav-ing it to cameras to remember."

The two men drank, both looking at Elizabeth. But Cheney knew Sanford was thinking of someone else.

Cheney was convinced that one of the great abilities of life, perhaps the most desirable one, was to appreciate life as it happened. He was a lucky man. And as he caught Sanford's sad face out of the corner of his eye, Cheney felt twice blessed.

To have Elizabeth. And to appreciate the fact that he had her.

The flickering candlelight cast Kimberly's body in flattering detail. From behind, her bare back arched, her dirty-blond hair barely touching her shoulders. Tony handled her gently, as one would handle a piece of art. His hands gently grasped her small round hips and pulled her closer to him, pulled himself deeper into her as she made the intimate sounds that lovers make.

He stroked her back, caressed it, outlining her spine with his finger. He was surprised at how smooth her skin was. Not that it was smooth, but that it was *so* smooth.

Without disengaging herself from Tony, Kimberly turned over so she was looking up into his eyes. Tony took in her small, firm breasts, flat stomach, and slim waist. He put her knees over his shoulders and pulled himself deeper into her. Her eyes fluttered and she moaned again.

Tony could not take his eyes off her.

And when he came, after she had climaxed several times, he collapsed next to Kimberly on sheets that were now tangled and soaked.

Kimberly cuddled up next to Tony and rested her head on his shoulder. Kissed him on the ear. And when Kimberly whispered the word "intermission" gently and sexily, Tony figured he was going to need a little inspiration.

In the candlelit room, he did not have to look very far.

The party went on for several hours, and each time Cheney bumped into his wife, she seemed happier and more confident than the last time. Each time she had an anecdote of someone else's reaction to her new look. Most people really couldn't pinpoint exactly what was different about her, only that she looked good.

It was nearly 1 A.M. when they said their goodbyes and left.

"You tired?" said Cheney as he looked at Elizabeth, who was leaning her head back on the car's leather headrest.

"I'm exhausted."

"I hope you have a little strength left."

"Don't worry, Cheney. You still get your reward." She paused and slipped her hand between Cheney's legs. "And so do I," she said, in a low, husky voice.

As Cheney ran a red light.

"Cops are really horny guys."

"Why would you say that?" asked Tony, as he lay nearly spent a second time. *Nearly* spent because this time he didn't come. Didn't want to. Well, wanted to but wasn't taking any chances on this respite becoming a second intermission. He was keeping a few bullets in the gun. Just in case.

"Oh, I don't know."

"You have sex with a lot of cops?"

"Plenty."

"What's plenty?"

"Less than a thousand," she said playfully. "But don't worry, I didn't have sex with any other cops . . . today."

"You know what this means, don't you?"

"What?"

"It means we *definitely* can't be friends."

"I thought we already had this discussion."

"Well, this makes it official. Once penetration takes place, that's it. All over, done, finished."

"So we're stuck now, right? I mean, we've got to be lovers, then."

"That's about the size of it," said Tony.

"Good thing you're such a good lover," she said, tickling his ear with her tongue.

End of intermission.

I wanna sigh in your arms. I wanna cry in your arms. I wanna lie in your arms. The lyrics of a song Elizabeth had been humming earlier played in Cheney's head as he busied himself in the kitchen putting together a small tray of delights. Petty had gone to her sister's for the night.

He removed a box, wrapped in a red ribbon, from a drawer. In it were two truffles, chocolate with Amaretto, Elizabeth's favorite. Four dollars a piece. They were concocted from chocolate actually made on the premises in a little shop in Brentwood. Elizabeth and Cheney went there whenever they felt like bestowing minor decadent pleasures on each other.

Cheney took a single red rose from inside the refrigerator and put it in a crystal vase. He set the vase and the box with the ribbon around it on a silver tray, which they had received as a wedding present.

This was going to be a night to remember. He tried to stop himself. Stop himself from creating unrealistic expectations. He had missed Elizabeth the past couple of months. They had acknowledged the fact that they had been drifting apart. Not because they didn't love each other. Scheduling. Professional demands. Hers this time, not his. But that would be over soon. Things were getting under control. He wanted tonight to be perfect.

They knew each other so well. Think of a number between one and ten, they had often challenged each other. Most of the time they could guess the same number. Other couples said they couldn't do it. Cheney and Tony Boston couldn't do it. Cheney knew what Elizabeth was thinking.

What she was thinking as she . . .

I wanna sigh in your arms. I wanna cry in your arms. I wanna lie in your arms. Cheney knew the song. Knew the last line.

I wanna die in your arms. He felt an arctic wave goose-bumping his flesh. The tray shook, and he dropped it on the hall table. He raced down the hallway toward their room.

"Oh, my God!" said Cheney to no one. Elizabeth

was lying on the floor, her mouth open, her eyes rolled back, and blood trickling from her lips.

Kimberly rolled her eyes back in her head as she climaxed again, this time pounding halfheartedly on Tony's chest. "Stop it! Stop it! I can't come anymore. It hurts."

Finally, Tony did stop. Again. He was amazing himself with this woman. She had inspired him to new heights. He lay down on his back and pulled her close to him, aware of the tiny earthquakes still exploding in her body.

As he lay there, her body shaking involuntarily next to his, drunk with the sensation of Kimberly holding him tightly between her legs for hours, Tony was thinking this just might be the best night of his life.

Then the phone rang.

And suddenly Tony realized that that was not true.

"I'll be right there," he said.

twenty

It all happened so fast.

Cheney administered CPR. Got her heart beating. Dialed 911.

Paramedics running through the house.

Lights flashing outside.

Neighbors gathered around.

Scribbling a quick note to Petty.

Riding downtown in the ambulance.

Meeting Dr. Blomberg in ER.

Watching Elizabeth being pushed on a gurney, unconscious.

In the car on the way home from the party she had said she was tired. A hint? Could he have acted on that information? Could he have saved her life?

Cheney had been in hospitals before. Standing around or sitting around, waiting to find out whether a person lived or died. A person he cared about: a fellow cop, a partner, his father, his mother. The waiting was gut-wrenching. All kinds of promises made, if only . . .

But this was different. This was Elizabeth. *My God, this was Elizabeth!* His wife. His young, healthy wife.

Cheney took a deep breath and said, "Oh, God." Again. He couldn't think of anything else to say. Or anyone else to say it to.

"Cheney!" said Tony, hurrying down the hall toward his friend.

Cheney looked up. He tried to smile, but the muscles in his face wouldn't work. He felt his eyes starting to tear. He swallowed hard, in an attempt to hold the emotions back.

"What happened?"

"I don't know. I went into the bedroom, and she was lying on the floor."

"I'm sure she's gonna be okay," said Tony.

Cheney realized that was what everybody always said when they could think of nothing else to say. He would probably be hearing it a lot.

"Yeah," said Cheney, nodding. "The doctors are with her now. I'm just waiting here. . . ." His voice trailed off. He wasn't able to complete the thought. He tried to focus on his immediate environment, but his attention was sucked back into the black hole. Into the nightmare.

"How long she been in?"

Cheney looked at his watch. "About an hour."

"Was she . . . ?"

"She never—that is, she *hasn't* regained consciousness since I found her. Actually, since before then. I was out in the kitchen." Cheney stared off into space.

"I was fixing up this little tray. You know, the one we got at our wedding?"

Tony looked at his friend. Knew what he was going through, or at least the process. Knew he was in shock. So he just nodded and said, "Yeah," even though he did not remember.

"You know, the silver tray?"

Tony nodded again.

"Yeah, well, I had truffles—the kind she likes, Amaretto, hand-made chocolates. . . ." Cheney spoke slowly, half to Tony, half to the institutional green wall opposite him. "I had a red rose in a crystal vase. Perfect. It was going to be a perfect night."

"Sounds very romantic."

Cheney turned to his friend with a pitiful look of desperation in his eyes. "It *was* romantic, Tony. It was going to be so romantic, you know? I mean, I love her, Tony. I love her so fucking much. . . .'

Cheney had cried twice in his life. The first time was when his first child was born. The second time was when his mother died.

This was the third time. He broke down and sobbed in Tony's arms, repeating his love for the woman who lay a few yards away behind sterile doors, fighting for her life.

And a big piece of Cheney's.

When the large double doors opened at the end of the corridor, Steven Blomberg and another man, an older man with a full head of white hair, walked toward Cheney, the doors flip-flopping closed behind them. They wore white coats, open loosely in the front.

But the only thing Cheney noticed was the fact that neither man was smiling. He stood, his mouth so dry he could hardly speak. Tony stood alongside his friend.

Cheney was full of questions, but he knew the doctors would need no prompting. They knew what his questions were. They also knew the answers. Or at least some of them.

"She's alive, Mr. Cheney," said the older doctor.

"This is Dr. Mendelsohn," said Blomberg. "He's a neurosurgeon." The introduction had come second, for obvious reasons.

Cheney didn't give a flying fuck who this guy was. All he wanted to know was how Elizabeth was. But the word *neurosurgeon* hit him as though he were a quarterback blindsided by a six-foot-six three-hundred-pound linebacker. He hadn't seen it coming. And when he felt the full weight of the blow, the effect was shattering.

"What else?" said Cheney, realizing there was more and, whatever it was, it was more difficult to say than "She's alive." And, Cheney knew, it would be more difficult to hear.

"She's in a coma," said Mendelsohn.

Cheney nodded as though someone had just told him his table would be ready in ten minutes. He was trying to absorb it all. Three hours ago he was dancing and laughing with his wife, and now she was . . .

"Is she going to—uh, I mean, how long before she . . . wakes up?" said Cheney, clinching his jaw to keep himself from breaking down again.

"We're not sure," said Mendelsohn.

"I mean, like, a day, three days, a week, two weeks?"

"We don't know."

"You mean it could be more than two weeks?"

"Yes."

It was a simple answer, but to Cheney it spoke volumes. "You mean she might not come out of it. Ever." It was not a question.

Sensing the explosive nature of the moment, Blomberg jumped in. "Mr. Cheney, it is my opinion that Elizabeth—"

What gave this guy the right to call her Elizabeth? thought Cheney. She's my wife! I call her Elizabeth. Her friends call her Elizabeth. You are not her friend!

"—will come out of this very quickly."

"What does quickly mean?"

"A few hours. A day or two," said Blomberg.

"But she might not come out of it at all."

"Let's not look on the dark side."

Cheney thought about telling Blomberg that he was living on the dark side now and probably would continue to be stuck there until Elizabeth opened her eyes again. But he didn't. Instead he said, "What about . . . permanent damage?"

"You mean brain damage?" said Mendelsohn.

Cheney nodded.

Mendelsohn sighed. Cheney didn't like the sound of it. "There's really no way to know until she wakes up. People have been known to come out of comas after very long periods of time and live productive lives."

Productive lives, thought Cheney. Isn't that what people always say about the mentally or physically impaired—they were rehabilitated enough so they could live productive lives? Elizabeth was a psychiatrist. She worked with her mind, with her brain, with her wits. She used that truly superior intelligence to solve other people's problems. If her brain was damaged, what would constitute a productive life for her?

"The preliminary tests and scans we've done don't show any appreciable damage."

"Appreciable?"

"There was some bleeding in the brain."

Bleeding? Cheney knew nothing about his wife's condition. "What happened?"

"In layman's terms, a blood clot traveled from your wife's chest—"

Mendelsohn called Elizabeth "your wife." That showed respect.

"—into her brain and exploded. *Exploded* is not really correct, but in layman's terms that's pretty much what happened."

Cheney stood there staring into Mendelsohn's eyes for a moment. There was something the doctor said. What was it? "A blood clot traveled from your wife's chest." *Chest?*

"Does this have something to do with her . . . breast surgery?"

Mendelsohn and Blomberg exchanged quick out-of-the-corner-of-the-eye looks.

"I'm not responsible for what happened to Elizabeth," said Blomberg.

"To be fair to Dr. Blomberg, Mr. Cheney—"

Who the fuck cared about being fair to Blomberg, the guy who was on such familiar terms with his wife? thought Cheney.

"—the condition that caused your wife's seizure would not have shown up in any examination Dr.

Blomberg conducted or could have conducted. It's a very tragic situation that could not have been diagnosed."

"It's just one of those things," parroted Blomberg.

Cheney felt like knocking him on his ass and sending him sliding back through the double doors. Just one of those things! Maybe it was just one of those things to Blomberg. The young doctor would go back through those double doors, take off his coat, put on his jacket, and his life would be waiting for him just as he had left it. He had had a tough day, but hell, things happen. Just one of those things.

Cheney's life wasn't the same as it had been a few hours earlier, and it might never be the same again. The heart had been carved out of it.

"Where is she?"

"She's in intensive care."

"When can I see her?"

"I want you to understand there's nothing you can do right now," said Blomberg.

Cheney tried to control himself. "And I want you to understand that I want to see my wife. As soon as humanly possible."

"Couple of hours," said Mendelsohn.

"Let me know. I'll be right here."

Mendelsohn nodded. Then he and Blomberg turned and walked back into the inner sanctum.

Cheney just stood there watching them go. Stood there until the doors stopped flip-flopping. Stood there frozen, feeling his heart beat, listening to the sound of it pumping in his ears, the distant sound of a doctor being paged. He was vaguely aware of his friend standing next to him. Glad he was there.

"You okay?" asked Tony.

"No."

"I meant—"

"I know what you meant, Tony," said Cheney, turning to his friend, a smile trying to work on his face. "Only one thing's gonna make me feel okay."

Tony nodded. "Hungry?"

"Not really," said Cheney.

"Then walk me to the cafeteria and watch me eat, okay?" Tony wasn't really hungry either, but he knew it wasn't a good idea to let Cheney stand in the hall-way paralyzed with fear, undecided about what to do next, knowing he was going to have to wait around for at least two hours before he could see Elizabeth.

Movement. Action. Tony knew what to do. So did Cheney, but in this case Tony was going to have to do it for him.

The cafeteria food was as bad as he expected, but Tony ate it as if it were prepared by Wolfgang Puck himself. He was doing everything he could to help Cheney remember there was a routine, a connection to real life he could grab onto when he felt himself starting to drown.

"Could you, ah, pass the salt?" asked Tony.

After a second's hesitation, the request registered and Cheney passed the shaker to Tony, who turned it upside down and sprinkled salt all over his scrambled eggs. He rarely used salt. He just wanted Cheney to pick something up and hand it to him. He could see his mentor fading in and out of reality like a picture tube starting to blow.

"You know, I was gonna call you tonight."

After a moment Cheney said, "Yeah?"

"Yeah. You mind if I ask you a couple questions about the Sanford case?"

Cheney sighed. "Sure, I guess. I don't know how much help I'm going to be right now, you know."

"Thanks," said Tony. He wasn't trying to be disrespectful. Left to sit there and think, there was nothing Cheney could do for two hours but consider all the horrible possibilities awaiting him in the intensive care unit upstairs.

"We've got another one," said Tony.

"Another what?"

"Another victim with her chest sliced up and fake blood under her toenails."

The information only half registered with Cheney. He nodded as though he understood.

"I'm planning to interview the roommate and the mother tomorrow. If you wanna come along—"

"I'm gonna stay with Elizabeth till she wakes up," said Cheney, with an almost childlike innocence in his voice.

Tony nodded. But he knew the hospital probably wouldn't let him stay with Elizabeth around the clock.

"You like Maui?" said Cheney, out of the blue. Out of the darkness.

"Never been."

"Beautiful. Great golf, great food, fantastic views. Elizabeth and I are thinking of getting a condo there in a couple years. You know, I think maybe we should go there when she gets out of the hospital. Perfect place to recuperate. Take some time, build up her strength again."

"Yeah, that sounds like a good idea. Hell, maybe

I'll take a week off and come over and play some golf with you."

"You're always welcome. Always." Cheney looked his friend in the eye.

The two men were silent for a moment. Cheney ran a plastic stir stick around the edge of his coffee cup. When he looked up at Tony, there were tears in his eyes again.

"I think I might be responsible for this, Tony."

"What are you talking about?"

"She said she wanted the operation for herself, not because I wanted it. I never told her to get the operation, honest to God I didn't, Tony. But maybe I wasn't paying as much attention to her as I should've been and—well, maybe she was just doing it to get my attention. I mean, why else does a woman have an operation like that? For her man, right? My God, Tony, I—"

Tony grabbed his friend firmly by the forearm and squeezed. "Stop it!"

"What do you—"

"Stop it, man! You had nothing to do with this. Nada, zip, zilch, not a fuckin' thing. You got that?"

"But—"

"You got it? You are *not* responsible for this! Do you understand?"

Cheney didn't answer.

"Elizabeth needs you, Cheney. But she doesn't need you wallowing in guilt. There's no way on earth you could have known what would happen. Elizabeth did what she wanted to do because—well, that's just the way Elizabeth is. She's strong; she does what she wants to do. She's independent. That's one of the things you love about her. Stop this horseshit right now. I don't wanna hear another fuckin' word about you having anything to do with what happened to her. You hear me?"

Cheney sighed again. Nodded. "You're right. Elizabeth needs me."

They both realized Cheney did not say that Tony was right about his not having any responsibility for what happened.

But it was a start.

It was nearly six in the morning when Dr. Mendelsohn came into the hallway to get them. No one spoke as the three men rode up in the large elevator.

When they reached the intensive care unit, Mendelsohn stopped and looked at Cheney. "I don't want you to be shocked."

"What do you mean?"

"I mean the last time you saw your wife she looked . . . well, beautiful."

Cheney thought about saying, She will always look beautiful, but instead he said, "What are you trying to say?"

"It's going to look worse than it is."

"I don't give a fuck how she looks as long as she's still breathing."

Mendelsohn pursed his lips a little, nodded his head, turned, and led the way into the ICU.

It was not the first time Cheney had been in an ICU. But it would be the first time he saw Elizabeth in such vulnerable condition. He braced himself. As much as anyone could.

Mendelsohn pulled aside a curtain and led the way to Elizabeth's bed. A nurse was sitting in a chair next to the bed, writing something on a chart.

Cheney looked at Elizabeth. His heart skipped a beat. Another. He gasped slightly, tried to cover it up. Why, he did not really know. Reflex. Never show weakness. It was all he could do to stand upright.

Elizabeth's head had been partially shaved for the battery of tests she had been given. She was pale, and without makeup she looked old. But it wasn't how old she looked that shocked him, but rather how incredibly frail she appeared. So helpless. In their short number of years together he had taken particular pride in trying to shield his wife from the various demons that roamed the cityscape of contemporary urban life. And to a great degree he had done so. But to see her so helpless, so ravaged, Cheney felt somehow was a reflection on his ability to protect her.

"Her vital signs are good and she's resting comfortably."

"Except for the fact that she's in a coma."

"I understand what you're going through, Mr. Cheney—"

"Have you ever looked down on your own wife, lying in bed in a coma?" challenged Cheney.

"Yes, I have."

Cheney took the point. "Sorry."

"You have nothing to be sorry about. I know what you're going through. The anger is just beneath the pain. I don't know if this means anything to you right now, but it might. Your wife didn't do anything to deserve this. And you didn't do anything to cause it."

Suddenly Cheney realized that Mendelsohn *did*

understand. Still, he did not ask what had happened to the doctor's wife. He took a deep breath, held out his hand, and said, "Thank you, doctor."

"I'm going home now, but I'll be notified instantly if there is an emergency. After you're . . . through here, I suggest you go home and get some sleep."

"I want to be here when Elizabeth wakes up."

"You will be," said Mendelsohn with a weak but sincere smile. "You will be." It was the kind of smile a coach gave his team when he knew they faced unbeatable odds but admired their courage.

Then Mendelsohn left, leaving Cheney and Tony standing beside the bed, the nurse still jotting notes on a clipboard, and Elizabeth sleeping.

Cheney had purposely not looked at Tony. He didn't want Tony to read his reaction to seeing Elizabeth. And he didn't want to see Tony's reaction. Tony cared about Elizabeth too. Cheney knew his friend was trying to be strong, but he knew seeing Elizabeth this way would affect him.

"I'm okay now, Tony," he said finally and turned to his friend.

"You sure?"

Cheney shook his head. "I'm not sure of anything right now. All I know is I'd like a few minutes alone with Elizabeth; then I'll go home, change clothes, and come back. I know how to reach you if I need you."

"You *will* call me if you need me."

"Yes, I will."

Tony extended his hand to Cheney, but Cheney ignored it. Instead he put his arms around his friend and hugged him. Then let him go. "Thanks."

"You'd do it for me, Cheney. We both remember

when you did." Tony was referring to the extra mile Cheney had traveled for his friend when Tony was going through his divorce. Cheney had been there to keep Tony from killing a man Dorie was having an affair with.

The two friends smiled at each other. Tony parted the curtain and left. The nurse looked up at Cheney, picked up her clipboard, and walked out.

Cheney walked closer to Elizabeth and leaned over. He touched her cheek gently. There was no response. Cheney thought of Sleeping Beauty and wished he could kiss her and wake her.

He kissed her softly on the lips.

She did not wake up. He was not Prince Charming, and she was not Sleeping Beauty. He was just some poor schmuck who lived his life as though it were never going to end.

"I love you, Elizabeth," said Cheney, picking up his wife's right hand and holding it between his two hands. "Please don't die. Oh, God, don't die. There are so many things I haven't told you, so many things we still have to do. And I don't want to do any of them without you. Please wake up.

"Please wake up," said Cheney, as a tear fell upon their gently interlaced fingers.

twenty-one

Petty was sitting at the kitchen table when Cheney got home. She looked up at him hopefully. He could see she had been crying. He walked over to her and took her in his arms.

After a couple of minutes, she got at least a partial grip on her grief and sat down at the table, looking at Cheney, whom she loved dearly in spite of the fact she tried unflaggingly to get his goat.

"She's in a coma."

Petty's lip started to quiver again. "What do the doctors say?"

"Nothing much. She could be out of the coma by the time I get back there, or maybe . . ."

Cheney couldn't bring himself to say the words.

After an awkward moment, he broke the silence. "I love her, Petty," he said, the words catching in his throat.

Through her own tears, Petty said, "She'll be back, Cheney. You gotta believe that. I *do* believe it. I've been praying ever since I read your note. Real hard. I know she's going to be okay."

"She looked so beautiful last night, Petty. I can't recall her ever looking more beautiful. Her eyes, the way she laughed. You know, I was watching her from across the room at the party, pretending I wasn't with her. Pretending I was seeing her for the first time. She was so attractive it was almost intimidating. I felt so lucky, so incredibly lucky that she had chosen me."

"She felt . . . she feels the same way about you, Cheney. I know that. You know that, don't you?"

"I suppose. You talked to Elizabeth a lot. Do you really, honestly believe she knows how much I love her?"

"I guarantee it," said Petty, tears running down her cheeks. "I swear she does."

Cheney smiled.

Petty took Cheney's hands and squeezed them between her own. "About what I said the other day, please forgive me. I was just running off at the mouth. It's part of my job to give you a hard time. Elizabeth told me over and over again that she wanted the operation for herself and it had nothing to do with pressure from you. Please forgive me for saying those things to you."

Cheney nodded, kissed her on the forehead, and walked out of the kitchen.

Upstairs, in the shower, he let the warm water cascade over him. He made the water hotter, turned around, bent his neck, and exposed it to the shower nozzle. He knew he should sleep but knew he could not.

He was afraid of what he might dream.

So he tried at least to relax, even for a few seconds at a time. In this case, until the hot water was gone.

He looked in his closet and chose a pair of stone-washed jeans Elizabeth had always said made his butt look cute, a white Guess shirt she had given him for his last birthday, a pair of beige Frye boots she had given him last Christmas, and a light-brown corduroy jacket, which she said made him look like Burt Reynolds, whatever the hell that meant. The only thing that mattered was she liked it.

He looked at himself in the mirror and sprayed on some Obsession Elizabeth had given him for their anniversary this year. He thought he looked good. He hoped Elizabeth would like what she saw when she opened her eyes.

"I'll be at the hospital if anyone calls," said Cheney.

Petty stood at the front door, not knowing exactly what to say. "Should I call Donald and Samantha in Maui?" Petty asked, referring to Cheney's son by his first wife and his daughter-in-law.

"They've been looking forward to this vacation for two years. Besides, there isn't anything they can do."

"Whatever you say."

Cheney kissed Petty on the cheek and left.

He was on his way out when Kimberly drove up, got out of her car hurriedly, and walked over to Cheney. It was an awkward moment for several reasons, all of them playing out in Cheney's head.

"I'm . . ." Kimberly shook her head, searching for the right word, one that conveyed meaning and did not sound trite or trivial. "I'm so sorry. Tony told me what happened."

"Yeah. I'm on my way back there now."

"I won't keep you. I just—well, I just wanted you to know . . ."

"Yes?" Cheney felt extremely uncomfortable. He wasn't sure why.

"I don't know, I just wanted to let you know I was thinking about you."

"Thanks. I gotta get going."

"Sure."

Cheney got in his car and pulled away. He saw Kimberly standing in his driveway, getting smaller in the rearview mirror.

Thinking about you? That seemed like a funny way to put it. It was probably just his mind playing tricks on him. Why had he felt so uncomfortable?

The truth was, what really made him feel lousy was standing there talking to a woman with whom he had had sex outside his marriage. The first and only time. And it had happened just a few days before his wife went into a coma. That was why he felt uncomfortable. Why he felt like a piece of shit. Kimberly Gary was a mirror that reflected the worst in him.

And it was the worst possible moment for such introspection.

Cheney checked with the resident before he went into Elizabeth's room. There had been no change. No news is no news, was what the doctor said. He also said that preliminary tests indicated there was no severe or organic brain damage, which was all to the good.

But it didn't mean anything unless Elizabeth woke up.

Cheney pulled a chair up beside her bed. There was another nurse sitting beside the bed. She also had a clipboard on her lap, but she was reading a Stephen King novel. She noticed Cheney, smiled, and said she'd be back in a minute or two.

Cheney picked up Elizabeth's hand and squeezed it. He looked at her face, which was as pale as he remembered it being last night.

He leaned over and spoke to his wife, knowing he must do so, or at least would feel more comfortable doing so, before the nurse returned. "I love you, Elizabeth. I love you more than anything in the world. I love you more than I've ever loved anyone else in my entire life. If I could trade places with you, I would. I swear to God, I would.

"But that isn't the way things work. Fact is, I really don't know much about the way things work, I guess. There's not really that much I care about if I can't share it with you."

Cheney heard footsteps approaching and turned.

"Is this where—" The young man carrying a bouquet of flowers saw Elizabeth, her head partially shaved, pale and drawn. "My God, Elizabeth!" the man said, gasping.

"Who are you?" Cheney hoped his words did not sound as gruff to the young man as they sounded to him.

"You must be Mr. Cheney," said the man. "My name is Taylor. Taylor Yates. I work with your wife."

"You work with my wife?" asked Cheney, puzzled.

"I don't actually work in the same office. I have a practice in the same complex. Everyone heard about what happened, and—well, we just chipped in and bought her some flowers. I had no idea . . ." said Yates, his voice trailing off, looking at Elizabeth with obvious difficulty.

"She's in a coma. The doctors say there's no apparent brain damage, and she could come out of it any minute."

"I'm sure she will," said Yates, as if he was sure of no such thing.

"I'll take those," said Cheney.

"Thanks," said Yates. He handed Cheney the flowers.

"I'll put them in a vase so she can see them when she wakes up."

"Great," said Yates, reaching deep and pulling out something he hoped passed for a smile. "Nice meeting you," he added as he shook Cheney's hand. He turned and walked out of the ward, his heels clicking on the hard floor.

Cheney thought he had met most of the doctors in Elizabeth's building. He did not remember meeting Taylor Yates. But then, that didn't mean anything. For the past two years, the building had become something of a pit stop for doctors on their way to someplace else. Elizabeth had been there four years, and she was fourth on the seniority list of the twelve practices.

Yes, Cheney thought as he sat down in his chair again, he would have remembered Taylor Yates.

Renee Hofstettler lived in one of the few remaining apartment complexes in Brentwood. Most had gone condo years ago, merely by applying a coat of legalese to the exterior and freezing out renters who couldn't afford a quarter of a million dollars for a place to live.

It was a two-story building on San Vicente near Bundy, about twelve units, Tony estimated. He parked his car in front of the building and walked up to the front door. The directory listed the name Hofstettler with a code next to it, not the apartment number, which Tony already knew because he had the sheet on her dead roommate, Jenny Clarke. The directory gave instructions for dialing in the code, which in Renee Hofstettler's case was 009. He picked up the phone and punched in the numbers, which, Tony knew, in turn dialed her phone. Which rang. And rang.

While he was standing there, phone in hand, a bleached blonde in a leather jacket, a sweater, jeans, and tennis shoes came through the door in a hurry, carrying two suitcases, each of which had clothes sticking out of the corners. Tony was hot in a sport coat and short-sleeved shirt. The only reason he wore the coat was to give himself the appearance of authority. You didn't go out interviewing people for the first time, intending to use your authority if you had to, in a short-sleeved shirt.

Tony figured the young woman was probably wearing the coat and the sweater because they wouldn't fit in the suitcases.

"You wouldn't happen to be Renee Hofstettler, by any chance?"

"Who, me?"

Tony recognized that as a distinct non-answer.

Hofstettler dropped her bags and took off running. Tony took off after her. "I'm a cop," he yelled.

He chased her around the corner of the building and down into the open parking lot underneath it. When she stopped next to her car, she squared around to make a stand. Scared, trapped, ready to fight.

Tony reached inside his jacket pocket and Hofstettler started to scream, but nothing came out. Tony withdrew his badge and flashed it. "I really am a cop. I just want to ask you a few questions."

Breathing hard, wanting to believe him, the young woman said, "Really?"

The apartment Hofstettler had shared with Jenny Clarke looked as if it had been ransacked by cops with a search warrant, but Tony didn't say so. He knew it had probably looked better before. When Jenny Clarke was alive and when Renee wasn't trying to get the hell outa Dodge. Alive.

Movie posters were on three of the four walls. Unframed or in cheap frames. Not classic movies. Movies with titles Tony didn't recognize. A bunch of CDs were scattered on the floor. That was easy enough to figure, or so the detective thought. The CDs on the floor were not Renee's. Or they were CDs she didn't want.

She puffed on an unfiltered cigarette and tried to get her breath. "I don't know nothin' about nothin'."

Tony thought about telling her that this was not a television show and she was not an actress. But he figured Renee would probably find both statements offensive. So he said, "What do you do?"

"I'm a singer. And an actress," she said, with what Tony perceived as a challenging tone. He recognized it. He had heard it before. Recently.

"Are you employed anywhere?"

"I'm also a dancer."

"Where?"

"Tiny's. It's near the airport."

Tony knew the place. He had gone there one night to a bachelor party. One of the detectives who worked for him was getting married, and his partner had arranged a final night of debauchery. It had been a long time since Tony had gone to a strip club. Things had changed. First of all, they didn't serve alcohol, at least this one didn't. Drinks, soft drinks, were $3.50 and watered down at that. Second, most of the girls looked like they were about fifteen years old, although he knew they had to be eighteen.

And they were nude. Completely nude. Live nude girls. And these days they did "lap dancing" and "table dancing" and "couch dancing." Basically, what that meant was for about twenty bucks a guy could have some eighteen-year-old girl, with a trimmed or shaved pussy and breasts out to here, give him one-on-one service in the middle of the club, in front of everyone. Service usually consisted of sticking her tits and pussy in his face. Close enough so he felt the manicured whiskers on his watered-down-Coke-dripping lips.

Tony had opted just to watch. And eventually to leave before anyone else. He wasn't a prude. He had seen more of the underbelly of life than any hundred men sitting at that club put together. But there was something repugnant about what was happening there. He couldn't put his finger on exactly what repulsed him the most. Certainly he felt bad that some women—girls—found such employment their best option in life. But he also felt pity for the men who sat there mesmerized by illusion, the illusion that some beautiful woman actually cared about them. Wanted them.

When he thought about it now, he did not feel as repulsed as he had that night. He just felt sad.

"How long had you known Ms. Clarke?"

"Six, seven months. I met Jenny in acting class."

"She was an actress?"

"Sure. Like me," said Renee, as though she felt it necessary to remind him.

"What happened, exactly, the night Jenny was murdered?"

"I don't know exactly what night she *was* murdered. All I know is, two nights ago is the last time I saw her."

"What happened that night?" asked Tony, knowing in fact Jenny was murdered that night.

"She just went out and never came home."

"Didn't you find that unusual?"

"You want an honest answer? Not really. Sometimes she didn't come home."

"Why was that?"

"Maybe she was out feeding the homeless. Whaddaya think she was doing?" Renee took a long drag off her cigarette.

"I don't know. Was she a hooker?"

"Nah. But she had it, guys wanted it, and if that guy could do her some good—"

"What do you mean, do her some good?"

"She's an actress, okay? You know, for an LA cop you ask a lot of stupid questions."

"Just bear with me a few minutes more; we're almost done."

"Good."

"Did she say *anything* about who she was going to meet?"

"Only to say he told her not to say anything. No wonder."

"Did she say anything else about who she was meeting?"

"Nope." Renee shook her head and smoked.

"You say Jenny was an actress and she had been— how shall I say this—going around with lots of people who could help her out. How was she doing?"

"What do you mean?"

"Was she making any progress? Making any movies?"

"Oh, yeah. She did her first real movie the last day I saw her. Two days ago."

"Real movie?"

"Well, she didn't count student films and, you know, a porno flick here or there."

"She did porno movies?"

"Not for a year or so. I think she only did a couple."

"What was the movie she just did?"

"Some vampire flick. She only had one day's work, but she had a speaking part. Something for the reel, you know?"

"The reel?"

"When you're in something, you put it on a video and get it edited together, so casting people can see your work."

"I see. How can I reach the company that was making the movie Jenny was working on?"

"I dunno. You could call her agent."

"You got his name?"

"Sure, we have the same agent, Jason Crown. His office is down in Venice: 555-9999. I got the number memorized. I'm always calling him, or at least his secretary. He never calls me."

"He called Jenny."

"Jenny slept with him a coupla times. Shit!"

"What?"

Renee stood and walked over to a small aquarium. "I forgot about Elmo."

"Elmo?" said Tony, standing and following her to the aquarium.

"He's a black goldfish. I can't just abandon him."

"No."

"But I can't take him with me."

Renee walked into the kitchen and returned with a lime-green commuter cup, scooped Elmo out of the water, capped the cup, and handed it to Tony.

"Hey, wait a minute."

"Just put him in a big jar. Here, this is a month's supply of food," she said, handing Tony a small container of flakes.

"I don't—"

"I really gotta go," said Renee. "If you need to reach me you can leave a message for me at Tiny's. I don't know where I'm gonna be stayin', but I work there five nights a week." She turned and headed for the door. "Ciao."

Tony stood there for a second trying to figure out how he got conned into taking responsibility for a black goldfish named Elmo.

* * *

Cheney was sitting next to Elizabeth's bed, monitoring every muscle twitch and eyelid flutter, hoping, praying it would be the prelude to her awakening. He was thinking about what he was going to say to her. He had made a mental list of all the things he wished he had said to her before. Included among all the good things were a couple of bad things, things Cheney felt he had to get off his chest. In time he would tell her about his one-night stand with Kimberly. It would not be the first words out of his mouth when Elizabeth opened her eyes, but eventually he knew he had to tell her.

He had friends, married friends, who had "arrangements." They had made agreements that one or both of the partners could have casual sex outside the marriage under certain conditions. Usually, there was to be discretion—that is, not to subject the other partner to the affair. Also, the person having the affair would be responsible for not allowing his or her own feelings to negatively impact the marriage. In other words, with the "right" to have sex outside the marriage came "responsibilities" to make certain the marriage was not harmed.

As wild as such arrangements sounded to people with more traditional marriages, Cheney had seen such relationships work and, in fact, outlast many other marriages.

But Cheney knew he did not have such an agreement with Elizabeth. It was not the act of having sex with Kimberly as much as it was breaking their agreement. The agreement had been, no sex outside the marriage. That was made explicitly clear by both parties before they exchanged vows. And that agreement had remained intact.

Until now.

"Cheney."

Cheney turned to see Jamison Sanford standing behind him.

"How is she?"

"She's holding her own," said Cheney, employing one of the many lame and meaningless phrases people use in such situations.

Sanford nodded. "Just thought I'd stop by, see if there was anything I could do."

"Thanks. Can't think of anything. But I appreciate the thought."

Sanford stared at Elizabeth. In an odd way, he envied Cheney. Sanford would have given every penny at his disposal to have a chance in a thousand, in ten thousand, that Barbara might open her eyes again. Smile at him. Take his hand and walk with him. Make love with him.

But there was no chance. She was dead. Buried. Beyond the reach of his money and influence.

"You're a lucky man, Cheney."

At the moment Cheney was feeling as though he were the most unlucky man on earth. He looked up at Sanford. "Why would you say that?"

"At the worst, you'll get to say goodbye."

Cheney was not ready to accept the fact that he might be saying goodbye, but he understood what Sanford meant. "She can't hear me," he said, swallowing hard.

Sanford put his arm on Cheney's shoulder. "She

hears you, Cheney. Don't let anyone tell you different." Sanford squeezed Cheney's shoulder, then turned and walked away.

Cheney turned back to Elizabeth and took her limp hand in his. "I love you, Elizabeth."

twenty-two

The offices of the Crown Agency were located in Venice above a kick-boxing studio and a fashionable vegetarian restaurant, just across the street from the World Gym.

The receptionist, a blonde in a tight miniskirt who looked as though she wouldn't know a word processor from a food processor, asked Tony if he wanted coffee, tea, or a soft drink. He declined everything. A few minutes later she showed him into the inner office and closed the door, managing to slip Tony a sexy look before she disappeared.

"So, you're a cop."

"Chief of detectives."

"So, you're an important cop."

Jason Crown had a ponytail, a three-quarter length coat as in *The Long Riders*, and an attitude.

Tony couldn't decide which he liked least.

"I just came from talking with Renee Hofstettler."

"Girl's got talent. You ever been to Tiny's out by the airport?"

"No. She said you were Jenny Clarke's agent too."

"That's right. Terrible tragedy. But it happens, you know. What can you do? You just say a prayer and go on." Crown nodded his head in what Tony thought was a very irritating manner. But everything Crown did seemed to rub Tony the wrong way. The way he put his feet up on the desk. Even the way his hair was slicked back in a ponytail, when his hairline was disappearing faster than a politician's promise.

"She was in a movie you got for her."

"First movie. Speaking part," said Crown, as though it would, or should, mean something to Tony.

"What movie?"

"Night of the Living Bra."

"Are you serious?" said Tony.

"It's a spoof of horror films. Spoofs are in. But not being in the business, well . . ." Crown smiled condescendingly, letting him know he thought Tony was, if not an outright idiot, at least uninitiated.

Tony felt like reaching across the desk and smacking him a few times just for the sheer joy of it, but there were too many lawyers in the world. Especially Crown's world.

"How can I contact the producers?"

"I hope you're not planning to make waves. I have a reputation here."

Tony didn't ask what that reputation was for, even though he had a couple of guesses he would have been willing to put money on. "No waves. Just routine. The woman was murdered. She was working for their company twenty-four hours earlier. I'm not going out to make arrests, I'm looking for information. Just like I'm doing with you. Very unintimidating."

"Well, in that case, the company's name is Golden Majesty Productions. They're out in the Valley. I think it's Canoga Park or something like that."

"You got the number?" asked Tony, even though it was obvious he did. The agent had done business with the company within the last week.

"Sure." Crown rattled off the number as he wrote it down on a piece of paper. He handed the paper to Tony, who pocketed it, stood, and walked out.

It was dark when Tony left the Crown Agency. Bodybuilders were on display in the three-story glass-enclosed gym across the street. Men and women. Bodies beautiful.

Tony felt his belt digging into his waist. Weight gain snuck up on you, he thought. One pound a month, completely unnoticeable unless a person was looking for it. A pound a month was twenty-four pounds in two years. Forty-eight in four. Forty-eight pounds and I'm a fat man, thought Tony Boston, as he watched men and women with chiseled bodies pumping iron and spotting each other.

He thought about Kimberly Gary's body. Now there was a body. Maybe she wouldn't have knocked Jason Crown's socks off, but fuck him, thought Tony Boston. Jason Crown was an asshole, and Kimberly Gary was better than the airheads with tits who got Crown's attention.

Tony was hungry. Felt like grabbing a burger. He was close to Tomy's. He thought about his waist. Thought about Kimberly Gary. Pinched more than an inch.

And walked into the vegetarian restaurant and ordered baba ganush and hummus. To go.

Cheney was sitting beside Elizabeth's bed when Tony walked in. Cheney looked up.

Tony smiled. "How's she doin'?"

"I've noticed more muscle movement the past few hours. Really, I'm not just—well, you know. . . . It's real movement," said Cheney, as though getting someone else to believe him would make it more real.

"That's a good sign," said Tony, even though he had no idea whether or not this was true.

"What's that smell?"

"Eggplant. I ate at a health food restaurant."

"Pretty strong."

"Yeah, well, least it's healthy. So, you going home pretty soon?"

Cheney looked at his watch. Sighed. "You lose track of time in here."

"You got any plans?"

"I don't know. I hadn't thought about it." Cheney had purposely not thought about what he would do after he left the hospital. Because the only thing he could think of was to go home and go to bed. To a bed that seemed so incredibly empty without Elizabeth.

"I was hoping I could coax you into going with me to talk to Jane Dumont's mother."

"Jane Dumont? Oh, yeah, right," said Cheney, the reality of the other world, the real world, coming back to him. "I don't know."

"I'd appreciate it if you came along with me. I'd like your take on things."

Cheney's initial reaction was just to shine it on, but he paused, mulled it over, and realized that anything that could take his mind off . . . things . . . for a few more hours would be a blessing. "Sure, I'll ride along."

During the drive over to Glendale, where Olive Dumont was staying in a Holiday Inn, Tony ran down his interview with Jason Crown. The motel was clean and bright. Mrs. Dumont said she would meet the officers in the bar.

For some reason, probably because he really hadn't thought much about it, Cheney expected some gray-haired old woman. But Jane Dumont had been only nineteen, and that meant her mother could look, well . . .

Like Olive Dumont. She walked into the nearly deserted bar and glanced around uncertainly. Young, in her late thirties, she was the kind of woman who took care of herself, worked out, and on a good day could, without blushing, field compliments from suitors who said that she and her daughter looked like sisters.

Cheney and Tony stood. She came over to the table, introductions were made, and the three sat down.

After the perfunctory yet sincerely felt preliminaries about the tragedy were out of the way, Dumont said, "Jane was not a tramp."

Cheney nodded, although he had no way of knowing one way or the other.

Tony, who was sipping a Bud Dry, said, "Would you say you were pretty close to your daughter?"

Dumont raised her eyebrows in a philosophical gesture. "Who's close to kids these days? I feel I was closer than most mothers. I mean, she told me things most kids don't tell their parents."

"Like what?" asked Cheney, starting to focus for the first time.

"Stuff about sex. Drugs. That kind of thing."

"Drugs?" asked Tony.

"She talked to me about how she was feeling. It's not easy being a parent. Maybe you two know that already. But it's a different world out there from the one I grew up in. You were a bad kid if you got caught smoking in the john or cutting class. These days, the only way you get a bad rep is if you kill somebody. Anything else is no big deal. Drugs, weapons, all kinds of sex—anything goes."

"What did your daughter say to you about drugs?" asked Tony. For the second time.

"She smoked a little dope now and then, nothing much. She asked me about cocaine. Sounds crazy, doesn't it? I mean, if I had asked my mother about cocaine she would have had me arrested. Seriously. But I don't live in Los Angeles. I can't be here twenty-four hours a day looking over my daughter's shoulder. I don't want her to do cocaine, but if I tell her it's going to kill her, she laughs in my face."

Cheney noted the woman still referred to her daughter in the present tense. He also knew this was not unusual.

"She tells me her friends do it, they function, some of them do really well. So, what's the big deal? she tells me. I tell her it's like playing Russian Roulette. You never know which chamber has the bullet in it.

Your roommate might not have a reaction to the drug, but you might have a reaction to it and die. It happens."

"What did she say?"

"She said, 'Mom, you did drugs when you were young.'"

"What did you say to that?"

"What can you say? She's right. I lived through it. It's like 'Do what I say, not what I do.' Or did. I don't do anything stronger than scotch these days. But my point is, Janie told me what was going on in her life. She confided in me. She told me I was her best friend."

Cheney didn't bother to say that a lot of kids need their mothers and fathers to be less of a friend and more of a parent.

"What did your daughter do for a living?" asked Tony.

"She was a model."

"A model? Was she doing anything else as a way to make money?" asked Tony. The sheet had listed her occupation as WAITRESS.

"She worked in a restaurant in Hollywood. The money was good. Pretty girls make better tips," said Dumont proudly.

"When was the last time you spoke with your daughter?"

Dumont picked up her drink and took a swig, then set it down again on the table. "The night she was . . . killed."

"Did she say anything that might give us any idea where she went that night?"

"She called me from a nightclub. It was noisy; I could barely hear her."

"Did she mention the name of the club?"

"Not that I recall."

"Was it the Orange Seahorse?"

"Actually, that does ring a bell. Yeah, I think that's it."

"What did she say?" asked Tony.

"She said she'd met some guy and they were gonna go somewhere."

"Did she say where?"

"No," said Dumont, shaking her head, trying her best to remember.

"Did she mention anything about the guy?" said Cheney. "Maybe she was trying to impress you about where the guy was taking her. Maybe the kind of car he drove. Maybe—"

"There was something," said Dumont. "She said the person taking her out was a big-time director."

"That's very interesting," said Cheney. "Did she say anything about him? A name? The name of any of his movies, maybe?"

Dumont squinted her eyes and scanned the memories. The painful memories. "She said something about his doing slasher movies. Does that mean anything?"

"It might," said Tony, exchanging a look out of the corner of his eye with Cheney. "It just might."

"The last day of Jenny Clarke's life was spent working in a vampire movie. Jane Dumont goes out with a big-time director who does slasher movies and nobody ever hears from her again. What do you think?" asked Tony Boston of his mentor as they drove back to the hospital.

"Sounds like something worth checking out."

"I've got the name of the movie company Jenny Clarke was working for. I'm going out there tomorrow morning. Can you come along?"

"I'm not sure."

"I really could use you, Cheney," said Tony, as much for his friend as for himself.

"We'll see. Give me a call."

Tony pulled up next to Cheney's car, in the hospital parking lot.

"Thanks, Tony," said Cheney, looking at his friend, who was dimly lit in the spill of the parking lot lights.

"No problem. I needed your help."

"Right," said Cheney, not bothering to argue. It wasn't necessary. They both knew. "Call me, okay?"

As Cheney got into his car to go home, Tony drove away.

Tony was thinking about Kimberly Gary and whether or not it was too late to call her. Or if it would be okay to just stop by. The hospital was only about ten minutes away from Kimberly's apartment building. He decided he wouldn't risk just showing up. Their relationship was too new. Nonexclusive. What if some guy was over there, some guy who had made a date with her two weeks ago, before she and Tony had gotten together? Tony knew he would make a scene. Partly because he was jealous, partly because what he had gone through with Dorie still haunted him. He would immediately assume the worst. It was better to call first. Much better to call first. But what if he called and she wasn't there? It was nearly eleven. He would assume the worst. Or what if he called and she said he couldn't come over? There could only be one reason, no matter what excuse she used. He would assume the obvious. Which was the worst of all.

Tony just drove home, had a beer, watched *Nightline*, and tried to go to sleep.

The first thing Cheney noticed when he walked in the house was the blinking red light on the answering machine. This morning the tape had been full of people calling to express their sympathy and to ask if there was anything they could do.

Cheney hit the MESSAGE button and the machine rewound. "Oh, Cheney, this is Beth. Frank and I are so sorry to hear about Elizabeth. Please call us if there's anything we can do." *Beep.* "Cheney, this is Lyle. Really sorry about Elizabeth, man. I know how you feel. I really do. Listen, if there's anything I can do . . . ? Call me, man." *Beep.* "Mr. Cheney, this is Dr. Mendelsohn." There was a pause. Cheney's heart stopped. "Please come to the hospital immediately." *Beep.*

Cheney was out the door before the next message came on. As he pulled out of the driveway it occurred to him that he should call the hospital first. But he did not. For two reasons. First, the car phone was in Elizabeth's car. Second, a part of him didn't want to hear the news, if it was bad news, over the phone.

So he just drove as fast as he could.

And prayed even harder.

*   *   *

Cheney parked in a no parking zone next to the entrance closest to Elizabeth's room, jumped out of the car, and slammed the door shut, not bothering to lock it.

He burst through the double doors, took the stairs two at a time, and ran down the hall like O. J. Simpson used to run through airports. He didn't care how it looked to those watching him. His eyes were focused on the double doors at the end of the hallway.

What waited just beyond them would change his life forever. Whatever way it went.

Suddenly, Cheney stopped short. His heart was racing and he was breathing hard. He took a deep breath and pushed open one of the doors.

Inside, several people—Cheney recognized Dr. Mendelsohn and Dr. Blomberg and two of the nurses— were standing around Elizabeth's bed.

Cheney moved—in slow motion, it seemed to him—toward his wife. He heard voices, but it all seemed like a dream, garbled and unintelligible. Perhaps he did not want to know the answer until the very last instant. If she was . . . if it was bad news, irreversible bad news, he wanted it postponed until the last second. When he left his wife a few hours earlier, she was alive. As he walked slowly toward her bed, she was still alive. At least in his mind.

Cheney got closer and closer to his wife. As he did, those gathered around the bed parted.

Finally he saw her.

She was sitting up, her eyes heavy-lidded. She looked tired, but . . .

She was awake! And when she saw Cheney she smiled and reached out her weary arms toward him.

Cheney sat down on the bed and held his wife as tightly as he dared, whispering in her ear how much he loved her and how he had missed her. She would have said the same thing to him, but she was crying too much to speak.

twenty-three

"You look like Christmas and the Fourth of July rolled into one," said Tony Boston.

"Better. Much, much better. They finally had to throw me outa the place. Mendelsohn wants to do some tests before he releases her."

"Incredible," said Tony as he pulled the car onto the White Oak exit of the Ventura Freeway. "And she seems . . . ?" Tony didn't know exactly what word to use.

"Normal? Yes. She's alert, bright, a little groggy, but Mendelsohn said she passed all the preliminary tests with flying colors. Far as he can see, there's no permanent brain damage and she can actually come home in a day or two."

"You're kidding!"

"I mean, she can't run any marathons for a week or so," said Cheney with a grin on his face, "but she can

◆ 349

sit in our bed and read and watch TV just as easily as she can sit in a hospital bed and do the same thing. Mendelsohn's scheduled an MRI for this afternoon. If it checks out, there's really no reason to keep her there. And you know Elizabeth. She wanted to come home with me this morning."

Tony laughed. He knew by the time Elizabeth got her strength back, she would make life miserable for the doctors and nurses if they tried to keep her an hour longer than she felt they should. It was good to see Cheney smile again. He was on top of the world. He had the demeanor and attitude of a man who had been to the brink and back and cherished whatever piece of life God gave him now.

Tony parked in front of a warehouse-type building in an industrial park in Canoga Park.

There was a line of oriental women in short black dresses and high heels. Each held a sheet of paper in her hands, which she appeared to be studying, although a few of the women seemed more concerned with making sure the seams in their stockings were straight.

"We're shooting a martial arts movie," explained Harry Corbin about the oriental women. He looked to be about forty-five, with salt-and-pepper hair and a pair of thick glasses that dominated his face. He wore a print shirt down to mid-thigh level, Italian shoes, and a pair of pants in which the crease was a distant memory.

On all four walls of his windowless office were posters of movies bearing the Golden Majesty Productions logo. There were about twenty-four posters, and in all but one there was a man holding a gun with a scantily clad woman on his arm. The sole exception was a poster with a woman getting her head chopped off with a sword.

"I don't mean to rush you," said Corbin, "but I'm really pretty busy. We start shooting in three days and I'm still casting."

Tony handed photos of Jane Dumont and Jenny Clarke to Corbin. He looked at them and handed the photo of Jane Dumont back to the officers. "I know her," said Corbin, holding up Jenny Clarke's picture. She's in *Night of the Living Bra*. What's this all about?"

"Both women have been murdered."

"My God!" said Corbin. It was interesting to see how a person who made his money selling fake violence reacted when confronted with the real thing. He looked again at Clarke's photo and handed it back gingerly, as though not wanting to catch some contagious disease.

"Who's directing the film?"

"Gino. Gino Marzetti. Why, you think he's got something to do with this?"

"We'd just like to talk to him, like we're talking to you."

"Gino's a weird guy, sure, but I really don't think he'd—well, you know."

"How's he weird?"

"He's a director. It goes with the territory, you know?"

"No, sir, I don't," said Tony.

"Well, being a director can be a real power trip. Everybody wants to be in the movies, so if you're actually directing movies, at any level, everybody's always kissing your ass."

"How is he more weird than any other director?"

"It's hard to explain. He's just fascinated with this stuff." Corbin tilted his head to take in the posters on the wall. "Some guys, they direct these movies and they want to move on, do something 'serious.' Like they know what the fuck they're doin'. I got a crew here could make you look like you know what you're doin'. Great crew. We got it down. Ten days, X number of feet exposed per day: voilà! we got a movie. We don't try to fool ourselves. People put us down, but we're makin' money while most of the studios are losin' their ass.

"Anyhow, Gino is good at the gory stuff. Damned good, probably the best in town. I let him expose a few hundred more feet of film with each movie, and he tries to stuff a little more 'art' into the picture. That's okay; least he gives me what I need to throw in a video box. Everybody's happy.

"But I always wondered why he doesn't move on, you know? I mean, he's really into making this shit. Don't get me wrong, it's okay with me. I mean, why not? I'm the one who benefits."

"Would you call Gino a big-time director?" asked Cheney, recalling Olive Dumont's comment.

Corbin smiled. "Big-time? Everything's relative. You're workin' on a student film, one of my films is big-time. You're an actress, you're goin' out with a director, he's a big-time director, period."

"Where can we find Gino?"

"Right now?"

"Yeah."

"He's shooting over at a bar on Van Nuys Boulevard." He looked at his watch. "Should be there for another four, five hours."

Corbin wrote down the address and gave it to Tony.

On the way out of the office, Corbin said, "If you or any of your buddies wanna pick up a few bucks moonlighting, doing security, I pay pretty good. It's easy work. Hundred and twenty-five a day and all the actresses you can eat."

"Thanks, I'll keep it in mind," said Tony as he and Cheney made their way through the maze of hopeful oriental women.

The Greenbriar Bar and Pool Hall was located on Van Nuys Boulevard, near Burbank. Several letters in the neon sign out front were flickering or burned out completely. A large truck was parked outside, along with a trailer and a number of vans. Street parking was impossible—unless, of course, you were driving a city vehicle. Tony stopped his car right in front.

Inside the bar, people were scurrying about, carrying this, yelling for that. A couple of guys were taping lights at odd angles around a Fussball table. A guy Cheney recognized but couldn't quite place was walking around with a script in his hand, talking and gesturing to no one. About a dozen other people were laying dolly track, moving equipment, doing sound checks, and generally looking very busy.

Cheney asked a long-haired guy wearing ripped jeans and a Guns 'n Roses T-shirt who Gino Marzetti was. The guy pointed out a man in the corner, who was talking animatedly with another man.

Marzetti looked to Cheney to be in his late thirties. There was a decent amount of gray mixed in with his naturally dark brown hair. He wore jeans, a plain black T-shirt, tennis shoes, and he looked fit. Not fit like Arnold, but fit like Mick Jagger. Slim, wiry, toned.

"Gino Marzetti?"

The man turned to look at Cheney and Tony. "Yes?"

Tony flashed a badge. For a reason. He wanted to see what it did to Marzetti.

It didn't do much. "We got permits up the fuckin' ying-yang. Talk to—"

"We'd like to talk with you. In private."

"What about?"

"Jenny Clarke."

Marzetti nodded. Giving nothing away. He turned to the man next to him. "You know what I'm looking for here, Steve," he said. "Just do it."

Steve nodded and walked away, leaving the director alone in a dark corner with the two cops.

Marzetti just looked at them. He wasn't squirming. He wasn't spilling his guts. He was going to let them start.

"How well did you know Jenny Clarke?"

"She was an actress in my movie. I met her, worked with her a little. That applies to about twenty different women, in this movie alone." Pause. "I make a lot of movies."

"She's been murdered." Cheney waited for a reaction. When it didn't come, he said, "You don't look surprised."

"I heard about it."

"From whom?"

"People on the set. Everybody knows about it."

"Corbin didn't know."

"Jenny was an actress. Corbin doesn't have a very high opinion of actresses. Unless the person's a star, he doesn't give a fuck. Besides, he makes a movie a month and this girl only did a couple days on one picture. He wouldn't have recognized her if she'd have walked up and introduced herself."

"You ever meet anyone by the name of Jane Dumont?"

"Nope," said Marzetti, shaking his head.

This guy is good, thought Cheney—if he's guilty. Or maybe he was really innocent.

"What if I told you I had a witness who could place you at the Orange Seahorse with Dumont the night she was murdered?"

"I'd say the witness was lying," said Marzetti, without missing a beat. Without even a betraying twitch. "Am I a suspect in Jenny's murder?"

"Why would you say that?"

"Because I'm not a fucking idiot, that's why. And if I *am* a suspect, I would be a fucking idiot to be sitting here talking to you without my lawyer."

All three men were silent.

"Look, if I can help you guys, fine. If you have any questions I can answer, fine. But don't come in here while I'm working and try to pin some bogus murder charge on me. I didn't kill Jenny and I've never met the other girl, whatever her name is."

"Where were you the night Jenny was murdered?"

"Look—"

"No, *you* look," said Cheney. "You come up with a good alibi and we're outa here and you have our apologies for spoiling your day. But this is serious business. It's real, not some make-believe bullshit. At least two women are dead, and we expect some straight answers from you. Especially since you've got nothing to hide."

"Everybody has something to hide, pal. Being a cop, you know that better than most people."

Cheney didn't respond. He just continued to look Marzetti in the eye.

"I was home. Alone. Like the movie," he said, trying to inject a lighter tone into the conversation. "I know that's not the right answer, but it's the truth. When I'm shooting, I'm doing twelve-, fourteen-hour days. The only thing I've got time to do is sleep, so I can get up the next day and do it all over again."

"So you don't have an alibi."

"No," said Marzetti sarcastically. "I guess I'm stuck with the truth."

"We're ready, Gino," said a woman wearing jeans and carrying an electronic bullhorn.

"I'll be right there."

The woman walked away, shouting orders to people around her, who instantly sprang into action.

"Look, I gotta get back to work. Time is money in this business. You wanna talk to me, call me at home." Marzetti withdrew a card and handed it to Cheney. "The number in the bottom right is my home phone."

"We just might do that."

"Be my guest," said Marzetti, as though he could not have cared less. Then he walked away. People gathered around him like lead filings attracted to a magnet.

The woman with the bullhorn said, "Quiet for

rehearsal!" and the bar, which an instant before had been full of metal clanging and people shouting and laughing, was suddenly as quiet as the beach at midnight.

The guy who Cheney saw earlier talking to the air stepped forward and said, to another guy, "Fuck you, asshole!" Cheney remembered where he had seen the man. He had been an actor on a late seventies situation comedy.

"What do you think?" asked Tony.

"I liked him better as a comedian."

Kyoko Rabinowitz did not look surprised to see Cheney when she opened the door. But then, Cheney didn't figure she would.

"Tell me about it," said Cheney, after he had taken a seat on the couch and she was sitting opposite him, her feet curled up under her in a rocking chair.

"Tell you about what?" she tried.

"Where Barbara went the night she was murdered."

"I don't know, I swear," said Kyoko.

"You know more than you told me. I need to know what you know. Now."

Kyoko stood. "You want some wine?"

"No, thanks," said Cheney.

She went into the kitchen and returned in less than a minute with a glass of red wine and curled her legs up under her again. "I promised Barbara I wouldn't say anything."

"She's dead. How much worse could it get?"

"It wasn't herself she was worried about. She didn't want to hurt Jamison."

"That's strange. She seems to have been involved in several activities that could have made him feel downright depressed," said Cheney sarcastically.

"You don't understand. This wasn't just an affair—I know that must offend your middle-class sensibilities."

"I'll have to wash my ears out before I go home."

"She was being blackmailed."

"By whom?"

"I don't know. Honest to God, I don't know. I know it had to do with something that happened to her before she married Jamison."

"How do you know that?"

"She said something like 'Even though it happened before I met him, it isn't the kind of thing a husband can easily understand. Even Jamison.'"

"Did the blackmailer have photographs?"

"I think so. I'm not sure. She never said exactly, and I never saw anything."

"Did she say anything else? Did she ever mention anyone in the movie business? Maybe a producer or a director?"

"No."

"Did she ever mention the name Gino Marzetti?"

"No. She never mentioned the person's name. But she did use the phrase 'the old days.'"

"What would that mean to her?"

"Vegas. We always referred to Vegas as 'the old days.'"

"So something happened in Vegas, before she met Jamison, that someone was trying to blackmail her about."

"Yes. I asked her about it, tried to help her, tried to get her to talk about it, you know? But she wouldn't tell me. She said it was her problem and she didn't want to get me involved. Then, like I said, she made me promise not to tell anybody. For Jamison's sake."

"I want you to think, Kyoko. Is there anything, I mean anything at all, that you can tell me that might point me in the right direction?"

Kyoko sipped her wine and rolled her eyes up, as though looking for answers on the dirty ceiling. After a few moments she said, "She used to call the guy from my phone."

"Tony? Cheney here. Look, I need you to run a phone number for me. My guess is that it's a phone booth, but I want to know the location. Meanwhile, I'm going to find out where Gino Marzetti was at exactly . . ."—Cheney looked at the phone bill Kyoko had given him—" two-nineteen P.M. on June twelfth."

"Got it. Meet me at Marty's in a couple hours."

Elizabeth had been moved to a private room. She was ready to go home and had made some noise about how she was a doctor and how Mendelsohn was just trying to pad his bill by making her stay in the hospital. But there was no way Mendelsohn was going to let her leave until he had checked the results of a battery of tests he had ordered done and, by this afternoon, completed.

Cheney found his wife in surprisingly good spirits, though a little restless. She asked him about the case. Cheney noted, with great relief, that she asked him precise questions that required accurate memories of what he had told her about Barbara Sanford's death and his subsequent investigation. Elizabeth's memory seemed to be perfectly fine.

"Sounds like you're on to something," she said, setting down her now-empty juice glass and wiping her mouth with a Kleenex.

"I can focus on the case more, now that—"

"I'm back?"

"Yes."

"It must have been very difficult for you."

"For me? What about you?" said Cheney.

"It was easy for me, Cheney. I was asleep. You were the one doing the worrying. You were the one pacing the floor, making deals with God."

"Does everybody do that?" he asked his wife, the psychiatrist.

"A lot of people do. What deals did you make, Cheney?"

"I said I'd give up drinking for eight hours straight."

"You really went out on a limb, didn't you, lover?" said Elizabeth with a big smile.

It was the smile Cheney had missed, desperately, during her absence.

"What about you? People often say this kind of experience changes them. Causes them to gives things a different priority."

Elizabeth's smile disappeared and her mood turned serious. "I thought about a lot of things when I first woke up. And lying here, I've had even more time to do a little soul-searching."

"Any earthshaking revelations?" asked Cheney.

"I don't know. I know we've gotten a little out of touch the past year or so."

"I know."

"We've got to be close again, Cheney. Not like it was before, because people can never go back. It's got to be something different."

"Better than it used to be."

"It can happen. But we've got to deal with the distance first. Talk about it. There are some things that need to be said."

Cheney knew this was true. He also knew it was not going to be easy. The thought of Kimberly Gary and what he had allowed himself to do struck him like an emotional lightning bolt. He knew that however small a part it played, it was, in fact, part of the distance, if only a symptom of that distance. But he knew his marriage could weather the revelation.

At least he hoped it could.

"Look, I've got to do a couple of things before I meet Tony. I'll be back tonight."

"Would you stop by the house and bring me my robe?"

"Sure," said Cheney. He leaned down and kissed his wife, smiled, and walked out of the room.

Elated that she had returned to him.

Afraid he might not be able to keep her.

Marty's in Brentwood was Tony and Cheney's bar. It was a serious place, for serious drinkers. Darkly lit, it had one TV with a sporting event always on in the background. Red vinyl stools and booths, a bartender in a white shirt, black vest, and tie. No trendy beers, only

American beers on tap. Wine was white or red and came from a jug. But if you wanted bourbon, vodka, scotch, or gin, you were in the right place. Generous shots, especially for the regulars. Guy came to Marty's, he came to drink. Alone or with his friends. Didn't matter. Beer nuts and pretzels were in dishes on the bar. No chicken wings or buffalo wings or Thai chicken pizza by the slice. Beer nuts and pretzels, take it or leave it.

The one exception to house rules was made expressly for Cheney, because he was a regular and, after all, when he was a *real* regular he was the chief of detectives, for chrissake, a fucking celebrity in a real man's bar. Exceptions were made for such men. So there was always a bottle of decent Chardonnay in the back of the refrigerator under the bar. Kendall Jackson was usually what Nicky, who bought the place from Marty ten years ago, stocked for the former chief of detectives.

Which was exactly what Cheney was drinking as he and Tony sat in a dark corner of the bar talking.

"Good news," said Tony, who had just arrived. Before sitting down he had grabbed a tap Bud Dry from Nicky, who said the first round was on the house. "The number you gave me is, like you figured, a phone booth. However, it's only about six blocks from where Marzetti lives." He noticed Cheney wasn't smiling. "What's wrong?"

Cheney exhaled deeply. "I just got off the phone with Corbin. He checked the schedule, and on June twelfth at two-nineteen P.M. Gino Marzetti was shooting in Agoura Hills."

"Maybe—"

"Forget the fact that it's about an hour away, no

traffic. He's got about a hundred witnesses. And whereas an extra or even an actor who's between scenes might be able to get away, the director is involved in every shot, every setup."

"Maybe it was during a lunch break."

"Lunch was at noon. They were shooting six A.M. till six in the evening. Dammit!" said Cheney, obviously frustrated.

"Where does that leave us?"

"The blackmailer Barbara called from Kyoko's house on the twelfth was not—could not have possibly been—Marzetti. Period."

"Maybe he's got an accomplice."

"Possible. But it's unusual for a serial killer to have an accomplice."

"Not unprecedented. Remember, the Hillside Strangler was really two guys working together."

"Anything's possible. But if we're dealing with one killer, which is the most likely scenario, Marzetti's got nothing to do with it."

"I dunno," said Tony. "There's something about the guy—"

"He's weird. But it's tough to get a jury to send a guy to the chair just because he's weird."

"It's been done," said Tony.

"Not by me," said Cheney. "And not by you. We're just going to have to try harder."

"Got any ideas?"

"I'll let you know."

"By the way, we're getting some help on this one. Two detectives, Talbot and Alvarez, heard about the case and volunteered their expertise."

"Which is?"

"Both of them have moonlighted as consultants for some movies and TV shows. Alvarez even sold a couple of scripts. They heard we were working on a case that might have some connection to the movies, and they offered to help."

"One thing. Get them to sign a waiver that they won't write a book, script, or whatever the hell else you can do these days to capitalize on this case. They won't sign, they're outa here."

Tony smiled.

"What are you smiling about?"

"Person might think you're still the boss."

"Sorry," said Cheney, laughing a little at himself. "You're right, though. Consider it done." Tony sipped his beer. "So, how's Elizabeth?"

"She's great. She'll be coming home soon. Her memory seems as good as ever. We're very lucky."

"So how comes you're not beaming from ear to ear?"

"No reason," said Cheney, not wanting to discuss the matter with Tony. Instead, he changed the subject. "How well do you know Kimberly Gary?"

"A lot better now than I did a few days ago."

Neither man spoke, although Tony was grinning like a kid who just got lucky with the best-looking girl in school.

"What's the matter?"

"Nothing," said Cheney.

"You should be happy for me. This is the first time since Dorie left me that I've been interested in someone."

"I *am* happy for you, Tony."

Tony thought about saying, You sure don't look it,

but he decided against it. Obviously, Cheney had something on his mind. Tony figured it had to do with Elizabeth.

"Did you know Kimberly very well before this case?" asked Cheney.

"Never met her before. She approached me. Introduced herself, gave me her card, told me to check her out."

"And?"

"I didn't do a deep background check, if that's what you mean. I called the *Tribune*, and they said they were happy with her work and she was a good reporter. Why?"

"Nothing," said Cheney, not ready to rain all over his friend's parade. Not yet, anyhow.

"At least she's up front about things. She needs a big story, something to put her on the map. She said she'd read the item in the paper about the death of Barbara Sanford, whom she had known—not really known, but known of—in Vegas. She recognized Barbara's photograph. She subsequently learned that her husband didn't buy the idea of hit-and-run. The murder of a person as prominent as Barbara Sanford was a story that could really do her some good. I know it sounds mercenary, but it also sounds like the truth."

Cheney was thinking maybe it sounded like something else.

Cheney said goodbye to Petty. He stuck the turquoise terry-cloth robe under his arm and walked out into the chilly night air. It was only about seven-thirty, but it was dark and unseasonably cold, around fifty degrees.

Cheney opened the car door and jerked to attention as he sat down in his seat. "What the fuck!"

"Cheney!" said Kimberly, as startled as Cheney was.

"What are you doing here? In my car," he said, almost as an afterthought.

"I'm sorry. I just needed to talk to you and—well, you didn't seem particularly friendly the last time we met. I was tired—I've been up all night—and I thought if I fell asleep in my own car I might miss you."

"Why didn't you ring the doorbell?"

"I don't know. I just thought it might be a little awkward. I mean, you have a housekeeper, and . . . oh, I don't know."

"What's so important that you need to talk with me right away?"

"It's about you and me," she began.

"There is no you and me. Look, Kimberly, I'm sorry about what happened that night between us."

"Sorry?"

"You know what I mean. And don't start playing dumb all of a sudden. You're pretty smart when you want to be."

"What's that supposed to mean?"

"It means you haven't been completely honest with me from the beginning."

"What are you talking about?"

"I mean you never said you knew Barbara Holgate."

"I said I might have bumped into her, but we never

really knew each other. Like people in your high school class. You knew them by sight, but you didn't *know* them. What are you trying to say?"

"I'm saying you manipulate people."

"Everybody manipulates people, Cheney. Or aren't cops that cynical." It was not a question. "I haven't hurt anybody."

"What about Tony?"

"What about Tony?"

"You're not going to hurt Tony?"

"I like Tony. I have no intention of hurting him."

"So, if you hurt somebody, as long as you don't intend to it's okay?"

"Look, Cheney, I see you're upset and I'm sorry if you're angry with me. Quite frankly, it doesn't make what I'm about to tell you any easier to say."

"Well, excuse me," said Cheney.

"I think I'm pregnant."

Suddenly the universe, at least the piece Cheney lived in, exploded into a trillion pieces. After a moment, he said softly, as though he didn't want anyone to hear, as though if he didn't say it too loud it might not exist, "How do you know?"

"I'm not positive. But a woman knows."

"C'mon, Kimberly. What are you—"

"I used one of those little testers you can get at the drugstore. The results came out positive."

Cheney sat back in his seat, let his head fall back, took a deep breath, closed his eyes, and tried to stop the world from spinning.

"What are you going to do?" asked Cheney, well aware of using the word *you* instead of *we*. For several reasons, not the least of which was that he knew

Kimberly would already have decided what she was going to do.

"I've got an appointment to see my gynecologist on Monday. Frankly, I hope I'm not pregnant."

"And if you are?"

"I don't know."

"So why are you telling me?"

"Who else could I tell? I felt really alone, Cheney. No, that's not it." She turned in her seat to face him. "I've spent a lot of my life alone. I can deal with that. I felt lonely. I'm not used to that. Besides, I just thought you should know."

"Tony said—"

"I know, I know," she said, nodding her head, anticipating what Cheney was going to say. "How do I know you're the father?"

"Something like that."

"I felt something happen the night we made love."

"Like the earth moving?" said Cheney sarcastically, not able to completely contain his anger. Part of that anger was directed at Kimberly Gary. Most of the anger was directed at himself.

"There's no reason to be sarcastic. I know I got pregnant then. If indeed I am pregnant."

Cheney just shook his head and breathed deeply again. The implications regarding his marriage, his relationship with his best friend, let alone his relationship with Kimberly and a new son or daughter were mind-boggling. Especially as he prepared to bring Elizabeth home from the hospital, where she had nearly died.

"Well, I guess I'd better get going," she said. She looked at Cheney and neither of them said anything.

Yet the silence was filled with unanswerable questions and unspoken accusations.

Kimberly got out and walked to her car, which was parked around the corner from Cheney's house. She got in and drove away. Cheney watched the taillights getting smaller and smaller in the darkness. He stared into the blackness long after they had disappeared.

And tried to figure out how he was going to convince his wife how much he loved her—while she was getting used to the idea that another woman was pregnant with his child.

"You're sure they know?" said Gino.

"I'm sure."

"What should I do?"

"All you can do is try to protect yourself the best you can."

"How?"

"They're going to be coming after you. You've got to make sure they don't find anything."

"What are you saying?"

"Everything they've got so far is circumstantial."

Gino sat back in his chair. The years, the sensations, the pain—it all surrounded him, enveloped him, like a comfortable old coat. Not particularly warm, not particularly attractive, yet somehow comforting in its familiarity.

As he laid his head back on the chair, it came back to him as clearly as always. For an instant he thought he could detect the smell of something fresh, and yet somehow rancid at the same time.

He could still see her through the window, as he

stood on his tiptoes like a child with his face pressed against the window looking in. Looking in from the outside.

And what he saw, what he felt at that moment, was the end of innocence. Forever.

Like a blind fighter, trained to fight like an animal against unseen opponents, knowing his punches landed, yet also knowing he would always lose, he kept lashing out, determined to answer the final bell on his feet.

The ghosts Gino fought were real. Flesh and blood. He could not defend his actions. No pugilist could *defend* beating another human being to a pulp in the squared circle.

Beyond a certain point, it was all instinct. And survival.

Gino was driven. By forces he could feel but not understand. Not completely. In each encounter he understood more and yet, somehow, less.

But it was all coming to a head. Now. After so many years.

"I love you," said Gino.

"I love you," she said, not bothering to append the customary "too." She felt her response was more sincere. Raw. Which was how she felt about him.

"One more time?" he said.

"One *last* time," she said.

Gino walked to the computer and hit a key on the keyboard.

Love.

The word appeared on the screen. Isolated. Black on white.

Became crimson on white. On black.

Two screens. Four. Eight.

Sixteen screens. Surrounded: 360 degrees.

Music. The sound, the feel of a single bass note. Deep bass. Pulsating rhythmically. From two speakers.

He pressed a button. Sixteen speakers.

He stood in the center, maestro to all sensation.

Love.

They were looking at the word on sixteen screens when they climaxed.

One last time.

twenty-four

"Thanks, honey," said Elizabeth, as she put on her robe. "I really missed it. I missed you, too." She leaned over and kissed her husband.

"I missed you."

"Dr. Mendelsohn says I can go home tomorrow."

"That's great," said Cheney. He felt as though he had been sawed in half emotionally.

"He said you could pick me up around ten, ten-thirty in the morning," said Elizabeth. "It'll be good to be back in our own bed."

"It'll be good to have you back."

"You know, it's the simple things I miss most. I miss you—not that you're simple, of course—and I miss the bed. I miss the smell of Petty's vanilla-flavored coffee when I wake up in the morning. I miss reading in bed, next to you, as you watch TV. I hope you're not insulted by this, but I miss lying next to you, reading, even more than I miss making love with you."

"Really?"

"It's hard to explain. No matter how much time people spend making love, it's never even remotely close to the amount of time they spend doing other things together. And lying in bed with you at night, reading or watching TV, my right foot always touching your left foot, knowing you're there even though I'm not concentrating on you one hundred percent, it's like . . ."

"Home," said Cheney.

"Yes," said Elizabeth, looking up into her husband's eyes. "You know, Cheney, I think I've been taking you for granted."

That was a line Cheney had been waiting to hear for months. But when it finally came, only moments after his conversation with Kimberly, all he could do was say, "I love you, baby," and kiss her on the lips.

Outside, in the hallway, Cheney leaned against the wall, lost in thought.

"Are you okay?"

Cheney looked up, a little startled, and saw Dr. Mendelsohn. "Yeah, I'm fine. Just a little tired, I guess."

"Of course. Well, at least we've got a happy ending. All the tests came back negative. There is no brain damage and, for all the trauma and drama, she's basically the same as she was a couple of days ago."

"Is there any chance of it happening again?"

"There's always a chance anything can happen to anyone. However, the test results indicate that chances of a recurrence are about one in a million."

"I appreciate what you've done."

"I really didn't do much. Elizabeth did most of it. With a hand from the man upstairs."

"I didn't think doctors believed in things you can't see under a microscope."

"Can't see love under a microscope, but I know it's there when I hold my daughter and when I make love with my wife. I think it's a little like that with God."

Cheney nodded.

"And if I'm wrong . . . big fuckin' deal," said Mendelsohn, as he turned and walked away.

"You look awful," Tony said, looking up at his friend.

"I guess the lack of sleep is catching up with me," said Cheney as he sipped tepid coffee from a Styrofoam cup.

He felt uncomfortable with Tony tonight, for the first time since they had met. What could he say? Oh, by the way, the real reason I'm feeling shitty is because your girlfriend told me she might be pregnant . . . with my kid. If she is, my wife might divorce me and things between you and me are never going to be quite the same. Besides that, everything's fine. How about you?

"Where'd you get the goldfish?" asked Cheney, indicating the small black goldfish swimming in a gallon jar on Tony's desk.

"That's Elmo. I really didn't want—"

Just then two people walked into Tony's office. Cheney had seen both of them around but had never spoken to either.

"Cheney, I'd like you to meet Detectives Jerry Alvarez and Cynthia Talbot."

Cheney stood and shook hands with both officers.

Alvarez was a husky Latino, who looked to Cheney to be in his mid-thirties. He was wearing a tweed sport coat, jeans, loafers, and a white shirt, no tie. A grin of recognition spread beneath his full black mustache. Everybody knew Cheney. Everybody, that is, who had been on the force for at least five years.

Detective Talbot had short blond hair. She also looked to be in her mid-thirties. She was wearing a navy-blue knee-length skirt that did not quite hide a pair of shapely legs beneath it, a matching blazer, a white blouse, and a pair of sensible, but not too sensible, navy pumps.

Alvarez was the first to speak. "It's like meeting a legend. Sir," he added hurriedly.

"Well, unlike most legends, I'm still alive."

Everyone laughed, even though Cheney had used the line before and was aware that it wasn't that funny. Cheney resumed his seat, and the two detectives turned their attention toward their boss.

"So, whatcha got?" said Tony.

"Here's the list we put together," said Alvarez, handing Tony two sheets of paper. "Every director associated with A- and B- slasher movies. And below. Which, essentially, means straight-to-video, sir."

Tony looked at the list. "This is a lot more than I figured. You get anything on Gino Marzetti?"

"Not a lot," said Talbot. "Certainly, no flashing red lights. He's made a number of these movies. The companies like him because he works cheap and he delivers. On time and on or under budget."

"I asked around about the guy," said Alvarez. "He's not really known in the mainstream Hollywood community, whatever the fuck that is. But the people who *had* heard of him didn't have anything bad to say."

"There's nothing in the computer on the guy," said Tony. "Not even an outstanding parking violation." He looked up at the two detectives. "Thanks. That'll be all."

Talbot and Alvarez smiled and nodded at Cheney again and left.

"They did this on their own time."

"Who says brown-nosing doesn't work."

"It's not like that, Cheney. At least Alvarez and Talbot aren't like that. I had them sign the waiver you told me to get them to sign. No problem. Signed it on the spot. They're good cops. So what if they make a buck consulting on cop shows? Big deal. I'd rather they pick up some money that way than a helluva lot of other ways you and I both know about."

"You're right. I'm just in a bad mood. Sorry." Cheney stood. "Maybe I better get outa here. It might be contagious." At the office door, he turned and said, "There *is* one thing I'd like you to do."

"Yeah?"

"I know you didn't find anything actionable on Marzetti. But see what else you can find out about the guy."

"Like?"

"Like where he's from."

"Why?"

"I'll bet you ten to one he's from Las Vegas."

Tony smiled and made a note. "What does your gut tell you about Marzetti?"

"My gut's kinda preoccupied right now," said Cheney.

Tony took that to mean that Cheney was thinking about Elizabeth. Which, in a way, was true. But that was only a small part of it.

Cheney looked at his old friend. "You and I are different now."

"What do you mean?"

"You're official, I'm working private."

"What are you getting at?"

"There are a lot of things you can do that I can't," said Cheney.

"So?"

"And there are a few things I can do that official cops can't."

"Such as?"

"Do you really want to know?"

Tony thought about that for a moment. "Not really."

"Good night, Tony."

Cheney didn't feel like driving straight home. He was trying to think and trying not to think at the same time. He figured that Marty's was his ultimate destination. He knew if he went home Petty would be there, and she would be so up and positive and full of optimism. Because she did not know the whole truth. He was the only one who did, and it was killing him.

He looked up in time to see the Silverlake exit off the Hollywood Freeway. What the hell, he thought. It was worth a shot. Marty's would be open for another four hours.

*   *   *

"What are you doing here?"

"I was just in the neighborhood."

"I'll bet," said Kyoko Rabinowitz. "Next time call."

"Can I come in?"

"I guess."

Cheney stepped inside. An incense Cheney recognized as Three Roses was burning in a small metal dish with Indian symbols engraved on the outside. He recognized the scent from the days when he was dating a hippie, when *hippie* wasn't a funny or pejorative term. That was a long time ago. But he still remembered the fragrance. On Kyoko's TV a view from a mountaintop was freeze-framed. There was a mat on the floor where Cheney figured Kyoko had been meditating.

"I didn't mean to interrupt. And you're right, I should have called first. But I really was in the neighborhood."

"Say ten Hail Marys, buy a dozen boxes of Girl Scout cookies, and you can consider yourself absolved."

Ah, if were only that easy, thought Cheney.

He sat down on the couch without being asked, and Kyoko dropped down onto the mat on the floor. She was wearing a short robe. Knowing her as he did, or as he remembered her from the backyard interview, he figured she'd probably been meditating in the nude when he knocked on the door.

"So?" she said, rather impatiently.

"Did you or Barbara know a woman about your

age by the name of Kimberly Gary? She's from Vegas."

Kyoko shook her head. "Never heard of her. Is that all?"

"No. The conversation Barbara had with the black-mailer, from your phone . . ."

"Yes?"

"What do you remember about it?"

"Nothing I haven't already told you."

"I want you to think about it again, focus on it," he said. Cheney knew from his twenty-plus years of experience that a lot of witnesses knew things they didn't know they knew. It had nothing to do with withholding information. It was just that they didn't remember—until someone made them remember.

"I already have."

"You meditate?"

"Yes."

"Pretend you're meditating. Take yourself back to that moment. Where did she make the call?"

"In my bedroom."

"Which is where?"

"Through that door," said Kyoko, pointing to a room off to her right.

"And you were sitting where?"

"Right where you're sitting."

"So you're sitting on the couch and she's on the phone in your room."

"Right."

"Was the door closed?"

"No."

"So you could hear what she was saying?"

"I guess."

"You must have been curious about who she was talking to. She had just made you promise not to tell her husband, under any circumstances, that she was being blackmailed. How did she sound to you?"

"What do you mean?"

"Did she sound angry? Did she sound polite? Did she sound scared?"

"She sounded angry."

"So you heard her voice."

"I suppose so."

"It's natural that she would be angry with someone who was blackmailing her."

"Yes."

"What did she say?"

"I don't know."

"Did she say a name?"

"No."

"Focus. Close your eyes."

Kyoko closed her eyes.

"Think about that time. Your best friend was angry. She was in the next room; you're sitting here on the couch. Her voice is loud because she's angry and you're sitting here catching bits and pieces of what she's saying. Tell me what she's saying."

"I don't know," said Kyoko, her eyes still closed.

"She's yelling at someone!"

"She's angry, yes."

Cheney noticed that Kyoko suddenly crossed her legs and sat in a meditation-type posture. She straightened her back. Put her right hand on her right knee, her left hand on her left knee, the index finger of each hand touching the thumb.

"She says his name!" Cheney shouted.

"No, she doesn't say a name."

"What does she say?"

"I don't know."

"Tell me what she says. You know!"

"I don't. . . ."

"Yes?"

"She says, 'Fuck you, bitch!'" Kyoko's eyes opened as she said the words. She looked at Cheney and smiled in wonder. "She was talking to a woman."

And for the first time in several hours, Cheney smiled too.

The man laid the knife against the struggling woman's left breast. Her hands were tied over her head and she stood on tiptoe.

"Good lord, Cheney!"

Cheney turned around, startled. "I didn't hear you come in."

Petty looked at Cheney as though he were some kind of pervert. "I always wondered who bought this kind of pornography."

"It's not pornography," said Cheney. "It's research for a case I'm working on."

Petty looked at him incredulously. "I'm glad Elizabeth isn't spending another week in the hospital. You could run amok." And with that parting shot and a dismissive and judgmental raising of the eyebrows, Petty marched out of the living room and into her own room.

The guy in the video store hadn't treated Cheney much better when he had checked out five low-budget slasher movies written and directed by Gino

Marzetti. When the clerk had asked him if he wanted a bag, Cheney got the distinct impression that the young man was asking, Would you like your pornography in a plain brown wrapper, sir?

Making ample use of the fast-forward button on his remote control, Cheney "speed-watched" all five movies by 1 A.M. Whereas they had different plots—not distinctly different, but different enough to give each film a different title—they all had similar elements. In each movie, the women who were slashed were always bound or tied up in some fashion. Each woman had lost the audience's sympathy in that she had cheated on a man before she was killed. Cheney thought this odd, because usually films manipulated the viewer into caring about the victim before he or she was killed, thus intensifying the audience reaction.

The villain in each of Marzetti's movies was usually the most fleshed-out character. And his good side was often accented. He was usually driven to his acts of violence by the woman's betrayal.

Another trait of the villains was that they seemed to really love women and appreciate their beauty. Their blind adoration always left them vulnerable to betrayal.

Cheney hit the OFF button and the TV went dark. There were no other lights on in the house. Petty was usually asleep before *The Tonight Show* was over.

As he sat there in the darkness, by himself, having filled his head with Marzetti's visions of life and death, love and betrayal, it occurred to Cheney for the first time that they were dealing not with a man who hated women.

But rather with a man who loved them. Terribly.

twenty-five

"A woman, eh?" said Tony Boston, repeating Cheney's words, not for the first time.

Cheney, Cynthia Talbot, and Jerry Alvarez sat in chairs opposite Tony, who was behind his desk. Cheney had just described his conversation with Kyoko Rabinowitz and his viewing of the Gino Marzetti film festival.

Alvarez, who once again wore his uniform of the day—jeans, white shirt open at the neck, and a tweed sport coat—spoke first. "I saw a coupla those movies. Sick, man. Sick."

Cheney didn't ask why Alvarez had seen more than one of Marzetti's movies if he'd had such an obvious thumbs-down reaction to them. People slowed down to see accidents. Didn't mean they liked what they saw.

"Marzetti's from Vegas," said Tony, smiling at his old mentor. "You were right."

"But he's got no record," said Talbot, repeating the bottom line of Tony's previous computer check.

"That's right. But I did a little more digging. He came here in 1986."

"Shortly after Barbara Holgate Sanford," said Cheney, not so much adding information to the pot as singing his verse in the round. But he didn't say that Kimberly Gary was also from Vegas. Not because Tony didn't know that already, because he obviously did. He didn't say it because ...

"Would you two excuse us for a second," said Cheney to Alvarez and Talbot. It was not a question. The two detectives grabbed Styrofoam cups of coffee and left, shutting the door behind them.

"This is about Kimberly, isn't it?" Tony was many things, but when it came to his job he was never stupid.

"I just think we should watch her, that's all."

"She insinuated herself into the investigation. I'd never met her before this case came up."

"She admits she recognized Barbara's picture in the paper and saw an opportunity," said Cheney, making an attempt to explain Kimberly's innocent involvement.

"She forced her way into your Vegas trip."

"Her references checked out at the paper."

"It's clear she knew Barbara Holgate."

"She says she knew *of* her. Had never spoken to her."

"Probably knew Marzetti."

"We have no proof of that."

Tony stopped and shook his head, not looking at Cheney. "She has no record." He looked up at

Cheney. "I checked. She got a speeding ticket in 1991. That's the worst thing she's ever done."

Cheney thought about adding the word "officially" but remained silent. Even if Kimberly was not a criminal, she would not be eligible for sainthood in this lifetime. What he said was, "So where do we go from here?" It was the appropriate thing to say. Tony, not Cheney, was in charge. Officially.

"We've got to keep an eye on her. Obviously, I won't give her any more information about the case."

"Does she know we know about Marzetti?"

Tony exhaled deeply, fingered his cup a little, then looked up at his mentor. "Yeah."

Cheney nodded and tried to make his expression appear nonjudgmental. Nothing Cheney could say would make Tony feel worse than he already did.

"Look, Tony, let's not jump the gun here. Everything's circumstantial at this point. Like you say, she's never been in trouble before. I just think it's smart to keep an eye on her, that's all. Let's leave it at that."

"Yeah," said Tony, not completely convinced. "I'll brief Talbot and Alvarez. Maybe they can find something on her that'll tie her to Marzetti."

Cheney looked at his watch.

"What time is Elizabeth being released?"

"About forty-five minutes."

"Then what the fuck are you doing here?"

"Right." Cheney stood and walked to the door. "Tony . . ."

"Yeah."

"Don't crucify yourself over this. First, Kimberly may be innocent. And second . . ."

"Yeah?"

"We all make mistakes," said Cheney. With conviction.

"Watch your step," said Cheney as he helped Elizabeth out of the car.

By the time Cheney had closed the passenger side door, Petty was hurrying out of the house. She approached Elizabeth gingerly, not knowing what she should or should not do. Didn't want to squeeze her too tight, touch her in the wrong place, hurt her in any way. Elizabeth made it easy. She opened her arms wide and enveloped the smaller woman, who hugged her back and started to cry. Neither woman said anything, except occasionally each other's name.

After taking Elizabeth's things into the bedroom, Cheney walked back into the living room, where Petty was waiting for him. She pulled him aside surreptitiously. "Did you hide your pornography?"

Cheney couldn't tell whether she was serious or not. To his surprise, he actually thought she was. "I told you those videos were research. But I returned them this morning."

"Good. My lips are sealed. You know tonight's my usual bridge night. But if you want me to cancel . . ."

"No, that's fine," said Cheney. Every Sunday night Petty played bridge with her sister and two other women. Cheney learned long ago that bridge was merely a euphemism for poker and that liberal amounts of schnapps and peach brandy were provided by her sister from a pot into which each woman contributed five dollars. Knowing this to be the case, Cheney always encouraged Petty to spend the night at her sister's place.

Upstairs, Elizabeth was lying on their bed, two large down-filled pillows behind her, propping her up. "It's good to be home," she said.

Cheney sat down on the bed next to her. "Not as good as it is to have you back home."

Elizabeth squeezed Cheney's hand. "You know, you'd think since I was sleeping like Rip Van Winkle, I wouldn't be tired. But I'm positively exhausted."

"Nothing on the schedule but rest and relaxation." Cheney looked at all the flowers on the table next to the bed. Flowers he had brought her, flowers people at work had given her. "Flowers look great."

Elizabeth looked at them. "They do, don't they. I love flowers."

"I know. And I love you."

Elizabeth looked at her husband. She didn't speak for a moment. Just looked at him. Took in his eyes, his face, his lips, his broad shoulders. His strong hands. His love. "It must have been very tough on you, Cheney," she said.

"Oh, it wasn't—"

Elizabeth held up her hand. "We need to start telling each other the truth."

Cheney looked at his wife, swallowed hard, and said, "It was the toughest thing I've ever been through. The most terrifying two days of my life."

Elizabeth's lips curled a little. It was not so much a smile as an indication that she understood. She nodded. "Last night after you left, I couldn't sleep. I tried to put myself in your position—watching *you* lie there, unable to do anything, not knowing if you were ever going to wake up. God, it must've been awful."

"But you. You were the one—"

"I was asleep, Cheney. I was the lucky one."

Silence.

"Anyhow," she said, "one thing I thought about this afternoon was that we need to tell each other the things that need to be said. We never know when something like this could happen again. There could be an accident. You could get shot. Plus, we're getting older; we just can't leave the important things unsaid."

"Nothing is more important, to me, than for you to know that I love you, Elizabeth. I have loved two women in my life, but I never loved anyone as much as I love you."

"I know—"

"No, listen, please. I know you know that I love you. But I'm really not sure you know how much. There's nothing or no one in my life, including myself, that means as much to me as you. I've known that since the day I married you, and I guess I figured you knew it too. But that's not good enough. When you were lying there, it occurred to me that you might not know how much I love you. And that . . ."— Cheney felt his eyes misting up—"that was a terrible thought. I just couldn't shake it. I love you, Elizabeth. I love you so much!"

Cheney embraced his wife. And she held her husband tightly. Trying her best, through her own tears, to tell him she felt exactly the same way about him.

*   *   *

"How late can you stay tonight?" Cheney asked.

"I can stay all night if you want me to," said Petty.

"No, that's fine. What time are you leaving for your sister's?"

"Eight o'clock. The game's supposed to start at eight, but Dottie—she's my sister's best friend—never shows up before eight-thirty. And I'm only fifteen minutes away, so leaving at eight gives me plenty of time."

"Great. I'd appreciate it if you waited here until I get back. Elizabeth is sleeping now, and I figure she'll be out for a while."

"No problem. I won't leave till you get back."

"I'll be back before eight."

As Cheney sat in his car, under the tree, a half a block south of Kimberly Gary's condominium, a lot of thoughts went through his mind. He realized with bitter irony that a life that had been solidly on track, predictable to the point of boredom, had suddenly become a runaway train, sprung from the tracks, careening into a chaotic and dangerous darkness. So much of his life, all the things that had meaning, were now subject to factors beyond his control.

George Winston was playing Pachelbel's *Canon* on the CD. There had always been one note, toward the end of the famous piece, that in Winston's interpretation sounded incorrect. But when he and Elizabeth had caught Winston in concert at UCLA last year, he had played it exactly the same way. Since then, Cheney had just chalked it up to the fact that Winston knew more about music than he did. Which, when you thought about it, would have been the short-odds answer all along.

All of a sudden, thousands of raindrops began to pelt Cheney's Mercedes. It happened like that sometimes. No warning. It came down in buckets. And if you were lucky you were standing someplace where you didn't get wet. Cheney remembered an old police captain who once told him, "The shit's gonna hit the fan, Cheney. Ain't nothin' you can do about it. The trick is figuring out where to stand so you don't get any on you."

Cheney was sitting there listening to George Winston, feeling melancholy, trying to figure out why his life had turned to shit and where he was going to stand when it all hit the fan—when Kimberly Gary walked out of her condo, got into her black Prelude, and pulled away.

Kimberly got onto the San Diego Freeway at Wilshire and took it south to the Santa Monica Freeway, which she took east, toward downtown. The rush-hour traffic was slowing by this time, ten minutes till seven. Cheney had a phone in the car and was prepared to ask Petty to sacrifice her poker—that is, bridge game—if that was necessary.

The rain had started late enough so that it just caught the tail end of rush-hour traffic, but it still slowed things down. LA drivers became wimps when it rained, like rain was some kind of road hazard. Cheney had driven in the Midwest, with the temperature at ten below zero, on a solid sheet of ice, people laying on their horns because the drivers in front of them weren't going the speed limit. Rain? Fuckin' rain? Why didn't they just pull over to the side of the road and start crying till the AAA towed them home?

Cheney shook his head. In spite of the soothing sounds of George Winston, he realized he was wired. When he was wired, he got cynical: about life, about politics, about driving in the rain.

He followed Kimberly as she transitioned from the Santa Monica Freeway to the Harbor Freeway north. The traffic ground to a halt as they slowly passed by the intimidating downtown skyline. Not intimidating when you compared it to Manhattan's skyline, thought Cheney, only compared to most any other city's skyline west of the Mississippi. In the rain, when traffic was slow. When your life seemed to be closing in on you and George Winston's melancholy music was playing on the CD.

When Kimberly pulled off at the Chinatown/Broadway exit, Cheney's heart skipped a beat. He had hoped—prayed—that she would not get off there. Hoped she would just keep on driving. Get off maybe in Pasadena or Glendale. Do some shopping and go home. No harm, no foul. Nothing incriminating about shopping, was there?

But she had turned off on the Broadway exit. Cheney followed, his wipers intermittently clearing the way, the glare of Chinatown neon fragmented into hundreds of tiny scenes by the drops falling, landing, and being swept away on his windshield.

Yet always in clear sight were the two taillights in front of him. Cheney tried to pretend he didn't know where she was going, but every turn mocked his game.

He followed her across the railroad tracks and away from Chinatown into the loft area. When she pulled up in front of 490 South Summerset, Cheney had already stopped a block back and parked, turning his lights off before Kimberly did.

He watched her run inside. Cheney knew the address. It was Gino Marzetti's building.

Perhaps it was because it was raining. Perhaps it was because . . . Cheney grabbed his temple and tried to massage some sanity into a mind in desperate need of something to grab hold of. George Winston was silent now. Cheney was about as alone as he had ever been in his life. Watching. Waiting. Waiting for the numbers in his life to add up to a sum. To a meaningful bottom line.

Cheney was thinking again about calling Petty when Kimberly ran out of the building as fast as she had run into it, jumped into her car, and drove off.

He left the CD player off. There was no background music that could give this movie a happy ending. Not anymore. Cheney felt like a fucking fool. A rather appropriate term, he thought, considering. . . . He had thought he was beyond that. But then, maybe no man was really beyond such things until he couldn't do it anymore. Maybe.

Maybe some men were beyond it for other reasons. Cheney used to think he was one of those men.

Kimberly was back on the Santa Monica Freeway heading west. Going home, Cheney figured.

He was a flawed man, always had been, and he knew it. Perhaps living with Elizabeth had provided him with a false sense that he had matured beyond temptation. The saying *There's no fool like an old fool* flashed in his head. How could he have been so fucking stupid?

The Wilshire exit came and went.

Where was she going? Maybe she was going to the club to play racquetball. Cheney wondered when Kimberly had purchased her membership. He had never seen her there before the day Tony had introduced her to him. At least he had never noticed her before.

Cheney had the sinking feeling that when it was all played out he was going to look bad. What had he been thinking? He knew, at least he used to know, that part of the con was getting you to think what you wanted to think.

Kimberly took the Sunset exit and headed west.

Toward Pacific Palisades.

Kimberly finally came to a stop in front of a large house with a semicircular driveway. Cheney pulled up a block behind her and turned off his lights. And waited.

This time Kimberly remained in her car, for fifteen minutes by the clock on Cheney's dashboard, before she drove away.

Cheney had thought about calling Petty, but when Kimberly drove away he didn't have to. The clock on the dash read 7:52.

It wouldn't take him eight minutes to drive one block and walk inside his own house.

"What do you think it means?" Tony asked. He had come directly from the club. Cheney had beeped him and he had arrived just as Petty was leaving.

They were in Cheney's study. Elizabeth was watching TV. Cheney sat in the swivel chair behind his mahogany desk, and Tony sat in a stuffed burgundy chair in front of the desk.

"I'm not sure. You got enough for a warrant on Marzetti's place?" asked Cheney, even though he knew the answer.

"No."

"If Kimberly told him we're on to him, he's going to cover his tracks so deep tonight we'll never uncover them."

"You mean he's going to destroy evidence."

Cheney nodded.

"I still can't get a warrant on what we've got."

"I know."

Both men sat in silence, each lost in his own recriminations. And in each man's private hell, Kimberly Gary danced somewhere in the flames.

"Can you get somebody over here to watch Elizabeth tonight?"

"Alvarez and Talbot?" said Tony.

"Okay." Cheney just looked at his friend.

"Are you sure?" asked Tony.

"I'm sure."

"I'll call Alvarez and Talbot." Tony stood and shook Cheney's hand.

Cheney walked his friend to the door and watched him drive off. And shut the door.

He had not made the final decision until . . . until he saw Kimberly drive up and park in front of his house. In front of the house where his wife lived.

At that moment, Cheney knew there was only one thing he could do.

twenty-six

"What do you mean, there will be detectives here until you get back?"

"It's nothing, really."

"C'mon, Cheney, I might've been asleep for a while, but I didn't wake up stupid. This is *me* you're talking to here. Elizabeth. A cop's wife."

"I need you to trust me on this, honey. I'm not in any danger, but unless I act tonight, we might lose a suspect."

"Does this have to do with the Barbara Sanford case?"

"Yes. Time to go earn my money."

"So what about the detectives?"

"Just a precaution. You know me—better safe than sorry."

"Get off it, Cheney, you sound like a public service announcement."

"Look, I'm just being cautious, that's all. I can end it all tonight. Hell, I'll be back in time to see David Letterman with you."

"I don't like David Letterman."

"Whatever. Cut me some slack on this, okay? I'm in no danger, really."

"Really?"

"Really."

After a moment Elizabeth said, "You never could lie." She smiled. "That's one of the things I like most about you." It had been a long time since she'd had to be a cop's wife. She knew there wasn't anything she could say that would change Cheney's mind. All she could do was make it easier for him. Support the decision he had already made. She knew the important decisions he made, as a cop and as a man, were never taken lightly. And if they weren't easy, they were usually wise.

"I love you, Cheney."

"I love you, Elizabeth."

And suddenly there was nothing else left to say. "I'll be back as soon as possible," said Cheney.

"Good luck, sir," said Jerry Alvarez.

"Don't worry about a thing, sir," said Cynthia Talbot. "I'll be inside with your wife until you return."

"Thank you, detective. That does make me feel better."

It took some of the pressure off, knowing that a policewoman would be in the house with Elizabeth and that Alvarez would be standing guard in the shadows outside. Just in case.

Cheney had instructed the two officers to be on the

lookout for two specific individuals, Gino Marzetti and Kimberly Gary. But no one, and Cheney could not have stressed this more strongly had he branded the instructions on their foreheads, was to enter his house until he returned.

By the time Cheney started toward Marzetti's Chinatown loft, the rain had stopped. It was nearly ten o'clock. The talk radio guy had a community leader on who was saying that black people could not be racist because they had no power. White hate was racism, black hate was justified rage. As a cop, Cheney knew there were wrongs on both sides and hate was hate whatever you called it. The bottom line was that everybody suffered. Especially the children. Everyone's children.

Cheney wondered what kind of rage made a man open up a woman's chest with a knife. Cheney had seen the photos. It was nothing less than rage. As a man, he wondered what could make Marzetti hurt that badly.

As a cop, Cheney was thinking about how to take him out.

"Can I get you anything?"

"No, I'm fine," said Elizabeth. "Thanks anyhow. Feel free to help yourself to anything in the kitchen. I think there's some leftover angel hair with pesto sauce in the fridge."

"Thanks, I already ate," said Cynthia. The two women had already gotten past the "Detective Talbot" part.

*   *   *

Cheney parked his car across from the three-story loft building where Marzetti lived. He knew Marzetti had the whole third floor. Lights were burning. On top of the building was a lighted sign for a brand of beer Cheney didn't recognize. A blonde in a string bikini was lying on her stomach, her top untied, looking seductively out on the world, which in this case was a vacant lot full of broken glass and shell casings.

On the radio the black community leader was telling the talk-show host, who was Jewish, that he would be willing to stop talking about slavery if the talk-show host would stop talking about the Holocaust.

Cheney was too young to remember slavery or the Holocaust. He did remember someone had once said that those who did not know history were doomed to repeat it.

But he remembered someone else saying that the only time you could live was now.

The station went to commercial.

And Cheney got out of the car.

"I love *Seinfeld*," said Elizabeth. Cheney had been good enough to tape the show over the past couple of months. They used to watch it together, the only network show they watched regularly.

"That was very funny," said Cynthia. "I've never seen *Seinfeld* before. I usually watch *Home Improvement*." She sipped a Diet Coke and scooped a handful of popcorn from the bowl of Orville Redenbacher's Smart Pop that Elizabeth had fixed. "A lot less fat and calories," she had said as she handed Cynthia one of the two bowls she brought from the kitchen.

* * *

As Cheney rode the freight elevator up to the third floor he didn't know what to expect. Which, he knew as a street cop, wasn't bad. A street cop lived in the moment. And either you were prepared or you weren't. For anything at any time.

Cheney, the former chief of detectives, the former street cop, felt prepared.

The elevator opened not into the loft but onto a twenty- or thirty-foot hallway that led to a blue steel door.

Cheney opened, then closed, the wrought-iron elevator door and walked toward the blue door. There was a doorbell next to the door. Cheney pressed it and waited.

For a murderer to open the door.

Cynthia Talbot opened the door.

"Everything okay?" said Jerry Alvarez.

"Fine. Everything's fine. Want some popcorn?"

"No, thanks. I ate before I came. Your walkie workin'?"

Cynthia picked up her walkie-talkie, pressed a button, and said "Hello" into it. The word resounded in Alvarez's walkie-talkie.

"I'm behind the rosebush over there," said Alvarez, pointing to a piece of manicured landscape near the west side of the semicircular driveway.

"Have fun," said Cynthia. Then she shut the door. And waited.

* * *

Cheney did not have to wait too long. When Marzetti opened the door on the second ring, he didn't look surprised.

"Cheney, right?"

"That's right."

"Come in."

Cheney walked in as Marzetti closed and locked the steel door. He looked around and realized he had entered another world. Marzetti's world.

Sixteen screens encircled the room. In the middle of the room was a console that had, at its center, a large computer monitor and keyboard.

"Welcome," said Marzetti.

Cheney was happy to get inside so easily. He considered it a distinct possibility that he would have to tap-dance around the rules of evidence, but since Marzetti did not deny him entrance, had in fact invited him in, Cheney figured he was at least one step ahead of the game.

"Nice place," said Cheney.

"Thanks."

Both men were silent.

"So, what are you doing here?"

"Do you know Kimberly Gary?"

"Why?" said Marzetti.

Cheney took that as an answer. "And you knew Barbara Holgate Sanford."

"What's this all about?"

"You're saying you don't know?"

"I'm saying you knocked on my door and I let you in. Beyond that . . ." Marzetti shrugged as if to say he didn't know what Cheney was getting at.

Both men eyed each other for a moment. Cheney

looked into Marzetti's eyes. If there was fear there, he could not see it.

"Have a seat," said Marzetti, waving a hand toward a chair near the console. Like an usher at a theater.

Cheney walked over and sat down in the chair, which resembled a theater seat.

"Welcome to the premiere," said Marzetti.

"What are you talking about?"

Marzetti walked over to the console in front of Cheney, stopped, looked at the detective, and smiled. Then he pressed a couple of buttons and suddenly a projector came on. But it was not like any projector Cheney had ever seen. About ten feet in front of the projector an image appeared, the image of a woman with her hands tied over her head and a man standing in front of her putting clothespins on her nipples.

"It's a hologram. Primitive compared to the holograms the studios can produce. But by using a few of my studio connections, and with my electronics and film background, I've been able to whip something up. It's rather impressive, don't you think?"

Cheney stood. In awe. The images were three-dimensional. Not on a screen but as though they existed in real life, floating free.

"Go on," said Marzetti, a smile of satisfaction splitting his face in two. "Touch it."

Cheney walked "into" the three-dimensional image, then turned to Marzetti.

"A special effect."

"It's amazing."

"But it's more than that, really." Marzetti walked over to where Cheney stood, touching nothing.

Gino reached out and grabbed a handful of air. "This is my life, Cheney. People are driven by their nightmares. By nightmares they can never completely come to grips with. Never remember in detail. This is my nightmare. My obsession." Marzetti walked through the holographic image.

"Most people are ruled by mental pictures they can't see. Me, I know what motivates me. And I've built a monument to it. To her. And I can look at it and walk into it, through it, and around it. Get to know it. Try to free myself from it."

"What's this all about?" asked Cheney.

"It's about love, Cheney. It's about love." Once again Marzetti waved a hand toward the chair near the console, and the detective walked over and sat down.

"So, what *is* this all about?" repeated Cheney.

"It's about real life. That's what any good movie is really about, don't you think?"

"I don't see a movie."

"You will. That's why you're here," said Marzetti with a knowing smile.

It was then Cheney realized he had been expected. Who had tipped Marzetti off? There was one obvious answer.

Marzetti sat down in a chair about ten feet from Cheney, a large remote control in his hand, and hit a button. Suddenly all sixteen screens flickered on. The screens were white with light, but they were blank.

"You know why I'm here," said Cheney. It was not a question.

"I do." Marzetti smiled. Confidently. "Do *you* know why you're here?"

Cheney did not respond.

"Watch the movie, Cheney. This is my life."

"I love *This Is Your Life*," said Elizabeth, who was old enough to remember the Ralph Edwards shows when they originally aired. Remembered the format, the sentimentality. She was glad the reruns were on cable and wondered when somebody would be smart enough to bring the show back.

"I don't remember Edwards," said Cynthia.

"Oh, he was an actor in the fifties."

"I was just a baby then."

Elizabeth just smiled. Suddenly she felt tired. Maybe it was the medication. Maybe it was something else.

Cheney recognized the images that began to fill the screens. Began to surround him in vivid color. He had seen those images played out again and again in Marzetti's movies. The helpless woman bound and vulnerable, the killer who tortured and eventually killed her. Who were they? Who were they to Marzetti?

"I loved her," said Marzetti. He was standing several feet from Cheney, the large remote in his hand, his eyes fixed on the large screen in front of Cheney.

"Who is she?"

"The most beautiful woman in the world."

"What's her name?"

"Denise."

"Denise who?"

"She was perfect, Cheney. May I call you Cheney? I understand people call you that."

"Sure." Who had told him that? Again, Cheney could assume only one obvious answer.

"If she was so perfect, why did you kill her?"

"Did I say I killed her?"

"Did you?"

Marzetti smiled. It was the saddest smile Cheney had ever seen. "I'm an artist." He laughed, and the sound echoed throughout the large loft. "I once had a relationship with a woman who thought that only people who painted pictures were artists." He shook his head as though in disbelief. "What in the fuck was I doing wasting my time with someone like that?"

"Why did you kill her?"

"I didn't say I did. But let's just suppose I did—for argument's sake. Do you believe in correction, Cheney?"

"Correction?"

"Of flaws. Of what stands in the way of perfection."

"What stood in Denise's way?" Cheney was trying to keep up and, at the same time, keep Marzetti on track.

"The obstacle that often stands in the way of beautiful women. You're a man, Cheney. Men know these things."

"What things?"

"I'm sure women want to be good, want to be faithful, but they just can't help themselves. Even good women."

"Why can't they be faithful?"

"Their bodies betray them. Certain parts of their bodies, you touch them and things happen. They can't help themselves. Even though they really want to stop."

Cheney noticed that Marzetti said *even though*, not *even if*. In his mind Marzetti believed Denise had wanted to stop.

"Who's the man?" asked Cheney, looking up at the screen, watching a man, whom Cheney did not recognize, putting clothespins on the woman's nipples.

"Pardon?" said Marzetti, as though he were coming out of a trance.

"Who's the man?"

"Who's that man?"

"That's John Garfield," said Elizabeth.

"I thought he looked familiar. Wasn't he in the original *The Postman Always Rings Twice*?"

With newfound respect Elizabeth said, "Yes. With Lana Turner."

Cynthia picked up her walkie-talkie, pressed a button, and said, "Jerry?" There was no answer. She hit the button again. "Come in, Jerry, this is Talbot." No answer.

Cynthia stood.

Elizabeth hit the mute on the remote. "What's wrong?"

"Probably nothing. Probably just a glitch in the walkies. Happens all the time," she said as she moved toward the front door.

Then she took out her gun and said, "Lock the door behind me."

*   *   *

Marzetti hit a button on the remote, and a steel bar slid across the door through which Cheney had entered.

"Just in case you're thinking about getting out of here."

Cheney reached for his gun, which he wore in an ankle holster.

"I wouldn't do that." When Cheney had turned toward the sound of the door bolting shut, Gino had removed a gun from under his jacket. "Slide it across the floor."

Cheney thought about his options. And slid the gun across the floor. Gino picked up Cheney's gun and pocketed it.

"What's going on here, Marzetti?"

"Like I said, this is a premiere. You're the first person to see the final cut."

"What if I don't want to stay?"

"You're a curious man. I think you'll want to see the ending."

"And if I still want to leave?"

Marzetti hit another button on the remote control. Instantly four blinking red lights went on—one near the door and three others, one each on the remaining walls. Beneath each blinking light was a bundle of three sticks of dynamite. Cheney didn't need a map for the rest of it.

"You won't do it," he said.

"Oh, really? And why's that?"

"Because you want people to see your movie. You blow us up, you destroy the film."

"I'm not stupid, Cheney. I have left instructions with a certain party."

"Kimberly?"

"You're a pretty smart fellow," said Marzetti with a sly smile. "The master is safe. The film will be shown. In fact, we're living out the last scene of the movie right now."

"What do you mean?"

"Life is not imitating art here. Life and art are the same thing. When my story is told I'll be famous. All my movies will suddenly hit the video top ten. I'll be like James Dean or the Beatles."

"You're a murderer."

"Even better. People are fascinated with murderers, Cheney. Or don't you watch TV or go to the movies? The public can't get enough of them. A film-maker who is also a murderer?" Marzetti smiled. "What could be more commercial than that?"

Cheney thought about arguing, but as crazy as it sounded, Marzetti was probably right. The first time one of his movies would actually make big money would be the week after . . . Cheney stopped that line of thinking.

"You'll be in the movie of my life. Not you, of course, but an actor playing you. It'll be a big part, too. You'll be in the grand finale."

Cheney tried to divert Marzetti's attention. He looked at the screen again. "Who's the man?"

Marzetti smiled. "You really want to know?"

"Yes, I do."

Marzetti's smile disappeared. "My father."

Elizabeth's heart skipped a beat when she heard the knock on the door. She had not returned to the living room. She was too scared. She had remained in the foyer, waiting for Detective Talbot's return.

"It's me—Cynthia," said a voice from the other side.

Elizabeth breathed an audible sigh of relief and opened the door.

"Everything's okay," said Cynthia. "Like I said, just an equipment malfunction. You got some coffee?"

"Sure. Let me get you some."

"A computer-enhanced version of my father, of course. Using old photographs of him, I was able to create a character that looks just like him."

Silence. Cheney was trying to take in the magnitude of the man's madness.

"I loved Denise," said Marzetti. "In the right way."

"You met her in Vegas."

"I was a photographer and a fledgling filmmaker. I paid the rent by editing at one of the local TV stations. I met Denise when I was giving a lecture at the university. A directing class. Back then people figured I was going to be the next . . . whoever. Anyhow, when I met Denise she was fresh, innocent. Very pretty. The world was all new to her." Marzetti looked up at the cop. "She hadn't been broken yet, you know?"

Cheney knew. He also knew that for most people it was just a question of when.

"She thought I was some kind of god. Sure, I liked the attention, but I really thought she was the most beautiful woman I had ever known, inside and out. Living in Vegas, I saw some lookers. But what's inside pulls the strings. Denise used to have something inside her, something good. I'd never seen something that good before. Never touched it before.

"Never touched it since."

"Good coffee."

"Thanks. It's actually left over from this morning."

"Is that vanilla?"

"Yes. Petty—that's our housekeeper—she always buys the vanilla roast. Cheney and I have learned to like it."

Cynthia looked at her watch.

"Hope Cheney gets back soon," said Elizabeth. It was a meaningless comment. Something to say when there was nothing to say. Wishful thinking. Elizabeth wanted to be in bed with her husband. Not necessarily to make love to him, but to hold him. So they could reassure each other that they were both alive. For another day at least. Another night.

Elizabeth was thinking about all that when they heard the knock on the door.

Elizabeth knew immediately that something was wrong. The walkie-talkie problem was supposed to be handled. Yet someone was outside knocking on the door. Someone who was probably not Detective Alvarez. Elizabeth was suddenly very frightened.

And Cynthia Talbot was moving toward the front door with a gun in her hand.

"Tell me what happened," said Cheney.

"What do you mean?"

"With Denise. And your father."

"Denise was a good girl. She couldn't help herself. She said so."

"She said so?"

"Yes."

"When?"

"That night."

"What night?"

"My father was scum. Always had been. Never wanted me around. Never wanted me, period, from what my mother said. Before she died."

"When did your mother die?"

"When I was ten."

Cheney had Marzetti talking. He was buying time. He had to figure out a way to get the remote control from Marzetti without blowing himself to bits.

"My father was a cop."

When Cynthia looked through the peephole in the door, she saw Kimberly Gary standing there. From a side window Elizabeth could see her too. Elizabeth and Cynthia looked at each other. Lots of questions passed between them. The main question was how she had gotten past Alvarez.

The answer was obvious.

Cynthia took a breath, flung the door open, gun in hand, and aimed it at Kimberly.

"Get down!"

"What?"

"Get down!" screamed Cynthia.

Kimberly complied and lay down on the front porch. Cynthia slowly edged her way out the door, holding the gun on Kimberly as she did so. Inching her way out into the yard, looking toward the place where Alvarez was supposed to be.

"Shit!" she exclaimed. She moved back toward Kimberly, picked her up by the collar, dragged her inside, and threw her against a living room wall.

"What's this all about?" said Kimberly, her voice trembling.

"Alvarez is dead," said Cynthia to Elizabeth.

"My God! What are we going to do?"

Cynthia looked at her watch. It was three minutes to eleven. "Tony'll be calling in three minutes. We'll wait."

Elizabeth sat down in her chair. Cynthia sat in a chair near Elizabeth, gun aimed at Kimberly's forehead.

"Your father did this to the woman you loved?" asked Cheney incredulously.

"My father liked to hurt people. He hurt my mother. He hurt Denise. He hurt me."

"How do you know he did this to Denise?"

"I saw him."

"You actually saw him do it?"

He followed her that night. Followed the woman he loved, the woman he adored. Followed her because even though he knew she loved him as much as he loved her, she seemed different these days.

At first Gino had not been able to put his finger on it. Her attitude changed. Subtly, but noticeably. A lover notices everything. She seemed courteous but distant.

Lovers were more than polite to each other. She had always been much more than courteous to him. Now she was polite. Which, in contrast, made her seem distant.

Gino was thinking about these things as he drove down Paradise Road, her taillights in his sight. She would not expect him to follow her.

When the taillights came to a stop, then went out, she was parked in front of a house. A house Gino knew well.

He had grown up there.

"What are you doing here?" said Elizabeth, trying to remain centered, feeling shaken but secure because Detective Talbot had the gun.

"You called *me!*"

"Shut up!" said Cynthia. "You killed my partner, you stupid bitch!"

The phone rang. Cynthia looked away from Kimberly for an instant.

Which was all it took. The athletic Kimberly leaped at Cynthia, swatting the gun away.

Before it went skittering across the carpet, the gun discharged and a bullet shattered the Tiffany lamp behind Kimberly's head.

Elizabeth screamed.

The phone continued to ring.

Kimberly dove at Cynthia and the two wrestled on the floor, rolling over and over, exchanging punches to the stomach and face as they fought.

Elizabeth got out of her chair and edged her way toward the gun, which lay next to the fireplace. She picked it up and yelled, "Hold it! Now!"

Kimberly and Cynthia stopped fighting and looked up at Elizabeth.

The phone continued to ring.

Elizabeth pointed the gun at Kimberly, who reflexively put her hands over her head. As she did, Cynthia nailed Kimberly with a right cross that knocked her cold, her head landing with a hard thump on the carpet directly in front of the fireplace.

Elizabeth handed Cynthia the gun and answered the phone. There was no one there.

twenty-seven

He waited for Denise to go inside. Waited another fifteen minutes before he got out of his car. Waited . . . for what?

For the end of the world. His world.

He walked around to the back of the house. Toward the room with the light. The shade was pulled, but if he stood to one side he could see inside.

Gino stood to one side.

And saw inside.

And what he saw changed his life forever.

There she was. Denise. Perfect, sweet, innocent Denise. She had come to him a virgin. In many ways. He knew this, not only because she had told him so, but because of the way she had bled when they did it the first time. Because of how tight she was. Because of the way she fumbled awkwardly and did not perform sex as the others had, as though it were a familiar and popular dance, the movements known to all. No, she had been a virgin. Had loved him enough to give him that special honor.

And Gino had tried to be worthy of that privilege. Had tried to show her how much he loved her. How much he respected her. In spite of the fact that she was taking her own time—her own sweet fucking time, to fully warm to sex. With him. He was thinking this as he looked through the shades into the dimly lit room. Into the shadows, the growing darkness. Into what would become the black hole that would inevitably swallow up every good and joyous emotion inside him. Swallow them whole and then, when he least expected it, regurgitate them in a reconstituted form, fouling the crippled life Gino had created for himself after that night.

It had been Christmas Eve when Gino stood looking into the window. At his father . . . with his sweet and innocent Denise. Gino's first movie would be entitled Christmas Mourning.

As Gino took in the sight of his lover in his father's arms, it appeared that she was having no trouble warming to someone else.

Gino watched as his own father, the man who had raised him, the man who had beaten his mother and drove her to an early grave—the man who knew that this woman was his son's lover—tied Denise's hands over her head and slipped the rope over a large hook that was screwed into the ceiling.

Denise stood in the middle of the room, on tiptoes, nude except for high heels. Gino could not understand what had turned his virgin queen into such a slut. Could not comprehend the transformation.

Then his father took two clothespins out of his pocket, the kind with the spring, and clipped one on each of Denise's nipples. It did not look excruciating, but the look on Denise's face was suddenly transformed and all at once he knew. Knew what his father knew. What Gino had not known. About women. About how their bodies betrayed them. How could he have been expected to know? Such things were never spoken.

All at once Denise's head fell back in ecstasy and she began to moan. The sound of that guttural, visceral ecstasy pierced Gino's heart like an iron stake driven home with a sledgehammer.

"I can't help myself!" she moaned. "It feels too good!"

At that moment Gino understood it was not Denise's fault. The monster who had destroyed his mother was destroying the only other person Gino had ever loved. Touching her in evil ways that a person as innocent as Denise had no defense against. His father knew her body would betray her.

That she was helpless.

"I felt so helpless," said Elizabeth.

"It's over now," said Cynthia, still breathing hard from her fight with Kimberly. "Strong little bitch."

"What do you think she was doing here?"

"I don't know. All I know is, you're lucky I was here. You got something to drink?"

"Like what?"

"Soda'd be fine."

"Sure. I'll be right back."

"I'll call Tony."

As Elizabeth left the room, Cynthia walked over to the phone.

*　　*　　*

Gino knew what he had to do. He was not thinking about what he had to do. He was running on raw emotion. Passion fueled his every movement. He entered the house through the back door. The back door of what used to be his own home.

When he appeared in the room, the action seemed to freeze for a moment. No one moved. Denise looked at him with humiliation and guilt, and yet there was something else in her eyes. Helplessness. Even in her moment of ultimate degradation, her eyes communicated that she still could not control herself. That she had crossed a border from which there would be, could be, no return.

And in that instant, everything became clear.

The look in his father's eyes was far less complex. Gino recognized it and closed in on it as any animal would. Fear attracted, demanded dominance.

And the rage of a lifetime was suddenly focused in his two fists as Gino began pummeling his father in the face until blood began to splatter from the red pulp with every blow.

While the virgin queen screamed helplessly behind him.

When he had finished with his father, Gino turned to his hysterical lover, who was by this time pleading for her own life. As he slowly registered the helpless look in her eyes, the sounds of her ecstasy still ringing in his head, he knew what he had to do.

He could make his perfect lover perfect again. He left the room for a moment, and when he returned he carried a knife. And with that knife he cut away the imperfections that had betrayed his lover.

That had betrayed him.

In spite of the passion that filled his limbs with adrenaline, he was careful not to dig the knife in too deeply.

Because he knew what he would do next. He would not pay for the crime these two had committed.

An hour later Gino put both bodies into his father's car and drove to a quarry ten miles outside of Vegas. He pushed the car into the quarry and it burst into flames. When it was found two days later, all that was left of the two bodies was enough bone and teeth to provide positive identifications.

The nightmare was over.

What surprised Gino the most was that it was not over. Besides the guilt, which he was able to rationalize away most of the time because of the injustice that had been done to him, there was another feeling. A feeling that at first he did not understand. A feeling he refused to accept. In the beginning.

But the more he resisted that feeling, the more it dominated his thoughts. Until he could no longer deny it.

He had been disgusted by what he saw through the window that night. He had been enraged by what he saw through the window that night. And . . . .

He had been aroused by it. The sight of the beautiful Denise, standing on tiptoes in her high-heeled shoes, her every muscle straining taut, her head thrown back in anguish and in ecstasy, the sound of her moans, which were a complex and erotic mix of pain and pleasure . . . he could not shake it. Could not deny it. And finally gave in to it. Acted it out.

Corrected the imperfection. Healed the body so it would not betray its innocence.

Made his virgin queen . . . a virgin again.

"Thanks," said Cynthia, taking the diet soda from Elizabeth.

Elizabeth sat down in a chair opposite Cynthia, who sat on the couch, near the still-unconscious Kimberly.

"What did Tony say?"

"He said he'll be right over. This place'll be swarming with cops in five minutes."

"Has he heard from Cheney?"

"Not yet. But I have a feeling we'll know something soon."

"So how did Barbara Sanford fit into all this?" asked Cheney, still trying to keep Gino talking. Trying to figure out a way to get the gun away from him.

"Besides being a young filmmaker, I was a photographer in Vegas. Women came to me all the time. Barbara looked just like Denise. Same features, same body type. The first time I saw her, I thought . . . Well, it was a startling resemblance. But she was just like Denise."

"What do you mean?"

"In the beginning, she was very innocent. But she fell into my trap. She could have escaped. She could have turned it down."

"Turned what down?"

"Temptation. I offered her free photographs if she would pose for me. Pose like a slut. What kind of woman would pose like that? Legs spread apart like a dog. The world is full of women like that. Too full. It's infested with women whose sexuality eats up society, feeds on it like a cancer. Women who use their sexuality to destroy, then blame men for making them do it."

"So you took photographs of Barbara," said Cheney, keeping Gino on track. Carefully edging closer to the madman. Getting ready to make his move. His best move. His only move.

"Dirty photographs. She didn't blink an eye. As long as she got what she wanted, she was willing to . . ."

"So you first tried to kill Barbara in Vegas."

"Very good," said Gino, as though giving praise to a promising pupil. "I tried to make the 'correction' after it was clear that she was like the rest."

"Like the other women you killed in Vegas?"

"Exactly like them. If Barbara had resisted temptation, even though she looked so much like . . . like Denise, she would not have had to die."

"Why didn't she report you to the police?"

"I wore a mask. Had to."

"What happened to Barbara on the Pacific Coast Highway?"

"As you probably already guessed, I sent her some photographs, the ones I took in Vegas. She didn't have any choice but to meet me. I told her she could have the negatives if she paid me a hundred thousand dollars. I knew she couldn't raise the money without her husband finding out."

"But you had another idea," said Cheney.

"I told her there was a certain kind of session I needed done. Two sessions, really."

"With her hands tied above her head, standing on tiptoes."

"I said she could wear a mask to conceal her identity. I'd give her one set of the old negatives after the first session and the other half after the second.

"The first session got a little rough. Left some

marks. She balked at doing the second session, so I suggested we meet."

"On the Pacific Coast Highway."

"It was near her house," said Gino, with a rare smile. Which flickered and died like a spark in the wind.

"She was very upset. Said she couldn't do the second session, because of the marks and the pain. She asked if there wasn't something else we could work out. I said I'd let her have the second set of Vegas negatives if she'd get drunk with me. In the car.

"Initially she refused, but the other two options—the money or a second photo session—made getting drunk seem like a pretty attractive choice. I finally got her so drunk she passed out."

"And that's where Kimberly came in," said Cheney.

Again the spark of a smile. "At the proper moment, Barbara was pushed into the path of an oncoming car."

"Your car."

"My car."

"How did you find Barbara?"

"Apparently Barbara got her photograph in the papers a lot. Society pages. I suppose it was fate. Suddenly, it all came back. My original intention was just to do it one more time. End it with Barbara. But—"

"You couldn't stop."

"I had hoped that I had fulfilled my—"

"Obsession?"

"—fantasy with Barbara. That first session I did with her was . . ." Gino stopped and shook his head as though in awe. "It was incredible. I hadn't performed any 'corrections' since I'd left Vegas. Frankly, I thought I'd left it all behind when I came to Los Angeles."

"Why kill her with a car? Why not kill her like the other victims?"

"If I had killed her and dumped the body, there would have been a murder investigation. But if I killed her and it went down as a hit-and-run, it would all be over."

"But it wasn't over, was it?"

"I don't think you really understand, Cheney. Our society is decadent. More decadent than any culture in history. And that decadence is killing us. One more bitch in heat, who spreads her legs because she can't help it and then blames men for her actions—who needs them? They're like a disease, Cheney. And I'm a surgeon. I can't cure the world, but I can cut out some of the cancer. Society will be a little less decadent without such women. They produce nothing except pain and heartache. Do you understand what I'm saying, Cheney? Do you really understand?"

Suddenly Cheney's foot sprang out from underneath him, catching Gino behind the knee and knocking him off his feet. The gun and the remote control hit the floor as Cheney enveloped Gino in a bear hug and pushed him up against an iron column. Cheney felt the air rush from Gino's lungs. As Gino collapsed, the two men hit the floor.

Gino was really no match for Cheney, even though he was younger. Cheney still ran four miles a day, at least four days a week, and the academy training never fully disappeared. He was working on muscle memory. And the only fighting Gino had done had been with himself. In his head.

Cheney nailed Gino with a left jab, which, Cheney could tell, broke the man's nose, then caught him with a right hook.

Cheney scrambled to his feet and grabbed the gun.

"Don't move."

"Or what?" said Gino, getting to his feet, blood dripping liberally from his nose.

"Or I'll give you a sneak preview of hell."

"Fuck you, Cheney! I'm not going in alive."

He made a move toward Cheney.

"Don't!"

"Fuck you!" screamed Gino and charged.

Cheney fired into Gino's chest. Blood spurted everywhere as the man went down.

Cheney tried to catch his breath, and it finally came. He was thinking now of three things: Elizabeth, the dynamite, and the legal ramifications of what he had just done. He would call Elizabeth to make sure Kimberly was not playing out her own end game. As for the dynamite, he would try to find some other way out of the loft or get somebody from the bomb squad on the phone.

As for the legal part of it, he had shot Marzetti in self-defense. He could make it work. Especially since there were no other witnesses and because the evidence of Marzetti being a serial killer was irrefutable. This was dangerous legal territory. But it was territory that Cheney, a former chief of detectives, was familiar with.

He could make it work.

He took another deep breath and picked up the receiver to call Elizabeth.

Which was when he felt something smash against the back of his head.

And he fell into a black hole.

Elizabeth stood at the window looking out into the darkness. "What's taking them so long?"

"It just seems like it's taking longer because you're afraid."

"Probably."

"There's nothing to be afraid of. Not anymore."

When Cheney came to he was looking up into Gino's crazy eyes. He tried to shake out the cobwebs. The only word that came out was, "What . . . ?"

"Please excuse the theatrics. I squibbed myself."

"Squibbed?" said Cheney, grabbing the back of his aching head.

"Sorry. Movie term. I had several blood bags attached to my body. You shoot a blank at me—from a gun I loaded with blanks and *let* you take from me—and I press a tiny remote control just up my sleeve and voilà! instant blood. Just like in the movies."

"What if I shot you in the face?"

"No cop is going to shoot somebody from that close a range in the face. Wouldn't look good. You're gonna shoot me in the chest, stomach, neck, whatever." Gino held up the gun Cheney had apparently shot Gino with earlier. "It's loaded this time." He raised the gun and fired it into the ceiling. A piece of plaster fell at Cheney's feet.

"Oh, and in case you're curious, the dynamite isn't really dynamite. But it sure looks real, doesn't it?"

"What's this all about?"

"I'm going to live through this, Cheney. You're not. That's what it's all about."

"How?"

"There's going to be a fire. Two bodies will be found. One will be identified as you. Tony Boston will know why you came here, and when a bullet from this gun—my gun—is found in you, and a bullet from your gun is found in me—well, case closed. It's a push. Your buddy will be sad, but that will be the end of it."

"I thought you said you were going to live through it."

"I am."

"But you said—"

"Yes, the bullet from your gun." Gino smiled. Holding the gun on Cheney as he moved, he walked carefully over to a black plastic tarp and pulled it back.

Cheney sucked air. Under the tarp was the body of a man with a bullet in his head.

"Good lord!"

"I sedated him before you arrived and shot him with your gun while you were unconscious. He was a homeless man I found wandering about near the bus terminal. A couple of days ago I took him in and offered to provide him not only with a few free meals but with some dental work as well."

Suddenly Cheney knew where Gino was going with this.

"When the dental work was done . . ." Marzetti smiled.

Cheney had underestimated this man big-time. Perhaps fatally. "You switched the dental records. Put his under your name."

"Interesting, isn't it? Breaking in and rearranging things instead of taking them."

"Surely someone will notice—"

"He and I both went to one of these cheap big-volume clinics. No one would recognize either one of us. Twenty student dentists, two hundred patients a day. I'm willing to take my chances."

And Cheney, the detective, knew the odds were stacked in Gino's favor.

"So when dental records are produced to verify my identity, the deal will be done."

Cheney tried to follow the logic, focus on the subtleties of Marzetti's plan.

Suddenly it hit him. Like a moving train. "Who would know exactly what dentist you've been to in the past week if all your records are burned in a fire?"

Gino smiled. It was the touché smile of a respectful opponent. "Obviously someone must guide things along a bit."

"Kimberly?" said Cheney.

"You're very smart, Cheney. Very smart."

And after a moment Gino added, "But not smart enough."

"I think I'll wait outside for Tony," said Elizabeth.

"I don't think so," said Cynthia.

And she pointed a gun at Elizabeth.

*   *   *

"She's the only one who really loves me, Cheney. Unconditionally. Do you know what I mean?"

Cheney nodded.

"She's not really my sister."

"Who?"

"She's my stepsister. We met when we were both teenagers. Not blood relatives. It wasn't a perverted thing. It was real love."

"I thought he loved me," said Cynthia. "Really loved me. He was my stepfather, not my father. That would have been perverted."

"When I told Cynthia what my father had done, she went crazy. Took it as hard as I did. Her mother— my stepmother—was weak. Out of the picture. A drunk.

"Cynthia was older. She was a cop. She guided things along downtown. Hid things, influenced opinions. She's very competent."

"I know," said Cheney.

"No real questions were raised over my father's death, and when Barbara filed a complaint with the Vegas police about the attack on her it got buried. After the second unsuccessful attempt to 'correct' Barbara, she left town. Right away. And I never saw her again."

"Until you saw her picture in the newspaper."

"Then it all came back." Gino looked at Cheney and cocked his head. "I couldn't help myself, Cheney. I swear to God I couldn't."

"You need help."

"I've got all the help I need," said Gino with a smile.

Cheney looked at the hologram again. "I can see the resemblance."

"What do you mean?"

"The resemblance between you and your father."

"What are you talking about? I'm *nothing* like my father. Nothing!"

"Same nose, same jaw. Maybe you just don't want to see it."

"My father was a drunk and a cheat. He hurt everyone who loved him."

"And you're a murderer."

"You don't understand."

"I understand you have become your father."

"I have not!"

"You have. So much so that now you even look like him."

"I don't!"

"You do. See for yourself," said Cheney, tilting his head slightly toward the hologram. His heart was pounding fast. He was running on pure adrenaline.

Gino turned his head for an instant.

An instant was all the time Cheney had.

An instant was all it took.

He reached out and slapped the gun out of Gino's hand. The gun discharged and Cheney felt a stinging sensation in his upper left arm.

This time Gino fought more powerfully. Fought for real.

Fought for his life.

In and out of the hologram the two men went at

each other. Cheney felt as though he were fighting three opponents—Gino plus the man and woman who, together, had destroyed Gino's life and finally driven him mad.

Using his knees, Gino pushed Cheney off him and dove for the gun. Cheney dove on top of him.

The gun discharged again.

Cheney staggered to his feet and looked down at his stomach and his blood-soaked shirt.

Gino's blood.

Cheney stood back from the scene, resting his weight on a desk, and looked at Gino lying beneath the hologram in a pool of spreading blood.

Two ghosts hovered above him like angels. Dark angels gone before him. Ready to take him . . .

To hell.

"You killed Alvarez," said Elizabeth, starting to fill in the blanks.

"When I went outside to check the walkie-talkies. Then I called Kimberly on my car phone, saying I was you. She had never talked with you, so she didn't know the difference."

"Quite a coincidence, you guarding me tonight, getting the opportunity to set Kimberly up."

"It didn't make any difference. We knew that sooner or later Cheney would go after Gino. Gino called Kimberly and told her to drive over to his loft earlier tonight. She buzzed his place, but he didn't answer the door. I knew Cheney was following her and I knew he suspected her. All he needed was a link between her and Gino. Tonight he got it.

"Any way it worked out, I would have killed Kimberly. She was the number one suspect. Originally, I planned to follow her to her house, shoot her, fire a couple of bullets from a gun into my car, plant the gun on Kimberly, and that would have been the end of it.

"But this works out even better." Cynthia pointed the gun at Elizabeth. "This is the gun Tony is going to find in Kimberly's hand. He already thinks she came here to kill you, because of what your husband did to Gino."

"What did he do?"

"Killed him. Terrible thing. Especially since he was killed in the process."

"Who?"

"Cheney."

"What are you talking about?"

"He's dead."

"No!"

Cynthia raised the gun and pointed it at Elizabeth's forehead.

The sound of the shot echoed off the living room walls, and blood splattered onto the carpet.

twenty-eight

When Cheney had called Elizabeth from Gino's loft, there was no answer. When he had called Tony, Tony could not be reached. But he had left Cheney a message: *Meet me at your place ASAP.*

When Cheney pulled up in front of his house, there were ten black-and-whites, three ambulances, and about fifty neighbors gathered in front of his house. Cheney parked the Mercedes in the middle of the street, jumped out, and ran toward the front door.

No one stopped him. No one stopped the former chief of detectives. Just as he hit the front porch, two attendants were walking out the door. Carrying a stretcher with a body on it. A body with a sheet pulled up over its face.

The attendants looked up at Cheney. Looked surprised. Was it surprise, thought Cheney, or panic? He could not help himself. Cheney pulled the sheet back and winced. Felt, and heard, air escape from his lungs. The woman's face was blown away.

"Oh, God!"

"Cheney!"

Cheney turned and saw Elizabeth running toward him. He ran toward her, taking her in his arms and holding her, careful not to squeeze her too tightly. But it took considerable restraint.

An hour later, in the kitchen, away from the lab guys tearing the living room apart and putting it back together, Cheney listened to Elizabeth and Tony recount the tale of terror that had played itself out in his living room. How with Cynthia holding a gun on Elizabeth, ready to put a bullet in her head, Tony had fired a shot through the living room window and killed Cynthia Talbot, Gino Marzetti's stepsister.

"When I called and didn't get an answer," explained Tony, "I got over here right away. When I saw Alvarez with a bullet in his head, I was expecting the worst." Which was exactly what he had found.

Elizabeth kissed Cheney and said she felt tired and would wait for him in their bedroom. He said he would be along shortly. He wanted to talk to Tony for a moment.

When his wife was out of the room, Cheney said, "I certainly had Kimberly pegged wrong."

"I'm glad. For a lot of reasons."

Cheney just nodded. "I'd like to talk to her. She still around?"

"She was here a little while ago. She got some

treatment for a bump on the head, but she didn't need to go to the hospital. Least she didn't want to."

"Thanks, Tony. I owe you."

"We're always even, Cheney, you and me. You know that."

Cheney hoped Tony would always feel that way.

Outside, next to the only remaining ambulance, Cheney found Kimberly. She had white gauze and tape on her left temple. She was sipping a cup of coffee.

"Hi."

"Hi," she said, looking up from the cup of coffee, which was sending a curl of steam into the chilly night air.

They talked for a few minutes about the obvious events of the evening then Cheney said, "Why did you come here earlier?"

"I just told you. Someone called me, identified herself as Elizabeth, and I came over. I had no idea the person on the phone was Cynthia."

"No, I mean the first time. A little before eight. You came by here and parked for a few minutes, then drove away."

"You were following me?"

"Yes."

There was an awkward moment of silence. "I guess I deserve that. Some of it, anyhow."

"Why did you come by?" said Cheney.

"I had something to tell you. I didn't see your car, so I just drove away."

"What did you want to tell me?"

"I'm not pregnant."

"What?"

"You're off the hook, Cheney. I'm not pregnant. I couldn't stand the suspense, either. I went to my doctor, he did a test, and at an additional cost to myself, or at least my insurance company, they were able to give me the results this afternoon. The rabbit lived, so to speak."

"I don't know what to say."

"You could say you're crushed that you and I won't be the parents of a beautiful and wonderful child, but I wouldn't believe you. Quite frankly, I'm glad it turned out this way. Now you don't have to say anything. No harm, no foul."

Cheney was silent.

"You know, Cheney, you really don't have to say anything to Elizabeth. Communication has its place, but a wise man once told me that part of the art of communication is knowing not only what to say and when to say it but also what not to say. I'm not talking about lying, Cheney. But some things just don't need to be said. It might make you feel a whole helluva lot better to confess, but all you're really doing is using somebody you love as a garbage dump."

"I don't know if I believe that."

"There's some wisdom there, Cheney. And my advice to you," said Kimberly, as she finished her coffee and tossed the Styrofoam cup into a trash can, "is to find it. Fast." She kissed him on the cheek and said, "I gotta go. I've got a story to write." She turned and started to walk away.

"What about Tony?"

She turned back around. "What about him?"

"Are you going to tell him?"

"Tell him what? That you and I had sex one night

when we were both drunk, before I started going out with him? Maybe I should give him graphic details about every man I ever slept with before him. Or maybe he just figures that's my business." She smiled. "I know I do."

Kimberly walked to her car as the last ambulance pulled away, empty, into the heart of the long dark night.

As Cheney lay in bed with his wife an hour later, he was thinking about how much he loved Elizabeth. About how little other things meant in relationship to that feeling.

And he was thinking about what Kimberly had told him.

"Cynthia told me you were dead," said Elizabeth, her head resting on her husband's shoulder. Her life had passed before her when she looked down the barrel of Cynthia's gun. Not her whole life, but chunks of it. The important parts. And Cheney was in almost every scene. She loved this man. Did not want to lose him.

It was strange, she thought, as she lay in his arms, how otherwise intelligent people could get so completely out of touch with reality.

Cheney was reality. Her feelings for him, his for her: they were real. She had taken the most important person in her life for granted this past year, maybe longer. She had explained to Cheney that it was work, something she had to do. And he had accepted that explanation, as she knew he would.

The late hours would end now. As she had always known they would, eventually.

"You know I love you, don't you?" she said.

"Of course. And you know I love you?"

"Yes, I do."

"So where do we go from here?" said Cheney, stroking his wife's hair, feeling her warm thigh resting on his legs.

"What do you mean?"

"You're the therapist. How important is the past?"

"It depends. Without it, people wouldn't have anyone else to blame for their failures, and talk shows wouldn't have any guests."

Cheney smiled. "Seriously."

"Seriously, I don't know. It's not as important as the present. Every once in a while the here and now presents a unique opportunity. Kind of a get-out-of-jail-free card."

"What do you mean?"

"Sometimes something happens. Some kind of realization, something traumatic, whatever." Elizabeth raised herself up on one elbow and looked Cheney in the eye. "Something happens that suddenly and dramatically puts things into a proper perspective."

"Like what's just happened with us."

"Yes. And no amount of therapy or digging up the past can cause that kind of impact."

"So we just go forward?"

"Starting this instant," said Elizabeth, kissing her husband lingeringly on the mouth.

Cheney reached over, turned off the tiny 25-watt light on the side table, and slipped the powder blue nightgown up and over his wife's shoulders.

And as they made love, holding each other tightly, passion surging the way it had when love was brand new, they both recognized that they were riding the wave of a new beginning. But it was better than a beginning. They knew each other.

They had lost each other. For a time.

Now they were reunited. In passion.

And in love.

True love.

When it was over they lay in each other's sweaty arms, two true lovers bathed in the afterglow of passion's prize, satisfied with the knowledge that some things, in fact, were better left unsaid.

Just before Elizabeth fell asleep, she noticed out of the corner of her eye that the roses next to her bed were now fully open.

The roses from Taylor Yates. Yes, she thought as she drifted off to sleep in Cheney's arms. . . .

Some things *were* better left unsaid.

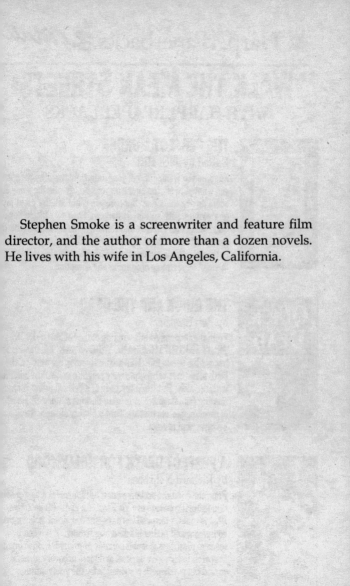

Stephen Smoke is a screenwriter and feature film director, and the author of more than a dozen novels. He lives with his wife in Los Angeles, California.

THICKER THAN WATER
by Bruce Zimmerman

From the Edgar Allan Poe Award-nominee comes a new thriller featuring San Francisco therapist turned sleuth, Quinn Parker, in another suspenseful adventure. This time, Parker's old pal, stand-up comic Hank Wilkie, invites him to Jamaica for a sunny all-expense-paid stay at the half-million dollar estate Hank has just inherited. It's just too good to be true.

THE WOLF PATH
by Judith Van Gieson

Low-rent, downtown Albuquerque lawyer Neil Hamel has a taste for tequila and a penchant for clients who get her into deadly trouble. *Entertainment Weekly* calls Hamel's fourth outing "Van Gieson's best book yet — crisp, taut and utterly compelling."